FORBIDDEN LOVE

BY MARGARET MCCULLOCH

CHAPTER ONE
Love and Passion

OLIVIA HOLLISTER MET Tom Bradford during her first year of college. As she stood before the University of Southern Georgia library, a tall man with broad shoulders walked up to her and started a conversation. His dark hair framed a handsome face with perfect teeth; and his blue eyes grabbed her as he introduced himself. She smiled and told him her name. Then he gave her a brief history of his life. He had always lived in Cedar Grove. He had an older brother and sister, aunts, uncles, and a slew of cousins who lived nearby. His mother and father lived near the city, but he spent most of his time at his apartment near the college. On weekends he stayed at his house on the lake that afforded him the quiet, peaceful atmosphere needed to concentrate on his studies. He majored in law and planned to work with his father's law firm after he graduated. Then he popped what, when, where questions about her life.

Olivia's father, Howard, worked at the post office in Boulder Bluff; and her mother, Mary, retired after teaching school thirty years. Her mother convinced her to major in education. Olivia wanted to get a job at the high school she had attended in Boulder Bluff, but she had two more years of college before thinking about a job. Her parents sent her to the University of Southern Georgia, because its broad curriculum offered the best education. In addition, the president of the University of Southern Georgia had graduated from high school with her father; and they had kept in touch over the years.

Olivia looked at her watch and saw that she must go to class.

As she turned to walk away, Tom touched her forearm and asked her to go out with him Friday night.

She hesitated before she accepted his invitation; then she gave him directions to her apartment.

Olivia made it to class in the nick of time and took her usual seat; but she had no idea what the professor talked about. She daydreamed about Tom Bradford through the entire lecture.

On Friday, Olivia rushed to her apartment and got ready for her date. When Tom knocked on her door, she tried to appear calm, but her heart beat in her toes. She liked everything about him, especially his good looks and personality.

As they drove, he asked where she would like to have dinner. She had no particular place in mind; she liked most everything from sandwiches to salads. He liked restaurants that served good steaks.

Outback Steak House in Cedar Grove had a full house; but they waited for a table. After they ordered, a man walked up to their table and shook hands with Tom. Then he looked at Olivia as he questioned Tom about where he found that beautiful woman. Tom introduced Olivia to Leonard West and explained that his beautiful woman appeared like magic at the right place and time; he took a chance and asked her to go out with him.

While Tom talked to Leonard about Bradford Law Firm, Olivia wondered how many other women appeared like magic before Tom at the right place and time. Leonard obviously knew Tom Well. She assumed that he worked for the Bradford Law Firm.

After they ate, Tom invited her to go to his house on the lake to have drinks. As he drove, she thanked him for the delicious steak dinner. She did not tell him that she lived on a budget and seldom ate steak.

Tom drove about fifteen miles from town before he took a left and drove down a narrow road shaded on each side by a thicket of pines mixed with oaks and maples. Fall had painted the thicket with streaks of orange, brown, and yellow; and the cool October weather brought a welcomed change from the summer heat.

Tom pulled up before a modern log house set on a rich green lawn; a lake peeped from the backside of the house that added to its beauty. Tom bragged on the big catfish and white brims in his lake. He liked to fish in his spare time.

Olivia moved her eyes from the lake to a small boathouse and pier. Beyond the boat house, a small house with a deck sat near the water.

Tom explained that Henry Gibson lived in the house. He kept up the grounds for all of their property. He pulled into the drive and quickly walked around the car to open her door. Warmth of his hand on hers made her feel giddy as they walked down a paved sidewalk toward rounded stone steps before the porch.

Olivia awed at his beautiful house as she moved her eyes from the gable roof above the second floor to the double windows across the front of the house. The cypress logs gave the house warmth; and the rockers with matching cypress swings on each end of the porch looked inviting. She followed him across the porch and waited for him to unlock the decorative wooded door with large panels of colored glass on each side. To the right of the entrance, a dining room took her attention with its long oak dining table and benches that shined like glass. She admired the cathedral ceiling, log beams, and the beautiful wagon-wheel surrounded by lights. Cornice boards covered with beautiful plaid material matched colors in the drapes and blended with the carpet, chairs, and couches. Deer heads, fish, and birds decorated the walls and showed his love for hunting and fishing. A beautiful stone fireplace warmed an open and spacious lower floor; a wide staircase with decorative posts led to bedrooms upstairs.

While Tom fixed drinks, she sat at the bar and admired the Maple cabinets that blended with tiles on the bar and the floor. She looked out the window and noticed the full moon gave a full view of the back porch and lake beyond.

He handed her a drink and she followed him to the couch in the living room. They talked about their classes, their families, places they liked to go, and things they liked to do.

Then Tom pulled her close and kissed her. Sparks flew and waves of pleasure swept through her entire body. Dazzled by his kiss, she pulled away from him and mentioned the research paper she had to finish before Monday. He cut off her next sentence with another kiss that made her want more than a kiss.

The clock struck twelve and she made excuses to go home; she must get up early Saturday and Sunday to finish her research paper.

As Tom drove her to her apartment, he talked about his classes. He also had work to do. One of his professors gave them a complex case to solve every day during the week; and they had to write details and quote laws that related to each case. He seldom had time to go out during the week.

The warmth of his arms around her and his goodnight kiss made her want to invite him to her bedroom. He asked her to go out with him the next Friday and she said yes. She thanked him for a wonderful evening and said good night.

She closed her door and leaned back with her head in clouds. When she heard his motor roar, she ran to the window and watched his tail lights disappear in the darkness.

After she went to bed, she could not sleep. She imagined sounds of his voice, warmth of his body, and his kiss. She felt as if she had met him before in another time and place; but she had never really met anyone like Tom. A fool blinded by feelings of love believed in magic, the beginning of a never-ending love.

The next week during class, she thought about Tom more than she should have. When she changed classes, she looked for him around every corner. At the end of the day, she looked for him in the parking lot, but she did not see him.

Finally, on Wednesday, Tom called and asked how she had been. Before he hung up, he reminded her of their date on Friday. He wanted to take her to his parent's lodge for dinner.

Olivia lived on dreams of seeing him again. On Friday, she met him at her door at seven o'clock. As he drove to his lodge, she felt nervous. She wanted to make a good first impression with his parents; she did not want to say the wrong thing; and she did not know how to act. They drove through an open gate and moved down a narrow winding road shaded by pines, a scene she had seen in a magazine. Beyond the pine thicket, more than a dozen horses grazed a large pasture before a blue lake that stretched beyond sight. Tall pine saplings formed a solid background behind the lake.

When Tom pulled into the drive, her eyes stretched with surprise. She had not expected such a large crowd; cars crowded the driveway and lined the road as far as she could see. Tom had a large family and more friends than he could count.

Before they walked up the step, a tall, stout man with fair complexion and bright blue eyes met Tom, shook his hand and asked him where he got that pretty woman.

Tom introduced Olivia to Whale Crawford as his good friend. Then he laughed and added that he picked up all pretty women he saw standing by the side of the road. He liked her looks from first sight and asked her to have dinner with him.

Whale laughed loud enough for everyone on the porch to hear.

Olivia felt embarrassed; but she brushed her feeling aside and followed Tom inside.

Mr. Bradford's tall, stocky frame looked like a giant next to Mrs. Bradford. He extended a warm hand to Olivia and introduced his wife. Tom had his father's dark hair, blue eyes, and handsome features. She imagined what Tom would look like at age fifty. Mrs. Bradford, a tall, neatly dressed woman, had a pretty face accented by dark hair streaked with gray. She also had a good figure to be in her early fifties; but she looked ten years older than Mr. Bradford did.

Mrs. Bradford led Olivia through a large foyer to a room packed with guest and introduced her to Tom's sister, Ellen, her husband, John, and their children. Ellen asked Olivia to sit with her. She looked nothing like Tom. Gray streaks in her dark hair made her look much older than her true age of thirty, but her personality made her vibrant. As they talked, Tom came in with his brother, sister-in-law, and their two children. Tom's sister-in-law, Penny, said very little; but his brother, Michael, took everyone's attention with his jokes.

Olivia liked Tom's relatives and they seemed to accept her as one of their family at first sight. She wished her parents could meet them. On the other hand, her father never found anything good to say about men she dated, especially men she liked.

Then Tom's best friend, Billy Miller, came in with his girlfriend, Lola Spivey. As Billy moved his tall, stocky frame around the tables, his dark hair fell over one eye and he looked like a hulk. He winked at Tom and laughed. Then he slapped Olivia's shoulder and said, "Tom always has a good looking pick up."

At first sight, Olivia wanted to slap Billy. His loud voice and laughter disgusted her. She wanted to ask the make and model of Tom's pick-ups. Instead, she pretended that she had not heard his smart remark and turned her eyes away from him.

Tom sensed Olivia's uneasiness; he quickly took her hand and led her toward the dining room. He made excuses for Billy's behavior; he simply wanted attention and said things to be funny; he seldom thought before he spoke.

With the crack of the door, the delicious aroma of fish made her mouth water. Tom bragged that his dad had the best cook in the county.

The crowd of strangers in the dining room soon made Olivia feel welcome, and she enjoyed their conversation.

With the call to dinner, guest lined up and Olivia fell in line ahead of Tom. She found it difficult to choose from the variety of salads and vegetables. She finally chose potato salad, slaw, and baked beans to go with fish and hush puppies. She followed

Tom toward a table near the back. As they walked by Billy's table, he said, "Olivia, you are too pretty for Tom to carry out in public. You are definitely not the kind of girl he takes to church with him."

Everybody in the room heard Billy; and his girlfriend laughed like a hyena. Olivia had never been more embarrassed in her life. She paused and stared at them with anger. She wanted to tell Billy to go to hell.

After she and Tom got seated, he whispered that Billy meant her no harm, and she must ignore him.

When Olivia first met people, she felt shy and had very little to say; but the friendly couple at their table saved the day with their conversation.

Before they finish eating, another acquaintance of Tom's came to their table with a wide grin and slapped Tom's back. Tom introduced him to Olivia as Ditto Frost. The weird acting man stared at Olivia while he talked to Tom about fishing. Minutes later, he disappeared as quickly as he came.

Olivia had never heard of anyone named Ditto in her entire life.

Tom didn't know Ditto's real name; everybody called him Ditto because he repeated everything at least two times. His parents lived two doors down from Tom's parents and Ditto still lived at home. In his younger days, he and his friends had carried Ditto with them to ball games and school events. Ditto helped him out now and then with odd jobs. He never finished high school and he usually went out with older women.

Olivia did not think Ditto's elevator went all the way to the top, but she remained silent.

After they had finished the main course, the waiter brought out a large tray filled with individual dishes of peach cobbler. Olivia felt stuffed, but she could not resist peach cobbler. After she swallowed her first bite of pie, she could feel pounds swell around her middle. She gained back all the weight she had lost that week.

They moved from the table to a large den, where the crowd had gathered. They listened to country music, danced, and talked. Tom danced like a cool breeze blowing over waves; he did not step on her toes one time, and she easily followed his lead. Tom liked George Strait; she liked "Carrying Your Love with me" best of all.

Suddenly the music stopped and everybody turned to see Billy at the stereo. He put on a different record and yelled across the room, "Olivia, if I said you had a beautiful body, would you hold it against me?"

Olivia stood and looked at him with shock. She turned back to Tom and whispered, "Billy has no respect for women. He needs to solve his problem."

Before Tom had time to answer, Billy cut in, pulled Olivia close, and swung her around.

Olivia swung at his face and shouted, "Get lost, you stinking Billy Goat. I don't want to dance with you! I don't want you to touch me! I don't want to be near you! I certainly would not hold my body close to you. Leave me alone!"

"If you shake that thing a little for Tom, you can get anything money will buy," Billy said and laughed.

"I know what you implied with your dirty mouth," Olivia said. Tom does not give me money, and I don't shake my body for any man, especially not for money. I don't want you to come near me again, Billy." As she walked back to find Tom, she felt as if everyone in the room whispered dirt about her.

She sat back down at the table with Tom and he acted as if he had not heard her argument with Billy. When she told him the details of their argument, Tom dismissed her words with a shrug of his shoulders and turned back to the others at the table. He bubbled with personality and talked about politics, weather, and latest gossip on campus.

Olivia felt jealous of the girls who crowded around Tom. He called them honey and darling, while they threw glances her way. She wondered how many of those girls had slept with him.

The guest left and Tom's family left soon afterward. Tom's father reminded him to lock doors, turn off lights, and the air conditioner before he left.

After they left, Olivia talked about how much she enjoyed dinner and the company of his family and friends; but she did not appreciate Billy Miller's rude remarks.

Tom explained that Billy ran his mouth to hear himself talk; she should pay no attention to anything he said. He added that he knew Billy like the back of his hand. They had been friends since grade school and finished high school together.

Time passed too quickly, and she realize that she had one drink too many. When she stood up, her head started spinning. Tom took her empty glass, went to the kitchen, and poured another drink. She pushed the drink back; she definitely did not need another drink; He insisted that she have one more drink and enjoy the night. After all, she had all day Saturday and Sunday to nurse her hang-over.

Before she finished the drink, she mentioned her blurred vision; animals on the wall seemed to move about and make weird noises.

Tom's hysterical laughter brought her back down to earth.

She realized the whiskey had gone to her head and made her completely crazy. She usually had one drink; she never drank three or four drinks made with strong whiskey.

Tom put his arm around her, pulled her under his chin, and kissed her.

Did her response to his kiss give him the wrong idea about her? Had she made the biggest mistake of her life? She straightened up and started a conversation about hunting and fishing.

Tom did not have much time to hunt and fish with all of his assignments at school; but he hunted and fished when he had free time. He and Billy liked to go deep sea fishing, too.

Olivia realized that she asked stupid questions more than once.

He pulled her close, put his face close to hers, and looked into her eyes for minutes before he covered her mouth with the most wonderful, gentle kiss that she had ever felt. She responded with a wildness that surprised her. He made her feel weak and crazy; she forgot that she had just met Tom the week before. She forgot that she had only been out with him twice and knew nothing about him. She simply forgot to care about the consequences of her action and what tomorrow might bring. She wanted Tom and she had never wanted anything more.

He finally pulled away and took her hand. Then they walked upstairs to his bedroom. She did not see the furniture or the floor plan upstairs; she only saw Tom lying in bed next to her; he made her feel wonderful, more wonderful than she had felt in her entire life. She expected him to tell her that he loved her, but he made no mention of love. She could not decide if she loved him or if he made her more passionate than she had ever been with another man. Her mother preached to her about love and passion; she believed the two emotions had nothing in common. Most men never fell in love; they felt only passion. Olivia seldom paid attention to her mother's sermons. She had finally found a man that made her happy, happier than she had ever been in her life.

The next week, she did not see Tom at school; but he called her every evening after she got to her apartment.

On Thursday, they had a dinner date, and she could hardly wait to see him. He picked her up at 7:30 and they went to Bulloch Country Club, where his father and all of his friends played golf, drank, and had dinner.

The restaurant served delicious steaks with salad, potatoes, and a choice of desserts. After dinner, Tom carried her to the Tavern, one of his favorite bars. They found a nice table in the back and enjoyed drinks while they listened to beautiful music. She related the songs to her feelings for Tom. Sting sang Every Breath You Take; Bob Seger sang We've Got Tonight; and Eric Clapton made the occasion extra special with his song, Wonderful Tonight.

After they left the Tavern, Tom carried her to his house on the lake. As usual, time passed quickly and she stayed later than she had planned. She got only five hours of sleep that night; but time spent with Tom made her forget her misery the next day.

Olivia fell hard for Tom Bradford. She had never been in love; she had never been in a relationship with another man like Tom. He knew how to satisfy her completely. Her wild and willing behavior as well as her eagerness to submit to his sexual desire must have made him feel like a stud. She thought about him every minute of the day, except the time she forced herself to study and listen to lectures in class. Her parents would fling a fit if she failed a course.

Before long, Olivia loved Tom so much that she wanted to be with him at all times; she wanted to scream how much she loved him when he made love to her. She loved him; he did not seem to care about sunshine or rain. When he did not show up on time for a date, she paced the floor with worry and cried. When he finally did show up, she melted to his embrace and forgot that he did her wrong.

Tom had more experience than Olivia did, and she wanted to please him. She read every book she could get her hands on about sex, especially the art of making love.

Every time Olivia had a date with Tom, she expected him to say the three magic words; she waited and wished, but he never said he loved her. One night after he made love to her, she felt so warm, so good all over, and she wanted him to know how she felt. She snuggled close to him, drew his face to her, and said," I love you, Tom. I fell in love with you the day we met on campus. I will love you forever."

He pulled her close, kissed her, and said, "Forever is a damn long time."

She froze and buried her head in her pillow. She felt as if the silence between would last forever. Then she felt him move. He sat on the edge of the bed and stared at the floor.

She got up, got dressed and asked him to take her home.

Back at home in her own bed, Olivia realized that she had been stupid to think that Tom Bradford loved her. His vocabulary did not include the word love; in fact, he had never been in love, had never told a woman that he loved her, and had never made a commitment to a woman. Why should he tell a woman lies about his true feelings? If he made a commitment to a woman, he could not keep his word. Tom wanted sex with no strings attached. Could she accept Tom's ways and enjoy the good times? Should she break up with him before he broke her heart? A one-sided love affair always ended in a broken heart, her broken heart. Now she knew how some of her love-sick friends felt when they split up with their boyfriends during high school.

The more she made excuses and tried to keep her distance from Tom; the more she wanted to see him. When he called or got near her, she tried to be less romantic to match his carefree moods; but she could not put on an act forever. She wanted Tom to love her as much as she loved him. When he kissed her and held her close, she submitted to his wishes. She felt love between them, but Tom still never mentioned the word love.

Olivia, a dreamer, wanted romance; realistic Tom never thought about romance; he never showed his emotions, unless he got angry. He took life like a grain of salt. He didn't know how to show his love or say the word.

Olivia hated the idea of being just another woman who Tom had sex with. She convinced herself that Tom loved her to calm her guilt for the way she acted.

Olivia learned right away that Tom liked to go to bars with his friends on weekends, especially on Saturday. This particular Saturday, Tom had asked her for a date.

After he picked her up, he announced that he had a surprise for her. She assumed that he would carry her to a nice restaurant for dinner, drinks, music, and dancing.

When Tom parked in the lot next to the Striptease Club and Bar, Olivia protested. "I am not going into the Striptease Bar with you. Take me back to my apartment."

"Come on, let's have some fun. I promised Billy, Whale, and Jordan that I would meet them here at eight o'clock."

"I don't want to watch women take off their clothes," Olivia said. "If I wanted to see a naked woman, I could take off my clothes and pose before my floor length mirror."

"Please come with me," Tom said. "If I don't show up, the boys will tease me about being hen pecked."

"If you want to be with Billy, Whale, and Jordan, take me back to my apartment."

"I will take you back home; but I have to go into the club and explain to Billy and Whale that I have a party pooper on my hands."

"I am not a party pooper; I would not be caught dead in that place."

Tom got out and stuck his head back inside the car. "I will be back in a few minutes."

Olivia watched him enter the Striptease Club and she tightened her mouth with anger. The longer she sat there the angrier she got. After thirty minutes passed, she thought of what she should do. Tom had taken the keys to his car with him. Another thirty minutes passed, and Olivia fumed. She got her phone and looked up the number for Bubba's Cab Service. She waited another fifteen minutes before her cab arrived, and Tom still had not come back to check on her. She got into the back seat of the cab and gave the driver her address.

Back at home, Olivia got dressed for bed and went to the kitchen to fix a sandwich. As she ate, she thought about how dirty Tom treated her. Like many times before, she promised herself that she would break up with him and find someone who treated her decent. Tom did not respect her.

After she ate and washed dishes, she went to the living room and watched television until she fell asleep on the couch. Hours later, the doorbell awoke her. She sat up and quickly gathered her composure.

As expected, Tom met her at the door. Then Billy, Whale, and Jordan came in behind him.

"We came by to see if you were home," Tom said. "When I got to the car and you had disappeared, I worried about you. I am glad to see that you got home safely."

"I got home safely in a cab with no thanks to you," Olivia said.

"Don't be mad, honey," Tom said. "Billy, Whale, Jordan, and I had planned this trip for weeks. I asked you to go with me."

"Forget about tonight," Olivia said. "I am ready to go to bed." She did not invite them to stay. The hands on the clock said one thirty in the morning.

Whale walked over to the couch where Olivia sat and threw down a Play Boy magazine with a naked woman's picture on the front cover. "You didn't get to see the show tonight, so I picked up a magazine from the grocery store for you to flip through."

"Take your stupid magazine with you, Whale," Olivia shouted. "I am not a freak; I don't sit around looking at naked women. Neither do I go to striptease clubs with a bunch of hoodlums to watch women undress."

"Tom says you write about love and romance," Billy said.

"What I write on my computer is my business," Olivia said. "I don't plan to publish all of the stories I write; but if I decide to publish, I will ask you first," Olivia said with sarcasm.

Then she turned to Tom and asked if he had read her manuscripts.

He denied having read anything. He had heard her talk about writing stories and poems.

Whale, Jordan, and Billy quickly made their exit; but Tom sat down next to Olivia and tried to kiss her. "I don't want to talk about this tonight," Olivia said. "Please go."

"Why do you want to spoil my fun," Tom said.

"I am not trying to spoil your fun," Olivia said. "Go have your fun; but you will not have fun with me at a striptease club."

"Goodnight," Tom said and he walked out the door.

Olivia got up and watched from the window as they drove away. She felt betrayed. Tom had read her manuscripts. How did he know about her love stories? When did he get on her computer? Then she remembered that she had flash drives laying around the apartment with her files on them. Tom had stolen her flash drive. Then she remembered that Billy had insinuated that men gave her money. She had written a story about a prostitute who had an affair with a man and gone into details about the woman's sexual encounters; but she never published the story. Tom had read everything on her computer and advertised it to his friends.

After she went to bed she could hear them laughing about the Play Boy magazine. She wanted to slap Whale; she never wanted to see him or Billy again. She really disliked both of them, but Jordan treated her with respect.

The weeks that followed made Olivia crazy. When Tom failed to show up for a date, she called him. If he did not answer his phone, she got into her car and tried to find him. When she failed her chase after him, she went back home and worried.

Then Tom finally came back to Olivia with his lies and excuses for being late for a date or not showing up at all. Tom won every argument; he convinced her to see things his way. She swallowed his lies and he continued the same routine. Afterwards, his lies hit her brain like a brick; but the next time he showed up; she went out with him again. She forgot his lies and her anger turned to a need for him that she could not resist. His touch and his nearness filled her with happiness that all fools dream about after they close their eyes to sleep.

Tom had Olivia under a mean thumb and deliberately did things to hurt her. He showed her and his friends his tough side. Tom made the decisions and she went along with his decisions. Nobody told Tom what he could or could not do. She cried often about things he said or did to hurt her; but Tom never cried. She began to wonder if he had a heart of stone. She wondered how a heart made of stone kept ticking. His heart beat for no one, except Tom. She definitely did not understand him.

When Tom came to pick her up on Friday, his good mood surprised her. He offered to take her anywhere that suited her fancy. She had no special place in mind; she did not care where they went as long as she went with him.

They laughed and talked as he drove to his house on the lake. That night made her happy. She enjoyed Tom's company more than three hours before they both fell asleep.

This fabulous ride she took with Tom on a smooth sailing ship over the calm sea soon met stormy weather with a crashing wave that threw her on the shore to spend the next weekend alone. What had happened to Tom? She watched cars pass by her apartment until she tired. Hours must have passed and Tom did not show. Olivia dressed for bed and sat down on the couch. She wanted to drive to the lake and introduce herself to the lucky woman. Instead, she paced the floor and worried with crazy thoughts going through her mind. She wanted to call him and tell him to never call her or try to get in touch with her again. She wanted to give him a piece of her mind; she wanted to slap his lying face; she wanted to hurt him. More than anything, she wanted to see him. God knows she loved and needed him.

Olivia did not see Tom at school the entire week; but she resisted her need to hear his voice on the phone. On Friday of that week, she rushed home and got ready for their usual date. She waited and wished for him to call; but his call never came. She felt miserable without him. She had never seen a more stubborn man. She hated him! She loved him! She did not know how she felt. She had no feelings.

Olivia realized that she had no future with Tom Bradford; but she loved him and wanted to be with him. The challenge of trying to change him frustrated her; but she kept trying. Her inability to let go of Tom made her a glutton for punishment.

CHAPTER TWO

For the Good Times

....

THE NEXT FRIDAY after school, Olivia called Emily, a close friend since high school. After graduation, Emily had moved to Rose Hill near Savannah and they did not visit often.

Emily shouted with happiness when she heard Olivia's voice. Right away, she asked Olivia to come and spend the weekend with her.

Olivia promised to be at Emily's house that evening around seven o'clock.

As Olivia drove toward Savannah, she noticed a beautiful blue lake near the road that reminded her of the times she had spent with Tom at his lake house. She slowed down and watched the skiers as the boats pulled them to shore.

One hour later, Olivia pulled into Emily's drive and admired the large, beige brick house with its three bedrooms and double garage. She especially liked the double windows across the front of the house; they gave plenty of light as well as a nice view of the neighborhood.

Emily met her with a tight hug and helped her with her luggage.

"I needed a shoulder to cry on," Olivia said.

Emily stepped back, looked at Olivia with concern, and said, "You never had problems in high school. I knew that love bug would bite sooner or later. Come on in and you can tell me about this lucky man."

Olivia followed her to the guest bedroom furnished with beautiful modern furniture. The curtains and carpet blended well with the throw pillows and paintings on the walls. Olivia unpacked her suitcase and went back to the kitchen to join Emily.

They talked while Emily fixed a bowl of chicken salad for them to have sandwiches for supper.

"Who is the lucky guy?" Emily said.

Tears ran down Olivia's face as she told Emily about Tom. His parents had money and they had spoiled him. She fell in love with him before she knew how he felt about relationships. Tom had never told a woman that he loved her; he did not want a commitment; he wanted sex and a good time. She tried to please him every way she knew how, but nothing she did made a difference. She had also tried to forget him, but she could not get him out of her head; she turned and tumbled without sleep; she thought about him constantly.

In a demanding voice, Emily told Olivia to call Tom Bradford and tell him to go to hell. She warned Olivia that he would never change. She thought Olivia deserved better and advised her to find someone who loved her.

Emily saw right away that Olivia's thick skull blocked her words. She wanted to throw ice in Olivia's face to get her out of her dream world. After they ate supper and cleaned the dishes, they sat in the living room and talked for hours before they turned in for the night. Emily finally told her she needed to go to a psychiatrist for counseling.

The next morning at breakfast, Emily told Olivia she thought Tom needed to grow up but some men never reached adulthood; they remained spoiled, selfish, and cold human being their entire life. Once again, she advised Olivia to never look his way again. Besides, he never told her he loved her or made a commitment to her. She added that Tom did not know how to treat a woman nor say words a woman needed to hear.

Olivia had no argument.

Emily broke the silence with her suggestion; she wanted them to go out to eat dinner, go shopping, and go to Sam's Club later that evening. She liked the band and the country music. Most of all, she liked to have a few drinks and dance.

They went to Shoney's for dinner, and Emily's company and the atmosphere helped, but Olivia never stopped talking about Tom. After dinner, they shopped most of the afternoon at the mall. Emily wanted a special outfit to wear to Sam's Club.

As they got dressed, Olivia admitted that she drank when she went out with Tom, but liquor made her do and say stupid things.

Emily suggested that a few drinks might be what she needed to get her head straight and forget that no good scoundrel. Emily called a cab to take them to Sam's Club. She never got under the wheel when under the influence of alcohol.

At Sam's Club, Emily and Olivia sat at a small table near the center of the club; but they could see the stage, the band, and the country singers. The music and the drinks put Olivia in the mood to dance. She naturally thought about Tom when Merle Haggard, sang, "If We Make It Through December."

As she sat and thought about Tom, a tall man with dark curly hair and blue eyes came to their table. He asked if she had reserved the chair next to her. She invited him to sit down. He introduced himself as Kirk Bentley and offered to buy drinks right away.

Emily and Olivia ordered a strawberry daiquiri and the drinks tasted delicious. Before they finished the first drink, another man came to their table and asked Emily to dance. She followed the man to the dance floor and left Olivia alone with kirk.

Kirk had a good personality and seemed to know how to treat a woman. After a few sips of the mixed drink and minutes of conversation, the band struck up a good song, and Kirk asked Olivia to dance. The singer did a good impression of Keith Whitley's song, "Don't Close Your Eyes". As his voice sounded around the dance floor, Olivia closed her eyes and thought about Tom. Then the singer sang, "It's Your Love", while Kirk held her tightly and whispered sweet nothings in her ear. He made her feel better, but she believed nothing he said.

Back at the table, Kirk kept Olivia busy answering questions about her family, home town, and her work. Then Kirk talked about his family. His parents lived in Tennessee. His father owned accounting firms in Tennessee and Florida. Kirk had moved to Florida to take care of their business there. He came to Georgia often to visit his grandmother who lived in the Rose Hill community.

They talked and danced until midnight. As they got up to leave, Kirk asked for Olivia's phone number; then he asked her to go out with him the next weekend.

Olivia gave his proposal little thought before she told him she had other plans the coming weekend.

On the way home, Emily called Olivia a fool for turning down Kirk's invitation. After they got home, they talked only a few minutes before hitting the sack.

The next morning after breakfast, Olivia packed and got ready to go home.

Emily followed her to the car and advised her to take care of herself, stop brooding about Tom, and go out with someone else.

Olivia made no reply; she thanked her for being the perfect host, smiled, and waved good-bye.

When Olivia got home, she unpacked her bags, picked up her cell phone, and paced from the bedroom to the living room. She sat down on the bed and stared at his name in her phone. Then she put her phone in her pocket and walked to the kitchen. She fixed a pot of coffee, sat down at the table, and took out her cell phone again. Finally, she got up the nerve to call Tom. After several calls to his cell phone with no answer, she called his home phone. She still got no answer. She finally decided to call his parent's home to find out if he spent the weekend with them. Her hands trembled; she did not know how Mrs. Bradford would react to her call, since she had visited the Bradford's only a few times. Tom answered the phone, but his voice held no excitement when she spoke." Tom, I have missed you the past weeks."

"We caught over three hundred fish this weekend," Tom said.

"Gosh, that sounds exciting," she said. "Where did you stay?"

"We stayed at the Saint Simons Resort on the Island."

"Who went with you?" she said.

"Just Billy, Josh, and several friends we meet at the club on the weekend," he said.

"Did you go out Saturday night?" she said.

28

"Damn, is this a multiple choice test? Can I answer each question with a yes or no?"

"You do not have to answer at all," she said. "I just wondered what happened to you. I haven't heard a word from you in over two weeks. You did not bother to call and explain why you broke your date with me."

"Where in the hell have you been? I called you Saturday, but you did not answer your phone."

"You should have called my cell phone," she said.

"I wanted to know if you were at home; that's where you should have been. What did you do this weekend?" he said.

She tried to avoid his question, but he asked again. Olivia could write fantastic lies on paper for her novels and fantasy stories, but she had always been truthful with Tom. She could not tell a lie and keep a clear conscious. She explained that she went to Rose Hill to visit Emily; they went shopping. Afterwards they went out to dinner. Later, they went out to Sam's Club to have a few drinks and dance.

"Did you have a swinging good time? Did lover boy step on your toes?" he said.

His sarcasm made her see red but she admitted that she felt terrible the entire weekend, because she worried about where he had gone and what he was doing.

"Don't worry about me; I am a big boy and I can take care of myself. Besides, you shouldn't feed me that bull shit; you knew where I went and why I went there."

"You never talk to me about where you are going and I don't know about your trips until after you have gone. You never ask me to go with you on these pleasure trips."

The line went silent. Then he said, "Olivia, would you like to go to a barbeque supper next Saturday? Henry cooks up some good barbeque, and our friends cook up some good trimmings to go with it."

In spite of his sarcastic tone, her spirits lifted and she said, "I would like to go to your barbeque."

"I will pick you up around four. The men folk like to get there early to have time to fish after they eat." He hung up before she had time to say anything else.

After she hung up, she still felt angry. Why did she feel the need to explain where she went and everything she did to Tom?

The next Saturday when Tom knocked on Olivia's door, she jumped up from the couch and ran to the door to greet him. He must have seen the eagerness in her eyes. He must have felt the love she felt for him. He stepped inside and neither spoke; he pulled her close and kissed her. She returned his kiss with a passion that begged him to make love to her.

He stepped back and said, "We had better stop this before things go too far. My folks never eat until I get there, and I do not want to keep them waiting."

As he drove, she slipped close to him and listened to him complain about the difficult bar exam that he had to take that summer.

Instead of going to his cabin on the lake, Tom headed toward his father's house on the lake across town.

Olivia wanted them to have some time alone. Now she had to act nice around his family and friends, listen to the men shoot the bull about golf games, and tell fish stories. Neither sport interested Olivia; Tom occupied her thoughts when she had free time.

As they turned off the main road, he pointed to his father's house in the midst of a thicket of oak trees. The lake ran from the side of the house as far as she could see ahead of them. Tom parked and they walked toward two shelters with shiny tin roofs. He talked about his younger days when his father carried him there to have picnics under the shelter and fish in the lake.

Olivia felt nervous. She always felt nervous around his parents and family. "Hold my hand," she said.

He laughed and said, "First day at school?"

She wanted to jerk her hand free and go back to the car; but her feet moved in time with Tom's steps toward the shelters. Tom threw up his hand to several of his friends who sat on the bank with fishing poles and lines cast. They walked on to a clear path before a sandy shore where women sun bathed. Olivia wanted to join them, rather than socialize with Tom's parents and family.

Before they reached the shelter, she heard laughter mingled with happy voices; smoked hams filled the air with a delicious smell. The atmosphere reminded her of her younger days when she spent the summer with her grandparents on their farm.

Tom's parents, sister, and brother seemed happy to see her again. She liked Tom's family, especially Tom's mother. She reminded Olivia of her grandmother, a person Olivia admired and loved more than anybody. Tom's father seemed like a down to earth person. He worked hard and provided well for his family, including Tom.

Olivia could tell by Mr. Bradford's conversations that he respected his law firm. He bragged about his business and his lawyers the entire hour before they ate. Olivia concluded that all of Mr. Bradford's employees came to the barbeque.

After the delicious meal; Tom and some of his friends went fishing; and Olivia followed a group of girls to the restroom to change into her swimsuit. They lay on the sandy shore near the water several hours. Olivia enjoyed their jovial conversation and jokes; but she had never liked beer. Beer tasted nasty and she swallowed two or three times to get it down, but she did not want to seem different. She continued to drink beer.

She felt as if Tom had dated some of the girls soaking in the sun. A few of the girls soon formed their own group; they whispered and stared at Olivia. She felt as if they talked about her. On the other hand, her broad imagination ran away with her at times. Besides, why should she worry about what they said or thought about her? She wanted to be like all of his other whores, the whores who whispered trashy things about her probably whispered trashy things in Tom's ear. She wanted to show Tom that she had no feelings for him. She did not need Tom; she did not need to hear his sweet words. She came to his party to have a good time.

Emily's voice shocked Olivia to a sitting position. One of Tom's friends, who knew Emily from high school, had called and invited her to the barbeque. She had jumped at the chance to see Olivia. She spread her towel next to Olivia and asked how she had been getting along with Tom.

"Tom thinks I am a push over," Olivia said.

As they laughed and talked, Olivia saw Ditto Frost walking toward them. She punched Emily and said, "Don't look now, but Ditto Frost is walking our way."

Emily laughed and said, "Who invited that weirdo?"

"Tom invited him. Do you know him?" Olivia said.

"I met him at a party when we were in high school. All of the kids made fun of him, but they liked to bug him by asking him stupid questions; they wanted to hear him say the same answer two times."

Ditto walked up to them and laughed before opening his trashy mouth. "Olivia you got some bowed legs; you got some bowed legs that look like Bowman's. His legs are bowed, too. He used to play basketball, though. They called him Bowman, because he had bowed legs. He played basketball, though."

Olivia jumped up and flipped him with her towel as she shouted, "Get away from me!"

He put his arms up in defense and said, "Don't hurt me."

Olivia flipped her towel at him again as she spoke, "My legs may be bowed, but I have good eyes. You are as ugly as a hedge hog and as blind as a bat. In addition, you are disgusting. I haven't done or said anything to you. Are you crazy?"

"Ditto doesn't have a chance with you or any other girl," Emily said. That's why he makes fun of girls. They won't pay him any attention."

"I think Emily likes you, Olivia. I think she likes you. Are you girls lesbians? You act mighty friendly, mighty friendly."

Emily laughed at his remark; but his trash disgusted Olivia.

"Olivia is my best friend," Emily said.

"I saw you rubbing Olivia's back with that oil. I saw you," Ditto said.

"Don't say anything else to him," Olivia whispered to Emily.

"Are you jealous because you can't get a girl to rub oil on your back?" Emily said.

"My girl rubs oil all over me; my girl rubs oil on me every day," he said and took off in a run back to the shelter.

"Why did Tom invite that stupid man?" Olivia said. "I cannot believe he mingles with human beings. He frightens me."

"Everybody thinks Ditto is weird; but the boys like to have him around for the show. They get a kick from his stupidity."

"I never laugh at children with disabilities; but Ditto is not a child and he has more than just a disability; I think he has a sickness that neither doctors nor pills can cure; and he probably never read a book. His trashy mouth makes me want to lash out at him. On the other hand, Tom's other friends are not quite right in the head, either. I think Tom likes friends who he can boss around," Olivia said.

"Ditto has always called girls lesbians if he noticed that they hung out together. I think he says off the wall things to girls, because they won't pay him any attention," Emily said.

"Which is worse being called a lesbian or a whore?" Olivia said.

"Some men make women the topic of their dirty conversations at bars, poker tables, and everywhere else they gather," Emily said.

"Tom falls into that category with all the other men, and he thinks he owns me."

"What did you say?" a deep voice sounded in Olivia's ears. She opened her eyes to see Tom standing over her.

Emily broke the silence with her smart reply, "Our conversation is personal. We have a woman to woman talk now and then."

"Come go with me, Olivia," Tom said. "I need to have a man to woman talk with you right now."

Olivia told Emily that she would call her later and she walked off in the sunset with Tom.

Emily saw that Olivia had been right about Tom. As she watched them walk toward the distant cabin, she wanted to rush after them, grab Olivia by the arm, and drag her away from Tom. He had no respect for Olivia and she should tell him to go to hell.

"How much have you had to drink?" Tom said.

"I had three beers, and I need just one more," Olivia said and giggled.

He opened the door to the cabin and she followed him inside. The small room turned in a circle about her. She had never seen this strange cabin. The room had no fine furniture; cans of food cluttered the counter; dust on the chairs stifled her. On the right wall, a white sheet covered a single bed.

"Who own this cabin?" Olivia said.

"Dad owns the cabin, but he uses it to store things mostly."

"Why did you bring me here," Olivia said.

"I brought you here to rape you," he said. "Now, get dressed and let's go for a walk. You cannot have another beer."

When they passed the shelter, the crowd had thinned. His folks had gone home; and only a few of Tom's friends remained. Olivia felt relieved that his folks left; she did not want to be around them with beer on her breath. She felt ashamed for having drunk too much.

Sunset fell on the tips of the trees and a flock of birds flew across the water in search of a nest for the night. The water quivered with quick ripples and sent waves to the sandy shore. They passed by two men who fished from the shore, while they chewed and spit tobacco. They walked on and Tom threw up his hand to a young couple with a little boy who walked back toward the shelter. Their two dogs apparently did not like each other. They barked, growled, and gnashed white teeth as if ready to fight.

Olivia wanted to get away from the dogs quickly. They walked more than a mile to reach the other side of the lake, where they had seclusion. She sat down next to Tom near the water's edge and they cooled their feet in the water. Then he put his arms around her and her heart quickened. She could not believe his romantic mood; she wanted to believe he had changed. She wanted to believe that he loved her; she wanted to believe he would say the three magic words. On the other hand, she wanted to forget the bastard. She had one drink too many.

Then Tom gently cupped her face and looked deeply into her eyes before he kissed her. Lost in the feelings of love, she wanted this minute to last forever. The sun's rays walked on the water and sparkled like gold. He got up and spread a blanket under a huge oak hidden by a cluster of smaller trees draped with gray moss. Then he came back and reached for her hand. She walked with him to the tree and they sat down. He had nothing to say; he wanted to make love to her and she wanted him as much as he wanted her. The liquor had gone to her head and made her too drunk to resist the pleasure of his arms around her. She acted like a cheap whore and he treated her like a cheap whore.

After they made love, they walked back to truck and Tom took her back to her apartment.

The next weekend Olivia got excited about her birthday. She could hardly wait to celebrate with Tom. He had called and asked her to go out with him on Friday, and she felt sure he had something special in mind for her birthday. She crossed her fingers with a wish for a birthday surprise. Maybe he would give her an engagement ring. On second thought, maybe he would take her out to eat at a special restaurant.

As she got dressed, she hummed a tune with the radio and wondered where Tom would take her and what he had for her birthday. She felt happy and good all over thinking about being with him. She looked at the clock and waited; she paced the floor and waited.

At nine o'clock, Tom had not shown up for their date. How could he stand her up on her birthday? Then she made excuses for him; his car broke down; he had a flat tire; something terrible happened; his family needed him. Then she cried and threw things. She went to the bathroom a dozen times and looked at her red, swollen eyes. Finally, she saw herself as Tom saw her, nothing but a pretty face. She lifted her dress and turned before the floor length mirror. Most men would like her long legs; but no man liked women with flat asses. She threw her dress down and looked down her shirt at her breast. Then she realized that none of these physical things really mattered to Tom. He did not care about a girl's figure, looks, or personality. He liked girls on the make for sex. After he tried one, he looked for a different more exciting girl.

The doorbell rang and broke her train of thought. She rushed to the door and there stood Tom with his friend, Billy Miller. They laughed as they staggered into the living room and the smell of liquor made Olivia cough. She stepped back and stared at them.

"We got stuck in the swamp," Tom said.

Billy laughed and his beer belly shook; he disgusted Olivia.

"We got bogged down to the damn axle."

"Why did you go to the swamp in the first place?" Olivia said.

"Our dogs got on a wild boar's trail, and we followed the dogs," Tom said.

"That boar hog got a head start on the dogs and us," Billy said and bent with laughter again.

"I imagine you trailed a young, wild guilt instead of a boar hog," Olivia said.

"The hog looked like a boar hog to me," Tom said.

"Tom is telling the truth," Billy said. That boar hog weighed more than two hundred pounds. I wanted to get a good aim at the devil, but we had to give up the chase."

Tom slapped Billy on the arm and they laughed some more.

"I'll bet that wild hog wallowed in the mud with both of you." Olivia said. She had never been angrier with Tom.

"When we started out of the swamp, we got bogged down in that mud and could not get out. We walked through the swamp for more than two miles and met up with Bryan Dennard and his hunting party. He called my brother, Michael, and he came to our rescue. That 850 John Deer strained its motor to get us out of that boggy swamp."

"What happened to your cell phone?" Olivia said.

"My cell phone went dead and Billy left his phone at home."

"How convenient! You two have a perfect answer for everything," Olivia said.

"We thought we had to spend the night in that swamp, and it is a scary place," Tom Said.

"Tom told you the truth," Billy said. "We got scared; that swamp is a scary place."

Olivia bravely stood up to Billy. "Have you been spending too much time with Ditto?"

"I recon we haven't run into Ditto in several weeks?"

"Ditto's habits have rubbed off on you, Billy. Why do you repeat everything Tom says?"

Billy saw the anger in Olivia's eyes and backed up. Then he quietly edged his way to the door and made a quiet exit.

Tom sat down on the couch next to Olivia, put his arms around her, and said, "Are you angry with me?"

His liquor breath told on him; she felt sure he had been drinking all evening. "Am I angry?" she screamed. "You never think about my sitting home wondering what happened to you. Why do you do me this way?"

"I did not plan to get bogged down in the swamp," Tom said. "Don't be nagging me about my hunting."

"I don't plan things like this, either," Olivia said. "I don't intend to sit home and wait for you to chase a wild boar hog ever again!" Tears slowly made a wet streak down Olivia's cheek. "You forgot my birthday. The card I got with cash from Mother and Daddy meant very little to me. I needed you, and I wanted to hear you say happy birthday."

Tom reached for her and said, "I'm sorry, Olivia. I will make it up to you. We'll celebrate your birthday tomorrow night."

Olivia jerked away from him and said, "Get your damn hands off me!"

He looked at his hands and laughed, "I do need to wash my dirty hands; but you should not act crazy and cry over a dumb boar hog?" He stood and looked at her for minutes and she said nothing. Then he pulled her under his chin and held on to her as if he would never let go.

"I'm not crying about the dumb boar hog," Olivia said. "I am crying, because you did not remember my birthday. You take me for granted. You do not care about me; and I have finally faced reality. I am the dumb little chick waiting with open arms after you go out and have a good time; after you have your way with other girls."

He said nothing, but he pulled her face to his and kissed her. Olivia melted to his embrace. Afterward, he said, "Baby, I didn't lie to you. You see, we planned to leave the swamp early, and I had plenty of time to get here for your birthday, but we got bogged down."

Olivia wanted him to hold her forever, but she pulled away from him. "Where is my present?"

"I slam forgot to go by my place and pick up your present," he said.

"You forgot my birthday!" she said. "You didn't buy me a present." She wanted to forget that he had no feelings for her; she wanted to satisfy her own need for him to hold her, kiss her, and make love to her. She wanted to feel his body melt to her, but she stopped; her pride kept her from letting him have his way. "Tom, I want you to go. I need to be alone and think things over."

"There is no need to think about what has already passed; you can't do a damn thing to change what has already happened," Tom said. "Hell, why can't you forget about the swamp and the boar hog?" He threw his hands to his side and walked out.

Olivia wanted to run after him and tell him she needed him to spend the night with her, but she did not move. Then she thought of checking the mud on his truck. She rushed to the door, but his taillights went over the hill. She went to the bedroom, threw herself across the bed, and cried. She tumbled the entire night without sleep and got up the next morning before her alarm sounded. She felt sure that Tom and Billy stayed out all night. Tom probably bragged that he had his woman under control. She spent the day wondering if Tom would call or come by to see her. She had sent him away. She should have told him to never come back again.

Olivia spent a miserable weekend. She did not feel like going to school Monday morning; but she had a test, the last test for the quarter. Her professor would not excuse absences other than death in the family or sickness.

As she backed out of the drive, she thought about driving by Tom's house out in the country. She decided not to waste gas. She had wasted gas on that five miles many times before. Tom would take delight in seeing her on that road.

Some fools never realize their mistakes; but Olivia realized her mistakes. She gave herself to a man who did not love her; worst yet, he did not respect her or care about her feelings. The good times and sex made him happy. She could let him continue to use her; or she could leave him alone. She decided that she would keep seeing Tom for the good times; he would never hurt her again.

CHAPTER THREE

Break up

....

OLIVIA DATED TOM more than two years before the final crash broke her heart. Several weeks passed and Olivia had not heard from him. She felt like an insane zombie. She had picked up the phone a dozen times, but memories of her past mistakes and her determination to stop this crazy one-sided love affair made her put the phone down. She would never call him again; but she thought about him constantly and worried that he had found another stupid girl; a girl ready to jump into bed with him.

Olivia had not kept up in class and worried that her grades would fall below requirements for the Dean's list. She had to get her mind back on her subjects, especially French. Her graduation would move up another quarter if she failed French.

That night she crammed for her French test and got less than three hours of sleep. When the alarm sounded, she felt like she had jet lag. She dragged to the shower and got dressed for school. She finished breakfast by seven and had a few minutes to spare. She drove by Tom's house and played her fingers on the wheel when she saw his truck in the drive. She resisted the temptation to stop and drove on to school. Tom's first class started at ten. He usually slept late.

That evening on the way home, she detoured and went by Tom's to see if he had gotten home; but she did not see his truck in the driveway. As she neared the crossed roads, she saw Tom at the stop sign. She turned left, stopped next to his truck, and let down her window.

He let his window down and looked at her as if she were a lost tourist who wanted directions.

"Tom, can we talk?" she said.

"I am all ears," he said.

Olivia pulled her car off the road and got into the truck with him. She tried to touch his hand, but he pretended to have an itch around his neck. Then he dropped both hands to the wheel as if trying to free his hands of her.

"Tom, I cannot go on like this," she said.

Tom sat like a stone statue and said nothing. She must have waited five minutes for him to say something; he remained silent and looked straight ahead.

"Tom, I am sorry that I made you angry, but you completely forgot my birthday. Instead of coming to see me, you went to the swamp and hunted boar hogs with Billy. You have never invited me to go with you on your fishing trips, either."

When he made no reply, she said, "What did you expect me to do?"

When he turned and looked at her, she read a message in his eyes. He wanted to tell her he loved her; he wanted to pull her close and kiss her. She never read him right.

She touched his face and said, "Tom, do you love me?"

He turned his face away from her and said, "I heard you had another boyfriend. I have friends who keep me informed. They saw you with another guy the weekend I went fishing, and I know everything about the bastard."

"I told you I went to Rose Hill to see Emily; I told you we went to the club. A man sat at our table and I danced with him, but that man did not mean one thing to me. I did not leave the club with him. Emily and I took a cab back to her house. I spent the night with her and came back home the next morning."

"I also heard that you have been with one of the professors at the university."

"Who told you that lie?" Olivia said.

"I cannot give you my informant's name," he said.

"Your probably have two informants, Billy and Ditto, those two idiot friends of yours. They are both liars and the truth is not in them," Olivia said. "Why do you hang out with those morons?"

"Either one of those boys would do anything I asked them to do. They care about me. If you cared about me, you would not be out kicking up your heels with a crazy, wild buck," Tom said.

"I don't know what you expect from me. You do not treat me decent. I am the rug under your feet that catches your dirt. I need a man who knows how to treat a lady; I need a man who loves me, and you apparently don't know the meaning of the word."

"I have to run some errands for Daddy," he said and pushed his foot to the gas pedal to tell her to get out and leave him alone.

Olivia humbly opened the door and made her way back to her car. She walked around the back of his truck, so he would not see her tears. Before she opened her car door, Tom put his foot to the pedal and disappeared.

As Olivia drove toward home, tears blinded her, and she did not have a Kleenex. Olivia decided that Tom accused her of being unfaithful, because he felt guilty for his own affairs. She could not imagine who told Tom every move she made. Billy did not go to the university; he worked as a mechanic at his father's garage.

The professor Tom accused her of dating had merely helped Olivia with her assignment after class. He had a wife and children. He had never said anything out of the way to her; he had never been romantically involved with her. She had heard the rumor the nosy liars spread about the professor and her. Olivia had been in the restroom stall when she heard the two girls gossiping. Unaware of her presence, they laughed and talked about the professor being sweet on his star student, Olivia Hollister. Olivia wanted to come out of the stall and face them with their lie; but she thought her denial would make matters worse. She never stayed after class again to get help; she never mentioned the incident in the bathroom to her professor; and the gossip finally ceased as far as Olivia knew.

That night, like many nights before, Olivia thought about the sheer hell Tom had put her through and what a fool she had been to keep clinging to that thin thread of hope for him to change. He had never admitted that he loved her; he had never made a commitment to her. He merely enjoyed being with her for a few hours each week to have sex. He did not want a woman to tie him down. Commitments led to responsibilities and he could not take on any responsibilities until he became independent. He depended on his father to pay his bills and give him money. He needed to study and pass his bar exam before he got serious about a woman.

Olivia made up her mind that she would finally end this crazy affair with Tom. She had wasted too much time on him already. She thought about the times she sat home and waited for him to come by or call to explain why he broke their date. She wanted to forget Tom and go out with other men for the good times. She never wanted to get hooked on another man; she never wanted to fall in love again.

The next evening, she called Emily and asked her if she wanted to go somewhere to have a good time that weekend.

Emily had a date on Friday, but she promised to call on Saturday.

To her surprise, Tom called on Friday and asked her to go out to eat Friday night. She hesitated and he said, "Olivia, do you have a hearing problem or have you crammed cotton in your ears?"

"The only problem I have holds the other end of the line," she said. She could not believe he laughed.

She took a good breath and said, "I guess I will go out with you."

"I don't want to cramp your style or break your arm to go out with me," he said and laughed. "I will pick you up at seven."

After she hung up the phone, she went to the bathroom, stood in front of the mirror, and talked to herself, "You are a stupid fool for going out with Tom again. I hate you for giving in to him."

On Friday when she met him at her door, she didn't feel the usual excitement; she felt numb.

Tom must have sensed a change in her, because he tried harder than usual to get her in a good mood by his jovial conversation and laughter; he even told several jokes, and he never told jokes. He carried her to The Meal House, where they served delicious steaks with all of the trimmings.

After dinner, they went to Shenanigans for drinks. When Bob Seger's song, "We've Got Tonight," sounded from the speakers, Tom asked her to dance. After several drinks, they left the bar and Tom carried her to his house on the lake. She melted to his embrace and followed him to the bedroom. They spent hours making love with naps in between.

Tom waited until the next morning to tell her his plans for the rest of that weekend. He had another fishing trip planned. His friend, Billy, planned to go with him to Saint Simons; they would be out of town until late Sunday night. He promised to call her when he got to Brunswick; and he promised to call her again Sunday night when he got home.

What could she say? She did not believe him. Neither did she trust him, but she kept her cool and went along with his fish tale.

Before lunch, he took her home. She invited him to come in and have a sandwich, but he made excuses. Billy expected him at eleven thirty.

She wished him good luck with the fish, got out, and walked toward her door without kissing him good bye.

Emily called shortly after Olivia got home. She asked if she wanted to go out Saturday night.

Olivia asked Emily to come spend the night with her; they would decide what to do after she got to her house.

Emily guessed that Olivia had another fight with Tom; she asked Olivia if Tom had asked her to go out lately.

Olivia admitted that she had gone out with Tom several times since they had talked.

Emily called her an idiot for seeing him again. Before she hung up, she said she would be at her house by six thirty that evening.

Tom called Saturday night and bragged about the fish he and Billy caught. He asked what she planned to do with the rest of the weekend.

She explained that Emily had come to spend the night with her; they planned to go out and eat dinner.

Tom asked if they planned to kick up their heels at the club.

She told him they planned to watch a movie at home.

Then he asked the name of the movie they planned to watch.

She told him they rented a movie called "Love, War, and Betrayal."

He seemed satisfied with her answers. He promised to call her when he got home. They would not get back into town until Wednesday or Thursday.

Emily and Olivia went to the Chinese Garden that evening for supper. They carried more food home than they ate, but they had Chinese chicken for dinner the next day.

Emily did not give Olivia any advice; she changed the subject each time Olivia mentioned Tom's name. She talked about the exercise club she had joined; she exercised every day after work.

Olivia did not have time to go out much during the week; she had to study to make the Dean's list, and keep her parents off her back.

On Sunday after Emily left, Olivia read her assignments for Monday's classes and started a research paper that she had to turn in by the following Friday.

Tom lied again; she did not hear from him Sunday night nor the week that followed.

When she called Emily and told her the way Tom had done her, Emily blamed her for letting Tom treat her dirty. She reminded Olivia that she had warned her about Tom, but she refused to listen to her.

To Olivia's surprise, Kirk, the man she had met previously at Sam's Club, called. She suspected that Emily had asked Kirk to call her. He talked about his job and asked how she had been. Before hanging up, he asked her if she would like to go out with him that weekend.

She made excuses with other plans she had, thanked him for calling, and hung up; but his call put her in a better mood. He made her feel beautiful, wanted, and important. At least, some men found her interesting and attractive.

Each day drug like a turtle with a broken leg, and Olivia merely existed from one day to the next. Another week came and went; she still had not heard from Tom.

The next Friday when Olivia got home, she braced her courage and called Kirk. He seemed pleased to hear her voice and quickly asked if she had changed her mind about going out with him. She replied that she would be delighted to go out with him.

He asked for directions to her apartment and told her he would pick her up at seven o'clock on Saturday. Before he hung up, he asked to think of a place that served good food and drinks. He also wanted her to think about a club for dancing after dinner.

On Saturday, when Kirk Bentley walked into her house, she liked what she saw. His dark navy suit with the white pullover turtleneck met fringes of dark hair on his neck and gave him sex appeal. Better yet, he took her hand on the way to the car and opened the car door for her.

Ruby Tuesday served delicious food. She ordered shrimp and a salad; Kirk ordered a seafood platter with all the trimmings. After they left the restaurant, Kirk carried her to Starkey's Bar for drinks. They laughed, talked, listened to music. Rod Stewart sang "Tonight's the Night," and Olivia smiled. Then he sang "Will You Still Love Me Tomorrow," and Olivia had another drink.

Three hours later, Olivia felt wonderful; but she had several drinks too many. She reasoned poorly and her vision blurred; but she saw the motel sign, "Hampton's Inn." She did not remember entering the motel room. She awoke to the sound of a television blaring. She sat up and looked around the room before she noticed the man lying in bed next to her. She checked her dress; she still had on her clothes, but she had spent the night with Kirk Bentley; she had slept in the same bed with him.

She shook Kirk and he sat up; he looked around the room and she turned her face away from him. She felt too embarrassed to look him in the face.

He sensed her embarrassment of this awkward awakening and put a hand on her shoulder as he spoke, "Olivia, you have nothing to be ashamed of; nothing happened." He explained that he did not feel safe under the wheel after they left the club.

She believed him, because she still had on her clothes, but she had spent the night with him and ruined their friendship.

Kirk seemed as nice as ever and as romantic as ever. He wanted to take her out to dinner, but Olivia wanted to go home, take a bath, and change clothes.

Olivia blamed her actions on Tom. Had he treated her decent, she would not have gone out with Kirk. She thought about Tom Bradford all the way home, but she did not know how she would tell him about Kirk.

The next weekend, Tom finally called, but he did not call to ask her for a date; he cursed her and called her a trashy whore. He claimed that he had tried to call her several times on Friday. Then he learned that she had gone out with the swinger again. He hung up on Olivia and did not call back.

After Tom hung up, the anger that had built up over time made Olivia scream. She promised herself that she would get her head straight and forget she had ever stooped low enough for Tom Bradford to get his hold on her. Tom could do as he pleased, but she had to walk the line. In Tom's way of thinking, women had no rights. She wondered how many women he went out with in Brunswick.

She did not hear from Tom that week. Then the weeks turned to months, and Olivia learned from friends that Tom had dated several other girls since he broke up with her, including Stella Shivers.

Olivia cried every day for months; the hurt would not go away. She thought about him every day, worried about his well-being, and had crazy visions of what might have been. She felt as if she would go off the deep end at times. She reached for the phone a thousand times, but drew her hand back. Her confused state of mind frustrated her and made her lose her appetite; she couldn't eat or sleep. She tried to keep busy to keep from thinking about Tom. She pretended that her feelings for him had only been passion, infatuation, and lust.

Olivia finally got used to spending most of her time alone. She studied and made the Dean's list every quarter. Several guys asked her for a date; but she turned them down. She feared rejection again; she feared getting hurt again.

Before the quarter ended, Emily contacted her and announced that she had met the man of her dreams and he had asked her to marry him. She had planned her wedding for the coming June and she wanted Olivia to be her maid of honor.

Olivia visited Emily on weekends to help her prepare for her wedding. In June, she spent an entire week with Emily. After Emily's wedding, Olivia felt more alone than ever. She went out with several men she had met on campus; but she did not find another man she loved. She would never find another man like Tom Bradford.

CHAPTER FOUR
The Perfect Storm

AFTER OLIVIA GRADUATED from college, she got a job teaching sixth grade at Boulder Bluff Middle School. She turned down her parent's offer to live with them rent-free and rented a nice house with a back yard pool near town. She liked the house and the pool as well as the location. She had less than a mile to drive to school. Best of all, she had her cat, Jasper, with her. He had lived with her mother while she attended college and her mother seemed reluctant to give him to her.

School started in September and slightly lifted her spirits. She got along better at work than at home all alone. Her mind stayed busy with her students, rather than useless thoughts about Tom.

As she sat before the mirror and applied her makeup, she took notice of each detail of her face. The tiny wrinkles around her eyes had turned to lines. She needed to make an appointment with a dermatologist for Botox. She applied a heavy coat of makeup, put on lipstick, brushed her long, dark hair behind her ears, and stretched her eyes to apply more mascara than usual. Before going to the kitchen, she turned before the mirror to admire the navy blue suit. Maybe she needed to lose a few pounds. Regardless of how skinny or how fat she got, Tom never noticed, but other men still found her attractive. She did not feel old; she still felt a need to party and dance. She had dated several nice men who had college degrees and good jobs, but she still thought about Tom. She assumed that he had graduated with a degree in law and worked for his father. She wondered if he had married.

Olivia had an unusually good day at school, the best day since she moved back to Boulder Bluff. Today the student cooperated and made her feel worthwhile as a teacher.

When she got home, she changed into a comfortable pair of slacks and a T-shirt. She usually walked a mile or more after school, but the dark clouds changed her mind about her usual routine. Instead, she settled in her nest on the couch. A loud clank of thunder reminded her that she had not checked on Jasper. He usually meowed and made a big fuss at the back door when she came home from work every day. She got up and rushed to the back door. When she opened the door, the wind almost took the door off its hinges. She found Jasper huddled in a tight ball in the corner of the porch. She reached down and cuddled him under her chin to calm his fright. She pulled with all of her strength to close the door and went to the cupboard to get Jasper a can of cat food. She put him down and he meowed hungrily as she emptied his food into the bowl. Then another loud crash of thunder startled her, and she dropped the empty can on the floor. Jasper disappeared beneath the barstools behind her. She called to him, but he remained under the stood in a ball. She picked up the empty can from the floor, threw it into the trash, and walked to the window. Rain whipped against the windows, thunder rumbled, and sharp lightening cut the sky like a flaming silver sword. She hated being alone during a storm. What would she do if she got sick and could not get in touch with her parents?

She walked back to the den and picked up the phone to call her mother; but the sharp flash of lightening made her drop the phone back in place. A loud noise startled her. She rushed to the double glass doors and saw the wind take the chairs from the patio. They flew into the air and tumbled into the pool; and limbs from the pines at the back of the house sailed in the air and landed all over the back yard. Black clouds rolled overhead and a flash of lightening slapped her in the face. She quickly moved back from the glass doors and watched rain pour from the sky and settle on the patio.

She went back to the couch and lay down. Jasper jumped up from his frightened squat, and jumped onto the couch close by her side. She talked to Jasper and tried to calm him.

Then all hell broke loose with sharp lightening followed by loud thunder that left her in the darkness. She cuddled Jasper under her chin and remained with ears for the wind and thunder. A few minutes later, she put Jasper down on the couch and felt her way to the kitchen closet, where she kept her oil lamps. She got two lamps from the closet and pulled her cigarette lighter from her pocket to light the wicks. The sweet smell of the oil filled the air as she placed one lamp on the bar. She lit the other lamp and its flicker carried shadows of objects that moved on the walls as she walked back to the den. She placed the lamp on the end table and its light fell on the stack of pictures of Tom that she have thrown in the trash. The picture on top showed a handsome man dressed in a black suit, white shirt, and red tie. His eyes seemed to focus on her. She liked his blue eyes, the first thing she and others noticed about him. She could imagine the warmth of his large frame next to her as she settled on the couch. At times like this, she needed him to comfort her and tell her some lies. Tom felt nothing for the women he had sex with; he used women. She wished she could feel nothing; she wished she could feel no guilt after she had sex with a man; she wished she could go out for a good time and forget the man's name. Would she ever stop thinking about Tom? She hated him.

She went to the couch, covered her head with a throw pillow, and tried to drown the sounds of the storm. Crazy thoughts crowded her mind; she saw the wind take the roof; she felt her body flying through the sky.

While Olivia worried about the storm, Scott Porter drove in the storm. At five o'clock that evening he crossed the Sidney Lanier Bridge in Brunswick and headed toward Porterville, his home town. Today his meeting in Brunswick had lasted all day. He wanted to get home before nine, but he had not eaten supper. He stopped in Garden City to fill up with gas. The clean town and nice restaurants looked tempting; but the dark clouds, rain and wind threatened a bad storm; he changed his mind.

After Scott left Garden City, the world turned darker, sharp lightening sliced the sky with a silver sword, and the cloud emptied torrents of rain that blinded him. He slowed to a crawl and strained his eyes to see the yellow line. He realized he had turned onto the wrong road when he did not see the sign for the interstate. He drove for miles and searched for a road that led back to the interstate. He could barely see and thanked God that the road had very little traffic. Then he hit a puddle and his tires skidded into the ditch. He mashed the gas, and the motor roared; but the car would not move forward. He put the car in reverse and tried to back out of the ditch, but the tires bogged deeper into the mud. He reached in his pocket and pulled out his cell phone to call a garage, but he had no service. He searched for his charger and discovered he had forgotten to bring it with him. He thought of getting into the back seat to sleep through the storm; but he needed to get back to his office to check on orders before meeting with his supervisors the next day. He expected a big order from the Sterling Company in California.

He got out of the car, braced himself against the wind, and bogged to his ankles as he moved toward the trunk. He quickly grabbed his raincoat and flashlight from the trunk. With his raincoat pulled close to his body, he moved the flashlight around his surroundings. He had never seen a darker night; stars failed to shine and the dark clouds swallowed the moon. He locked the car and started walking. He had walked less than a mile when he saw a dim flicker of light ahead. He flashed light in his steps and kept walking. He soon reached a house that sat back from the road. He walked up the driveway and reached stepping stones that led to the steps. He climbed the steps and knocked on the door.

Loud raps at the door startled Olivia. She sat up on the couch and looked around the dimly lit room. The shadows on the walls frightened her; but the caller at her door frightened her even more. She sat quietly and prayed for the caller to go away; but he knocked again. Then he called out loudly, "Is anyone home; please help me."

The urgency in his voice made her brace her courage; she got the lamp from the end table and slowly made her way to the door. She held to the doorknob several minutes before she got up her courage to open the door. Maybe her daddy had come to check on her. Her hopes rose as she pulled the door back.

A tall, slender woman with long, dark hair faced Scott Porter with a frightful gasp. She quickly slammed the door in his face and pushed the night latch in place. She could not see the man's face; but she realized that the tall stranger with water dripping down his face looked nothing like her daddy. She had never been more afraid in her life; and her neighbors lived more than four blocks from her house.

Scott Porter spoke with that same urgency in his voice. "Miss, I lost control of my car and landed in the ditch. The battery on my cell phone is dead. Would you please call a garage and ask them to send a tow truck to pull my car out of the ditch?"

Olivia's voice trembled as she talked to the man through the door. "My home phone is dead and I have no electricity; but I will try calling on my cell phone."

"Thank you," the man said.

Olivia went back to the den, got her cell phone, and made her way to the kitchen to find the phone book. She called two different garages, but she got no answer. She went back to the door and with the bad news. She explained that most businesses in the city had probably closed for the day. They talked through the door several minutes before Olivia finally took a chance and opened her door to this stranger.

He thanked her as he followed the flickering lamp to the living room, where she offered him a chair.

She set the lamp on the coffee table and said, "I wish I could do something to help you."

As she sat there with the stranger, terrible thoughts raced through her head. Did he intend to kidnap her? Did he intend to rape her? Did he intend to kill her?

He got up, walked over to the couch and held out his hand to her as he spoke, "I am Scott Porter. I hated to disturb you, but I didn't want to spend the night in my car."

His gentle voice made her trust him. "I am pleased to meet you, Mr. Porter. My name is Olivia Hollister."

"You must be terrified being here all alone in this storm," he said.

"My husband is usually home before now. I am worried that he got stalled in the storm, also."

"I got on the wrong road and searched for a sign to get back on the interstate. What town is this?"

"Boulder Bluff is only a few miles from here." she said.

"I have been to Boulder Bluff many times," he said. "Porterville is only twenty-five or thirty miles from here."

"You need to get out of those wet clothes," she said. "Come and I will get you some dry clothes." She remembered that she had one of Tom's old sweatshirts and a pair of his jeans that he left at her apartment.

She led him to the bathroom and he waited for her to find dry clothes for him to wear. She came back with the sweatshirt and jeans, gave him the lamp, and felt her way to the kitchen to get the other lamp before she went back to the living room.

A few minutes later Scott Porter came back into the living room. He thanked her for the dry clothes and remarked that they fit him perfectly.

She could not believe that this stranger wore the same size clothes as Tom. Then she blurted, "This is the craziest thing I have ever done. I invited you into my home and I don't know you from Adam."

"I am much younger than Adam and as harmless as a butterfly," he said. "In fact, I have never talked to Eve or any other woman in the dark." He laughed and she felt more at ease.

"I have never talked to a man in the daylight or the dark that I did not know well," she said.

"There is a first time for all things," he said. "I guess we can sit here in the dark and talk through the storm. What do you do for a living?"

"I am a school teacher," she said. "What do you do for a living?"

"I trade horses," he said and she could see his mouth break in a smile.

"Don't tease me at a time like this," she said.

"Seriously, I own Porter Manufacturing Company located in Porterville. I stay busy from daylight until dark every day during the week and sometimes on Saturday and Sunday."

"Porterville sounds like an interesting name for a city," she said. "I think I have been through Porterville on my way to the Savannah Mall."

"The city is named for Edward Alexander Porter, a distant relative of mine. He fought in the Civil War," he said.

"You must have a very profitable business," she said. "What kind of garments do you make?"

"My company specializes in shirts for teens, all styles, all colors, and all sizes. I will send your husband a new shirt and pair of pants to replace these."

"Don't bother," she said. "I lied to you about my husband. I am not married. I was in a serious relationship with Tom Bradford during my college days but things did not work out for us. Tom lives in a different town and a different world from mine."

"I am sorry to hear that. You must be going through a tough time." He could see the outline of her beautiful face in the flickering lamplight. She had dark hair, and he imagined that she had fair skin and blue eyes. Her eyes probably stared at him with fright.

She wanted to ask him about his family; instead, she talked about Tom and how dirty he had treated her.

Silence settled between them for minutes, and then she said, "Have you eaten supper?"

"I have not eaten since lunch, but I do not want to impose on you anymore than I have already."

"I wish we could go out to eat; but everything in town is probably closed, since they have no electricity. If you come through Bolder Bluff often, you should try the food at Southern Grill. They have vegetables, meats of your choice, salads, sandwiches, and desserts. I guess we must settle for sandwiches tonight. Come, let's go to the kitchen and find some cans to open."

She carried the lamp to the kitchen and set it on the bar. He stood next to her and she had to look up to him. He looked to be six feet tall and had broad shoulders like Tom. Why did she compare this man to Tom? She must not let her imagination get out of control and end up in the bedroom with this stranger.

She offered him a chair, but he sat down at the bar. He did not mind eating at the bar.

She searched the cabinets and pulled out cans of sardines, tuna, ham, and soup. She called out the choices and he told her that beggars could not be choosers.

Then she remembered that she had no way to warm the soup. She put the canned goods back in the cabinet and searched the refrigerator.

He watched her slender figure bend and turn as she set the food on the bar. She had a good figure to go with her beautiful face; but he had no right to look at her with sex on his mind. He dismissed his lustful thoughts and asked if he could help her with anything. As he started to get up, Jasper let out a loud meow and scampered across the kitchen. "My God, that cat startled me! I must have stepped on his tail."

"I forgot about Jasper; he likes to get under the bar stools when I am in the kitchen. Sit back down. Two fools fumbling around in the dark make double trouble," she said.

She did not know how many years had passed since she had let herself go and say what she thought without thinking, and she felt good.

She set mayonnaise, lettuce, tomato, ham, baloney, and turkey on the bar. Then she moved the lamp to the cupboard and pulled out a fresh loaf of bakery bread. "There, that should do it. What would you like to drink?"

"I like most anything to drink."

"Cold beer, wine, tea, or coffee; but the coffee is cold, too," she said.

"Beer will do fine," he said.

She pulled out a six-pack and set it on the counter. Then she fixed herself a glass of tea.

"This sandwich is the best cold cut I have ever tasted," he said.

They laughed, talked, and laughed some more. In fact, she laughed too much; and she did not want to give this man the wrong impression, but she liked everything about him. He had a good personality and reminded her of Tom.

As if he read her mind, he said, "You make me feel at ease, and that is something to brag about. I seldom have a loose tongue with women I don't know, but I feel like I have known you all my life."

She did not know what to say and he must have sensed her reaction.

"Are you still in love with Tom?" he said

Her silence made him quickly ask a different question, "Would you go out with Tom if he came back?"

"I don't want to get involved with Tom again, unless he changes his ways." she said. Then she asked herself why she talked to this stranger about her relationship with Tom Bradford.

They talked long after the wind, rain, and lightening ceased; but he told her very little about his personal life, and had said nothing about his family. The lights came on with a frightening flash and two strangers faced each other with happy and content faces. Neither of them noticed that the storm had calmed.

Astounded by the beautiful woman sitting across from him, Scott stared at her for minutes before he spoke. "You are more beautiful than I imagined, and your beauty shines under the lights." He thought she had the most beautiful face he had ever seen, and her dark hair shimmered around her shoulders.

"Your kind words make me blush," she said and pushed a hand over her hair. "I must look a mess."

"From my observation, Tom lost a very beautiful and kind woman when he broke up with you. I would come back to you on bended knees."

"Tom saw me in a different light, I suppose." Olivia said. At the same time, she thought about Scott Porter's handsome face. He had smooth skin, dark eyes, thick brows, and dark hair.

Scott looked at his watch and said, "I have no excuse to hang around longer. I need to use your phone."

He stood up and Olivia could not help but admire his broad shoulders and tall, slender figure. "She pointed to the phone on the table beyond the couch. "I don't know if my house phone is working or not, but I have a cell phone you may use."

"Do you have a phone book handy?"

She got up, went to the kitchen, and came back with the phone book.

The phone works," he said with excitement as he looked up the number. He called Davis' Garage and paused to ask Olivia her address. He came back and sat down across from Olivia to wait. Mr. Davis knew Olivia and knew where she lived. He would be there in about an hour. He had another call to answer first.

While they waited, they talked some more. He asked if he could call her sometime, and she quickly grabbed a piece of paper, wrote down her number, and gave it to him.

When the tow truck pulled into Olivia's drive, Scott got up and said, "Thank you for everything; I enjoyed your company and the food; I would have never made it through the storm without your help. I would like to take you out to dinner sometimes."

"I will give your invitation to dinner some thought; but you do not owe me anything. I am glad that I could help." As she watched him walk toward the tow truck, she closed the door and leaned back with a sigh. She hated to see him walk away. Until tonight, she had never seen a perfect storm.

She closed the door, checked the night latch, and went to the bathroom to take a bath. Minutes later, she sang a happy tune in the shower. Mr. Porter's visit had put her in a good mood. Then she thought of the foolish thing she had done; she had opened her door and invited a stranger to come into her home. Had she lost her mind? Luckily, he had been the best thing that had happened to her since she broke up with Tom.

After she dressed for bed, she thought about Scott Porter instead of Tom. Why had Scott not mentioned anything about his personal life or his family? She feared that he had a wife and children. She must forget about Scott Porter. She had promised herself that she would never fall in love again. Now she found herself dreaming about a stranger she had just met.

CHAPTER FIVE

Life after Tragedy

IN THE MEANTIME, Mr. Davis pulled Scott Porter out of the ditch with ease. Scott paid him in cash, thanked him for coming to his rescue, and drove away. At Boulder Bluff, he got on the interstate and headed to Porterville, Georgia, a small southern town south of Savannah.

As Scott Porter drove toward home, he thought about Olivia Hollister. For the first time since he married Laura, he found himself strongly attracted to another woman. Should he feel guilty about the good feeling he got when he looked at Olivia? Why should he feel guilty? Laura never spoke to him or reacted to his kind advances. He treated her like a queen and spoiled her like an only child; he made sure she had her favorite foods served at least once a day; he gave her cards on special occasions; he bought her flowers, candy, pretty gowns, and fruit baskets. Laura paid no attention to him or anything he did for her. He felt like throwing up his hands in defeat. Did he have a future?

His mind flashed back to their first date, their wedding day, and the five happy years they had together. They got married in the Methodist Church that Laura had attended all of her life. Then Laura Joined the Baptist Church where Scott attended. They followed the principles of Christianity, read their Bibles, and went to church every Sunday. Laura played the piano for the church choir. They had everything a young couple could ask for and they lived the good life. Laura liked their beautiful home; and she kept it neat and clean. She decorated, cooked, and worked in the yards. He hired Mrs. Louise Sanders, who had helped his mother raise him, to help Laura with the house and cooking, especially when they had dinner parties. Scott drove a new truck and bought Laura a new car every when she wanted one. They had many friends and Scott had political pull in the city as well as the State. He played golf every week at the Ocmulgee Country Club with the mayor of the city and tax commissioner as well as his other friends. They drank beer at the club and had lunch together. After hours, he and Laura often went to expensive restaurants in the city or the country club to have dinner and drinks.

Since high school, hiking had been one of Laura's favorite activities. She often spent the weekend on hiking trips with her friends. She especially liked the scenic routes on the trails in North Georgia. When they had long bus rides, they carried tents and spent the weekend.

Laura liked the hiking trips to Stone Mountain best of all. In fact, she had hiked more than a mile on the Walk-up Trail to reach the top of Stone Mountain; she had walked the five miles Cherokee Trail around the base of Stone Mountain; she had hiked the near one-mile loop on the Nature Garden Trail; and she had hiked the mile long Songbird Trail.

He could still hear the laughter and excitement in Laura's voice as she described the scenic routes shaded by Georgia oaks, hickory trees, and native plants. She mimicked the sounds of songbirds, talked about where they camped, their cookouts, sky rides, cruises on the riverboat, duck tours, tours through an antebellum plantation, and activities at the crossroads. She especially liked the fine restaurants, movie theaters, and places to shop.

One weekend Laura went with a group of friends from the First Baptist Church on a hiking trip to her favorite place, Stone Mountain, Georgia, near Atlanta. Laura stumbled and fell face first on a ragged granite rock. Her friends called an ambulance, and they carried her to the Grady Memorial hospital in Atlanta, where she got the best of care from doctors, nurses, and attendants. The hospital also had the best medical supplies and facilities. In spite of the best of care Laura's brain injury paralyzed her, and Doctor Sidney Ricks gave Scott no hopes of her recovery.

Laura's accident changed her life forever; her condition changed his life forever. Laura could not speak, use her arms or legs, and had no control of her bodily functions. Scott placed Laura in the Hillcrest Manor Nursing Home in Porterville, where the nurses cared for her as they would care for a newborn baby. They bathed, dressed, fed and comforted her; they gave her medication to make her rest.

 He loved Laura as much as a man could love a woman. He kept up his hopes for her to get well and come back home. He stayed by her side every day for more than a month. He slept only a few hours every night, took a bath, got dressed, and picked up something to eat on the way back to Hillcrest Manor. Back by Laura's side, he held her hand, and prayed for her to call his name, tell him she loved him. At times, her fixed stare at him gave him hope; he thought she recognized him; he thought he could read the look in her eyes that said she loved him. Sometimes she opened her eyes, but she stared at nothing each time he visited her.

After Laura's accident, Scott found himself all alone in a large two-story house that seemed empty without her. The home he and Laura once loved had become the loneliest place on earth. He walked from one room to another as if he would find Laura there. He felt shocked; he felt devastated; more than anything, he felt angry. He had long known humility; he had long known hate; but he had never known the loneliness that he felt without Laura. He could not think straight; everything he looked at reminded him of their happy times together; especially their wedding pictures that covered one wall.

Scott remembered the first day he walked into that empty house; he could not stay there. He turned with anger and rushed out the back door, walked across the porch to the shed, and grabbed the hoe as it were a weapon, and went to the garden. He always planted a garden in the spring. The once healthy plants had practically choked on weeds. He chopped the weeds and dug at the earth as if to tear it down to thin dust. The weeds tumbled here and there, and the leaves quickly withered. He trampled the fresh bed of dirt and fought through another green forest. Sweat poured from his brow and ran down his face, and blisters swelled his palms, but he felt no physical pain. He worked and sweated until the sun fell and darkness forced him to go back into his empty house. He could actually hear Laura in the shower; he could feel the bed dip as she slipped into bed next to him; he could feel her snuggle close to him; and he could smell her clean sweetness. How he wished Laura could have given him a child. At least, he would have that part of her to help him make it through each day. Laura wanted to get pregnant right after they married. When all else failed, they both went for fertility treatments. As a last resort, they asked for insemination of his sperm into and Laura; but nothing they tried worked magic.

He had changed many of his ways since Laura's stroke. He did not have her to tell him which shirt went with the pants he chose; he did not have Laura to tell him which shoes to wear; and he did not have Laura to help him write his speeches for the meetings with stockholders every month. Many times, he would sit up on the side of the bed and cover his face with his hands to grab his composure and face reality.

The months changed to a year with no good news or hope for Laura. Would he ever live a normal life again? Why had God put a burden too heavy to carry on his shoulders? How could he live without Laura's love and affection? He needed her; he needed to feel her warmth close by his side; he needed her to sit across the table from him at meal time; he needed her opinion about his business; he needed her understanding; most of all he needed her love. He wanted to scream and vent his anger. He did not know how much longer he could take his terrible situation.

Finally, he realized that Laura would never recognize him again; she would never get any better; she still breathed, ate, and existed; yet, she died the day she had the accident. He could do nothing to help her, except pray and pay for her care. He prayed every day for her to get well; but God did not answer his prayers. He thanked God for the years He had given him with Laura; but he did not understand why He took her from him.

The Porterville city limits sign brought him back down to earth in his car driving toward home. When he walked into the empty house, he felt more restless than ever. He got a beer, sat down in his chair, and thought about his situation. He felt sorry for Laura, but the good feeling he got when he looked at Olivia made him lust for her. He could not stop thinking about her. She did something to him that no other woman had ever done before, including Laura. He needed Olivia; he wanted to hold her in his arms and make love to her all night. He had to have her.

He continuously asked himself what he could do about his situation; he came up with not good answers. He got up and paced back and forth across the room. He needed to talk to someone. The hands on the clock told him he had waited too late to invite a friend over for a beer. He walked to the kitchen, got another beer, and went back to his chair. After the third trip to the kitchen for a beer, he fell asleep. He awoke to the dong of the clock as it struck eleven times.

After he went to bed, he told himself that he must get his head straight and make the best of a terrible situation.

The next morning, Scott went to Hillcrest Manor to visit Laura. He felt guilty about not having visited her the day before; he felt guilty about the good feeling he got when he looked at Olivia. As usual, he walked into Laura's room, leaned over and kissed her cheek, sat down in the chair next to her bed, and held her soft, warm hand. Like all the other times since the accident, Laura stared at nothing and showed no feelings at all for him. That part of his life ended the day of the accident; and he did not know what to do about the life he had left.

As he sat and looked at her blank stare, he thought about how much he loved her; but she could not love him back. He thought about their wedding vows: to love, honor, cherish, and keep each other for better or for worse until their death. Things could get no worse. Laura could not keep her vows. Who wrote those wedding vows? How could he divorce his helpless wife? Laura had been a devout Christian; she had been faithful and lived by God's commandments. She had attended church three times a week and lived a righteous life. Why did God punish the Godly and bypass the sinners. Laura's condition made him think that God had no mercy for the true believers; He tested true believers. According to God's word, he had sinned already. How could his thoughts about Olivia be a sin? Should he ask forgiveness for a sin he had not yet committed.

Scott kissed Laura on her forehead and left to go to work. He pulled into the paved parking area, surrounded by a forest of green pines, and found his marked space before the large brick building. He sat there and looked at the building and the parking area filled with cars. He employed over one hundred workers, which included tailors, cutters, packers, office workers, and truck drivers. Porter Manufacturing had grown since Scott Porter Senior's death. The small town had a population of less than ten thousand, and his factory supplied many of the citizens with jobs, especially the women. Like his father, he specialized in shirts for teenagers, but he also made pants, shirts, and bathrobes that suited the older generation. He shipped shirts and pants to popular department stores all over the United States, Canada, China, and Japan. Cheap labor in Japan and China made it difficult to offer American goods to these countries, but the wealthy businessmen in other countries liked his products; their trade kept him in business.

Was his hard work and responsibilities worth the money? He no longer had Laura to share his fortune with. How he wished his parents were still living. He missed them so much. His daddy taught him everything he knew about running the business and he paid him a good salary. None of his high school friends made as much money as he did. Money motivated Scott to work harder. At first, he carried bundles from the cutting room to the sewing room. At age fifteen, his father taught him how to sew; he could sew better than the best tailor in the state could. Before he turned eighteen, his father gave him a raise and assigned him to train new employees. He taught them how to cut, seam, and pack. Before he graduated from high school, he knew how to run every machine in the factory and could do any job better than the any employee his father hired.

Scott finally got out of his truck, walked down the sidewalk lined with neatly trimmed hedge, and entered the building. Tropical plants decorated the entrance and spread a clean smell around the room.

His secretary, Jan Langley, greeted him with a cheerful good morning and said, "Did you have a nice trip to Brunswick."

"I got stalled in the storm for a spell, but I finally made it home."

"I am glad you got back home safely," she said. "The storm blew down trees and power lines around my house. We had no electricity for several hours."

Scott did not mention the time he spent with Olivia Hollister in the dark. He simply said, "We don't know how lucky we are to have electricity until we are caught in the dark."

She laughed and watched his tall figure disappear down the hall. She wondered how he kept such a good sense of humor. She did not know what she would do if her husband, Leonard, had an accident that paralyzed him. She had already turned forty-five, more than fifteen years older than Scott Porter. Women noticed his handsome features, good build, and the way he carried himself. All of his employees loved him. He had the reputation for being conservative; but she admired a man who knew how to handle his money. Besides, he gave thousands to charity every year. When she asked for donations, he never turned her down. He also spent money on his friends and gave his employees a bonus every Christmas. She visited Laura often and wanted to do something for her. What could she do? She felt sorry for Scott. On the other hand, he wanted no sympathy or pity. She turned back to her computer and continued posting debits and credits.

As Scott unlocked his door, he took out his handkerchief and wiped the dust from his nameplate that read: Scott Porter, President of Porter Manufacturing Company. Just inside, he hung his hat on the hook next to the door, walked across the plush carpet to the window, and opened the rich green linen curtains. The window gave a nice view of the parking lot and the surrounding area.

As he sat at his desk, he looked around the room at the colorful paintings that Laura had chosen for his office. He thought he should change everything around him that reminded him of Laura.

The stack of mail on his desk took his attention. After he went through the mail, he called his secretary, Jan, and asked her to set up a meeting for nine o'clock with his supervisors in the conference room.

At the meeting, Scott talked about production and asked them to turn in monthly reports before the end of the day, including orders, shipments, and inventory.

After the meeting, Adam Sinclair walked with him through the plant. The cool cutting room had long tables marked at the edge for measuring large rolls of cloth. He and Adam stood and watched the employees bring in rolls of cloth and place them on the tables. Then they set an electric machine to roll out the exact number of yards or inches needed to complete each job. Each cut of cloth supplied cloth for a certain number of shirts or other garments. The cutters rolled and cut cloth all day. After they cut, the shirts and garments out, they placed them in a rolling cart and the bundle boy rolled them to the machine room.

Scott and Adam walked on to the Machine room to check on progress. They never saw idle workers. Five rows of machines, with adequate room between each row, filled the well-lit room from wall to wall. The sewing room had an assembly line of sewing machine operators who sewed pockets, collars, zippers, sleeves, and labels before sewing the fronts and backs together. One tailor sewed one part of the garment and passed it on to the next tailor to sew another part. This process continued and ended with a finished product.

They left the machine room, and went to the steam room, where five employees handled large pressers and ironed out the wrinkles in the finished garment. After they pressed the garments, bundle boys moved them to the packing room.

In the large packing room, workers folded, bagged, and boxed the garments for shipment. As they walked back toward Scott's office, he told Adam that he liked the shipping department best of all in his younger days. He enjoyed packing the boxes and slapping mailing labels on them.

Adam Sinclair told Scott the employees worked extra hard to make production. He added that production for the month increased from the previous month.

Scott agreed with Adam. All of his employees seemed dedicated to their jobs. He added that money always motivated him to work harder; and their salaries depended on their production. The more garments they put out, the more money they made; and the more money Porter Manufacturing made.

Back in his office, he looked up Olivia Hollister's address on the internet and left his office. At Jutland's Florist, he ordered a dozen red roses, wrote a note on the card, and handed Jane Jutland a piece of paper with a name and address for delivery. Jane paid little attention to the name on the piece of paper, since Scott often sent flowers to his employees and friends

After going to the club for lunch, Scott went back to his office. As soon as he settled behind his desk, he read his mail. The large order from Sterling Corporation made him smile. He called Adam to his office, informed him about the order; and they talked about an hour.

Scott worked later than usual on accounts to keep from having useless thoughts about Olivia.

After he left his office, he stopped by the club and ate supper. Joseph had already left and he missed talking to him. His other friends had finished eating; but they stayed and waited for him. He took an empty chair at their table and joined their conversation while he ate.

At the same time that evening, Olivia pulled into her drive and discovered a white box sitting on her front porch. She pulled under the garage, rushed through the house, and got the package. Back inside, she noticed that the package came from Jutland's Florist; she guessed the contents of the box before she opened it. She pulled out the vase of beautiful roses and marveled aloud at their beauty. The note made her smile, "Thanks you for being a friend when I needed one most. Scott Porter." She set the arrangement on the table in the living room, stood back, and looked at the roses. Tom used to give her roses, too. Why did she continue to compare others to Tom?

She went to the bedroom, changed clothes, and walked her usual mile. She liked to watch the animals along the way. Sometimes she saw a rabbit hop, stop, and listen; at other times, she stopped and watched a squirrel scamper up a tree. Most of all, she liked to listen to birds sing.

On the way back home, she stopped at the wooden bridge and sat on the rail to rest. Water flowed over the huge rocks and they looked like whales jumping in the stream. For some reason, the scene put her in a useless romantic mood.

Two days later, Scott still had not heard from Olivia. He thought she would call and thank him for the flowers; he thought she would call and invite him to come for dinner. He longed to hear her voice. Everywhere he went, he saw her face in the crowd. He had never met a more beautiful woman. He knew other beautiful women who could satisfy his sexual needs with no strings attached; but something about Olivia made her different. He could not forget her; he wanted her more than his next breath.

After he went to bed at night, he lay in the darkness for hours and thought about Olivia. Then he dreamed about her. He sat up on the edge of the bed and buried his face in his hands. He decided that he would ask Olivia to go out for dinner to show his appreciation for her kindness; but he must not think about having sex with her; he had a wife; he had responsibility to the Baptist church to fulfill his duty as a deacon. As an out-standing member of the community, he must keep up his good name. He must pray about his situation; he must ask God to help him forget her. Then he thought of the times he had called on God to help Laura get well. Each time he prayed this prayer, he remembered his mother's words: "God does not answer selfish prayers."

On Sunday, Scott went to church to ease his guilt. He pretended to enjoy the social gathering, but he no longer enjoyed going to church.

On the way home from church, he asked himself what other Godly men would do in his shoes? Would they think about having sex with another woman? Most men needed companionship; most men needed a woman to love; most men needed a family, and he no longer had a family. His friends sympathized with his situation and pretended to understand, but they had no idea how miserable his life had become. He had an empty, worthless life without a woman to love. He must keep his desire to make love to Olivia a secret.

At the same time, Olivia thought about Scott Porter. She walked around the room and observed the students while they took their weekly quiz. The bell rang before most students finished their quiz. She assured them that they could finish their quiz the next day. She stayed busy the rest of that day with her lecture and writing notes on the board.

When Olivia got home from school, she stuffed a load of clothes in the washer and went to the kitchen. Grilled chicken and a garden salad sounded delicious. Before the chicken browned, she found herself daydreaming about Scott Porter. She wished he would call.

After she finished eating, her wish came true. She rushed to the living room and looked at the caller identification. With a pounding in her chest, she took a deep breath and answered with a cheerful hello.

Scott thanked her once again for her kindness the night of the storm. She thanked him for the beautiful roses and they talked a few minutes about their work.

After Scott hung up, he felt disappointed. He thought she would invite him to come over for a cup of coffee or a beer. Did she still love her ex-boyfriend? Was she involved with someone else? He had no right to question her about her life.

Scott had been wrong to think that Olivia had no interest in him. The sound of his voice made her have chill bumps and feel warm at the same time. She liked talking to him; she liked him more than she wanted to like him. He had renewed her spirit and put a skip in her step. She crossed her fingers with wishes to meet Scott Porter again soon. Then she thought about his family. She must ask questions the next time he called.

On Friday after school, Emily called with shocking news. She had filed for a divorce. Olivia pulled the phone away from her ear and looked at it with shock; she could not believe her ears. Olivia asked her to come for a visit and they could be lonely together.

Emily promised to come on Saturday for a visit.

At twelve o'clock on Saturday, Emily arrived. They went to Saxby's and talked while they enjoyed salad and chicken strips. Olivia learned why Emily wanted out of her marriage. Her husband never went with her anywhere, not even to her parents' home on Sunday. Emily liked to dance and dine; she liked to go out for dinner; she also liked to have a drink or two after dinner. Her husband changed into a couch person after they married, and Emily missed the good times.

Olivia complained about the way Tom had dumped her. She had heard that he had dated many other girls since she left Cedar Grove, including Stella Shivers.

Emily advised her to let go of her bottled up anger and live again. If she sat at home and thought about the past, she would never have a future with the right man, a man who appreciated her and liked to do the same things she liked. She suggested that Olivia go out with different men to discover what she had been missing.

Olivia finally got up the courage to spill the beans. She had met Scott Porter, a handsome, kind gentleman who she wanted to go out with, but she knew very little about him. He had sent her a dozen roses.

Emily shouted, "Thank God!" Everyone in the restaurant turned and stared at them.

After they finished eating, they drove to the mall in Boulder Bluff to shop. As usual, the mall bustled with shoppers. Emily wanted a new pair of shoes to match an outfit she had.

When Emily dropped Olivia off at her house, she said, "Call me and keep me up-to-date on Scott Porter."

"I will call and let you know if he asks me for a date," Olivia said. "I enjoyed our time together; we must go out more often."

As Olivia watched Emily drive away, she silently wished she could be more like Emily, more daring and ready to take chances; but Olivia feared she would step off the deep end if she went too far.

CHAPTER SIX

Unexpected Proposal

WHEN OLIVIA GOT home from work, she dressed in comfortable jeans and pull over to relax a few minutes before she cooked supper. She picked up the Boulder Bluff daily news from the end table and lay back on the couch to read. She had not finished the front page before the doorbell took her attention. The thought of seeing Scott again made her heart quicken. She jumped up from the couch and made her way to the door. When she looked through the door peeper, she got the shock of her life; there stood Tom Bradford dressed in a nice suit, white shirt, and tie. She thought her heart would literally beat out of her chest. She took a deep breath and unlocked the door. Too shocked to speak, she stood and stared at him. His handsome face nor his good physique had changed.

He smiled and said, "I should have called; but I knew you would hang up on me. Besides, I wanted to see you in person and talk with you."

"I am surprised to see you," Olivia said and invited him to come inside."

She offered him a chair in the living room and asked if he would like something to drink.

He asked if she had a beer handy, and she trailed off to the kitchen. She needed something stronger than a beer, but she did not have any liquor. She handed him a beer and he deliberately brushed his hand down her arm before taking the beer. She pretended not to notice, but she definitely felt his magic touch. She sat across from him and asked how he had been. He had graduated, passed the bar exam, and worked with his father at Bradford Law Firm. They had a good business and he stayed busy.

He soon changed the subject to her life since they parted ways. In fact, he wanted to know every detail of her life and daily routine. She explained that she taught the sixth grade at Boulder Bluff Middle School. Her job required a lot of patience and over time; but she liked her job. She had made many friends and she loved her students. She also brought him up-to-date on her parents and asked about Mr. and Mrs. Bradford. She soon ran out of things to say and felt awkward with him sitting in her apartment. After all, she had not heard a word from him in more than two years.

He walked across the room and held his hands out to her. Like a fool, she took his hand and he pulled her from the chair. Then he pulled her close and kissed her with a wildness that made her lose her good sense. His kiss brought back memories of the first time he had kissed her, and she had flash backs of their good times together. She finally pulled away from him and asked if he would like to have dinner with her.

He wanted to take her out to dinner. She did not tell him that she usually cooked her meals to save money for rent and utilities. She looked at her dress; she would have to take a bath and dress if they went out to a restaurant. She suggested that they call a restaurant and order something to go. He said food to go would be great; and he offered to go and pick up their order. She could not believe the change in him; he never liked to order meals to go before.

She heard Jasper meowing, excused herself, and found Jasper huddled under a chair in the dining room; he would not come to his food. He seemed to feel Tom's presence and he did not like Tom. She squatted down and petted Jasper to assure him that he had nothing to be afraid of.

She went by the bedroom, grabbed her purse, and went back to the living room. Tom stood and took her hand as they walked to his car. He drove to the Chinese Garden and they ordered chicken to go. While they enjoyed dinner, Jasper disappeared from sight. They talked about old times. He helped her clear the table and followed her back to the living room. When she started to sit back down in her armchair, he grabbed her hand and led her to the couch. She wanted to stop before things got out of hand; she made excuses about having to get up early and looked at her watch. He took her hint, kissed her good night, and told her he had enjoyed being with her.

Before closing the front door behind him he said, "Olivia, I miss you; I miss what we had; I want you back." He rushed down the steps before she had time to put up an argument.

After Tom Left, Olivia lay in bed and thought back to the time she and Tom first met. Two young and foolish people who liked to have a good time. Then she fell madly in love with him; her love for him seemed like a hypnotic drug that gave her a wonderful feeling for a short time and almost killed her when it wore off. Tom had never had a serious relationship and never made a commitment to her. The good times with Tom ended and they went separate ways. She assumed that he still played the field and planned to remain a bachelor the rest of his life. Now Tom had returned and he still turned her legs to jelly. Why had she kidded herself? After all these years, she still loved him; she would always love him. Memories of their times together made her have chills. She could feel the warmth of his body; she could feel his kiss; she yearned for him to make love to her. He could talk her into climbing Mount Everest, and heights terrorized her. What would she do if he came back and asked her to go back to him? She could not deal with his heart of stone. She did not want to get hurt again. What did tomorrow hold? What did he want from her? Was he the same old Tom who wanted sex and a good time? Why did he come back after she met Scott Porter? What would she say to Scott if he called her again?

The next evening after work, Tom called. He asked her to go with him to the mountains the following weekend.

After minutes of silence, she refused to spend the weekend with him. Instead, she invited him to come have dinner with her Friday night.

After she hung up, she went into the bathroom, looked in the mirror and talked to the crazy woman looking back at her. "You are a fool if you go back to Tom Bradford! He makes you crazy! He wants to control you!" She flipped her hand at the woman in the mirror and said, "What will be, will be." She had not changed. Tom still had her under his thumb. She got dressed for bed and lay on the couch with Jasper under her chin as she watched television. When the phone rang, she expected to hear Tom's voice.

Instead, Scott surprised her. "Hello, beautiful. Do you feel as good as you look?"

She did not know what to say; her heart beat in her toes as she spoke, "I feel fine. How have you been?"

"I called to ask if you would like to go out to dinner with me tomorrow night."

Olivia did not want to tell Scott that Tom had come back; she did not want to tell him she had invited Tom to dinner. She simply said, "Could I take a rain check on your invitation? I have already made other plans for tomorrow night."

"I understand," Scott said. "I should have called earlier. I will keep in touch."

After he hung up, Olivia asked herself why she had not told Scott about Tom. She had looked forward to Scott's call; she had turned him down; and he would never call her again. Was she ready to go back to Tom? Her previous experience with Tom made her distrust him. He had earned the reputation for being a lover boy. After he had sex with a woman, he ditched her. She had been innocent, loving, and trusting in her relationship with Tom; she gave her heart and soul to him and expected his love in return, but he used her for his gain and made her look like a fool. The bad picture he painted of her covered his own wrong doings. He advertised secrets she shared with him. He had treated her as he would treat a retarded child. Was he still a cheat and a liar? She never wanted to make the same mistake again.

Tom Bradford spent the weekend with Olivia and completely changed her loneliness and depression to happiness. He bragged on her cooking after they ate, and Olivia appreciated his manners. She had never spent a more romantic weekend with Tom. They talked about old times, drank beer, listened to music, danced, and made love. Tom Bradford had changed to this wonderful man who acted as if he adored her.

On Monday, Olivia over-slept; she had only thirty minutes to get dressed and get to school. She rushed to the shower, threw on her clothes, and combed her hair. Before she left for school, she ran to the bedroom and to let Tom know she had to go to work and promised to call him at recess.

When the students had their ten-minute break at ten o'clock, she called Tom. She wanted him to feel at home. She had plenty of cold cuts in the refrigerator to make sandwiches for lunch.

Tom had to go back to Cedar Grove to meet with a client. He thanked her for a wonderful weekend; she had made him a happy man. He would call her when she got home that evening.

Olivia pulled the phone before her and stared at it with disbelief. Why had he never told her before that she made him happy?

One night in bed with Tom made Olivia fall in love all over again. She had never really gotten over him to begin with and found that she loved him even more. He made her happier than she had been since they broke up. He softened her heart for the long haul.

After the second date, Tom said the three magic words. He admitted that he had loved her from the beginning of their relationship; but he could not make a commitment to her. After all, he had no job making his own money; his father supported him; and he had school as well as his future on his mind.

Olivia fell for his story. As long as Tom loved her and satisfied her in bed, she did not need romantic scenes and gestures at other times.

On Christmas Day, Tom proposed; and Olivia shouted with happiness. The carat diamond he slipped on her finger made her eyes widen with excitement and happiness. She realized that lawyers made much more money than poor school teachers made. She had to pinch pennies to have enough money to make ends meet every month.

Olivia's parents liked Tom; her mother catered to him by cooking special dishes he liked. She wanted the best for Tom and paid him more attention than she paid her own daughter.

Olivia planned a big church wedding for the following July at Cavalry Methodist Church, the church she had attended with her parents all of her life.

When school turned out in May, Olivia told the principal that she would not be back the next year. The principal as well as all of the teachers were happy to hear that

Tom had proposed to her. Her friends at school knew about Tom and how much she loved him. They offered to help with the wedding and bridal shower that Olivia and Tom's mothers had already planned.

Olivia worked during the entire month of June to make her wedding perfect. Her mother and Tom's mother pitched in and helped with the invitations and decorations. Tom's mother hired a professional photographer to make the wedding pictures; she also hired Knox's Catering for an elaborate reception. They invited more than one hundred people to the wedding.

Olivia shopped for a wedding dress three days before she found the perfect dress. She turned before the mirror and smiled as she admired the satin dress covered with lace. She turned to get a side view of the A-line skirt that fell on her feet and carried a three yards train. Most of all, she liked the low cut princess style bodice with the tiny pearls that covered the front. She held out her arms to admire the long sleeves that tapered to a point at her wrist. The dress fit perfectly. As she got dressed, she thought about how many months it would take to pay off her credit card. More than one hundred dollars a month for an entire year. She did not want Tom to pay for her wedding dress. Then she remembered that she would not have rent or utilities to pay after she moved into the house with Tom; she would have money left over every month for the first time since she moved out on her own.

During the last week of June, Olivia moved out of her apartment. The next week, on the fifth day of July, she and Tom got married. More people came to their wedding than they invited. People filled the seats in the church, stood on the sides, and behind the back pews. Olivia's silky black hair bounced around her shoulders and framed a beautiful face as she held to her father's arm and walked toward the altar. Tom smiled and looked at her as if he adored her. Her smile let him know that he had made her the happiest woman in the world.

After a honeymoon cruise for seven days in the Bahamas, Olivia moved into the lake house with Tom. She liked the house, and she had only two miles to drive to Cedar Grove High School, where she taught English. Tom still worked with his father at the Bradford Law Firm that had been in Tom's family over fifty years.

Olivia had a full schedule during the week at school; but she quickly learned to live a different lifestyle after school. She went to the gym one day every week; she and Tom went out to eat two or three times a week. Tom had a very good income and gave her a generous allowance to pay the bills and buy groceries. They could afford many luxuries that most people do without. She had a house cleaner that came in once a week to clean, wash, and iron. Tom still had Henry to keep the yards and tend the garden. Tom always planted a garden in the spring.

Olivia had to get used to her new social life, also. She had lived alone and had grown used to the quiet, peaceful life. Olivia had never been a daily drinker; Tom went for his bottle when he got home every evening. Tom wanted to be in control of the show when he entertained. On Saturdays, they often had dinners for lawyers and accountants who worked for Bradford Law Firm as well as special clients. They also had dinner parties for their friends. Olivia got accustomed to the business dinners and parties. She quickly learned how to mingle with the crowd and be a good host. Tom seemed proud to show her off to his friends, and she felt proud to be his wife. She did not like the women who flirted with Tom; but she pretended not to notice. Sometimes Tom hired a band; other times they had a DJ to play music. They danced, played cards and other games, and went swimming.

On the weekends, when Tom did not have a party, he carried her out to expensive restaurants or visited friends.

On Sunday, they went to church. Olivia moved her membership from the Methodist church to the Baptist church that Tom attended. She got along well with his parents, sister, brother, and their children. Mrs. Bradford did little things to make life easier for Olivia. She baked cakes for them and sent gift cards for them to have dinner at expensive restaurants. She even booked and paid for hotels on the beach for them to spend weekends and vacations. Mrs. Bradford treated them like spoiled grandchildren, and Olivia liked her special treats. In spite of the changes for Olivia, Tom made her happy and they had a good life.

Tom's mother became one of Olivia's best friends. She taught Olivia how to cook some delicious foods that went together; and Olivia like to cook special dishes for Tom. He especially liked his mother's pizza and spaghetti. Mrs. Bradford made pizza dough that tasted better than any Olivia had ever tasted; Olivia had not mastered the secret to her pizza or spaghetti. Mrs. Bradford's Italian grandmother passed the secret recipes down to her mother.

Olivia heard the garage door slam and she rushed around the kitchen to check on dinner. She did not have dinner ready. She turned from the stove to see Tom standing in the door. He smiled and said, "How is my beautiful wife?"

"When I get the food on the table, I will tell you," she said.

"I know the food will be delicious. You have learned to handle that frying pan like a professional."

He walked up to her, pulled her to him, and kissed her long and passionately.

"My steak!" she said, and grabbed her turning fork.

"Turn it off," he said as he unbuttoned her blouse.

"You will have soggy steak."

"I don't want any steak; I want you," he said and pinched her.

"Don't pinch me!" she said.

He ran to the bedroom and she ran after him. Their playful tussle ended with a wild and passionate need for each other. He made love to her with gentle touches and sweet kisses that sent her to the wild blue yonder.

An hour later, she reheated the pan and finished frying the steak.

Tom made their first anniversary special. He bought her a dozen red roses and took her to Nicks for dinner. He ordered a Margarita before ordering dinner and she ordered a frozen daiquiri. The both had a garden salad and seafood platters with shrimp, fish, and fried oysters. After dinner, they spent the night at the Gulf Place, an elaborate hotel with top service and fantastic rooms. They made love and talked about their future most of the night.

That first year married to Tom had been the most wonderful year of her life. Tom fussed over her and treated her like a queen. He often sent her flowers or special little gifts with sweet love notes. He had bought her so much expensive jewelry that she did not know what to ask for at Christmas time. Tom seemed content and happy. Likewise, she lived for Tom, and he relished her attention. She thought of him as her pillar of strength; and she looked forward to the time they had together.

CHAPTER SEVEN

Marriage on the Rocks

DURING THE MONTHS that followed, Tom continuously talked about starting a family. He complained that he wanted children before he got too old to raise them, but Olivia could not work magic and get pregnant. She thought something must be wrong with her, but Doctor Collins, her gynecologist, assured her that she had no female problems. He believed that stress prevented her from getting pregnant and advised her to relax and let nature take its course. How could she relax with Tom's complaints? Each time he brought up the subject, Olivia cried. Tom apologized and promised not to bring the subject up again, but he did not keep his promise.

Olivia liked living on the lake, but Tom decided they needed to move to Cedar Grove to be near his office. He often got calls after hours and needed to refer to client's records.

Tom brought stacks of house plans for Olivia to choose the design of the house and the floor plan she wanted. He would settle for the house she chose; but he wanted a workshop next to the garage. In his spare time, he liked working with wood. He had a natural talent for building things. He had built tables, a doghouse, a boat, and several birdhouses.

Their new house quickly took shape and Olivia liked the floor plan. She often drove into town to the lot where the carpenters worked on their new home. Their contractor, Joel Foster, checked everything behind his workers. He walked through the house with Olivia and showed her what they had finished and what else they had to do. Olivia chose the color of paint she wanted for each room and picked out the cabinets she liked.

The next week, Olivia went by their new house every day after school. As she and Mr. Foster discussed the built-in bookcases in the living room, Tom walked in the front door. Mr. Foster shook his hand and they talked a few minutes about the house. The carpenters would have everything finished by the end of the next week.

That night, Tom accused her of being too friendly with Mr. Foster. She stood and looked at him with disbelief. How could he accuse her of being romantically involved with another man? Women flocked to him everywhere they went and when they had dinner parties. He danced with other women often; but she seldom danced with another man.

The next week, Olivia did not go by their new home. The day Mr. Foster and his construction crew finished their house, Mr. Foster lost control of his truck, ran off the road, and hit a tree. He died from his injuries at the hospital shortly after they got him to the emergency room.

Olivia felt depressed about Mr. Foster's death; she felt sorry for his wife who had a young son in fifth grade. Mr. Foster had just left their house when he had the wreck. She wished they had never hired Mr. Foster in the first place; she wished they still lived at the lake.

The next week after school, Olivia went by their new home; but everything outside and inside the house reminded her of Mr. Foster. The wide porch set with decorative columns, the beautiful kitchen cabinets, the ceramic tiled bathrooms, the hardwood floors in the kitchen and dining room, and the stone fireplace with arched bookcases on each side.

Tom did not like for her to mention Mr. Foster's bad luck. After all, he nor Olivia caused his accident.

Olivia paused before the winding staircase before she climbed. In the master bedroom, she walked to the glass sliding doors and looked out at Henry Gibson, the Gardner. He had planted shrubbery around the house and had started on the rose garden on the right corner of the house. She wanted to move into the house before the roses bloomed; but she wanted to wait until she had the drapes made and hung. She also wanted to shop for things she needed for the kitchen and bathrooms. She pulled out her tape, measured the glass door, and went to the other bedrooms to measure the windows.

Back downstairs, she walked through the den to the glass sliding doors to get her measurements. Out on the patio, she admired their beautiful pool. Tom liked to have pool parties. He had a nice grill already set up on the patio.

The following weekend, Olivia went shopping and bought material for all of the windows with matching spreads, pillows, and dust ruffles.

In June, Tom and Olivia celebrated their second anniversary in their new home. She bogged in the plush carpet in the living room and admired everything in the room. Tom had furnished the entire house with expensive furniture. Light from the chandelier in the center of the room shimmered and threw light on eighteenth century art that decorated the wall. Tom hired a man to hang the paintings and the solid mint green drapes that she had made. They blended perfectly with the couch and chairs. She walked on through the den and took notice of the colonial furniture and antique rug that blended perfectly with the drapes. Upstairs, she walked through each bedroom and took notice of her new curtains. The master bedroom had beautiful French provincial furniture. The yellow curtains blended perfectly with the beige carpet; and the pillows she made for the chairs gave contrast and color to the room. She walked on to the guest room and admired the brass bed, and antique chest, dresser, and night stands. She made blue sheer curtains and made a blue velvet cushion for the white rocking chair that gave the room a flare of elegance. She could see the room transformed into a nursery. She did wish she could have a baby. Tom wanted a baby even more than she did.

Olivia still thought about Mr. Foster. She saw his son almost every day at school; and she wanted to reach out to him and say something to comfort him. Olivia wished they had not built a new house. Maybe Mr. Foster would still be alive.

Olivia missed living on the lake; but Tom liked their new location in town. She tried to adjust to her new home for his sake. Being near Tom made her happy, but the new home had nothing to do with her love for Tom. If she lived in a shack with Tom, she would be happy.

After they moved into their new home, Olivia noticed that Tom seemed restless. He worked after hours at his office. When she asked him why he worked late every night. He claimed that he had to work overtime to write briefs and catch up with his paper work.

Then Tom had more business trips than usual. She missed him on the weekends. Then he had business trips that lasted the entire week. He never discussed his plans with her beforehand; and he never asked her to go with him on trips out of town.

Tom's sudden change puzzled Olivia. She worried that their problems stemmed from the fact that she could not get pregnant. She wanted to take a fertility drug; but Tom's behavior made her change her mind. He had become more distant and did not talk to her all. She had to literally pull words out of his mouth. She feared Tom would leave her, and she would have to raise the child without him.

When summer came, Tom did not want to take a vacation as they usually did. They still had the same friends, but friends could not make their problems disappear. They still went to church and painted a pretty picture of the perfect family. In fact, they seldom missed a Sunday service. Olivia became more restless with every passing day. She wanted more from Tom than he wanted to give.

The weekend rolled around again and Olivia wanted to spend it with Tom; but he had to go out of town again.

Olivia got up at the usual time on Saturday. She took a shower, went to the kitchen, and made coffee. As she sat at the table drinking her coffee, she read the Macon Telegraph. Bold headlines described the plane crash that had taken a family who had gone to the Bahamas on vacation. She wondered when Tom would get back. She always worried when Tom took business trips, especially when he flew.

Tom finally made it home on Sunday. When she questioned him about his trip, he gave her short answers. His bad mood lasted all that week. Every time she tried to make conversation with him, he made excuses to get away from her and went to his workshop. His saws still hummed when she went to bed that night.

As time went on, things between Tom and Olivia got even worse. When Tom had time he could spend with her at home; he went out with his friends and stayed out late. His behavior made her angry and sick; she lost her appetite and lost weight; but Tom did not notice. She asked him to go with her to talk to a marriage counselor; but he flatly refused. He put her down every time she opened her mouth; and every time he opened his mouth, he told a lie. She hated a liar. His actions spoke even louder than his lies. He seldom made love to her and never kissed her His lack of affection made her hurt all over. She needed him to hold her, caress her, and kiss her with passion. She needed his understanding and compassion. When she forced herself on him, he accused her of taking sex pills and said they had made her act crazy. She had never heard him say anything so ridiculous. She hated him when he ridiculed her; she wanted to slap him. He made her feel inferior and unworthy, like a cheap whore without morals. He sent her on a trip through hell.

Tom stayed angry and Olivia felt as if she would go crazy. She did not understand what had changed him. She had done nothing to make him angry. She had done nothing to hurt him; she loved him too much to hurt him, but he obviously did not care about her or how much he hurt her. She prayed that he would change; she wanted their marriage to work. They made vows for better or worse and she got the worst. She had always given more to their marriage than her fair share; but she got nothing in return. She learned to expect nothing good and she tried to endure the bad. He had led her down the garden path; but she never smelled the roses.

The next Sunday, Tom came in from his business trip around suppertime. Olivia had supper ready when he came into the house. As he passed the kitchen door on his way to the bedroom, Olivia spoke to him; he barely spoke and walked on down the hall to the bedroom with his suitcase.

She called him to come eat supper and waited to eat with him. She walked down the hall and heard water running in the shower. She put the food in the oven to stay warm and sat down at the bar to have a cup of coffee. She must have waited thirty minutes before Tom came in dressed in his gold bathrobe. He rudely asked what she had cooked for supper.

She tried to please him; she had cooked his favorite meal: mashed potatoes, hamburger steak, creamed corn, and tossed salad. She set the food on the table and poured Tom's coffee before taking her place.

After he said the blessing, she asked about his trip.

He blurted that he answered questions and listened to clients complain about their settlements all day on Saturday.

She reminded him that his clients paid him a chunk of cash to answer their questions and listen to their complaints. They wanted a fair settlement with their insurance companies.

He gave her a sullen look and filled his plate. He seemed to enjoy his meal, but he barely looked up at her while he fed his face. Olivia ate much slower than Tom did; she like to talk while she ate, but Tom had little to say. Before he finished eating, she got up and put a delicious looking peach cobbler on the table.

"I don't want any dessert," he said."

"I thought you liked peach cobbler," she said.

"I don't want any dessert," he said. He pushed his plate back, got up from the table, got a beer from the refrigerator, and walked toward the living room.

Olivia sat at the table and looked at the food on her plate; she had lost her appetite. How could Tom be so rude to her? He did not appreciate the things she did for him; and he never thought of anyone, except Tom. His nasty attitude and mean disposition made Olivia scream inside. He seemed to take for granted that she required no attention and no rewards. He assumed that she would always be there ready to please him.

When Olivia finished the dishes, she went to the living room to sit with Tom. She found him stretched out on the couch sound asleep. She let him sleep and went to get a bath. She dressed in her blue lace gown to get Tom's attention, but she fell asleep before he came to bed.

Olivia awoke when she felt the bed take a considerable dip with Tom's weight next to her. His clean skin smelled good. She snuggled close to him and tried to encourage him to make love to her. He pulled her to him and his hot breath aroused her sexual desire. He made love to her; but he definitely did not have sex on his mind. She turned over less than satisfied and stared through the darkness. He wanted nothing to do with her. What had happened to him? She had put his wishes and needs before her own; she had tried to please him; she tried to be nice to him; she had been too nice to him. She realized that no one respects a person who gives and stoops. She asked herself why she wasted her life on a man who left her out of his life completely.

The next Friday, Tom had to go to Atlanta to meet with a client; he would not be back home until Monday evening.

Olivia became extremely angry. Did he think she was stupid? She felt sure that he had a woman with him on his business trips. His clients met him at his office when they had business to discuss. Something or somebody had his attention. He never spent time with her anymore. She had no way of knowing where he went or who he went with. She accused him of having an affair.

He denied her accusations and claimed that he had no interest what-so-ever in another woman. Then he turned the table and accused her of having an affair. He even called the names of men around town who she had been with.

After Tom left, Olivia had never felt more lonely or depressed. Being alone in this big house drove her crazy. She went to the phone and called Emily; but she had a baby that took up most of her time. She could not come to visit as she did before she married. She advised Olivia to hire a private detective.

Olivia hung up and called three other friends who lived in Cedar Grove, but they made excuses. Neither did they invite her to come to visit them.

She wondered what ever happened to Scott Porter. She thought back to that one time them met and how much she enjoyed his company. She had been a fool to believe Tom had changed. She understood why people got addicted to alcohol and pills. She went to Tom's liquor cabinet and drank three shots of Tom's 100 proofs Old Grand Dad. If she had not passed out on the couch, she probably would have gone and searched for Scott Porter without feeling guilty. Why should she sit at home, while Tom enjoyed the company of another woman?

In spite of Tom's change for the worst, Olivia still loved him. What could she do to make things better? Was Tom's interest in other women her fault? Did his inability to get her pregnant cause their problems? Her doctor had told her that she had no female problems. She kept praying for him to change back to the man she married.

Olivia spent her lonely weekends writing, a hobby she started in high school. She stored her poetry and novels on her computer and wanted to get them published someday. Tom did not like her hobby and he never encouraged her write or try to publish her work.

One day after Tom got home from a business trip, he found Olivia at the computer and started yelling. "Why in the hell do you waste your time writing that silly poetry and those crazy love stories?"

She looked at him with anger. He had been reading her literature before they married. "Writing helps me get through lonely weekends at home, while you go out and have a good time with other women," she said.

Her reply made Tom angrier; he rushed over to the computer and jerked all of the wires from their sockets in the back of her computer.

She screamed at him to leave her computer alone. He jerked the computer from the desk, carried it to the garage, and set it on one of the shelves with the garden tools. When he came back, Olivia had moved the monitor and all of the cords he had ruined to the guest bedroom.

Olivia did not speak to Tom the following week. She carried her computer to Radio Shack for repairs and replacement of the broken cords that Tom destroyed. From that day forward, Olivia did all of her writing in the guest bedroom out of Tom's sight. She changed her password and hoped he would not completely destroy all of her years of hard work.

To her surprise, Tom stayed home the next weekend. He apologized to her for losing his temper and ruining her computer.

Olivia could not understand why he got angry in the first place. Writing had been her hobby since high school. Besides, her novels and poetry came from her imagination and had nothing to do with him. She thought he should be supportive rather than critical of her work.

Tom promised to never interfere with her computer again. He asked her to go out to dinner on Saturday. After they got back home, they watched a movie, laughed, talked, and loved like old times.

Tom's good mood lasted only a few weeks before he started his trips out of town again on the weekends.

After Tom left for the weekend, Olivia worried about his affair. His woman must have hidden talents that she did not have.

Olivia tried harder than ever to hold their marriage together. She did not question Tom about his trips out of town, and she tried to do things to make him feel wanted and needed. Each time she tried to get close to him, she could feel him stiffen. He acted as if he wanted to get away from her. Memories of the times Tom had done her wrong, the lies he told her, and the hell he had put her through flooded her mind. He acted as if he owned her and tried to control her, while he ran free to do as he pleased. He had made a game of their convenient marriage, and his game thoroughly disgusted her. She decided that Tom's second childhood came early and she had enough of his childish behavior. She had never begged a man to love her and did not want to play his game any longer. If Tom wanted his whore, he could have his whore. If he wanted his wife, he could make the next move. She moved all of her personal belongings out of their bedroom and took the guest room.

On Sunday, when Tom came home, Olivia did not have dinner cooked and she did not speak to him.

When Tom walked into the bedroom, she heard him cursing. He came back to the living room and stood before her with a face filled with anger. He raised his voice and asked why in the hell she had moved out of their bedroom.

Olivia calmly lowered the book she had been reading and exclaimed that she did not know what he wanted from her; she did not know how to please him. She added that she had done everything she could do to make their marriage work; but he obviously did not want a wife. She reminded him of the times she had tried to get close to him and he turned away from her; she reminded him of the times that he refused to discuss his business trips with her and left her completely in the dark as to what went on in his life. Last but not least, she told him that she wanted a man she could trust; a man

FORBIDDEN LOVE

who loved and appreciated her. He had proven to her that he did not care about her; he only cared about himself. Finally, she told him that they no longer had a marriage and she wanted a divorce.

"I love you, Olivia. I have a lot on my mind; I have to carry a big load that you would not understand."

"Tom, I am not stupid. I do not expect you to admit that you have been seeing someone else; but I know. A wife always knows. If you want a divorce, I will leave; but you cannot sleep with another woman on the weekends and stay married to me."

To her surprise, Tom sat silently and did not deny that he had been seeing someone else; he did not want a divorce; he wanted them to work things out. He practically begged her to stay with him and promised to try harder to be a better husband.

He walked over to her, held out his hand and pulled her to him. His kiss and his passion made her crazy. He promised to make things better and include her in decisions he made from that day forward.

Tom's actions during the months that followed made Olivia happier than she had been since she married him. She went to work every day and Tom came home at five. She wrote a menu for the cook every day to make sure that Tom had his favorite dishes cooked when he got home. They ate together, went to movies, had parties, visited friends, went to church, and enjoyed life as they had when they first married. She worked hard to keep their marriage together, because she loved the ground Tom walked on.

CHAPTER EIGHT

Caught Cheating

THREE MONTHS LATER on a blue Monday, Olivia awoke at six o'clock with a splitting headache. She took two Tylenols and got dressed for work. Her children got one day behind when she took a day off; they needed her. She made it through the first two classes and went to tell the principal, Mr. Danbury, that she must take the rest of the day off.

When she went into the house, she noticed Tom's coat on the hall Tree. She wondered why his car had not been in the garage. Had he come by the house after she left for work? He always dressed in a suit, white shirt, and tie when he went to the office.

Olivia went to the kitchen to get a glass of water to take pain medication. When she turned on the tap, she looked out the window and all of the blood drained from her head with the shock. A provocative blond sat in Tom's lap as he relaxed before their pool in his lounge chair.

Olivia felt angry; she felt too shocked to move out of her tracks. She stood there and stared at Tom and his whore several minutes. She could not see the woman's ass, but she could see her legs swinging to the side of Tom's chair. What should she do? She wanted to go to bed and forget what she saw; but she had to face Tom; she had to let him know that she knew about his whore. She set her glass down on the cabinet with a bang, rushed out the back door, and slammed it with the force of a lumber Jack. The woman's bikini left nothing to the imagination; it barely covered her nipples and definitely took Tom's attention.

The loud bang of the door got their attention. The blond immediately jumped like a leaping frog and groped for her towel lying in the chair next to Tom's.

By this time, Olivia stood before them and shouted, "Get your ass out of my yard and away from my house before I start shooting!"

Olivia had the urge to grab a wad of the woman's blond hair and force her into the pool. Instead, she rushed back into the house. She felt sick on her stomach as she made her way to the bedroom. The unmade bed with its tussled covers and the whore's clothes scattered all over the floor around her bed made her furious. She rightly assumed that they had already had sex in her bed. She went to the bathroom and sat down on the edge of the tub. She had to face that whore again. She did not know if her legs would carry her back down the hall.

Olivia got up, flushed her face with water, and buried her head in the towel. The picture of Tom's whore sitting in his lap flashed on her brain and made her want to fight. She wanted to kill her. She held her head and cursed. She never wanted Tom to touch her again.

Minutes later, Olivia let the towel fall from her face and grabbed her composure. She held her shoulders straight, and marched back down the hall to face the whore. Before she got to the back door, the whore zipped past her and ran to the bedroom. Olivia followed the bitch and watched her rushed around the bed to pick up her clothes.

"Get your fat ass out of my house! If you ever set foot near my door again, I will kill you," Olivia said. The close-up of the blond brought memories of the first time she met the bitch. Stella Shivers used to come to Tom's parties when they were in college. She didn't like her then; now she hated her.

Olivia stood like a planted stump in the doorway as the whore rushed past her. When the front door slammed, Olivia breathed a sigh of relief. She walked to the living room window and watch the bitch run down the steps. She made her way across the lawn, crossed the street, and got into a white Chevrolet parked next to the street in front of the line of houses. Olivia prayed that their neighbors did not see the sorry bitch run away from her house.

Thank God, the bitch had left her home, but she still had to face Tom. He sat in the same lawn chair with sunglasses covering his eyes. She stood before him and cursed him for everything she could think of. He reached and got his beer sitting next to his chair, took a sip, and put it down. Then he lay back as if she had not spoken and never replied. What could he say? Olivia caught him with Stella; he could not deny her charges.

Then Olivia shouted for him to get out of her sight before she did something she would regret.

She slammed the back door behind her and went to the kitchen. Olivia fixed a pot of coffee and sat down at the table. She wanted Tom to leave her alone with her misery. She wanted nothing to do with him. Besides, words between them would solve nothing. She had faced reality; Tom did not give a damn about her. Why did he ask her to marry him? She had been a fool to accept his marriage proposal. Tom would never be faithful to a woman. Tom came into the world with an inborn instinct to run wild. All of his trips out of town had been an excuse to be with his whore, Stella. God only knew how many other women he had slept with.

Olivia wondered how long he had been shacking up with Stella. She had a thousand questions on her mind. Had he been shacking with Stella all during their marriage? Was this the reason Tom liked to have parties for his friends? Did everyone in town know about Tom's affair? Before she and Tom married, Stella Shivers got engaged to, Willis Johnson, a friend of Tom's. Was her engagement a cover for her affair with Tom?

An hour must have passed before Olivia heard Tom's footsteps coming down the hall. Then the front door slammed. Olivia jumped up and ran to the front window to see who came to get him. A black Lexus pull into the drive; Tom got into the car, and it pulled away. His father had come by to pick him up. Olivia realized that Stella had picked up Tom at his office and brought him to their bedroom to have sex. Then they went for a swim in their pool. They probably had sex in the pool, too. She got up and walked around the room. She had to get a hold on her thoughts or go completely insane.

Olivia went to the kitchen, got a cup of coffee, and came back to the couch. Tears rolled down her face as she looked around the room at the beautiful furniture, their wedding pictures, and pictures of his parents and hers. She had gradually begun to trust him again, and he had been sleeping with the whore all of this time. His promises meant nothing more than dust in the wind.

Tom's whore shattered Olivia's dream of making her marriage work. Tom had hurt Olivia the last time. His having sex with that whore in her bed upset Olivia more than his meeting women at a hotel. She thought of Tom as a sorry sleaze ball; a big bag of wind with bad oxygen. He had destroyed her life. She had often heard that a thin line separated love and hate. She realized at this minute that Tom broke this thin line. She hated the bastard; she detested him. He had been sleeping around on her for years, while he accused her of being unfaithful. His accusations eased his own guilt. How could he act so calm and so innocent? He had kept everything a secret from her. When she accused him of having an affair, he denied having looked at another woman. She hated a cheat and liar. Had he been honest with her, she would have gotten out of his way; he could have avoided the scene in the bedroom.

Olivia realized that their marriage crashed long before she caught him with Stella. She should have ended the relationship the first time she suspected his running around on her. She saw clearly now; Tom could not be faithful. Olivia had prayed for him to change; things did get better for a while. Tom never really changed; he covered his tracks well.

Olivia cried and asked herself questions. What would she do? She hated to divorce Tom. What would she tell Tom's parents? They had been good to her. She could never tell them about Tom's affair; she loved and respected them. Maybe she should quietly leave Cedar Grove and go back to Boulder Bluff. With her out of the picture, the gossip would be about her having left Tom. They would never know about his affair. She would not have to explain Tom's affair to his parents and friends; she would not have to tell her friends at school. She wanted to save his face as well as her face.

Olivia did not want to hire a lawyer until the end of the school year; she didn't want to break her contract. She must stay in Cedar Grove until school turned out for the summer. Afterwards, she would hire a lawyer and get a quick divorce. What would she do after the divorce? She could not run back to Mother and Daddy. They had their own problems. Besides, she did not want to listen to her mother blame her and give her useless advice. Since the day Olivia came into the world, she never did anything right in her mother's eyes.

Olivia dismissed her thoughts of the future and went to take a shower. As she turned and soaped, she tried to scrub Tom's dirt from her body. She got out of the shower, got her robe from the closet, and went to the guest bedroom and looked around. She did not want to go into their bedroom, but she had to move again. She pushed their bedroom door back with anger and looked around the room. The tumbled covers on the bed made her sick on her stomach all over again. She went to the closet, grabbed her clothes from the rod, and carried them to the guest bedroom. Then she went back to the bathroom, took all of her belongings, and carried them to the bath next to her new bedroom, where she intended to live until school turned out for the summer.

An hour later, she had everything organized. She turned the covers back to sleep and ease her troubled mind; but she could not sleep. Would she ever sleep again? Would she ever forget Tom and find happiness again? She wanted to forget all things that had passed and start a new and better life. The life she had lived up until this day had been the pits of hell. She wondered if she would ever be free from doubt. She doubted everything and everybody. He made promises to break; he gave gifts to take back. Some saw man as basically good; others saw man as basically bad. She saw Tom as a sorry bastard, as sorry as they come.

Hours must have passed before her cell phone awoke her. Tom's voice made her heart beat in her ears. She took a good breath and asked what he wanted. He asked if he could come over and talk. She hung up on him and lay back on her pillow. What in the hell did he have to say? Then she thought about the house; Tom must be worried about what she would ask him to give up, but she wanted nothing from him; she wanted her freedom.

The next day, Tom sent her a dozen yellow roses with a note. "Olivia, please forgive me for all the hell I put you through. I don't give a damn about Stella Shivers, and I wouldn't have gone with her had I not been drunk out of mind. I don't want a divorce; I want you back. We need to talk about us and try to make our marriage work. I would like to take you out to dinner Friday. Please call me."

When she got home from work, Tom called and asked if she received her flowers. He mentioned that he remembered how much she liked the yellow roses he had sent her once before.

She thanked him for the roses. Then she told him that all of the flowers in the world could not change her mind. She would never forget the emptiness that drained her when she saw him with Stella.

He explained that he had too much to drink and did not realize what he was doing.

She told him that his excuses did not change the facts and she hung up on him.

The next morning before she got dressed for school, Tom called again. That evening when she got home from school, he called again. Every day that week, he called and asked her to at least talk to him, listen to what he had to say; but she quickly let him know that she had nothing to say to him.

The next Monday evening, Tom paid her a surprise visit.

"Could I come in?" he asked in a humble voice.

"Sure, come in. I just put coffee on," she said.

He sat down at the dining room table in his usual place, and she pulled out a chair across from him.

"How have you been?" he said.

"I guess I will live," she said. "How have you been doing?"

"I've been working, eating, and sleeping."

"I guess everyone works, eats, and sleeps; but very few men bring their whore home with them," she said.

"Olivia, I am so sorry you saw me with Stella. She suggested that we come here. We had spent the night together and had started drinking before breakfast. The alcohol fogged my brain. I would have never done such a thing in my right mind. I love you, Olivia. I came to ask your forgiveness for my stupidity. If you will let me come home, I will go to a counselor; I will go to Alcohol Anonymous; I will do anything you ask me to do to save our marriage."

"Tom, do you expect me to forget what I saw? I cannot block the pictures of you with that bitch from my head. No matter how much I try to busy my mind, I still see you with that whore. Would you forgive me if you caught me with another man and knew I had been having sex with him all during our marriage? I will never trust you again. You did not marry a stupid idiot; but I have been stupid to put up with your affair all of this time. You accused me of doing things that I never dreamed of doing. I have never run around on you; I never looked at another man with desire, because I loved you and wanted only you. Can you honestly say that you ever loved me?"

"I have loved you since our first date. I admit that I fooled around with other women, but I did not love them. I love only you; I want to come back home and make our marriage work."

His sweet words did not soften Olivia, and his money could not buy her. "Tom, don't sit here and lie to me; you will never be true to me nor anyone else you have a relationship with. You are a thrill seeker. I don't know why you chose a career in law; you break man made laws and God's laws. You like to do anything that is forbidden," she said.

"Forbidden by whom?" he said.

"Adultery is forbidden by God and by spouses like me who get hurt. I certainly do not condone your affair with Stella or any other woman while you are married to me."

"Forgive me for my forbidden sins," he said. "I will do anything to keep you."

"You don't mean a word you say, Tom. I cannot count the times that you have hurt me. I no longer feel any love for you; I feel only bitterness and resentment for the years I have wasted with you. You have made the public think that I am a sorry woman, and I will never forgive you for the lies you have told on me. I want a divorce."

He sat silently and looked down at the floor for a long time. Then he agreed to move out.

While Tom packed his clothes and personal belongings, Olivia went to the kitchen and mixed a strong drink of bourbon and coke.

When Tom came through the living room on his way out, he looked at her with pity, and said, "If you change your mind, call me. I will keep in touch. Take care of yourself."

From the window, Olivia watched Tom put his suitcase in his car. She felt as if her world crashed around her. Her heart beat in the top of her head. She did not know if she could free herself from the load of garbage Tom buried her under. Her mind turned with memories of the last year she and Tom lived together. He had treated her like dirt; he had even gone on vacation without her.

A squirrel caught Olivia's attention as he darted freely around the oak tree in the front yard; then a red bird flew from one of the limbs, dipped to the ground, and grabbed an acorn. The squirrel zipped higher up the tree and peeped down to see where the red bird had gone. Animals fought to survive at times; but they had no emotional problems. They lived a free, peaceful life. Her marriage to Tom had been anything but peaceful for the past two years. The kind words, laughter, and happiness had long passed. His mood went from good to bad and from bad to worse. Tom acted as if he wanted revenge for a terrible wrong he suffered. He punished her for hurtful things others did to him. She had never done anything to hurt him. She had never harmed a soul, and she had always tried to practice honesty and do the right thing. Honesty and truth did not faze sociopaths or psychotics; they liked to destroy lives.

After losing Tom, Olivia stopped living; she existed from one day to the next. All of her friends seemed happily married, and she had nobody who cared. She stopped visiting her friends and family. On Sunday, she still went to church, and she went to the grocery store only when she had to go.

At the end of each day, Olivia could hardly wait to go home and go to bed, but she never slept. She lay in bed with her head covered and felt sorry for herself. Then she thought of those less fortunate and stopped her brooding for a short time. At least she had plenty of food to eat; she had a nice warm home with a shelter over her head. She must get used to living alone and take one day at a time.

Olivia needed time to erase memories of Tom; she still missed him; she still loved him. How could she forget him? Late in the evening, she got lonely and depressed. She would stand at her bedroom window and look out as if she could see Tom turn into her drive. Some nights she would walk to the window and listen to the animal sounds and murmuring from the woods, deep in the woods. Many nights after she went to bed, she would stare through the darkness and imagine Tom lying next to her. She could feel his arms around her and the warmth of his body submerge her with delight. She could hear him breathe and feel his warm breath; she could hear his voice. At times like this, she wanted to remember only the good times and feelings of love they shared over the years. Their first anniversary still brought back good memories. She had thought long and hard about what she had done or what she did not do to make him turn to another woman.

On the weekends, Olivia slept late and ate brunch. She tried to stay busy with chores to keep from thinking. She walked aimlessly around the house and tried to remember why she had gone to the bedroom. Then she remembered; she had to wash the bed sheets. As she stripped the bed, her eyes fell on the pictures stacked on the dresser. The top picture of the tall man with bright blue eyes and strong arms held to a beautiful woman with dark hair falling around a happy face. That picture held years of good and bad memories. Tom's handsome face, good physique, and charming personality made her fall head over heels in love with him. At first, she thought she had made the perfect choice, but things turned sour after their first year of marriage; then things got better; then things got worse. Each time she entered the bedroom, that picture caught her eye. When she moved, she planned to store all the pictures of Tom in a box and put them away forever. The sight of his face made her more depressed.

The twilight turned to darkness and the sun rise fell on another lonely day. Olivia had the same empty feeling that she had since Tom moved out. She clung to his memory as a climbing vine clings to bricks. The no good scoundrel did not deserve a second thought. He had caused her unbearable pain and withered her spirit. He had never loved her. She had been a naive, stupid fool. She had learned from her mistake with Tom, and this lesson made a big change in her. A man would never hurt her again, because she would never fall in love again.

CHAPTER NINE

The Divorce

....

AFTER OLIVIA FILED for a divorce from Tom, she lived in sheer hell. The next evening when her doorbell rang, she thought Tom had come to talk about the divorce settlement. Instead, she met Tom's brother, Michael at the door. She wondered why he had come. She had no qualms with Michael; he and his wife, Penny, had always been nice to her when they came to parties and when she saw them at Mr. and Mrs. Bradford's home. She invited him to sit in the living room and took a seat across from him. She tried to make conversation about his wife and the kids. She also asked about Mr. and Mrs. Bradford.

She soon ran out of things to say and Michael broke the silence with his shocking words, "Why don't you and me go somewhere cozy and exciting for the weekend?"

Too shocked to reply, Olivia sat and stared at him for minutes before she spoke, "I was not aware that you ran around on your wife, Penny."

"You know how it is; she went with some of her friends to the beach this weekend; I got lonely sitting home all by myself."

"I really don't know how it is Michael. I don't go out with married men. Have you taken up your brother's bad habits?"

"Tom had never taken women serious, until he married you. I am nothing like Tom. In fact, I have never asked a woman to go out with me since I married Penny."

"I guess there is always a first time for everything; but you have asked the wrong woman. How did you know that Tom wouldn't be home?"

"I wanted to ask you out and I took my chances," he said.

"I think you should go, Michael. If I were you, I would not advertise this visit. If Tom sent you to snoop for him, you can tell him that I don't play the same dirty games he plays and he can go to hell."

After he left, Olivia leaned against the door with shock. Had Tom's married brother asked her for a date? She felt sure that Tom had sent him to snoop. She had just caught Tom with Stella and he wanted to get the goods on her. Had he learned his dirty tactics in law school? Maybe she should have studied law. She wanted to call him up and curse him for a poor example of a man.

The next Saturday, Tom's mother came to see her. Olivia tried to act as if nothing had happened. Before Mrs. Bradford got seated, she apologized for Tom's behavior. She did not blame Olivia for wanting a divorce, but she loved her and would miss her. She had talked to Tom and asked him to apologize and try to make things right between them.

Olivia let Mrs. Bradford know that there was nothing Tom could do to make things right between them. He had made his choice and she wanted nothing more to do with him. She explained that she had filed for a divorce.

Mrs. Bradford cried and offered to help Olivia and give her anything she needed to get a new start.

Olivia thanked her and asked her not to take blame Tom's mistakes.

Olivia thought she would never stop talking. When Mrs. Bradford started to leave, she hugged Olivia and told her not to worry about a place to live; she would personally see that Olivia got the house and all of the furniture.

Olivia explained that she wanted to buy a smaller house near Boulder Bluff, and she planned to move during the summer.

Then Mrs. Bradford told her she would make sure that Tom gave her a settlement to cover a new home.

When Olivia opened the door for Mrs. Bradford to leave, she grabbed Olivia again and cried. She told Olivia that she loved her and if she ever needed anything to call her. She asked her to please come and visit her.

Olivia cried with her, but she never wanted to enter the Bradford home again.

After she left, Olivia felt relieved that Mrs. Bradford knew everything. She had not bad-mouthed Tom to his mother. She did not tell her how angry she got when she caught him with Stella Shivers; she did not tell her that she really hated Tom for what he had done; She did not tell her that never wanted to see Tom again; she did not tell her that the quicker she signed the divorce papers and left Cedar Grove, the better off she would be.

The next week, Olivia got calls from several men who wanted to go out with her. She hung up in their face. One of the men talked vulgar to her and mentioned that hot chicks like her turned him on. She cursed him and told him she would call the cops if he called her again.

After she hung up, she worried. Did Tom put these men up to call her? What could he gain from hurting her? She had not asked for the house or a large settlement.

Then the worst happened. She had just come in from school and forgot to lock the door behind her. She changed into comfortable clothes, turned on the television, and sat down on the couch to enjoy a glass of lemonade and watch the evening news. She looked up and saw Ditto Frost standing in her living room. He frightened her to silence.

He looked at her and grinned; then he said, "Olivia, come and go with me to the bathroom."

Olivia had never been angrier nor more frightened. She finally said, "I don't have any business going to the bathroom with you. Get out of my house."

He ignored her and disappeared down the hall.

Afraid to move, Olivia sat like a frozen mummy. Then she heard his heavy footsteps coming back down the hall. He walked out the door and closed it behind him. Olivia jumped up from the couch and locked the door. Then she ran to the phone and called the local police.

An hour must have passed before an officer arrived. He shook her hand and said, "I am Henry Bates. Did you call to report an intruder?"

"I called to report an idiot who walked into my house without an invitation." Then she told him what Ditto Frost said to her.

He shook his head and said, "Ditto Frost is a weird character. We had complaints from another woman who claimed that Ditto made a pass at her and she had to fight to get away from him. I think her father put an ass beating on Ditto Frost."

"Why don't you do anything about Ditto's weird behavior?"

"You can take out a restraining order to keep him away from you and your property. If you take out a warrant for his arrest, his folks will hire a lawyer and everything you say will be your word against his. You will also be required to testify in court if they make a case against him."

"I will take out the restraining order," Olivia said. "I don't want to go before a judge."

After Officer Bates left, Olivia walked back and forth across the room; she needed a dose of calm and peace that did not come in a bottle. She would never find happiness as long as she lived in Cedar Grove. Tom left peacefully, but he still controlled her. Why was he trying to drive her crazy?

The next week, the harassing phone calls stopped and Ditto Frost got his warning. Olivia still did not feel safe; but she wanted to make the best of the situation and stay in Cedar Grove until her contract expired at the end of the school year.

Then Olivia got a shocking phone call. When she saw Penny Bradford on her caller Identification, she could not imagine what she wanted. Had she found out about Michael asking her for a date? She felt reluctant to answer, but she finally said, "Hello, Olivia speaking."

"Olivia, this is Penny. How have you been doing?"

"I can't say that I am happy, Penny. Are things good between you and Michael?"

"Michael and I get along pretty good. You know we have three children to think about. I called to tell you that they found Stella Shivers dead this morning."

Olivia felt sick on her stomach. She sat down on the couch and asked Penny what happened to Stella.

"They don't know for sure what happened to her. They found her on the floor in her bedroom. Rumors are going around that she died from sniffing too much cocaine."

"My God, I was not aware that Stella sniffed cocaine. Did you know about her drug problem?"

"Everybody knew Stella had a drug problem; she had a drinking problem, also."

"I can't say that Stella and I were friends; but I am truly sorry that she died. How old was Stella?"

"She must have been our age. I would say she was twenty-five years old. I wanted you to know," Penny said. "You take care of yourself and visit us sometimes. Michael's mother loves you like a daughter, you know."

"Thanks, Penny, for the invitation; but I don't feel comfortable around Tom's folks now that Tom and I have split up."

"You can still call and talk to me anytime," Penny said. "I know how Tom treated you. If Michal treated me like that, I would leave him and take my kids with me. I wouldn't live with him another minute if I caught him running around on me; and I don't blame you for your decision to divorce Tom. I will miss seeing you when we go to Mr. and Mrs. Bradford's for Sunday dinner. I wish you good luck with your new job next year, and I hope you find happiness with a decent man."

"Your words mean so much to me, Penny. Thanks for calling." Olivia hung up and stared at nothing. Was Tom sniffing cocaine when he shacked up with Stella? If he got on cocaine, he had a worse problem than she thought he had. She had been stupid to stay with Tom and waste her life. She had given her heart to a narrow-minded fool and had been blind to the truth. The time had come for her to make some changes in her life. She must stop existing and start living. She must do what she must do to be happy before her life slipped away.

Gossip about Tom's affair and Stella Shivers' death kept lines busy. His affair had definitely been more than a friendly meeting in the park. Several of their friends had called Olivia to let her know that they knew about Tom's affair with Stella; they wanted to tell her, but they did not want to hurt her. One of her college friends told her that Tom shacked up with Stella after Olivia moved back to Boulder Bluff.

Olivia added nothing to their gossip. She informed them that she did not want to talk about Tom. After all, gossip that went from one to another turned to lies that got bigger with repetition, and one could not separate the truth from the lies.

Several friends called and offered a shoulder to cry on. They wanted to know what she planned to do, where she planned to live; they even asked if she and Tom would ever get back together. She explained that she would continue to teach school at Cedar Grove High School until the end of the school year; then she planned to move back Boulder Bluff, her hometown.

Olivia hated Tom for what he had done to her; but she hated his so-called friends who gossiped about him, too. They only pretended to be his friends.

When Olivia called Emily and told her about Stella death and the rumors about how she had died, Emily did not seem surprised. She knew Stella used cocaine and abused other drugs, also. She knew, several of Tom's friends who used cocaine; but she claimed that she had never seen Tom use the drug and she knew nothing about his habits. In her opinion, Tom probably used cocaine if he stayed around Stella. .

Olivia admitted that she hated Stella; but she hated to see any young person die. She worried that the public would somehow connect Tom to Stella's death and get him into trouble since they were seeing each other.

Emily could not believe that Olivia still dwelled on Tom and worried about what he did and where he went. She advised her to forget that sorry bastard and move on to a greener pasture. Then she explained she could not come for a visit. She had her hands full with her little girl and did not like to leave her with her parents for the weekend.

Two weeks before school turned out for the summer, Olivia signed the divorce papers. Her lawyer, Quincey Maddox, thought she settled for less than she deserved, but Olivia did not want to fight Tom in court; she did not want the house; she wanted a settlement, part of the furniture, and some of the paintings. She planned to move from Cedar Grove to be near her parents. Tom agreed to give her the settlement she asked for without a fight and agreed for her to live in the house until school turned out for the summer. To her surprise, he also paid the lawyer's fee.

Olivia did not want to face her mother with the news of her divorce. She thought a phone call would make things easier. To Olivia's surprise, her mother already knew about her divorce. Tom had already called and told her. The phone went silent for minutes. Then her mother wanted to know why she divorced Tom, and talked about what a good man she had lost. Olivia told her she did not want to talk about Tom or the divorce on the phone. She explained that she would be home after school turned out for the summer.

After post planning, the teachers and faculty had a dinner in the school cafeteria. Before they ate, Principal Danbury thanked the teachers and staff for a successful year and spoke briefly about the next school year. Then he spoke directly to Olivia and wished her the best at her new job. After dinner, they all wished her well and said their goodbyes.

Olivia had tears in her eyes as she drove away. She left Cedar Grove behind, but she carried memories of Tom Bradford with her to Boulder Bluff and went to stay with her parents until she could find a house and move out on her own.

CHAPTER TEN

Ghost House

OLIVIA'S MOTHER AND father welcomed her home and seemed happy to have her under their roof; but her mother immediately questioned her about her divorce from Tom. What happened? Did she not love Tom? What did she plan to do?

Olivia did not tell them about Tom's affair; she simply explained that she and Tom could not get along and agreed to disagree. Then she quickly changed the subject to the good smells coming from the kitchen. She followed her mother to the kitchen and set the table for dinner. The beef roast, creamed potatoes, fresh corn, and green beans tasted delicious.

While they ate lunch, she told them she needed to stay with them until she found a house of her own. Her father tried to convince her that she did not need a house; he wanted her to live with them. They had plenty of room and she could live free of charge and save her money. He added that a house payment, utility bills, and taxes would take every penny she made every month.

Olivia explained that she wanted to move out on her own; she did not want to impose on them. Tom had given her enough money to pay cash for a house; but she wanted to get a mortgage for the house and make monthly payments if she could get a loan with low interest. She could draw interest every year on the money Tom gave her to help pay for the house.

Her father thought every couple in the world should live the same way he and her mother lived. Her mother had settled happily with her teachers' retirement, and her father planned to retire from his government job with the post office at the end of the year. They enjoyed life, visited, went on vacations, and stayed busy with activities in the church.

On Monday, Olivia went to the Boulder Bluff Board of Education to apply for a job. She asked about a teaching position at the middle school, since she had taught there previously. The secretary asked her to fill out an application and she would call and let her know something after the board meeting the following week.

The next day, Olivia drove around town and looked at houses she had seen advertised for sale on the internet. She did not want to live in the city limits; but she wanted to avoid a long drive to work. She looked at three different houses, but she did not like any of them. She finally found one house outside the city limits that she liked. The sign on the front lawn said for sale or rent. She got the phone number and called Rotwell Real Estate Agency. Mrs. Pittman made an appointment to show her the house the next day at one o'clock.

The next day, Olivia arrived at the house before Mrs. Pittman. She walked from the front to the back and noted details of the house. She liked the looks of the house; it appeared to be in excellent shape on the outside.

Minutes later, she met Mrs. Pittman at the front door and she showed her the inside of the house. Olivia liked the large living room with its stone fireplace. Mrs. Pittman pointed out the beautiful chandelier in the dining room and moved on to the small kitchen and adjoining breakfast area that suited Olivia's needs. Next, she followed Mrs. Pittman down a hall and showed her the three bedrooms. The master bedroom had a full bath; the other two bedrooms had half baths. Then they went out the back door and stepped onto a large back porch that pleased Olivia. Several pecan trees shaded the porch from the evening sun. Last of all, they went upstairs, where a large, unfinished attic had enough space for four large bedrooms. Mrs. Pittman explained that the couple who built the house had planned to finish the upstairs, but the company the man worked for transferred him to another state and they had to move. Olivia liked the large attic; she could use it for storage.

Olivia spent most of the next two days with Lawyer Kimmo's who prepared the paper work for the house. The deed, closing cost, and lawyer's fee made Olivia see dollar signs; but her complaint did not change the price she had to pay. She reluctantly signed the papers and went back home.

The next week, her father and a friend of his went with her in his pickup truck to Cedar Grove to move her personal belongings. When she saw that her piano had disappeared, she wanted to call Tom and ask what he did with her piano. She dismissed the idea and pointed out to her father which pieces of furniture she wanted to take. She also got her picture album and two paintings that she especially liked.

The next week, the secretary for the board of education called and told Olivia that all teaching positions had been filled for the middle school; but they had a teaching position open for third grade at the elementary school. Olivia told her she wanted the job and she would be there the next day to sign her contract.

Olivia stayed with her parents and spent the entire summer painting, cleaning, making curtains, shopping for kitchen supplies, and furniture. The house had a washer and dryer that she planned to use until she had to buy new appliances.

Two weeks before school started, the furniture company delivered her furniture, and she moved into her new home. Her father installed rods for curtains, and her mother helped her hang them as well as get other things in order.

Later that evening, Olivia drove back to her parents' house to get her cat, Jasper. His meows begged for her attention and interrupted her mother's questions. Her mother loved her soft loveable Jasper, too. Olivia had carried Jasper with her to Cedar Grove after she married Tom, but his allergic reaction to cats forced her to carry Jasper back to her parents.

Olivia took Jasper into her and he seemed pleased. He settled right next to her on the way home. She had bought Jasper's favorite food and a few toys to play with. He especially liked the ball with its pull string.

Olivia thought she would feel better after she moved into her own house; but the devil lived with her. Everything that could go wrong went wrong. Right away, she discovered that one of the burners on the stove had burned out; the wall on the front in the living room had no electric plugs; the light switch in the dining room had a loose connection, and the lights blinked constantly. Worst of all, the thermostat on the hot water heater had burned out, and the water got hot enough to boil a chicken. She had to remember to turn the heater on and off each time, she showered. Then she started to do the wash and discovered the washing machine had a broken knob. Now she knew why the former owner had left the stove and washer. She expected something to be wrong with the dryer, too. She went to the kitchen, got a pair of pliers, and gave the metal stem on the washer a twist to the wash cycle. She threw the pliers down with anger. If the real estate agent had been honest with her, she could have called an electrician to check the lights and install a new water heater and stove before she moved into the house. Now she had to go shopping for appliances and find an electrician.

She went to the living room, lay back in the recliner, and compared everything in the house to her life; both had fallen apart and needed repairs. It seemed that she never reached set goals. Just before she reached the finish line, a tall wall of stone appeared from nowhere and blocked her path to success.

Jasper seemed to sense her sadness and jumped into her lap. She sat there for some time and rubbed his fur, while she felt sorry for herself. Then she looked at the other side of the coin. She should be thankful for her good health, the nice roof over her head, and food to eat. On the other hand, the food would likely make her sick, and the roof would leak when it rained. How could things get worse? Tomorrow had to be a better day.

She got up and turned on the radio, and tried to get in a better mood by listening to music. The sad country songs made her think back to times she had danced with Tom. Whitney Houston sang, ""I Will Always Love You," and she cried. Tom called her a dreamer; she called him a realist. He proved to be as realistic as an old rusty screw. Why should one replace a rusty screw that still worked?

Before going to bed, she went to take a bath. The cold water fell on her nakedness and quickly brought her to her senses. She turned the water off, got out of the shower, and went to turn on the hot water heater. She had to wait thirty minutes before she could wash away her sweat. She finally got a bath and dressed for bed. Then she went to the kitchen and fixed a sandwich for supper.

The next morning she made sure the hot water heater had heated up before taking a shower. The warm water sprinkling her body felt refreshing. After she soaped her body, the water stopped all together. She got out of the shower and wrapped a towel around her soapy body, and went to check the electric box. She knew nothing about electricity; the wires looked like other electrical wires she had seen.

She went back to the bedroom, dressed, and went outside to check the pump. Nothing seemed wrong with the pump. She still had no water; she had a miserable itch all day from the soap that coated her skin. She called her father and he came right away; but he found nothing wrong with the pump. He called an electrician, but he could not come until the next week.

Late that night as she got dressed for bed, she heard the pump come back on. She turned on the hot water heater and waited for the water to get warm.

After she bathed and started to get out of the tub, she heard loud banging in the attic above the bathroom. She yelled to the intruder to go away, quickly grabbed a towel, ran to the bedroom, and got her twenty-two pistol from the nightstand. After shooting through the bathroom ceiling, the noise stopped immediately. Even with the gun in her hand, she felt too afraid to check out the attic. She left the bathroom and checked every room in the house. Then she went back to her bedroom and locked the door. She forgot Jasper; she had fixed his bed in the den. She eased back to the den and disturbed his sleep by moving his bed to her bedroom. The ghost disappeared and she finally fell asleep.

The next day, Olivia went to Lowe's Building Supplies and came back home with a new stove and hot water heater.

On Monday, Ray Harrell, an electrician her father had hired, installed her new appliances and checked out the lights. Mr. Harrell had appointments every day that week; but he promised to come back the next week and fix the lights and put plugs on the outside wall.

That night, Olivia awoke to the sound of footsteps coming from the attic right above her head. Jasper sat to attention and meowed. The footsteps walked across the attic; then they disappeared. Too scared to move or speak, Olivia lay still and listened for hours before falling asleep.

The next morning, Olivia called her mother and told her about the noise she had heard in the attic. Her mother believed in ghost. She thought the ghost did not want Olivia to take up its space. Olivia did not believe in ghost. On the other hand, she knew of no one who would want to scare her for no apparent reason, unless Tom or one of his girl friends came for a visit.

The next week Mr. Harrell came back and ran new electric wire to the dining room to stop the blinking light and put two electric plugs on the outside wall.

In spite of the improvements, Olivia still felt uncomfortable in the ghost house.

The first day of school made Olivia happy and nervous at the same time. She got up earlier than usual and had time to enjoy her breakfast. As she drove to school, she prayed that she liked her job.

The secretaries and the principal welcomed her and the office staff offered to help her get the supplies she needed to decorate her room and bulletin board. The principal announced a meeting in the library at eight thirty. First of all, he introduced Olivia and five other new teachers. Then he talked about objectives, lesson plans, and activities scheduled for the coming year. Olivia could not have asked for a more helpful and friendly group of teachers to work with. She met several teachers her age and they talked during lunch. When they learned that she had recently divorced her husband, two of them consoled her. They had been there and done that, also. They all encouraged her to find someone new. One of teachers admitted that she stayed with her husband more than three years after she learned about his affair. After she divorced him, he wanted her back, but she could not live with a man she did not trust. At the end of the day, Olivia felt better about her situation.

Two days later, the students returned to school. Olivia liked the third grade. The students seemed anxious to learn, and she wanted to do everything she could to make learning fun. She stayed after school most days to prepare activities for the next day.

The ghost returned almost every night. Olivia called Emily and asked if she believed in ghost. She definitely believed in ghost and suggested that Olivia talk with the previous owner about the history of the house. If they had never heard the ghost, Tom had tried to scare her.

That night, Olivia turned and tumbled for hours with thoughts about Tom. Why would he try to scare her? He did not want her to come back to him. He did not love her; and she did not need him. She had never been able to share her secrets, fears, wants, and needs with Tom. She needed a man who loved and respected her; she needed a man who treated her as an equal; she needed a man who had an imagination and a romantic nature; she needed a man who liked to do the things she liked to do; she needed a man who could tell the difference between fiction and truth and had the guts to deal with both. Most of all she needed a man she could trust and a man who trusted her.

Olivia hated to call the previous owners to ask about ghost; she did not want them to think she had lost her mind, but she needed some peace of mind and a good night's sleep.

Mrs. Pittman, the realtor gave her the previous owner's number. Mrs. Langley seemed reluctant to answer Olivia's questions. She did not believe in ghost. Olivia kept prying and she finally admitted that she and her husband had often heard loud sounds coming from the attic. Her husband believed the wind made the sound when it blew through the vents. The house had two vents on the front and two vents on the back. Then she said that she had heard about some strange and terrible things that happened on that place before they built their house. The people who once owned the land tore down an old house; the house tumbled and heavy boards fell on their little boy; he died before they got him to the hospital. After this happened, they dug a well and built a wooden curb around the well. Their eleven years old daughter climbed up on the top board of the well curb, fell into the well, and drowned before they could rescue her.

More frightened than ever, Olivia thanked Mrs. Langley and hung up the phone.

The weeks to follow, Olivia heard the same strange noise coming from the attic. The wind did not blow at all times. She could not live in that house. On the other hand, she must wait until school turned out for the summer to start house hunting again.

Olivia tried to forget the ghost living in her attic, but she heard him make his rounds every night. She did not talk to her friends at school about the ghost. They might think she had bugs in her head. Tom accused her many times of letting her imagination run away with her. She kept the attic door locked, as well as the doors downstairs. She let the ghost do as he pleased; but she could not wait to get out of that house and find another place to live. During the day, her job and the students occupied her mind; but every night the ghost visited a little after midnight.

The next Monday, Olivia got up early to have coffee and toast before getting a bath. As she poured her coffee, the pop of the toaster startled her, and she spilled coffee all over the cabinet and floor. Jasper ran under the table with the commotion. As she cleaned up the mess, she asked herself why she jumped at the sound of every little noise. The ghost had not harmed her; she had never been afraid of Tom. She got her toast from the toaster and sat down at the table. The dry crumbs seem to stick to her esophagus. She took a large sip of her coffee and glanced at the clock. She had over an hour before she had to be at work. When she awoke early, she usually went to her computer and brainstormed ideas for a story. Then in the evening, she would go back and improve on her ideas. When she started to sit down at her computer, she noticed that someone had turned it on. She never left her computer turned on. Had the ghost tampered with her files? Had the ghost been reading her files? Her mind flashed back to the times Tom had told his friends about her love stories. Then after they married, he complained often about her writing and had pulled all the wires from her computer. He never encouraged her to publish her stories; he criticized her for writing stupid stories. He often accused her of being paranoid. She dismissed the thoughts of Tom and the ghost, opened a new file, and wrote almost two pages before she left for school. The ghost mystery like her life, had no end.

On the weekends, Olivia worked in the yards. She went to the storage rooms under the garage, where she kept her garden tools to get the loppers to trim shrubbery. Her loppers had disappeared. A thief had stolen her brand new loppers. When she complained to her mother about the thief, her mother thought she had misplaced the loppers. She told her not to jump to conclusions. Her mother made her angry; she reminded Olivia of Tom who blamed her for everything that went wrong. At times, he acted as if she made up things to complain about and simply ignored her.

On Sunday, Olivia slept late and had a late breakfast. She had not finished eating before her cell phone interrupted her. She expected to hear her mother's voice; instead, she heard Tom's familiar voice. First he asked how she had been doing. Then he asked about her job. Last, but not least, he asked about the house she bought.

Before she explained all of the things that had gone wrong, he wanted to know why she bought a house with an unfinished attic; he added that he had given her enough money to buy a new house.

Shocked by his knowledge of the attic in the house, she asked how he knew about the attic.

He bragged that he had his sources and they kept him informed.

She tried to explain that the price of the house made her buy it quickly; besides, she needed a place to live before school started. She admitted that she wanted to look for another house when school turned out for the summer.

Before Tom hung up, he told her he missed her and she could move back into the house with him.

Olivia flatly refused his offer; she didn't want to take a chance on love again. She would never consider going back to him.

He wished her the best and hung up.

Olivia lost her appetite; she sat and stared out the kitchen window. Now she knew that Tom had something to do with the ghost in the attic; he wanted to scare her; but she could do nothing about his foolish pranks. Did he really think she would go back to him? She felt good about turning him down; she felt strong again.

Two months before the school year ended, Olivia put a large "For Sale" sign in her front yard. She wanted a prospective buyer before she looked for another house.

To Olivia's surprise, a couple came and asked about the house the next week. She showed them the house and they wanted to buy it right away. She explained that she must find a place to live before she could move out of the house. They asked her to hold the house and call them when she got ready to sell.

Every day after school, Olivia drove around Boulder Bluff and looked for another house. She spotted a beautiful, two story brick home just outside the city limits. She liked the idea of being out of the city limits and away from the noisy traffic in the city. Best of all, she liked being even nearer to the elementary school. She called the realtor, Mrs. Crafton, and asked for an appointment to see the house the next Saturday; she asked her to meet her at nine o'clock.

As she followed Mrs. Crafton up the steps, she looked up at the boxed windows on the second floor and back down to the small porch. The long windows on each side of the wooden door gave a flare of elegance to the house. They entered a large living room with a small fireplace and moved on through the kitchen, breakfast area, and dining room to a hallway that led to a large bedroom on the ground floor. Then they climbed the stairs and looked at two bedrooms with a bath and walk in closet in each room. Olivia liked the floor plan and the house looked brand new with freshly painted walls and new carpet throughout, except in the ceramic tile baths. The master bedroom on the ground floor had a door on the back wall that led to a large back porch and patio surrounded by a fenced in back yard.

Mrs. Crafton explained that she had shown the house several times in the past month and two couples seemed interested, but they had not been able to get a loan.

Olivia expected the asking price for the house to be at least one hundred fifty thousand; but the couple who owned the house wanted to sell the house quickly, because the man retired from the Coca Cola Company in the city. He and his wife had already moved back to Virginia, where they both grew up. They wanted one hundred twenty-five thousand for the house.

Olivia promised to call Mrs. Crafton the next day and tell her what she decided about the house.

When Olivia got home, she called the couple who wanted to buy her house to let them know that they could move the last week in May.

They wanted to arrange a meeting that weekend to close the deal. The couple had no trouble getting a loan and Olivia closed the deal. She would have taken a loss to get rid of the ghost house; but the couple had not asked her to lower the price. Olivia sold the house for two thousand dollars more than she had paid; but she had that much in the curtains and repairs.

When school turned out for the summer, Olivia's father hired two men to help him move her furniture and appliances into her new home.

One week later Olivia went to her parent's and got her cat, Jasper, to spend the first night in her new home. She pulled up before the red brick house and studied it for minutes before she pulled under the double garage. Her eyes moved across the lawn to the leaves piled up around the oak trees and the limbs scattered about the yard. She also needed to trim the hedges and replace the straw in the flower beds. She liked roses; Tom used to buy her roses for special occasion. She let the garage door down and sat in the car for some time and thought about the times she had tried to live with Tom and the times she had moved to start over again.

She hated going into the house. She wondered if Tom knew she had moved into another house. She felt as if Tom, the ghost, had followed her to this house and loomed from the dark corners.

After she unlocked the door, she paused before she stepped inside. The darkness and silence scared her. She flipped on the kitchen light and walked from one room to the next. The movers had placed the furniture in the exact spot she wanted each piece; but she had beds to make and clothes to organize.

After she took a bath, she ate a sandwich for supper and went to the living room to watch television. Jasper joined her on the couch and snuggled under her arm to sleep. She awoke at twelve thirty, turned off the television, and went to bed. She lay awake for an hour and listened for strange noises. Luckily, the house had no ghost; but old habits die hard.

The next day Olivia went to buy groceries and canned goods to stock her new pantry. As she shopped, a handsome man with sandy hair and a stocky build walked up to her and said, "Olivia Hollister, how good to see you. I have not seen you since high school. You are still as pretty as a picture."

Olivia did not recognize him at first. Then she smiled and said "Nick Jolly, it is nice to see you, too."

They talked a few minutes about back then, and Nick asked if she had a husband. She did not feel up to talking about her divorce from Tom. She admitted that she had married a man she met in college, but things did not work out. To her surprise he had the same experience. His marriage lasted less than a year. She looked at her watch to let him know she wanted to part ways. He quickly asked if she would like to go out and have dinner sometimes. She told a big lie about being in a relationship with someone else. As she started to walk away, he said, "If things don't work out with the lucky guy, call me. I know you still like to dance."

She smiled and said, "I do like to dance, and I will keep you in mind."

As Olivia drove home, she remembered that Nick always showed her a good time when they dated in high school, but the thought of starting a new relationship scared her. Then she thought about Scott Porter. If he came around again, she would jump at the chance to go out with him.

On Saturday, Olivia usually met her parents at Morrison's for dinner; but her mother called to cancel plans. Some of her friends from out of town had called and wanted to come for the weekend.

Olivia drove through town and passed by Morrison's. She did not want to face the large crowd; she wanted a quiet peaceful table at the back corner of a small restaurant. She pulled into a parking space at the Steak Place. A waiter showed her to a choice table in the smoking area. The windows gave a nice view of the residential section surrounding the restaurant. She ordered corn, cream potatoes, and roast beef with sweet tea to drink.

While she waited for her order, she watched the traffic in front of the restaurant. She moved her eyes down the long row of cars to note the color and make. She looked for Tom's car every time she went to town. He had apparently kept tabs on her since she moved to Boulder Bluff. Why did she give the sorry bastard a second thought? The waiter brought her food and she forgot Tom. She had an enormous appetite and ate more than she had eaten in months. She ordered another glass of tea to take with her.

On the way home, she turned on the radio and listened to country music. She smiled when the announcer played Gloria Gaynor's famous song, "I'll Survive." She tapped her fingers to the beat and sang with the radio. Slowly, but surely she would survive without Tom Bradford.

Olivia spent the summer measuring windows, making curtains, and shopping for odds and ends she needed. She tried to find material similar to the material she used in the other house; but she settled for different patterns. When school started back in September, Olivia had curtains and everything organized in her new home.

CHAPTER ELEVEN

Reunion by Fate

IN THE MEANTIME, Scott Porter still thought about Olivia; but he remained faithful to his wife, Laura. He visited her every day and made sure she had everything she needed to make her comfortable; but his visits made him more depressed than ever. He still hated to go home to that empty house. Many times, he went back to the factory and worked to avoid the lonely silence in the house.

The days drifted to weeks; months passed to a new year. Then spring melted winter with warm sunny days that filled the air with sweet blooms and covered the earth with green plants. As Scott walked to his truck, birds tweeted happy tunes from the trees and butterflies flitted their beautiful colors around the azaleas. Sweet tunes nor beautiful flowers made Scott happy anymore. All excitement has gone out of his life; and his days of happiness ceased to exist.

When he got home every evening, he mixed a strong drink to help him make it through the night. In spite of his hang over the next morning, he continued to drink until he fell asleep. He usually got a good night's sleep; but he still got up tired and depressed. His depression showed in his reactions to his friends and his employees. His friends encouraged him to play more golf and enjoy life. How did they expect him to enjoy life? Then he remembered what his mama once said: "The past is just a memory; but you must stay focused on your duties at the present to be successful and have a good future."

How he wished his parents were still alive. He had no close relatives who lived nearby. Laura's parents had grown distant since her accident, and they did not visit her often; they never visited him. Laura's sister, Lisa Cane, came every day for several months after Laura's accident; then she came only once every two or three weeks. Scott seldom ran into Lisa; she visited Laura before he got off from work. Lisa had barely spoken to him since he dumped her and married Laura. In their teen years, Laura and Lisa had been close. Lisa often bragged about being two years younger than Laura was. Laura got her degree in fine arts and Lisa got a degree in architecture. Lisa worked with a company in Atlanta as a designer until she divorced Robert Cane. Then she moved back to Porterville and worked with Interior Designs.

Summer came with hot breezes that wilted the blooms of spring and parched green crops before maturity. Scott still stuck to his boring routine. He went to work at six-thirty, left work at five-thirty, went to the Ocmulgee Country Club to eat with his friends, visited Laura, went home, and drank liquor until he fell asleep.

Tonight, he resisted that strong drink of whiskey to put him to sleep. Instead, he put on a pot of coffee, and took a bath while his coffee perked.

He sipped his coffee, relaxed in his recliner, and thought about his predicament. If he continued to feel sorry for himself, he would go insane. He must make some changes and enjoy life before he got too old to get around. After two cups of coffee, he got dressed, and went back to the club to talk to his friends.

When Scott got back home, he went to bed and slept better than he had slept in months. Maybe things would get better.

As Scott drove toward his office, he tried to think of something positive, something that would make him feel better. His mother had taught him not to dwell on his problems. She believed in doing good deeds for others to forget his problems.

Scott invited all of his supervisors to have dinner with him. Tomorrow, he would invite his secretaries to have dinner with him. He would continue this thoughtful practice every day until all of his workers had been invited to have dinner with him.

On Friday Scott had to go to Savannah to pick up supplies. He looked forward to his trip out of town. He felt relieved that he did not have to spend the night at home; he also had a good excuse for not visiting Laura. He usually felt guilty if he did not visit her every day after work; but his visits meant nothing to her. He needed the warmth, love and understanding of a woman who could take Laura's place. He knew many available women who were anxious to please; prostitutes, whores nor trashy women measured up to his expectations. He wanted a special woman with morals, a woman like Olivia Hollister.

Two years had come and gone since the night he met Olivia Hollister. After all this time, he still thought about her. He had called her a dozen times but she never returned his calls.

When he reached the Boulder Bluff sign, he turned off the interstate and drove to Olivia's apartment. The elderly lady who answered the door informed him that she had lived in the apartment more than one year; she did not know Olivia Hollister.

Scott thanked the lady and left. He felt sure Olivia had gone back to her old boyfriend, Tom; but he would never know for sure, unless he asked questions and got answers. The hands on his watch pointed to twelve and he thought about the Southern Grill, a restaurant that Olivia had recommended the night they first met. He drove around town until he found the restaurant and parked.

At the same time, Olivia had gone to the Southern Grill to eat lunch. As she mixed her salad and poured on the dressing, the deep voice that came to her ear made her put her fork down.

"What a nice surprise."

She turned to see Scott Porter with a broad smile on his face.

"Scott Porter, how nice to see you," she said with wide eyes of surprise. He looked more handsome than she remembered in his navy suit, white shirt, and red tie that peeped from his unbuttoned coat.

Before she invited his company, he pulled out a chair and sat down across from her.

"When I walked into the restaurant, I saw you and I could not believe my eyes. How have you been?"

"I have been doing fairly well. How have you been?"

"I have been working, eating, and sleeping," he said. Then he quickly changed the subject. "What are you eating for the main course?"

"Salad is the only thing I ordered," she said. "I like their garden salad. Besides, I want to lose about ten pounds."

"You don't need to lose weight," he said. "You are as beautiful as I remembered."

After he ordered, he said, "What on earth happened to you? I called you several times and you never returned my calls."

"I did not know you called," Olivia said. She knew immediately that Tom had checked her cell phone the first night he visited her. Then after she went back to him, he came in with a new phone as well as a new number.

"Several weeks later, I went by your apartment and learned you had moved. Where have you been?"

"I am sure you would not want to hear about the last two years of my life," she said.

"I think you went back to your old boyfriend," he said and smiled.

"I not only went back to Tom; I married him."

Scott's face fell and he said, "I guess I should not be sitting here in public with a married woman."

"My marriage to Tom lasted only two years. I am back in Boulder Bluff for good. I bought two houses before I found one that I liked. The first house had ghosts in the attic."

Scott laughed and said, "Do you believe in ghost?"

"I never have before, but this house gave me the creeps."

"Do you like your second home?" he said.

"So far, I am pleased with the house. I have only a few miles to drive to school each day."

"Are you at the same school?"

"I am teaching at the elementary school now. Before, I taught at the middle school."

"I have thought about you often and would like to spend some time with you. Are you dating anyone now?"

"No, I have not been that brave," she said. "I stay busy with the kids at school all day. When I get home, my life is so boring that you would not be interested."

"I am interested in anything you have to say," he said.

"We don't have time to get into the story of my life," she said.

He sat and looked at her for minutes as if reading her mind. "Don't tell me that a beautiful woman like you have been sitting home since you divorced Tom."

She told him a convincing lie, "I did not say that I had been sitting home. I have been out a time or two with my friends."

"Let's make that three times," he said with a broad smile. "I want to take you out on the town. I never repaid you for the kindness you showed me the night of the storm."

She did not want to seem anxious; but she wanted to go out with him.

Before she had time to answer, he said, "You have nothing to worry about; I like to show off a pretty woman with no strings attached."

She glanced at her watch and said, "I am running late; the students will climb the walls." The principal had never fussed at her about being a few minutes late, but she liked to be back at work on time. As she got up to leave, he said, "You did not say you would go out with me."

"I would like to go out with you, Scott."

"Would you like to go out tonight," he said. "I can get a room at Hampton Inn."

"If you need to go home, I understand," she said. "We can go out tomorrow night."

"I don't need to go home. My supervisors can handle the work load. I will see you tonight at seven," he said.

"I look forward to seeing you," Olivia said. The she remembered that he did not have her address. She got her small pad from her purse, wrote down her address, and smiled as she handed it to him. "This might help you stay on the right road."

He knew why she had said that; he got on the wrong road the night they first met. He smiled and said, "Thanks, I forgot that you had moved."

When she went to pay her bill, the waiter told her that the man at her table picked up her ticket when he first came into the restaurant. She looked back at Scott, smiled, and moved her mouth with, "Thank you."

On the way back to school, she felt as if fate had brought Scott Porter back to her. How could she explain their strange encounter at the restaurant after more than two years? Why did he pick that particular restaurant to have lunch? Until now, she had not believed in fate. She had finally met a man with manners and he showed respect for women. Scott seemed too good to be true. Then she remembered what her mother once told her: "Olivia, if a man seems too good to be true, he probably is too good to be true. You can compare most perfect men to those sweepstakes you get in the mail. They promise you the big prize and you end up with a big bill for something that you did not order."

She gave her student their worksheets and assignment to answer questions for the review chapter. As they worked, she walked around the room and thought about Scott.

After school turned out, Olivia rushed home to get ready for her date. She made it home in less than twenty minutes; the evening traffic slowed, and she did not catch any red lights.

When the doorbell rang at seven, her heart pounded with excitement. She opened the door and faced a handsome man dressed in an expensive black suit, white shirt, and red tie.

She felt as if she looked too casual in her slacks and pullover. She invited him to sit in the living room and dashed to the bedroom to change clothes. She chose a navy blue dress with white trim and matching coat. Then she kicked off her flats and slipped on a pair of navy heels.

When she walked back into the living room, he whistled and said, "What a change! You need to wear dresses more often. You get more beautiful each time I see you."

"You look very handsome, too," she said.

He stood up, took her hand, and kissed her on the cheek.

She could feel her face grow warm; and her heart beat in her toes as she smiled up at him. She felt like a teenager going out on the first date; but she had grown much wiser since her last date with Tom. She walked ahead of him and picked up her purse from the hall table.

As they walked to the car, he squeezed her around the waist and made her have love chills. He opened the door and got under the wheel. Then he looked at her and said, "I have thought about you a long time. I have looked forward to taking you out since the first time I laid eyes on you."

As he drove, he asked where she would like to have dinner.

Any restaurant suited her; she liked vegetables most of all.

"Do you like Mexican, Chinese, or plain old sloppy Joes?" he said.

"I guess I am a plain old sloppy Joes' girl," she said.

"Let's have seafood," he said as he took a right down Maple Street.

They pulled into the parking area at Red Lobster and walked into the restaurant. A waiter dressed in a black tuxedo met them. He ushered them to a table at the back of the elegant dining room. Large globe lights hung from a sunroof ceiling in the center of the restaurant. White linen tablecloths covered the tables, and candles flickered on each table.

Scott studied the menu and she studied him.

"What would you like?" he asked.

She wanted to say soup and salad from Shoney's, but she pretended to study the menu trimmed in gold with a gold price tag beside each entrée. She could not believe that one lobster with salad cost forty bucks. If she ate one of those lobsters, she would probably throw up.

"I think I will have the lobster," he said.

"There is too much to choose from. I always fail multiple choice tests."

He laughed, took her menu, laid it aside and said," I will order for you. Do you like lobster?"

"I like lobster," she said. She dared not tell him that she never ordered expensive items on the menu.

After Scott ordered, he asked the waiter to bring a bottle of the best wine in the house. The waiter smiled and said, "Yes, Sir. Our wine is the best."

Scott talked about his job and his business trips to New York and New Jersey. He added that he lived out of a suitcase sometimes, but he liked the money.

He asked if she would like to go to the movies. She suggested they go back to her house and watch a movie; she had Netflix.

Back at home, Olivia asked Scott to make himself comfortable and she disappeared to the bedroom to change into a comfortable knit pullover, jeans, and flat shoes. She stood in front of a chalkboard all day, and her feet hurt.

She left the bedroom and went by the kitchen to get beers. She came into the living room, handed a beer to Scott, and sat down on the couch next to him. He immediately put his arms around her and kissed her. Then he cupped her face in his hands and told her he had never kissed a more beautiful woman. He kissed her again and she wanted more than a kiss; but she wanted him to respect her. Thoughts of his making love to her scared her; but she had grown wiser and stronger after Tom broke her heart. She had learned her lesson the hard way; men judged women by their weaknesses, while they did as they pleased. Men never worried about their reputation. In fact, men measured their manhood by the number of women they tucked under the sheets.

Olivia picked up the television monitor, flipped to Netflix and asked Scott what kind of movie he wanted to watch. He liked romantic movies and murder mysteries; but he mostly wanted to be near her. She smiled at him as she settled for a romantic movie.

After the movie started, she went to the kitchen to pop some popcorn. This gave her an excuse to get away from him for a few minutes. She came back with popcorn and cokes and they talked during the entire movie.

Olivia talked about their meeting again after more than two years. She asked if he believed that fate brought them back together.

Scott admitted that he had been to the Southern Grill each time he passed through Bolder Gap. She had told him that it was her favorite place to eat; but fate must have played a part in their happy reunion.

Olivia talked about Tom and the years she lived in Cedar Grove. She left out the heartbreak and loneliness she suffered after they broke up.

Scott still had not told her much about his life. She knew when he graduated from high school and college; she knew the names of his friends; she knew his parents had both died; but she did not know if he had been married and divorced. She felt sure he had a girlfriend. When she asked about other women, he avoided her question with his answer. He had never been with another woman as beautiful as the woman sitting next to him. Neither had he been with a woman who made him feel as good as he felt being with her. He pulled her close and said, "I want you so much that I can hardly stand being away from you. Let me make love to you."

"I want our relationship to mean more to you than a one night stand with sex and nothing more."

He pulled her close and kissed her between words, "I love you, Olivia. I have loved you since the night we met. After you didn't answer or return my calls, I backed away, because I felt like you needed more time. I wanted to call you; I wanted to see you."

Then she explained that she tried to make her marriage work and thought Tom would change; but things got worse with every passing day. She admitted that she had thought about him often when Tom left her home all alone.

Before he left, he held her a long time and asked if he could see her again the next weekend.

She reminded him that Thanksgiving came the next week; and school turned out on Wednesday. She asked him to call and they would make plans for the weekend.

He laughed and said, "School teacher make plans for all things."

His words made her laugh, too; but he had spoken the truth; teachers had to make plans for their students and got used to planning everything else.

He promised to call her the next day. As he walked toward the door, she wanted to scream for him to come back; she wanted him to take her to bed, but she stood strong and did the right thing. She closed the door and walked to the window to watch him drive away. She did not want to fall in love again. She had been attracted to Scott at first sight; Tom came back and put a stop to her relationship with Scott before it got started. Did Tom know that Scott had called her? She felt sure that Tom erased all of her calls from Scott that she never got.

CHAPTER TWELVE

Romantic Thanksgiving

ON SATURDAY, OLIVIA awoke with Scott on her mind. She went to the kitchen, fixed a cup of coffee, walked to the window, and looked out at the world. Sunrise peeped through the trees; and their leaves flamed with beautiful streaks of orange, yellow, and brown. She liked fall; but she dreaded spending Thanksgiving Day with her parents and all of her kin folks, cousins and aunts. Her Aunt Isabell and Sophie would run her into the ground for divorcing Tom; and she hated answering their questions about her personal life. If she invited Scott to have Thanksgiving dinner with her; she would have a good excuse to stay at home for Thanksgiving.

That night, Scott called and asked if she had made plans for the weekend.

She had made plans for Thanksgiving and she wanted him to come on Thursday and have Thanksgiving dinner with her.

"Having Thanksgiving with you would make me the happiest man in the world," he said. "I wanted to ask you to go out with me on Thanksgiving, but I assumed that you would have dinner with your family; I didn't want to spoil your tradition."

"I usually have dinner with my parents; but I had rather have dinner with you. I promise to cook the traditional Thanksgiving dinner with turkey and all the trimmings; but you must carve the turkey," she said.

"I would settle for hot dogs and slaw to be with you," he said.

"I want you to have a good Thanksgiving dinner," she said.

"I will be there early on Thursday and help you with dinner," he said.

After she hung up, she called her mother to cancel Thanksgiving with the family; she explained that she had special company coming to her house for dinner.

"Who is the lucky man? How old is he? Where does he live? What does he do for a living? Has he been married and divorced? Does he have children?"

"Why do you question me about who I invite to dinner?" Olivia said.

"I do not want my daughter to invite a stranger off the street to have dinner at her home," her mother said.

"Mother, I have to go. I will talk to you later," Olivia said and she hung up.

Scott called Olivia again Sunday night. He could tell by her exciting tone that she loved him as much as he loved her. He felt happier than he had felt in over two years. Then he worried. How could he tell her that he had a wife? How could he make her understand his situation?" If he told her about Laura, she would ask him to leave and he would never see her again. He did not want to lose her. He thought about her every minute of the day; he could not stay away from her. He could not give up the best thing that had happened to him since Laura's accident. He must keep his wife a secret in order to spend time with Olivia.

Scott called Olivia every night that week and asked if he could come to see her. She explained that she had no time to socialize. She had to clean the house, shop, and plan for Thanksgiving dinner.

On Tuesday after school, Olivia went shopping and bought everything she needed for the perfect dinner. That night, she cooked a cake for her students.

After school on Wednesday, Olivia's students enjoyed cake and punch. As they left class, their excitement and laughter echoed through the hall. Holidays always brought a lot of excitement. Olivia felt excited, too. The sound of Scott's voice on the phone made her knees weak. Why did she fall in love again?

On Thursday, Scott knocked on Olivia's door at ten o'clock in the morning. He kissed her, wished her a happy Thanksgiving, and handed her a beautiful fall arrangement, a horn of plenty.

She bragged on his perfect choice, set the decorative piece in the center of the dining room table, and asked him to make himself comfortable in the living room.

He offered to help her with dinner; but she didn't need any help. She already had the turkey ready to carve, but she had to bake the dressing, green bean casserole, and potato pie. She would join him shortly.

When Olivia walked into the living room, she heard Scott talking on his cell phone. After he hung up, pulled her down on the couch next to him and said, "I want to take you to my place near the beach in Brunswick. You need to get away a few days and relax. I think you will enjoy the scenery. I have a beautiful lake behind my house. We can spend the entire weekend relaxing and enjoying each other's company. I have already called Bo Walden, the man who keeps my place up. He will cut plenty of wood for us to burn the rest of the week."

"I did not know you had a place near the beach in Brunswick, but the trip sounds delightful," she said.

An hour later, Olivia went back to the kitchen to put dinner on the table and Scott followed her. They laughed and talked as he carved the turkey. Olivia noticed that his carving skills looked professional. Then he put ice in their glasses and poured the tea.

After they finished eating, he bragged on her dinner. He had not had a Thanksgiving dinner that delicious in years. Then he mentioned that her dressing tasted like his mother's.

As they cleared the table, Olivia suggested that they take the left-over food with them for supper.

He suggested they take only enough for one meal; he wanted to grill steaks one night and he wanted to take her out to eat. He had a freezer and pantry packed with food. They could cook breakfast every morning.

He helped Olivia clear the table pack and store the food. As she washed the dishes, he stood right next to her and dried them.

Olivia had never had a happier Thanksgiving.

As Olivia packed her clothes, she felt excited and relieved. If Scott felt free to go away with her and spend the weekend, he definitely did not have another girlfriend or wife.

Scott loaded her luggage and came back to wait for her. She checked everything, got her purse, and held Scotts hand as they walked to his Cadillac. He opened the door for her and she took a comfortable seat with a relaxed breath.

"Would you like to take the long scenic route, or the short cut," he said.

I am anxious to see this fabulous lake," she said. "Let's take the short cut."

They drove more than fifty-five miles from Olivia's house to his place near the beach in Brunswick. As he drove, he talked about his business and his employees. She wanted to ask him about his women, but she could not bring herself to face him with such personal questions.

Scott neared the entrance to his estate and stopped to open a chained gate. He motioned for her to drive through. After he locked the gate, he took the passenger's side and gave directions. As she drove toward his house, she admired the pines, and large cypress trees that shaded thick underbrush. They passed a shelter covered by a shiny tin roof with long tables and benches that he used for cookouts. Behind the shelter, a lake stretched east and west out of sight. Then they came to a large, two story house with cedar siding. He asked her to drive around to the back and park in the garage.

"After we get unpacked, we can go for a boat ride on the lake," he said.

Just inside the door, a staircase led to the top floor. The floor plan reminded her of a fictional scene she had written in one of her love stories. As she walked ahead of him through the foyer, he placed his hands around her waist and turned her to face him.

"I love you; you are so beautiful," he said.

"I cannot deny the fact that I am getting older," she said.

"I am also getting older. We must not waste one minute of our time together," he said.

She wanted him to kiss her, and he did. He kissed her with a need for her that lasted and started over again. He did not stop; his actions made her anxious for him to make love to her. In spite of her need for him, she didn't want to rush things; she wanted this night to be perfect.

He must have read her thoughts, because he quickly walked ahead of her to show her around the house. A beautiful stone fireplace in the center of the living room blazed and made the house warm and cozy. Couches on each side of the fireplace blended with mint green curtains. Blinds beneath the curtains gave the room privacy and warmth. Animal skins of beautiful colors decorated the walls. The zebra skin took top prize for its beauty; but she hated the thought of taking an animal out of its skin. A large cherry desk took the far corner of the room. The adjoining dining room had a long mahogany table surrounded by eight matching chairs and two captain's chairs. They walked on to the den and the walls of the large room had mounted deer heads, antlers, fish, foxes, wolves, and wild cats. Then he led her up a beautiful staircase and showed her three bedrooms furnished with expensive wood furniture. She expected to see elephants and tigers, but he had no mounted animals in the bedrooms.

"I rent the house during deer hunting season; the men love this place; they like to fish most of all."

"You have a beautiful home. I can see that you decorated the house for sportsmen."

After they unpacked and stored the food in the refrigerator, he took her hand and they walked out onto a back porch. The steps led to a boat ramp with a boat waiting for the sightseeing tour down the lake. She took a seat and he sat next to her.

The boatman turned and looked at them, and Scott said, "Bo, this is my friend, Olivia."

Bo tipped his hat and said, "Nice to meet you, Miss Olivia."

Then Bo slowly backed up and edged the boat down the lake. He carefully twisted and turned the boat between the thickly settled cypress trees. The tall trees looked ancient. The sights and sounds of nature surrounding them amazed her. Frogs and crickets echoed through the trees, and the flapping wings of a thousand birds made a frightening sound that fell from the sky. The white birds resembled laughing gulls and their wide wings carried them with rhythm in a circle and back toward a thicket of trees to roost.

The boatman hit the front of the boat with a large wooden paddle and the birds took flight again.

"What kind of birds are they?" she said.

"Grebes," he said. They like lakes and fresh water streams. They migrate before Christmas to a warmer climate."

"Georgia is pretty warm. Maybe they will stay," she said.

"Late in the evening, the birds amaze me. I have never seen a more beautiful sight than a flock of birds sailing across the lake."

She asked about the alligators, and Bo bragged that he had tamed the alligators. Then he called the names of different kinds of fish that made their home in the lake.

The scenery and the boat ride with Scott Porter sitting close to her made this the most romantic and peaceful place on earth. She could not remember feeling more relaxed and at ease. She looked ahead and saw a deck with a walkway for anglers to cast lines.

"This beautiful lake takes my breath away," she said.

"The low level of the water and the lily pads has ruined the beauty of the lake. I came down here in the summer and worked to clear out some of the lily pads, but they have grown back thicker than ever."

"You must not destroy nature's way of putting oxygen into the water," Olivia said.

"I stir the water to keep up the oxygen level. I don't need the lily pads."

Bo continued to move slowly down the lake for more than a mile, and the distant trees wrapped up the sun's warm rays in its shadows.

"I guess we had better head back. Darkness is catching on, and we don't have lights on the boat."

As they moved back up stream toward the pier, the roaring motor boat silenced their conversation as well as the croaking sounds of frogs. The birds had perched again on their roost and made no movement as the boat passed.

Bo told Scott to call him if he needed anything. Then he made his way up the stone steps. At the top step, he turned and said, "Miss Olivia, the next time I will take you to the end of the lake."

"Thanks, Bo," she said. "I enjoyed the ride."

They climbed out of the boat, walked up the steps, and met a wide sidewalk that led to the house. Before they climbed the steps, the moon shed sparkles on the water and shadows from trees surrounded the lake with a blanket of warmth and security.

She followed him across the porch and waited for him to unlock the door. Before going inside, he pulled her close, kissed her, and whispered sweet nothings in her ear. Best of all, he told her he loved her. Then he looked beyond the porch and pointed toward the sky, "Look at that moon."

"Very romantic," she said and smiled up at him.

"Do you want to sit here on the porch a while or go inside and sit before the fire.

"Let's go inside. The weather feels a bit chilly."

Scott grilled steaks for supper; she baked potatoes and made a garden salad. The delicious meal made her full and lazy. She wanted to sit and do nothing, but she insisted that she wash the dishes. Scott helped with the dishes. Then he fixed drinks, and they went to the den to watch television.

Olivia had not drunk mixed drinks or liquor since Tom deserted her. She could not drink like a normal person and worried that the liquor would make her act crazy. She did not want to give Scott the wrong impression. Liquor made her talk too much and say the wrong things. Liquor made her think about having sex, become aggressive, and act like a seductive whore.

When Scott asked to refill her glass, she pulled her glass away; she could not drink much without getting crazy.

He wanted her to get crazy; he wanted to make love to her. He took her glass and came back with it filled to the brim.

If she sipped the drink slowly, she could stay in complete control of her actions. She intended to keep her mouth shut. Before she finished the second drink, her head felt dizzy.

Olivia liked the sound of Scott's voice and his laughter. She did not want to hide her feeling for him; she wanted him to make love to her; she would do anything he asked. Once again, this fool in love forgot about consequences of her actions. She could hear his proposal; she could see him waiting at the altar for her. Their wedding would be special; she would wear a long satin gown. The music would be sweeter than a blue bird's song. He would take her hand, slip a gold band on her finger, and vow to love and keep her. The feel of his arms around her and his kiss made her feel wonderful. She wanted to push him away; she wanted him to take her to bed and make love to her all night long.

Then she felt the warmth of his body against her nakedness as they fell on the bed. How would this end? Scott still had told her nothing about his life. Did she care? Could she walk away afterward and never look back?

Euphoria filled her with the incredible sensation that surged through her from head to toe. Scott made love to her the way she had dreamed he would. Her moans of pleasure excited him even more. He gently stroked her hair and whispered words of love. They talked until they both fell asleep.

Scott fixed eggs, grits, bacon, and toast for breakfast. After they ate, they went back to bed. She had never had sex with a gentler, more caring man. She once thought that no man could satisfy her, except Tom. She thought she loved Tom; but she had never been in love, until now. They slept and made love until after twelve o'clock.

She fixed turkey sandwiches for dinner. Then they went for a walk around the lake. They came back and sat in the porch swing until the chill ran them inside. Then they watched a movie.

Late that evening, she found hamburger meat in the freezer and everything else she needed to make spaghetti. While the spaghetti simmered, she made a garden salad, baked potatoes, and browned the rolls.

An hour later, she called Scott to dinner. He bragged on her spaghetti. She liked a man who showed appreciation for a woman's efforts in the kitchen. Maybe he bragged on the meal to show good manners; maybe the meal tasted delicious.

After they cleaned the kitchen, they watched a football game on Television. Then they went to bed and made love.

The time she spent with Scott that weekend in Brunswick made her happier than she had ever been in her life. She loved him completely; she wanted to stay with him forever; she wanted to spend the rest of her life with him. She dreaded going back home.

Before they walked out the door, he kissed her. She told him that he made her feel loved and needed. She thanked him for a wonderful weekend. She added that she could live there forever and never tire of the atmosphere. She did not tell him all the wonderful things she thought about him. He treated her special, the way she wanted to be treated. She had found the man of her dreams at last; and she wanted to spend the rest of her life with him.

Before they got outside of Brunswick, Scott told her he wanted to take her to Seafood Delight, a restaurant that specialized in lobster. He said he always stopped by there to eat on the way home from Brunswick.

They pulled into the parking area of the Seafood Delight and she admired the large sign with pictures of sea animals.

She asked Scott to order for her. He ordered lobster with all the trimmings and a bottle of wine.

Before the waiter brought their order, a tall handsome man with sandy hair walked up to their table and slapped Scott on the shoulder. "Scott Porter, I did not expect to see you here," he said. Then he looked at Olivia and smiled. "I did not expect this beautiful woman to be with you, either."

Scott looked as if he swallowed a wad of cotton. He said, "This is a friend of mine, Olivia Bradford, and he introduced the man as Joseph Harrington, his lawyer, friend and golf partner.

Joseph mentioned that they had missed seeing him at the country club the last week; Scott quickly explained that he had been out of town on business.

Olivia felt uneasy as they talked about things back in the city and Scott' business. She excused herself, went to the bathroom and called Emily. When she told her how Scott reacted to his friend and what his friend had said, Emily thought that Joseph's statement about Scott's beautiful woman sounded normal and she should play it cool for a while before she started popping questions about his life.

She told Emily she would call her later and hung up, but she still worried about Scott's reaction when Joseph walked up to their table. She wanted to know everything about Scott. He had never mentioned his family; when she had talked about Tom, Scott quickly changed the subject.

While Olivia went to the restroom, Scott talked to Joseph about Olivia. Scott trusted Joseph and had already thought of talking to him about Olivia, but he did not know how to tell him. He asked Joseph what he would do if he sailed in the same boat.

Joseph admitted that his sailboat would sink to the bottom of the sea.

When Olivia got back to the table, Joseph got up and said, "I will see you tomorrow at the club for dinner."

"I look forward to dinner," Scott said.

Joseph turned to Olivia and said, "I am pleased to have met you, Olivia. Scott knows a pretty woman when he sees one. You two have a nice evening."

Scott told Olivia that Joseph seemed like a brother. They had been through high school and college together. He had majored in accounting, while Joseph majored in Law. He called on Joseph for all legal advice.

Olivia smiled and said, "What would we do without friends?"

When they got to Olivia's house, Scott carried her bags to the living room. Olivia complained of having a headache. He pulled her close and asked to spend the night with her and cure her ache.

She thanked him for the wonderful weekend; but she felt exhausted and needed some rest.

He kissed her goodnight, told her he loved her, and looked forward to seeing her again soon. He seemed to understand; but she sensed disappointment when he told her goodnight. Before he closed the door behind him, he promised to call her the next day.

After Olivia went to bed, she thought about Scott. He made her feel beautiful, wanted, and needed; but he still had told her very little about his life. Why had she spent the weekend with him before she knew everything about him? She must not see him again until she checked his background. Had she already gotten in over her head?

CHAPTER THIRTEEN

Heartbreaking Secret

EARLY THE NEXT morning, Scott called and asked if she would go out with him that evening.

She wanted to see him more than anything; but something told her to turn down his invitation. Then she thought about how wonderful he made her feel. She had fallen in love with him; she wanted to believe that he loved her as much as she loved him. She felt sure that he would dump his girlfriend for her. On the other hand, he might be married. Then she concluded that he could not be married. He had spent the entire Thanksgiving with her. If he had a wife, he would not be free to spend days away from home. Besides, he wanted to see her again the next day.

Scott did not call again the next two days and Olivia almost went crazy. When her phone rang Thursday evening, she rushed to answer it.

"Hello, sweetheart," he said, and her heart went to the races.

Then he talked about how busy he had been and asked about her week at school. He hoped he had given her the time and space she needed to get back on track.

She told him she had a good week at school; but she thought about him more than she should have.

He told her how much he had missed her and wanted to see her. Then he asked her to go out with him on Friday.

Olivia quickly agreed and he told her he would pick her up around seven.

On Friday, Scott acted happy and well-mannered as usual. After they ate dinner, he asked if she wanted to go to a movie. Olivia suggested that they go to her house and talk.

Back at Olivia's place, she went to the kitchen, got beers, and joined him in the living room. He kissed her on the cheek as she sat next to him on the couch. Then he set his beer on the end table, cupped her face in his hands, and told her she was the most beautiful woman he had ever made love to. Then he told her he loved her. Afterwards his kiss made her want to go to bed with him, but wanted him to tell her more about his life. She moved away from him and folded her legs between them on the couch. She did not know how to ask the questions on her mind, but she could not live another miserable night without knowing more about this man she had fallen in love with.

"Come here," he said, and pushed her legs to the floor. "I want to kiss you again."

He kissed her again and she gave in to his wishes. Before she lost her senses, she said, "You make me crazy; I don't want to get carried away."

"You make me crazy, too," he said. "You do something to me that no other woman has ever done; you carry me to a place made in heaven." He pulled her closer and she almost gave in to him completely.

She pushed him away again and he said, "What is wrong, Baby?"

"I might ask you the same question," she said. "Are you involved with another woman back in Porterville?"

Scott picked up his beer, took a big swallow, twisted the can with both hands and stared at the floor.

His action and silence tore Olivia's heart out. She wanted to scream at him; she wanted to slap him.

He turned to her and his eyes begged for understanding as he spoke, "I did not mean to fall in love with you. I have thought about you for more than two years. I thought I would go crazy if I never saw you again."

"You did not answer my question. Who is the lucky woman?" she said and tears pressed her eyes.

He reached for her, pulled her close, and kissed her with a passion that made her want him; but she jerked away from him and demanded that he tell her about the other woman in his life.

"Olivia, I cannot do anything about my predicament."

Olivia shouted, "What on earth do you mean? Is the woman pregnant? Have you promised marriage? "

"I am married, Olivia."

Olivia felt as if her heart would literally fall out of her chest. She jumped up from the couch and tears rolled down her cheeks as she screamed at him, "Get out!" She started to the door and he ran after her.

"Wait, please let me explain," he said.

"There is nothing to explain!" she shouted. "Why didn't you tell me you had a wife? Have you lost your mind?"

"I did not tell you, because I fell in love with you the first time I saw you. I could not get you off my mind. I fought with my temptation to come back to see you the next day. I tried to forget you. I made trips out of town to forget you. The more I tried to forget you, the more I wanted to see you again. God knows, I have never loved anyone as much as I love you. Each time I drove on the interstate near Boulder Bluff, the temptation to pay you a surprise visit made me crazy. I forced myself to keep driving toward home. I prayed for God to help me forget you; I spent sleepless nights thinking about you. When I ran into you at the Southern Grill, I cannot explain the good feeling I had to see you again. I needed to see you; I needed to hold you and tell you how I felt about you. I wanted to tell you about Laura; but fear of losing you made me so scared that I decided to take my chances and keep you as long as I could before telling you about Laura."

"I cannot see you again. I am a decent woman with good morals; I also have pride. You have treated me as you would treat a prostitute or cheap whore who cares not about the men she goes to bed with. Get out of my sight and do not come near me ever again!"

Olivia got up and Scott stood next to her. "Baby, please forgive me for not telling you about my wife. I did not mean to hurt you; but you have not let me explain the story behind my silence."

Olivia shouted, "There is nothing to explain; and there is no excuse for your silence. You are a married man! I would never willingly have an affair with a married man. You used me; your fling with me is over!"

"My wife had an accident that injured her brain and paralyzed her. She has been unable to speak or move for the past three years. She does not recognize me, her family members, or anyone else. She seems healthy otherwise, but she must have constant care for all of her basic needs. The nurses at Hillcrest Manor have taken good care of her, but she does not improve. I sat by her side every day for months. I only left her bedside to get something to eat, take a bath, and check on my business. When the doctor told me that she would never recover, I went back to work. I still visit her every day, but the doctors have given me no hopes for her to get any better. "

Olivia could feel his pain. She dried her tears and looked at him with compassion as she spoke, "I am terribly sorry about your wife. I can only imagine the misery and pain you live with; but you still have a wife. I must not see you again."

He put his hand on her shoulder and said, "Please say you will see me again. I love and need you. Can you at least be my friend?"

"I cannot be your friend; I am in love with you. Our friendly chats would quickly lead to sexual desire," she said.

"I can understand why you don't want to see me again. I should have told you, but my selfish need for you made me lose my good sense. I would not hurt you for anything in the world. I wanted to make you happy, as happy as you made me."

"You have already hurt me; you have hurt me more than you will ever know," she said. "I ache all over."

"We need to talk about this some more," he said. "I will go now, but I want you to think about my situation. I fell in love with you. I am so sorry that I hurt you, but I hurt knowing that I can never see you again. I need to talk to you every day. I will call you tomorrow."

"Scott I have nothing more to say to you. I want you to go."

He got up and walked behind her to the door. Before going out, he said, "I will always love you. Please try to find it in your heart to forgive me."

She did not answer his plea; she quickly closed the door, ran to her bedroom, fell across the bed and screamed. She felt numb all over; she felt completely insane. How did she get herself into this big mess? Why had this happened to her? How could she deal with the terrible hurt? Scott Porter treated her special and she thought he loved her. She believed that she had finally met the perfect man, a handsome prince, a decent man, and the man of her dreams. She thought they had a future together. Why had she fallen in love with the wrong man again? She had jumped out of the frying pan and fell head first into the fire. How could she pull herself out of the flames?

Olivia finally sat up in bed, wiped tears on the sleeve of her pajamas, and took a good breath. Stupid fools never change. She should have listened to her mother.

The hands on the clock said two AM in the morning. She drug out of bed and took a shower, but she felt no better.

She finally drifted off to sleep. Her wonderful dream about Scott Porter ended like all other sweet dreams. She buried her face in her pillow and cried some more.

At the same time, Scott lay in bed, smoked, and thought about Olivia. She made him feel like a man; he wanted to touch her; he wanted to hold her in his arms; he wanted to make love to her. He could not stay away from her. He wanted to go to her this minute. He wanted her so much that he could feel her bare warmth next to him. His lustful feelings made him believe that he could satisfy her and sweep her off her feet. Instead, he had made her unhappy and miserable. He hated himself for hurting her. He wanted to marry her, but he could not ask her to marry him right away. She refused to see him again, but he would never stop trying to get her back. He would call her every day, buy her nice gifts, and send her flowers.

CHAPTER FOURTEEN

Shocking Christmas Gift

ON MONDAY MORNING, Olivia awoke with the blaring alarm at six fifteen. She fumbled for the sound and turned over for another wink. She felt drained; she wanted to call in sick, but she had no lesson plans prepared for a substitute. She dragged out of bed and went to get a quick shower. After she got dressed, she went to the kitchen for a cup of coffee before rushing out to beat the morning traffic.

The December chill hit her in the face as she walked out into the garage. She hated cold weather. During the winter months, she wanted to hibernate. Her break-up with Scott had made facing winter even worse.

Her students noticed that something bothered her and asked questions. After she gave them their reading assignment, she sat down. One child came up to her desk and placed her hand on Olivia's as she spoke in a soft voice. She wanted to know who made her cry. Olivia thought she had covered her swollen eyes with make-up. She forced a smile and complained of a headache. She could not tell her student the truth; she had fallen in love with a married man who tore out her heart.

That evening when Olivia got home from school, Scott called. She expected his call; she told him she did not feel like talking, and she never wanted to see him again.

After she hung up, fantasies about him drove her crazy. She told herself that he loved her; but his poor helpless wife needed him. Fools in love believed anything that suited their fancy; she must never speak to Scott Porter again.

She went to the kitchen, pulled down a bottle of wine from the cabinet, poured a tall glass full and drank it down in minutes. Then she went to the living room, lay down on the couch and fell asleep. The loud ringing of her home phone awoke her. She sat up and picked up the phone from the end table. Tom's voice surprised her; what he said shocked her.

"Olivia, that man you are dating is married."

"Well, well, if isn't Tom Bradford."

"Well is a mighty deep subject; two wells in one sentence are two mighty deep subjects," Tom said. "I am not joking around. Scott Porter is married."

"Seems that you and Scott Porter have a lot in common," Olivia said.

"What do you mean by that smart remark?" Tom said.

"Tom, you know what I mean. Scott Porter is running around on his wife. Don't you remember when you screwed around with Stella Shivers?"

"Don't throw that bull shit up to me. I didn't give a damn about Stella; and Scott Porter doesn't give a damn about you. I called you, because I care about you and I don't want you to get hurt again."

"Tom, you have no business checking up on me. Before we married, you got drunk, stood me up, and treated me like a cow patty that spoiled your shoes; you threw me in the corner of the porch. After we got married, you still treated me like dirt. You made me feel like the rug under your feet; You went out of town every weekend, ran around with sorry women, and did as you damn well pleased, while I sat at home and waited with open arms for you to come back. Don't preach to me about anything that I do; I am no longer your concern."

"Olivia, I told you I was sorry for the way I treated you. I see my mistakes now, and I still care about you. Scott Porter is a millionaire; he thinks he can have what he wants and whoever he wants by snapping his fingers."

"Scott Porter is a good substitute for Tom Bradford. You also have money and think you can buy and own people. You can't own me anymore. Good bye, Tom." Olivia hung up on Tom.

Minutes later, the phone rang again. Olivia said, "Tom, I don't want to talk about Scott Porter. How do you know so much about him, anyhow?"

"I have my sources," he said.

"I sure need to know the names of your sources; maybe they could bring me up to date on your latest fling."

"I don't have flings anymore, and I don't want you to have a fling. What are you going to do about the crazy bastard?"

"I guess I will settle for second place. Do you remember Stella Shivers? She is dead now and I am sorry about that; but that does not excuse what she did. She loved you and waited for her chance to spend every weekend with you, and you were married to me."

"Your affair with Scott Porter is forbidden and breaks the laws of man and God. Those are your own words, Olivia. You accused me of being a thrill seeker and preached to me about adultery and the forbidden. Now you are doing the same thing," Tom said.

"If I changed for the worst, you changed me," Olivia said. "Besides, Scott's situation with his marriage is totally different from our marriage. You had me, a perfectly normal and healthy wife."

"Tell Scott Porter to go to hell," Tom Said. "He is treating you with disrespect and I don't like him."

"You are a fine one to talk about respect for a woman. You need to take a leap for hell with Scott Porter," Olivia said and slammed the phone down.

Tom did not call back; neither did Scott call. Olivia felt more alone and depressed than she had ever been in her life. She felt the need to hear the sound of a voice; she felt the need for love and understanding. She wished she could talk to her mother; but her mother made her want to scream. She could not take her mother's criticism and smart remarks. She answered her mother's questions, but she never volunteered personal information.

After she went to bed, she wanted to call Scott; but she resisted the temptation and watched movies until she fell asleep.

The next morning, the doorbell awoke her. She threw on her house coat and ran to see who had called at seven in the morning. She peeped to see a young boy. He held an arrangement of yellow roses. When she faced the boy, he politely said,

"Good morning, Miss," and he pushed an expensive vase with a dozen yellow roses toward her. She thanked him and closed the door quickly.

In the kitchen, she set the roses on the table and tore into the small card.

"Olivia, I love you more than words on paper say. I pray that you find it in your heart to forgive me for being so selfish. As I told you before, I did not mean for you to get hurt, but I could not stay away from you. After we spent the weekend together, I fell deeper in love with you. I want to marry you and spend the rest of my life with you, but I cannot make that commitment to you today. I wish you would agree to talk to me so I could explain things. At least, answer my calls and talk to me on the phone. I love you so much. Scott."

Olivia cried as she walked to the living room with the vase of roses. The card touched a soft spot in her heart and meant more to her than the roses.

On Sunday, her mother called and asked her to come have dinner with them. She had not called that week, and she had been worried about her.

Olivia made excuses; she had been busy with school work; but she promised her mother that she would come and have lunch with them.

When she walked into her parent's door, her mother bugged her about going to church.

Olivia complained that she felt like an outsider in a crowd, especially since she divorced Tom. Most of her friends in Boulder Bluff had married and had children; she had nothing in common with them anymore.

Her mother had a delicious dinner, fried chicken, corn, potatoes, corn bread, and apple pie for dessert. Olivia tried to appear happy, but she could not wait to get back home. She stayed to help her mother clear the table and wash the dishes. Then she made excuses to go back home.

Back at home, she walked to the window and looked out at the world. Winter had stripped leaves from the trees and white velvet clung to their naked branches. Silver frost covered the once green lawn; she shivered with the thoughts of winter that brought cold winds, snow, and ice. Last winter had been the worst and longest winter she had ever known; this winter would be even worse.

She dreaded Christmas; she had no desire to have Christmas alone; she had no desire to decorate the house, especially not the outside; she had no desire to visit her parents and exchange gifts. She needed comforting arms around her; she needed a few kind words; and she needed someone who needed her. What would she do at Christmas?

When she lived with Tom, he hired a man to put up Christmas decorations outside; and he made their house the showplace of the season. Olivia decorated the inside; and Tom always helped her decorate the tree. At Christmas time each year, he never failed to tell her that he wanted her to get pregnant. She soon realized that her inability to have children made Tom get interested in other women.

She took a bath, got dressed, and went to the mall to shop for a Christmas tree and a wreath for the front door. She had no intentions of stringing lights and putting elaborate decorations outside.

Before going to bed on Sunday night, she had finished decorating the tree and had a beautiful wreath on the front door with a flood light that made it visible.

On Monday at school, the secretary called her to the office. Tom had sent her yellow roses. Olivia looked at the roses with shock. Why had Tom sent the same color roses in an almost identical vase to the ones that Scott sent? Tom had his sources; she believed his sources kept tabs on her.

Mrs. Walden, the school secretary got up, put her hand on Olivia's shoulder, and said, "Olivia, are you alright?"

"I am fine," Olivia said.

"Those are the most beautiful roses I think I have ever seen. I wish I had a man who loved me enough to send me roses. I do good to get daisies or tulips on my birthday. Sometimes I get them again on Valentine's Day."

They both had a good laugh and Olivia carried the roses to her room to read the card. "Dear Olivia, these roses cannot make up for the hurt I caused you; but I sent them to let you know that I still love you and I want you back in my life. I did not realize what I lost until you left me with a void in my life that I can never fill until I get you back. You are a beautiful and wonderful person, and I was a fool. I will never give up on us."

Love, Tom"

That weekend, Olivia visited her parents again. Her mother questioned her about her depressed state of mind; but Olivia lied and told her she felt fine.

Olivia's father seemed more understanding, but she could not talk to him about Scott. He would flip out if he knew she had gotten involved with a married man. He would threaten to kill Scott; in fact, he might do more than threaten him.

When Olivia got back home, she went to bed. She thought about what she should do. She definitely needed to go to a psychiatrist. She could see herself on his couch; she could hear the questions he asked; she could see his expression as he tried to analyze her answers.

She turned over and tried to think positive; she must be strong and work things out on her own. She could not go to a psychiatrist; she would lose her job. She had to work to pay her bills and keep living.

On Monday after school, Olivia could hear her house phone ringing before she got the door open.

"How are you doing?" Scott said.

"How do you think I am doing? I think I am losing my stupid mind."

"Please say you will see me. I will not touch you. I have to talk to you. Go with me back to Brunswick next weekend. We can go out to eat and talk. Who will know where we go and what we do?"

"I will know where we go and what we do, and I could not live with my guilt," she said. "I will not sneak to see you; I will not settle for an affair with a married man. I think I deserve better."

"Olivia, I love you, and you love me. We need each other. What we do is none of anybody's business. Please talk to me. I cannot let you go," he said.

"I will talk to you on the phone; but I cannot talk to you in person."

"Can I call you every day?"

The long silence let him know that she had no answer. "Good night, baby; I will call you tomorrow."

After she hung up the phone, she called Emily and told her the shocking news about Scott.

Emily advised her to stay away from Scott Porter and never speak to him again on the phone or in person.

Then Olivia made excuses for Scott's actions by explaining his wife's accident that left her paralyzed.

Emily believed that Scott would divorce his wife if he really loved Olivia; and he should not let his wife's condition hold him back.

In spite of Olivia's determination to forget Scott, wishful dreams disturbed her sleep. He stood in the doorway and asked why she fought her feelings for him. He told her that he had the same feelings and nothing would make them go away. He begged her to let him make love to her. Her heart beat faster and faster as he walked toward her. He took her in his arms, held her tightly, and told her how much he wanted to make love to her. Unable to resist him, she fell against his shoulder; he cupped her face gently and kissed her. She felt weak, wild, and wonderful. She gave herself to him; and she felt wonderful. When she awoke, she felt ashamed and hated herself for her dream about him.

At the same time, Scott thought about Olivia. When he went to bed at night, he stared through the darkness with thoughts of her. He liked her looks; he liked her figure; he liked her common sense; he loved her. He could go out with a whore and satisfy his sexual craving; but he wanted the woman he loved. She was refined, educated, and beautiful. He liked her long legs and slender figure; he liked her soft, smooth skin; he liked her auburn hair that shined with golden glints; he liked her green, observant eyes. In fact, he liked everything about Olivia; she fascinated him. Best of all, she had a good personality and they always had interesting conversations. He had a taste of her love and he wanted her for keeps. How could he keep two women? If money could buy her, he would offer her a million.

Scott stayed busy with his work during the day. After work, he still visited Laura and watched her lay there with that fixed stare.

On Sunday, Scott missed Sunday service. He hated sermons about sin. He felt guilty about his sins and did not want to listen to a sermon about sin. In his younger days, he liked church. He remembered his mother's devotion to the church. She held his hand as they walked to her favorite bench on the second row. He also remembered the mean eye his father gave him when he misbehaved in church.

After he and Laura married, they attended church every Sunday. Then her accident changed him; he dreaded going to church. Why should he keep going to church when he could not live up the teachings of the Bible? On the other hand the hypocrites in the church did not live up to the teachings of the bible either. Hypocrites outnumbered the true Christians; and he wanted to point a finger in their painted faces; he wanted to shout their sins to the congregation. The hypocrites amazed him; he called them the great pretenders. He could see Mrs. Etheridge sitting on the front pew. She claimed to be a born again Christian. She sang her heart out for the glory of God and acted like a saint at church. When she got home, she found it difficult to practice what she preached. She had earned an honest reputation for being the town gossip. She stayed on the phone and spread rumors about everybody who had attended church that Sunday.

Barker Waltham and his wife, Lilian, sat on the second bench from the front and praised the Lord; but they had never lived by the Ten Commandments. Mr. Waltham stole every penny he could get his dirty hands on, and his wife covered his dirt by telling lies on others. She wore the scarlet letter under her coat. What brass they had on their faces!

Then there were the Godly men. They had their little wives sitting right next to them, while each of them suffered for a woman who knew how to love them and make them feel needed. He knew how they felt; he needed Olivia's love to cure his suffering. He really did not care what folk in that church thought about him anymore. He loved Olivia and would do what he had to do to get her back into his life.

While Olivia still wanted to see Scott, she tried to keep her mind busy with the students. They got excited about Christmas holidays. They each took turns and

told what they wanted for Christmas and what they would do during the holidays. One child remained seated at his desk and held his head down with embarrassment as he told the class that his daddy had lost his job. He could not afford to buy Christmas presents for him and his other eight children. His mama promised to cook them a chocolate cake and a good dinner on Christmas day.

That evening after school, Olivia went shopping for the boy's family. She carried a box filled with canned goods to the family; and she had never seen a more grateful family.

When school turned out on Friday for Christmas holidays, Olivia went home and went to bed. She did not want to think about Scott Porter.

On Christmas Eve, Olivia got a small package in the mail. She rushed into the house and checked the package return address before opening it. What had Scott Porter sent her? She opened the package, dug through the shredded paper and found a blue velvet box. A card dangled from the side that was tied with a red ribbon around the box. She opened the box and gasped with shock at the large diamond. She put it on her left finger and it fit perfectly. Then she opened the envelope and read Scott's letter inside the Christmas card. "My darling, Olivia, I hope you will wear this engagement ring until I give you the band to go with it. I do want to marry you, and I will marry you one day soon if you will still have me. I love you with all of my heart and I miss you more than you will ever know. I hope you have a good Christmas, and I hope you will let me come for a visit during the holidays. I love you, Scott."

Had Scott Porter lost his mind? A married man had given her an expensive diamond ring. Even if she kept the ring, she could not wear it out in public. She could see her friends' reaction to the diamond; she could hear the questions they would ask about the wedding that would never take place. She pulled the diamond ring off, placed it back in the velvet box, and closed the drawer with anger. She intended to give the generous gift back to Scott Porter. Did he think he could buy her love?

Back in the kitchen, she sat at the table and drank coffee. The diamond ring did not leave her thoughts. Why had Scott sent an expensive diamond ring in the mail? She wondered if he had insured the ring.

Then her mind drifted back in time. Tom had also given her an expensive ring. After she divorced him, she offered to give the ring back to him, but he refused to take it; he wanted her to keep all the gifts he had given her as a reminder of his love for her. Olivia wanted to slap him, but she said nothing. Then after their divorce, she had gone back to his house to move her furniture and Tom had taken her piano, the piano he had given her on their wedding day. She did not trust him; she did not believe a thing he told her.

Since Tom had done her dirty, she sold his wedding rings and used the money to buy a new bedroom suite. Now she had gotten an even more expensive ring from Scott Porter; but she had no intentions of keeping it.

She walked back to her bedroom, got the velvet case from the chest drawer, and slowly opened it to look at the ring again. Then she placed the ring back in the velvet box and put it back in the chest drawer.

On Christmas day the sound of the doorbell seemed like a distant drum. She looked at the clock and wondered who came visiting at six thirty in the morning. She drug out of bed, put on her housecoat, and ran a hand over her tumbled hair as she walked to the door. She looked through the door peeper and there stood Scott. He held a beautiful potted purple orchid with yellow tips. Her heart beat in her toes. She slowly opened the door, and drew her arms around her waist.

"Merry Christmas," he said. "May I come inside? This cold wind is rough."

She invited him to come inside, the biggest mistake she had made since they met the first time.

He kissed her on the cheek and pushed the orchid toward her. She took it, bragged about its beauty, and mentioned that no one had ever given her an orchid. She added that orchids must be a rich man's choice of flowers.

He wanted her to have the prettiest and the best, regardless of the cost.

In the kitchen, she placed the orchid in the window and complained about her potted plants dying; she did not have a green thumb and had little luck with plants.

"You have a magic touch with me," he said and smiled.

She ignored his remark and poured him a cup of coffee before sitting down at the table across from him. He bragged that he had the most beautiful woman in the world sitting across the table from him.

She avoided his eyes that looked at her with a need that she understood.

"I received a surprise gift from you yesterday in the mail. When I opened that little velvet box, the beautiful diamond took my breath away. I stood there and stared at the ring with shock. I cannot accept such an expensive gift from you; and I want you to take it back."

He got up, walked around the table and stood behind her. She felt his warm hands on her neck as he lifted her hair. Then he kissed her on her neck. The touch of his lips on her skin set her on fire; she twisted in her chair and asked him to sit back down. He sat back down and questioned her about how she had been and what she had been doing on the weekends. She admitted that she had been miserable; but she tried to make the best of a bad situation. She finally suggested that they sit in the living room. Before they made it to the couch, he swung her around to face him and kissed her. She felt wonderful; numb from her head to her toes; and she wanted him, but she needed to get far away from him. Like a fool, she stood there and he kissed her again; then he kissed her again. Her better judgment told her to run; but she froze. She needed him; she wanted him to hold her and make her hurt go away. She finally came to her senses, grabbed her composure, and pushed him away. Then she asked him to sit down. She wished to hell that she had never laid eyes on the bastard.

He sat on the couch with thoughts of her sitting next to him, but she took an armchair across the room and remained silent. He did not blame her for turning away from him; but he knew that she loved him just as much as he loved her. He finally broke the silence; he asked if she wanted him to leave.

She said nothing; but she did not want him to leave. He had confused her and made it impossible for her to make the right decision. She loved him so much that she hurt all over; she loved the ground he walked on.

Once again he talked about his wife, Laura, and went into details about her accident. Although he had nothing to do with his wife's accident and her condition, he still felt responsible for her. If Laura could only recover, do things on her own again, and live a normal life without his help, he would divorce her and marry Olivia in the blink of an eye.

As Olivia listened to his unfortunate situation and watched his expression, the sadness in his face made her more understanding; she felt his heart break and suffering; but she felt her heart break and suffering even more. She hurt all over. She wanted him, but she wanted all of him. She must do the right thing and stop this nonsense. She thought about the diamond and rushed to her bedroom to get it. She pulled the chest drawer open and had the little blue velvet box in her hand when she felt his warm breath on her neck.

He took the velvet box, set it on the chest, and whispered in her ear, "Baby, I just want to hold you in my arms. I will leave if you really want me to go."

She screamed inside; she wondered how she could live without ever seeing him again. Then she thought about his situation. She admired him for his concern and care for his wife; but he no longer loved Laura. Like all other men, he got over his wife after she got sick and helpless.

She stepped away from him and handed him the blue velvet box. Then she asked him to leave.

He took the velvet box, placed it on the chest and pulled her close as he whispered how much he loved and needed her. Then he found her lips and her strength left her; she melted to his embrace. He kissed her gently and pushed her down on the bed. She had dreamed of this moment, his kiss, his touch, his lovemaking, but the real Scott felt more wonderful than he felt in her dreams. She responded with a need for him that gave him the best feeling he had had since the last time he made love to her.

After he made love to her, she snuggled close to him and said, "I do not have a Christmas present for you."

"You are the best Christmas present I could ask for," he said.

She did not bring up the subject of his wife or his friends. She lay in his arms and his sweet words and caresses surrounded her with a cloud of love. She felt more relaxed than she had felt since the last time she lay in his arms.

Before they fell asleep, he said, "I love you, Olivia. I cannot stop loving you. I would do anything you asked me to do. I would come to you any time of the day or night that you need me. If you run me off a thousand times, I will come back to you."

Olivia did not fall asleep right away. She lay close by his warm body and thought about the stolen moments with days and weeks between that she would not see him at all.

The next morning, Olivia awoke before Scott and eased out of the room to let him sleep. She went to the kitchen and hummed a song as she made coffee and cooked breakfast. Scott took away her depression and made her feel wonderful. She wondered if his friends knew about her. His friend, Joseph, had probably spread the news about their affair to all of Scott's friends. She thanked God that Scott lived in Porterville. She prayed that her friends had never heard of him. She must keep her affair with Scott a secret from her parents, also. They would disown her and tell the preacher everything about her personal life. Their harsh actions would force her to move to another city or state far away from home.

When Scott came to eat breakfast, they talked about plans for the day. Olivia always went to see her parents on Christmas day to exchange gifts. She did not want them to come calling with questions about Scott's being there.

Scott needed to deliver gifts to his friends, but he asked Olivia if he could come back that evening to go out for dinner. He suggested they spend the weekend at his place in Brunswick. She smiled and told him this might turn out to be the best Christmas ever.

That evening, Olivia returned home and packed her bags to go with Scott to Brunswick. They stayed at his place until New Year's Day. He spent the night at her house on Monday and she returned to school on Tuesday.

From that time forward, Scott called her every day and spent every weekend with her. She felt happier and more content than she had felt those miserable months she spent without him.

CHAPTER FIFTEEN

Pregnant and Single

THE COOL BREEZES of spring brought hungry animals from their dens and filled the air with the sweetness of flowers and green plants that soon covered fields and gardens. Olivia felt happy in the spring, especially since Scott Porter came back into her life.

On the way to school, Olivia rolled down her window to take a breath of fresh spring air. She had never seen anything more beautiful than the blooms of spring. The flowering plants on the green lawns before the homes on Windham Street took her breath. Her parents lived in a neat house but not as elaborate as many of the homes with their decorative columns and expensive windows and doors.

She watched the weeks turn to another month, but she felt content now that Scott came back into her life.

Then that stone wall appeared again and blocked her path to happiness. She wrung her hands with worry. She had missed two periods and felt as if she would go insane. She needed to talk to someone. She could not tell Scott; he had a helpless wife who needed him.

If she told her parents, her mother would shame her and blame her; and her father would go into a mad rage with threats to kill Scott.

She could not talk to her best friend. Emily would advise her to keep the baby and put it up for adoption; she did not believe in abortion.

Olivia had to keep her pregnancy a secret. She cried and cradled her stomach with love for her baby. She wanted to keep the baby, but she did not want to be a single mother; she could not take care of it and give it a good life. She wanted her baby to have a father. If her baby had no father, people would ruin its life by pointing fingers and poking fun at it. On the other hand, she did not want Scott to feel obligated to marry her. She wanted him to marry her simply because he loved her and wanted to spend the rest of his life with her. She had too much pride to come right out and ask him to marry her.

Everybody in Boulder Bluff would soon know about the bastard child she carried for a married man. They would look down on her and shame her; they would mark her as a whore, slut, and trash. She would carry their scars the rest of her life. She must have an abortion; she had no other choice. She would take a few days off from school, plan a trip to the beach in Savannah, and no one would ever know her secret.

On Friday evening, Scott got there at the usual time. She pushed her heart out of her stomach before facing him. Her eyes met his and the drawing power of love made her heart flip with rapid thuds. She wanted him as much as ever. She wanted him to take her into his arms, hold, and comfort her.

"Hello, beautiful."

His eyes adored her, but she did not want him to come near her. She did not trust him.

"I do not feel very beautiful," she said as she walked ahead of him toward the kitchen. She went to the sink and wet a dishcloth to wipe the table. He walked up behind her, moved his hands down her hips, kissed her neck, and whispered words of love around her ear. The warmth of his breath made her head spin and gave her a sweeping chill. She side stepped to the table. He grabbed the wet cloth, sailed it across the room, and embraced her with a kiss that made her lose her senses. Then, he ran his fingertip down her nose and around her lips. "I've missed you this week. I could not wait to see you. Let us forget about dinner. I want to make love to you."

Sparks of excitement flickered in her eyes and her heart thumped in her stomach as that fiery feeling of love overcame her anger and made her forget all things, except Scott.

With a breath of happiness, he held to her as if he would never let go. "You feel so good. Damn! You're Purdy!" He twined her hair around his finger, let go and kissed her between whispers, "I want you, baby. I love you. I've loved you since the moment our eyes met."

His lips smothered her reply. A good feeling rippled through her. She wanted him to make love to her quickly.

He took her hand and she followed him to the bedroom. Just inside the bedroom door, she pulled off her clothes, and he pulled her to him. He kissed her as he guided her to the bed. She clung to him and repeated, "I love you."

Her beauty and the warmth of her body next to him made him crazy. She screamed his name before the same good feeling consumed him. She snuggled close by his side, closed her eyes, and thought about the high price she must pay for only a few minutes of pleasure; she must destroy the innocent baby growing inside of her womb.

He sensed her worry and nuzzled the tip of his nose to hers. "A problem of yours is a problem of mine," he said. "When I get worried, I work to forget my problem. You could go to the gym and hit a punching bag; you could run around the block; you could beat the hell out of me."

She made no reply, and he said, "Are you one of those rare birds who flap heavy wings of burden and never let go of problems?"

She still made no reply and he shouted, "Please tell me what is wrong with you. If you tell me what is bothering you, I will solve your problem!"

"If is a small word; yet, it has much strength," she said. "If I had not gotten involved with you in the first place, I would have no problems. You are a married man and you will never be free to marry me."

"I stay with you as much as I can, and I do everything I can to make you happy. You seem happy most of the time. What happened to put you in this bad mood?" he said.

She turned to him with a blank stare, fell against his chest, and said, "Are you ready to make me your wife?"

"I wish we could get married tomorrow," he said.

"I am pregnant!" she said in a whisper as if others listened to her shameful secret.

His heart beat in the top of his head and his brains splashed his skull. His did not know what to say. If he said anything at all, he would say the wrong thing. He wanted children; he had prayed many times for his wife, Laura, to get pregnant. The thought of Olivia carrying his child filled him with pride and happiness; yet, he felt terrified. He could not make a commitment to marry Olivia right now. If he divorced Laura in her condition, the whole town, her family, and all of his friends would turn against him. "I need some time to think about what we must do about the baby," he said.

"You never intended to marry me!" she shouted and jerked away from him. "I was a fool to look at you a second time! Get out of my house and leave me alone! I never want to see you again."

"I love you too much to leave you."

"What do you know about love? You know nothing about me."

Tears filled her eyes and they sparkled. He had never seen her more beautiful, and the urge to grab her, hold her in his arm, comfort her, and kiss her overwhelmed him. He reached for her hand and she jerked away from him. "Don't touch me." She rushed from the room and he ran after her. "Baby, listen to me. I need some time to make plans for us."

She laughed with mockery and screamed, "You have run out of time with me. When I discovered that you had a wife, I should have cut off my relationship with you forever. You do not love me! I am pregnant and you put your wife's feelings ahead of mine. You have said that your wife is helpless and does not recognize you. I have decided that I do not know you, either. Your wife has nurses to care for her. I need you more than your wife needs you; but I will find a way to survive without you. Go and leave me alone. I never want to see you again."

His heart jumped and his pulse quickened "I do love you; I love you and nobody else."

"Words are cheap. If you really loved me; you would marry me and give our baby a name; you would give your child a father. You cut out my heart with your words and I feel nothing for you. I cannot brush away hurt as if lent upon my figure. Let me drown in my tears alone."

"Our baby will carry my name," he said. "I promise that I will marry you."

"Your lies have soaked in here!" she said and hit her chest.

"Listen to me. I am happy that you carry my child. I want our baby as much as I want you. I want to be a good father, but I need some time to think about what I must do. I want to go about the divorce from Laura in the right way."

Olivia had believed his lies many times before, but she saw clearly now. Scott would never divorce his wife. "Scott, I will tell my child that his father went away to war and never returned. I do not want others to poke fun at my child and call him a bastard. I want my child to have a super life and a good self-image. I never want to see you again! Get out of my house; don't come near me ever again!"

"Your words make me hurt all over. I want to be a part of my child's life," he said.

"Your words have cut me down since the day I discovered you had a wife. I am tired of your promises. Do you think your wishes are all that matter? You cannot have a wife and me at the same time. People will mark me as a kept woman, your whore."

"I cannot leave you like this," he said and pleaded with her to let him spend the night. "I love you, Olivia."

She slapped at him with both hands and mocked him, "I love you is such a romantic lie. Get away from me! Let me drown in my sorrow."

He watched her cry and he wanted to hold her in his arms and make the hurt disappear. "My life would be nothing without you. I love you more than anything," he said and reached for her hand again.

She jerked her hand back and shouted, "Get out of my house!"

He stopped and looked at her for a long time, but she would not look at him. She walked to the window and stared at the darkness. He slowly turned away from her and walked to the door. He looked back at her with sadness before closing the door behind him.

She watched his tail lights disappear in the night as she had done many times before. She would never see Scott Porter again. She wanted Scott to stay with her, but she still had pride. She had been in love with two different men, and they both used her. She knew about heartbreak and disappointment; her dreams never came true. She remembered the day Tom left; she remembered the day he came back; and she remembered the day he left again. Why had she been such a fool? How could she be so stupid? She let sorry men control her heart, mind, and soul. She had only stolen time with Scott. She had been a fool; she must forget Scott Porter. Would she ever regain her sanity?

Scott did not remember the drive back home. Restless with worry, he went to the refrigerator and got a beer. What would he do without Olivia? If he did not have Olivia in his life, he would be nothing; he would live a miserable life. Porter Manufacturing Company, his fine home, and all of his money meant nothing without Olivia. She meant more to him than material possessions. On the other hand, he had to work and make money to support two families. He had a child on the way and he did not want Olivia to work outside of the home.

At the same time, Olivia paced the floor and cried. She did not believe in abortion, and she would feel guilty, but she had no other choice. Her parents would never agree for her to have an abortion, but they would not agree for her to put the baby up for adoption, either. If she waited another week, the doctors would refuse to abort her baby.

Scott's need to be near Olivia drove him crazy. He walked around in circles and held his pounding head. He could still see her crying; he could still hear the anger in her voice. He must go back to her, persuade her to talk to him. He picked up the phone and called her.

When Olivia answered the phone, he did not say anything right away. He just listened to her voice. Finally, he said, "Olivia, I love you."

"You are a liar!" she shouted and slammed the phone down. She lay back on her pillow and thought about how much she hated him. How could she hate and love him at the same time? She wanted to call him back, tell him to come this minute. She would lose him forever if she let her foolish pride stand in the way. Like a desperate fool, she picked up the phone; she quickly put the phone down. She lay back, closed her eyes, and prayed for him to call back.

In the middle of the night, a loud knock on the door made Olivia sit upright on the couch. She got up, rushed to the door. When she saw Scott, she quickly locked the screen. "You are not welcome here! I have nothing to say to you," she said.

"I don't like this screen between us," he said. "Could I please come inside?"

"You have a wife, and you have made your choice," she said and turned to walk away.

"I only have the responsibilities for a wife," he said. My wife is helpless; she does not know me; she cannot speak nor move on her own. I have stayed married to her, because I made vows to keep her until my death."

"Regardless of your excuses, you are married."

"Olivia, I would do anything for you; you are my reason for living."

"You are a liar," she said, crossing her arms. "Go away and leave me alone!" Once again, she watched him drive away. She had once been sure of his love and believed his lies; she would never believe him again.

CHAPTER SIXTEEN

Attempted Abortion

························

THE NEXT MORNING Olivia called Emily. She explained that she planned to have an abortion in Savannah to keep the secret from spreading around Boulder Bluff and back to her parents.

Emily advised her to talk to Scott about her plans to have an abortion. He had a right to know.

Olivia's loud reply surprised Emily. Why should she get permission from Scott Porter to have an abortion? He had not asked her to marry him. Besides, he should have told her about his wife. If she had known about his wife, she would not have gotten involved with him.

Emily agreed that Scott should have told her about his wife before she went out with him; but he did not want to lose her and he did not want to divorce his helpless wife. He felt sorry for his wife and he also felt responsible for her needs.

"Scott Porter can go to hell," Olivia said. This is my body and his mistake. I will do as I please."

Emily reminded Olivia that she had been suspicious about Scott's secret past. She had advised her not to go out with him again; but she had not taken her advice. Regardless of what had happened, Scott still had lawful rights as the baby's father to know about the abortion and give his consent.

Olivia screamed at Emily, "I am not telling Scott anything!" and she hung up.

Two days later, Olivia had an appointment at the abortion clinic in Savannah. As she drove toward Savannah, she placed a gentle hand on her stomach to calm the life that made her stomach quiver. Voices in her head urged her to go back home and forget about the abortion; but she had no other choice.

In the meantime, Scott drove toward Savannah and worried about Olivia. Emily had called and told him the shocking news. If Olivia had an abortion, he would blame himself. He wanted her to have his baby. He had to find her, tell her he loved her, and tell her he wanted to marry her. He could do nothing for Laura; but he could not do without Olivia. His love for Olivia and this baby meant more to him than the slanderous lies Laura's family and friends would spread after he divorced Laura.

At the same time, Olivia found a parking place less than a block from the clinic. She grabbed her overnight case, and walked down First Avenue.

At the clinic, the receptionist gave Olivia a dozen papers to fill out. Afterwards, the receptionist directed her to report to the out-patient desk. They assigned her to a room, where they prepared her for the procedure. Then they left.

An hour later, a nurse came in and gave Olivia a shot that numbed her senses. She could feel the movement as attendants wheeled her into the operating room. The bright lights blurred her vision, and human forms dressed in white uniforms crowded around her. Monitors ticked in her ears like a thousand clocks.

Then she heard loud voices and a commotion around her that puzzled her. She raised her head to see a tall man; he wore a gray felt hat like the hat Scott wore. He pushed the nurses aside and Olivia saw Scott's face. The nurses ran behind him and pulled on the tail of his suit.

Scott gave the nurses a hard shove, ran to Olivia and shouted, "The worst thing about dying is to have never been given a chance to live. Have you thought about giving our baby a chance to live?"

The doctor turned to his attendants and shouted, "Call security! Tell them to get this idiot out of my operating room."

Scott yelled at the doctor. "You cannot perform this abortion without my consent! I am the baby's father, and I have my rights. I will sue you and this hospital for more than it is worth."

A white mask covered the doctor's face; but his eyes grew wide with fear. Silence settled around the room as the nurses exchanged glances.

Then the man's loud voice came clearly to Olivia's ears, "I'm going to kill myself if you kill our baby!"

When Olivia heard Scott's threat, she quickly removed her feet from the hard, cold stirrups, sat up on the edge of the bed, and said, "Get this needle out of my arm. I cannot go through with the abortion."

When she walked out of the clinic, Scott threw his hat to the wind and ran to her. He swung her around, pulled her close, and said, "Thank God, I made it here in time."

"Take me home," she said.

He sat under the wheel, pulled her under his arm, and the sweet smell of her cleanliness made him crazy. He brushed his lips from her forehead to the tip of her nose and their lips met with a hungry desire. "Baby, I thought I had lost you forever," he said. "Um, I want you." A warm chill ran around her neck as he kissed the cleavage of her breast. She longed to be in bed with him. He kissed her again and moved his hand under her dress. She twisted and squirmed with desire as he caressed her. "You are making me crazy," she said. "Take me home."

As he drove toward home, the words he spoke in that clinic played in her head like a stuck record: "The worst thing about dying is to have never been given a chance to live." She felt as if nobody ever gave her a chance to live, either.

"What are you thinking?" he asked.

"How did you know my plans to have an abortion? How did you know where I had gone?"

"Your friend, Emily, called and told me you had gone to Savannah to have an abortion and she thought I had a right to know. Having an abortion is a serious procedure; Emily worried that you might regret your decision later. She wanted me to talk to you before you went through with the abortion. I did have a right to know your plans to abort our baby. I am the baby's father."

"I am the baby's mother; and I have a right to have a husband before I give birth to a child that I will have to raise on my own. Maybe I should have told you, but I am at my wits end. I do not know what I will do. My baby needs a father and you are a married man who will remain married until death do you part."

"I promise you that I will marry you soon," he said.

"Action speaks much louder than words. I can no longer live on promises. You must leave your wife, and marry me; or you must leave me, and stay with your wife. It seems that you have already made your choice."

"I do not have a wife. You are the love of my life. You are more a wife to me than Laura has ever been. I love you more than anything on this green earth, and I want to marry you."

"I need security and love. Most of all, our baby needs a father."

Scott stayed with her that night and promised her the moon. He wanted her to move into the house with him until he could build them a new house; he wanted them to get married; he wanted her to quit teaching school and stay home with the baby.

Scott's words sounded like a sweet melody that he had played a thousand times; but one never tires of sweet melodies.

She had two more months to teach before her teaching contract ended. She did not want to move into the house with him. He should move in with her, since no one knew him in Boulder Bluff.

The next morning, he had to go to work; but he assured her that he would take responsibility for his child and her. He promised to be back that night and they could talk about the baby. He kissed her and stretched his arm until her hand dropped with his steps.

After Scott left, Olivia felt happier than she had been in weeks. She thought about making wedding plans. In the back of her mind, where she stored all of those unwanted thoughts, doubt clouded her dream and she faced reality. Scott had not asked her to marry him; he had only said he wanted them to get married and had asked her to move into his house with him. Scott would never divorce Laura; he felt responsible for her.

She sat down on the couch and embraced her stomach with love for her baby. A painful lump closed her throat when she thought about the abortion. If she had gone through with the abortion, she would have never forgiven herself.

That night, Scott came in humming a tune. He peeped into the kitchen, and held up a bottle of white wine. "Hello, beautiful. I want to celebrate; we are having a baby. I feel like making love to you all night."

"We are not having a baby; I am having a baby, and I cannot drink alcoholic beverages."

"I will fix you some grape juice, and you can pretend that it is wine," he said.

She laughed and asked what he would like for supper.

He wanted to go out to eat or order something to take out. They needed to spend some time together; he had to go to Savannah the next day on business.

The next morning before Scott left, he asked her to tell the principal that she would not be back the next year. He mentioned her moving into the house with him but she refused his offer. He finally agreed to move into the house with her; he could spend every weekend with her. He also wanted to be there for her when she needed him and make sure she went for her doctor's appointments.

Scott kept his promise and stayed with her at least three times each week, mostly on the weekends. He made her feel like a queen and treated her wonderful. She could not live without him. He made her happy; yet, she felt sad. She wanted Scott to marry her before the baby arrived. If they could get married, their life would be perfect. Then she realized that Scott would not marry her as long as his wife still breathed. As he had said, his wife had no life; she merely existed from one day to the next.

CHAPTER SEVENTEEN
Angry Parents

OLIVIA STILL DID not know how she would face her parents with the news of her pregnancy; but she could not hide her pregnancy much longer. Her observant mother had already noticed that she had gained weight. She visited her often during the day. Scott stayed with her mostly at night, but he dropped in sometimes to have lunch with her. She did not want to answer her mother's questions if she walked in and found Scott there with her.

Her parents did not think couples should live together before marriage; and they certainly did not believe that couples should have children before marriage. When they heard the rest of her story, they would fling a fit and go into a rage about her immoral and sinful life with a married man.

She must ask Scott to go with her to tell her parents. After all, he got her pregnant; and he should take on part of the responsibility for her pregnancy. She often pointed fingers and placed blame; but she could not blame Scott; she had been stupid.

That weekend, Scott went with Olivia to visit Ralph and Mary Hollister. They met her with open arms; but their eyes questioned her about the gentleman standing next to her. Olivia quickly introduced Scott; and her father extended a warm hand; but her mother merely greeted him. Then her mother asked if they would stay and have dinner with them. Olivia explained that Scott had to go to work; they would pick up something to eat on the way home.

Mrs. Hollister invited them to sit in the living room. While she questioned Olivia about how she had been and about her job, Mr. Hollister talked about politics, the weather, and the latest news. Then he questioned Scott about where he lived, what he did for a living, and his family.

Olivia interrupted her father with an explanation of how she and Scott met. Then she mentioned Porterville, his hometown, and Porter Manufacturing Company. She paused before telling them the rest of the story. She finally said, "I am pregnant, Daddy; Scott and I cannot get married right away, because he is married. His wife had an accident; she cannot move or speak. Scott had to put her in a nursing home."

Silence fell around them and Olivia's father stared at Scott with anger and disbelief. Olivia's mother got up and left the room without an explanation. Olivia looked from her father to Scott; they stared at each other and neither spoke.

Scott finally broke the silence with his question, "Mr. Hollister, what would you do in my situation?"

"In the first place, I would never get myself into your situation as long as I am married to Mary Hollister."

"I'm going to marry Olivia," Scott said.

"You are a liar; you will never marry Olivia. You played my daughter for a fool, but you are the fool. Only a foolish man would get another woman pregnant when he already has a wife to support. A man who denies his wife is a coward."

"I do not deny my wife; I provide the best of care for her. I did not intend to get involved with your daughter; but I fell in love with her and I could not stay away from her."

"A smart man's actions are not beyond his control," Mr. Hollister said.

"Your anger is well deserved, but I plan to marry Olivia as soon as I get things worked out for my wife."

"Your promises are not worth the breath wasted to speak them. Go back to your wife and forget about Olivia! Her mother and I will take care of her and the baby. I am not a rich man, but we will find a way without your help."

"I take full responsibility for our baby and Olivia. I will pay the doctor and the hospital. Money is the least of my worries."

"We do not need your money; your money can not buy my approval for you to live with my daughter out of wedlock. I forbid you to see her again. I want you to leave this instance and stay away from my daughter."

"Please don't forbid me to see Olivia," Scott said. "When I get Laura situated, I plan to marry Olivia. I hope we can marry before she has the baby."

"How many women have you fooled already? How many wait for your hand in marriage?" Mr. Hollister said. "If you lied to Olivia to get your way, you will lie any woman who suits your fancy. I know men like you. You play dirty; I do not like your dirty games."

"Our baby will carry my name; our baby will inherit all that is mine. My daddy would turn over in his grave and curse me if I did nothing for my child. He taught me to be honest and always do the right thing."

"Would your daddy turn over in his grave if he knew you committed adultery and got the woman pregnant? Would your daddy turn over in his grave if he knew he had a bastard grandchild on the way?"

Scott's face turned red and his eyes blazed with anger as he jumped up, went toward Mr. Hollister, and shouted, "Don't call my child a bastard! I will give my child my name."

"What is your definition for a child without a father?" Mr. Hollister said.

Olivia pulled him back and stopped him from throwing a fist to Mr. Hollister's nose.

"I do not want to fight you," Mr. Hollister said. "I am not a violent man; but I am a vindictive man. I have nothing more to say to you. Get out of my home and leave my daughter with us. We will take care of her."

Olivia wanted to scream at her father; she wanted to tell him to shut up; she wanted to tell him that Scott loved her and planned to marry her. She pulled on Scott' arm and asked him to go outside with her. Scott sat down next to her on the steps, took her hand and said, "I love you. Please don't leave me."

"I will never leave you," Olivia said.

Mr. Hollister came out on the porch, walked past them down the steps, walked around the oak tree and kicked at acorns with anger. Then he came back and stood before them as he spoke, "You are not in love with Olivia; you are in love with your money. You are afraid that your wife's family will try to take your money if you divorce their daughter and I don't blame them."

"Money has nothing to do with my situation. I love Olivia more than anything in the world. On the other hand, I cannot live on thin air. I have to keep my business going. I have to have money to give my wife the care she needs; and I have to have money to look after Olivia and the baby. I want them to have the best."

"If you want the best for Olivia and your baby, you will do the right thing and marry her. She needs you more than your wife needs you. From what you have told me already, your wife is cared for by nurses in a nursing home."

"I am aware of Olivia's needs, and I will see that she has the best life possible. I have asked her to quit work and stay at home with the baby. I will pay all of the bills."

Mr. Hollister swung his heels against the porch foundation, looked up with a squint against the sun, and said, "You need to marry Olivia and give your child a father. I doubt that you will ever marry Olivia. Your word means nothing."

"I am as good as my word," Scott said. "I am going to marry Olivia as soon as I get things situated in my life."

"Have you thought about how much Olivia will suffer for bearing your child out of wed lock? She keeps telling herself that you will marry her. She believes your lies, because she has no other choice."

Olivia realized that neither her father nor mother would accept Scott. She wished now that she had not told them about Scott and her pregnancy. She wanted to go home and forget their protest.

Mr. Hollister walked back up the steps, turned back at the door, and said, "I want you to leave right now, Mr. Porter. If you do not get out of my sight, I will call the cops to throw you off my property."

Olivia gave her father an angry stare and said, "Where ever Scott goes; I will go, also. If you will not accept Scott, I will no longer consider myself your daughter. We will go now, and we will not bother you or Mother again.

Scott took her hand and they walked toward the car. After they got into the car, she moved close to him. He leaned over and kissed her.

Her father slammed the door and never looked back. He went to the kitchen and sat down at the table.

Mary turned from the stove and asked what happened.

He told her they had raised an idiot for a daughter; she left with that sorry son of a bitch who had ruined her life as well as their lives.

Mary thought they should ask the preacher to have special prayer for Olivia at prayer meeting on Wednesday night.

He felt sure that prayer would not stop Olivia from having that little bastard she carried in her belly; and prayer would not stop her from living with that sorry son of a bitch. He sat with a worried brow. Then he suggested that they get a court order to have Olivia put in a mental institution. He believed they should take that baby away from Olivia and raise it as their own. After all, their daughter had lost her damn mind and did not have sense enough to raise a child.

Mary tried to convince him that they could do nothing about Olivia's affair with a married man, except pray for her and ask God to help her make the right decision.

Mr. Hollister argued that Olivia could not make the right decision; the bastard would never marry her and she would be left a single mother with a child to raise on her own.

On Saturday, Olivia got up at her regular time; she and Scott had breakfast together before he went to work. He suggested they go out for dinner that evening and take in a movie.

After Scott left, Olivia's mother paid a visit. When Olivia opened the door, her mother stormed into the house, turned on her and shouted, "Why are you letting that man spend the night with you?"

"I do not think my personal life is any of your business, Mother."

"You are my daughter; I make your business my business," she said. "Have you lost your good mind? You are pregnant for a man who has a wife. You have no morals what so ever. You have ruined your life for good this time. You should force him to marry you with demands for money. When you get into a man's pockets, he comes across and does the right thing. His helpless wife is no better than you are. Your daddy and I talked about this situation most of the night. You have as much right to have a husband as his precious wife. Have you talked to Tom? If he knew about your being pregnant for a married man, he would put Mr. Porter in his place."

"What I do is none of Tom's business, and you have no right to bring his name up. Tom's infidelity brought on my divorce from him. How can the pot call the kettle black?"

"Tom cares about you; he has called and asked me about you many times since you divorced him."

"Mother, Tom cares about Tom and no one else. You nor Tom have any business prying into my personal life."

"You are my daughter," Mrs. Hollister said and I have the responsibility of seeing about you. You don't need this big house, either. You need to move in with your father and me. You need someone to take you to the doctor; you need someone to buy things the baby needs; you need someone to take care of the baby."

Olivia could not take her mother's demands any longer. She shouted that she liked her house; she loved Scott; and she planned to live with him until the end of time. She added that she had not become helpless; she could drive herself to the doctor; she could buy everything the baby needed; she did not need her money; and she did not need her help to care for her baby. She asked her mother to leave.

Before her mother reached her car, Olivia shouted, "Have a good day, Mother."

Olivia fell back in the recliner and stared at the ceiling. She felt as if she had no rights to speak her mind in her own home. Her mother spoke to her as if she were still her dependent child; but her mother nor father had given her a dime since she finished college and got a job. She paid her own way; and her mother had no apron strings attached to her. She loved her mother; but she hated the way she tried to control her life. She could not have a decent relationship with Scott as long as her mother stuck her nose into her personal life.

That evening, she and Scott went out to dinner, took in a movie, came home, and went to bed early.

Olivia still went to work every day; she hid her belly fat with suits, dresses with matching coats, and loose tops. She assumed that her friends did not know about her pregnancy. If they did, they never questioned her. The month before school turned out for the summer, she told the principal that she would not be back the next year.

Mrs. Hollister kept close tabs on Olivia. She called every morning, until Olivia got tired of her harassment and stopped answering the phone.

CHAPTER EIGHTEEN

Cruel Visitors

AFTER SCHOOL TURNED out for the summer, Olivia had plenty of time on her hands to work in the yards and cook. She became a professional cook and liked to try different recipes. Scott never complained about the meals she prepared; he liked most everything, except spinach.

The next morning after breakfast, Scott walked behind her chair, and kissed her. "I love you. I hope you have a good day."

"Drive carefully," she said. "I will see you at six."

She got up from the table and walked to the window. Bamboo and weeds had taken over her rose garden. She wanted to work in the yard before the sun got unbearable. She walked back to the kitchen, put the dishes in the dishwasher, and filled her thermos with lemonade and ice.

Dressed in a pair of jeans, a cotton shirt with long sleeves, she slapped her straw hat on her head, and went to the garage to gather her garden tool. After she hitched the wagon to the lawn mower, she drove to the rose garden in the front yard and began digging.

By ten o'clock, the temperature felt like ninety degrees. She propped her shovel against the wagon, pulled off her hat, wiped her face on her sleeve, and drank some lemonade. She wanted to finish cleaning the rose garden before lunch, but she had to dig deep to get the bamboo roots.

After a short rest, she returned to her chore. As she plunged the shovel deep into the earth, a shiny gray Lincoln pulled into her drive. She propped on her shovel and stared at the two men as they walked toward her. She thought her eyes played a trick on her. Then a loud unpleasant voice shouted, "Hey Olivia, do you need some help?"

Olivia froze in her tracks; she would never forget Billy's voice. She turned to see Tom, with his friend, Billy Miller, at his heels. After all of this time, she could not believe that Tom had come to pay her a visit; neither could she believe that he brought his idiot friend, Billy, with him.

When they got within feet of her, Billy said, "If you will put down that shovel, pick up that hoe, and put it to use, I will call you what you are."

Billy's loud laughter followed his smart remark and made Olivia furious. She felt as if flames of fire licked her face. She propped on her shovel and stared at Billy. Fire blazed from her eyes as she shouted, "You sorry, stinking, Billy Goat! You have always treated me with disrespect and you know nothing about me, unless Tom told you lies about me. I should call the cops and have you thrown off my property. Get out of my yard!"

"I was only kidding," Billy said. "I meant you no harm. Tom asked me to come with him to see about you. Tom has always had good things to say about you. He still loves you, Olivia, and I care about you, too. We are both concerned about your health and well-being."

"If you don't get away from me, I am going to smash your ugly, stinking, Billy Goat face with this shovel," Olivia said and raised the shovel to hit him.

Billy backed up and said, "Wait, Olivia, I didn't mean to make you angry." Then he turned and ran back to Tom's car.

Olivia propped on the shovel and said, "What are you doing here, Tom?"

"Your mother called and asked me to come and talk some sense into your thick skull. She said you would listen to me. I didn't tell her that I already knew about your affair with Scott Porter; I didn't tell her what I thought of him. If you ask me, he is a nut case!"

Olivia's eyes shot daggers at Tom. She wanted to slap him; she hated him more this minute than all the years she lived with him. She pulled off her hat, threw it into the wagon, and shouted, "You have some nerve coming here to give me advice. Did you tell my mother about your affair with Stella Shivers and all those other women you shacked with while you were married to me? Did you tell my mother that your affairs caused our divorce? You have no business talking to my mother; and my mother had no business telling you anything about me. I am no longer your concern."

"Olivia, I will always love you. If you will come back to me, I will marry you and give your unborn child my name. I promise to be a good father."

"How can you stand there and make such an offer. What about being a good husband? I was the rug under your feet. I will never go back to you, Tom. I love Scott and he loves me. He is a good man. Most important of all, he is the father to my child, and we plan to get married as soon as he gets things situated with his wife."

"That son-of-a bitch is a lying bastard; he will never marry you, Olivia. Who does he think he is? You deserve better. You are my wife and I want you back! We had something special, something that I never had before I met you nor after I lost you."

"Your fling with Stella ruined our marriage. You lied to me every time you opened your mouth. I do not believe one word you say. I forgive you for the things you said and did to hurt me; but I will never forget what you did. Please go and say no more."

"If you change your mind and want to see me, call me," he said. "I would do anything to make up for my mistakes."

Olivia watched him walk toward his car and the memories of her past flashed in his footsteps. She remembered the times that the sight of Tom made her heart beat with love; now she felt nothing for him.

Long after Tom left, Olivia stood in the same spot. She felt numb all over. Had she imagined Tom Bradford's visit? Did Tom really tell her he loved her and wanted her to come back to him? Did he want to marry her? Did he want to claim Scott's baby? She thought about the good times, but her mind wandered to the time that things got bad between them. His actions should have been a red flag, but she loved him and refused to admit that their marriage would never work. She finally got tired of his ignoring her and became indifferent. Then she caught him with Stella Shivers. That day changed her forever, and she finally admitted that Tom never loved her to begin with. Then insight hit her like a flash of lightening. Tom wanted to claim the child she carried as his own, because he could never have children.

She gathered her garden tools, put them in the wagon and drove the lawn mower toward the shed. Her cell phone rang and she stopped the lawn mower to see who called. When she saw Tom's name, she let the phone continue to ring. She had nothing to say to him and she prayed that he would not cause even more trouble for her.

She went back into the house, took a bath, and walked around in a daze for hours. She felt confused and angry. She felt like pulling her hair; she felt insane. Then she thought about her mother; she felt betrayed. Her mother had no right to call Tom. Her mother blamed her for all things that had gone wrong in her marriage to Tom.

When Scott came home, she wanted to tell him about Tom's visit; fear of his reaction made her keep silent. She must never tell Scott about Tom's visit. She might lose him forever.

The next evening before Olivia started supper, she sat down at the table to thumb through her new recipe book, "Cooking with Martha Stewart." She decided she would try Martha's recipe for baked chicken with seasoned potatoes that would go good with a garden salad.

The doorbell interrupted her thoughts; Scott never rang the doorbell. She expected her mother or a salesperson when she opened the door. Instead, she faced Reverend Pierce. She thought he must have the wrong address. She had not attended church with her parents in over three years. In spite of her reservation, she greeted the Reverend and invited him inside. He followed her to the living room and sat down in an armchair across from her. He turned down her offer for a drink and twisted in his seat as if uncomfortable.

Olivia broke the silence with her questions about church members that she remembered. She expected his invitation to church; instead, she got the shock of her life.

"Olivia, I remember the sweet, innocent, young lady who used to come to church with Ralph and Mary. From what I have been told, you have changed into a completely different person."

Olivia laughed and said, "Are you sure your memory is not playing tricks on you, Reverend Pierce?"

"Your mother and father are concerned about you. They do not approve of your living with a man out of wedlock. I understand that the man is married, and you are carrying his child. They asked me to come and pray with you and try to convince you to do the right thing. Your mother and father kneel at the altar and pray for you every time they come to church. We also have set aside a special prayer service for you every Wednesday night."

Olivia sat and looked at him with shock. She wanted to tell Reverend Pierce to get out of her home; he did not know her or understand the situation. Instead, Olivia said, "I am not against praying, Reverend Pierce. In fact, I pray every day; but my parents have no right to advertise my personal life to the public. I do not want my name mentioned at your service again."

"You give me no other choice, Olivia; I must remove you from our church roll."

Olivia got up, looked at Reverend Pierce with anger and said, "Remove me from your church roll if you must. Your decision to do so will not hurt me, but it will hurt you. I think you should go before I call the cops to throw you out. In God's eyes, one sin is no greater than another sin is. You should clean out your own closet before you judge me. This also goes for my mother and father as well as the others in your church who have judged me. To quote a famous passage, "He who lives in a glass house should not throw stones. " Do not judge me or pray for me before cleansing your own soul of sin, Reverend Pierce." She stood and asked the preacher to leave before Scott got home. She added that Scott hated trouble makers.

Olivia walked to the front door, opened it, and paused with angry eyes still on the reverend. I have one other thing to say to you, Reverend Pierce, "If I found fault with everything that others do and say, I would bite my tongue to force silence, fall on my knees, and pray."

Reverend Pierce looked like a wounded dog with his tail between his legs as he made his way to his shiny black Buick, the expensive car the members of his congregation gave him as a gift for Christmas that year. She had heard her mother joyfully brag about the gift and how proud Reverend Pierce had been to get the car.

Olivia felt more anger than she had ever felt in her life toward her mother and father, but mostly her mother. She wanted to give her an angry piece of her mind; but she decided to wait and talk to Scott. He would know the best thing to do in this situation.

When Scott got home, Olivia met him with the news about Reverend Pierce's visit. She cried as she told him the things the preacher said to her. He tried to comfort her and told her not to worry about what he said. They loved each other and their life should not concern others. Scott could not believe her own mother had betrayed her; but he blamed himself for her tears.

After supper, they sat in the living room and talked over an hour. He still had not made up his mind to get a divorce and marry her. They could move to Porterville if she would only agree to move into the house with him.

He finally said that the more they stirred the gossip, the worse it would get. They should ignore the preacher's visit and not say anything to her parents about their betrayal.

CHAPTER NINETEEN

A Precious Gift

ON SEPTEMBER 28, 1986, the nurse came into Olivia's room and laid her beautiful son in her arms. Her baby's soft warmth, sweet smell, and the way he grasp her finger filled her with love, a love that only a mother knows. That minute she bonded with her bundle of joy with a need to protect him. God had given her a precious gift and she would try to be the best mother in the world. She wanted him to have a good life, a life better than her life had ever been.

The baby had all of Scott's features and this made him a proud father. He stood by her bedside and bragged that he had a son, the smartest little boy in the world. He bent over, kissed Olivia gently, and whispered, "Thank you for giving me a son. I love you more than anything in the world." Then he pointed to her flowers on the table by her bed.

"Gosh, the roses are beautiful. Thank you."

Then he said, "I know we have talked about all the names in the book; but I would like to name our son Alexander Porter. You know, they named Porterville after my Uncle Alexander."

"I had not thought of that name; but I like the sound of Alexander and so shall it be.

Scott put his hand on him and said, "We can call him Alex; but he will be Alexander the Great."

They both laughed and Scott took his son in his arms and held him until the nurse came in and took him back to the nursery.

When Scott brought Olivia home from the hospital, Mrs. Louise Sanders met them at the front door. She cleaned and washed for Scott once a week, and he wanted her to stay with Olivia until she felt like taking care of the baby and doing the house work.

Olivia loved Mrs. Sanders from the first time she spoke to her; but she wanted to take care of her baby. She agreed for Mrs. Sanders to stay with her two weeks to clean the house, wash, and cook.

Before Mrs. Sanders left, she took Alex in her arms, hugged him, and talked baby talk. She asked Olivia to call her anytime she needed help with the baby or housework.

Olivia stood next to her baby's bed and looked at him with pride. His beautiful little face looked so much like his father. He also had dark hair like his father. She gave him plenty of attention. He especially liked Olivia to rock him and sing to him at night. He seemed happy and content most of the time; he cried only when he wanted to eat; needed a dry diaper; or did not feel well. Luckily, he had not been seriously ill since he came into the world. He had the measles and mumps with a high fever; but Olivia fussed over him and nursed him back to health quickly.

After the baby came, Mr. and Mrs. Hollister visited almost every week and practically begged Olivia to let them keep their grandson. They encouraged her to get away for a while. After all, she stayed right by the baby, and they thought she needed a vacation.

Olivia quickly let them know that she would take Alex with her when she went on vacation.

She thought about her mother's betrayal and the ugly things they had said about Scott. Her father still had no use for Scott, but he did not criticize him; he wanted to visit his grandson.

Scott got up at five each morning, except on Sunday, when he slept late and had breakfast with her and Alex. He had said that Sundays belonged to his family. He loved Alex as much as Olivia did.

After breakfast, Scott went out to get the Sunday paper and came back to the kitchen to read while Olivia cooked dinner. As she moved around the stove, Scott looked up from his paper and asked if he could help her with dinner.

She assured him that she had everything under control.

He lowered his paper, smiled, and mentioned the delicious smelling squash casserole. Then he said, "Why don't we hire Mrs. Sander's full time. You need some free time to relax, shop, and travel."

"A full time maid would cost a fortune," she said. She really did not want a maid. She enjoyed managing the house and looking after Alex.

"I can afford two maids if you wish," he said. "I want you to be happy."

"You and my son make me happy. I can manage the house and our son. I could not leave Alex with angels in heaven."

"Louise Sanders is an angel; she raised me and kept the house for Mother all of my life. She could, at least, do the house work and cooking."

"I am not reaching for the moon, the sun, or the stars. I only want us to be married so I can be your wife and tell my son he has a father."

"I want to marry you, Baby; but every time I walk into my wife's room and see her lying there dependent on others for the life she has left, I hurt all over. I don't think I could live with my guilt."

Olivia felt his pain; but she felt her pain and needs even more. When she made no reply to his excuses, he said, "Give me a few more months, and I will marry you. I don't know how the public will react to my decision. If push comes to shove, I will sell Porter Manufacturing. We can move to another city far away from here."

"I never get my hopes up anymore," she said. "Besides, I could not ask you to sell Porter Manufacturing and give up what you have worked for all of your life. You have to make a living for two families now."

"I would give a million dollars if I could marry you right now," he said. "I love you so much."

After they finished eating, he stood behind her chair and massaged her shoulders. She stood and turned to him. She needed to feel the comfort of his arms. His lips found hers and set their world ablaze with a wonderful feeling that flamed toward the heavens. Minutes later, he took her hand and led her to the bedroom.

"I want you," he said. "Don't you want me?"

"That is not a good question?"

His gentleness as he unbuttoned her dress made her crazy. Then he slowly pulled it over her head and she wanted to jerk the dress off quickly. Then he unhooked her bra, pushed it down, and admired her nakedness. She squirmed for him and cuddled close to him. The warmth of her body and the sweet smell of her skin made him wild with passion. She became weak with the warmth of his kiss, and the pleasure she experienced in his arms made the hell she lived through worthwhile.

On Monday after dinner, Scott called and complained about problems with machines, paper work, and inventory. He had to work until midnight to get caught up and would be unable to come spend the night with her and Alex.

Olivia pretended that she understood. They exchanged the usual words of love before she hung up.

Then early the next morning, the phone awoke Olivia at six-thirty in the morning.

Scott apologized for calling so early, but he had a virus and he did not want to expose her and Alex.

Olivia remained silent for minutes; she did not believe him, because he had not been to see them the day before. She accused him of neglecting her and the baby; she accused him of running around on her.

He did not know what to say about her sudden outburst of anger. He promised to call her the next morning.

Before he spoke his usual words of love, she slammed the phone down with anger, pulled the cover over her head, and cried.

An hour later, she heard Alex crying and jumped up to see about him. After she fed him breakfast and gave him a bath, she put him back to bed to take his usual nap. Then she went and got the laundry. She cried and slung Alex's diapers as she folded. She leaned over his bed, looked at him, and said, "You are sleeping like a good little son, the son of a worthless tramp. How I wish you had a father. You will never have a father. It does not matter that I have no husband, but my son needs a father."

She did not want her child to grow up in that gossiping town. She did not want people to make fun of him and call him a bastard. She wanted him to have a super life with a father to show him how to do things. His future would depend on impressions he learned as a child. She wanted him to have a good self-image, a trusting nature, and to be brave and patient. She wanted him to see the beautiful things in life; she wanted him to hear sweet melodies; most of all, she wanted him to have a good self-concept. Olivia quietly closed Alex's door and went to the kitchen.

The next evening, Scott called and told her he felt much better and would be at her house before six.

When he walked into the house, his eyes moved from her head to her toes. The sight of her sexy body in her tank top and shorts made him want to take her to bed. He kissed her and told her how much he had missed them. He reached for her again, but she pushed him away.

"Is Alex awake?" he asked as if nothing had happened.

She flew past him without an answer.

Scott rushed ahead of her and stood at Alex's bed.

Alex kicked and laughed as if to say, "I love you, Daddy."

Scott picked him up, kissed him, and said, "I miss you so much. I hate to be away from you and your mother." Then he danced about the room and held Alex above his head as he spoke, "You're a sport! Daddy's going to make a fine fisherman and hunter out of you."

Scott saw that Olivia looked at him with disgust. He pulled Alex back to his shoulder and said, "I love your mother. Did you know that? She has a hard head that does not soak up my words easily."

Olivia threw Alex's bottle across the room and milk puddled in the shattered glass as she shouted, "I hate you, Scott. You take my words as grains of salt. Get away from my son!"

She went toward them, and Scott pulled Alex close as if protecting him from harm and backed up. Then he shouted, "Olivia, stop it! You don't know what you are saying."

"I know well what I am saying. I want you to get out!"

Scott lay Alex back in his bed, pulled Olivia close, and said, "Listen, Lady, I love you, damn it! Don't you know I've loved you from the minute I laid eyes on you?"

Alex pulled up and fumbled at the wooden rails with little noises of happiness.

Scott already had her blouse pushed down over her shoulders before she jerked away from him.

"I have to fix Alex another bottle." She picked up the shattered glass from the puddle of milk and left the room. She came back with a roll of paper towels and another bottle. She placed the bottle in Alex's hands, and said, "Go back to sleep, Sweetie."

Alex let go of his bottle and moved his arms and hands aimlessly about as if he did not want to go back to sleep. Then he babbled loudly as if to say, "Get me up from here."

Olivia pushed his dark hair back and said, "Mama's little boy must take a nap."

As she started out, Scot grabbed the wad of paper towels from her hand and threw them in the garbage can next to Alex's bed. Then he pulled her into his arms in a gentle embrace before he kissed her.

"No," she mumbled with pleasure. "We must not. The baby is watching us."

Scott urged her with another kiss, and whispered, "My son approves of every move I make; he wants me to please his mother."

The wonderful feel of his arms around her made her heart beat fast. He took her hand and she followed him to the living room. He pulled a quilt from the back of the couch, spread it on the floor, and pulled her down next to him. Hot tinges shot through her and made her too weak to resist him.

Afterwards, she snuggled close to him and said, "I love you, Scott; but I think we should get married, especially since we have our son's future to think about."

"I love you and my son more than anything on earth. You will be my wife someday." He paused a few minutes before his question. "Baby, why don't you trust me? I will never look at another woman as long as I have you."

"I am sorry I accused you of cheating on me; but your promises to marry me have not materialized. I learned the hard way that men cannot be trusted."

"Olivia, I am not just another man. I love you; we have a son together. I will marry you as soon as I can."

She heard Alex quarreling and got dressed. As she walked toward Alex's bedroom, he followed and admired her legs and figure. He had found the perfect woman; one day she would be his wife.

At Alex's door, she put a hush finger to her lips and peeped at him; he lay quietly and played with his rattler. She quietly closed the door and said, "He will go back to sleep if we go away."

Alex's eyes followed them to the door, but he did not cry. He shook his rattler and quarreled at the birds that flew in a circle above his bed.

Olivia started down the hall toward the kitchen. Scott asked if she minded if he took a nap before dinner. He had not slept much the last two nights.

She told him that she did not mind at all if he took a nap.

He asked if she would like to go out to dinner. She told him she had rather he go pick up something; she didn't want to take the baby out in soggy damp weather.

Scott slept three hours. When he awoke, he could hear Olivia singing to Alex, "Mama's going to buy you a July Fly."

He stood in the doorway and listened until she finished her song. Then he said, "I am so lucky to have a son and a woman who loves me."

Scott left and came back with chicken dinners and a salad from Chick Filet. She sat quietly across the table from him to enjoy dinner.

Alex slept about an hour before Olivia heard him quarreling. She went to him, cuddled him to her breast with loving care, and hummed a tune.

After they ate lunch, Scott talked Olivia into going for a ride. He thought she needed to get out more. She had stayed right by Alex since the day he came into the world. Olivia enjoyed the scenery around town. She especially liked riding in the park. When Alex got older, they could go to the park and have a picnic.

The next week, Scott spent the night with them every night. They talked about getting married soon.

CHAPTER TWENTY
Anonymous Threats

THREE YEARS LATER, Scott still had not divorced his wife; but Olivia seldom mentioned marriage to him anymore. She had accepted the fact that her life with Scott would be shared with time for his wife. Besides, he spent more time with Alex and her than he spent with anyone else. She prayed that he would marry her before Alex started to school. Why did he not realize that Alex needed him more than anyone else?

As she looked down at her son's beautiful face, she ran a gentle hand over his silky dark hair with thoughts of his future. Would he ever have a father to look up to with pride? Could he go to public places with his father without whispers behind his back? She often thought of moving to another state to raise Alex and spare him embarrassing encounters that he likely faced. At the door, she looked back at Alex and quietly closed the door behind her.

She should have listened to her father. He had warned her that she should face reality. He had never heard of a man leaving his wife for another woman, unless the wife caught him cheating.

She reminded her father that Scott's wife lived in a nursing home; she depended on Scott for her next breath. He felt responsible for her.

Her father did not agree with her thinking. He believed that his daughter deserved more respect than Scott had shown her, and Scott should marry her and give his grandson a real father. He thought Scott used his wife's condition as an excuse to get out of marrying Olivia.

"Father, I love Scott; he makes me happy. We are getting married very soon."

Her father walked away from her, shook his head, and said, "Hog wash!"

Olivia could not leave Scott. He controlled her mind and her body. Her love for him was greater than her fear of her child's future.

When Scott came in from work, he forgot about his business and devoted his attention to Olivia and his son. Scott reminded her of her grandfather. She had loved her grandfather and had spent the summer with him every year during her younger days.

In the morning, when she awoke the quietness in the room made her anxious. She closed her eyes and imagined Scott lying in bed next to her. She longed to feel his warmth submerge her with delight. Scott would not return from New York until Friday. He called her every day, but she wanted him to come home. She missed and needed him desperately.

Porter Manufacturing required a lot of Scott's time and hard work; but he had one of the most profitable businesses in the State. Olivia hated his business trips; but she did not fuss. He provided well for her and Alex. Besides, he usually asked her to go with him when he had to go out of town. She seldom went with him to the northern cities, especially in the winter; she hated to carry Alex out in the freezing weather. They had been with him several times during the summer months to the beaches on the southern coast. Alex liked to play in the sand and splash the water. He adored Alex and spent as much time with them as possible with his job and sick wife.

In the kitchen, she soaked up the morning sun streaming through the windows and listened to country music while she cooked breakfast. She wished Scott could eat breakfast with them.

Before she got Alex's grits and eggs mixed and stirred, the phone rang. Scott' voice made her feel better. He told her how much he loved her and asked about Alex.

She explained that she had Alex's breakfast ready, but she had not got him up, yet.

He said he would call her later and hung up.

After breakfast, Emily called and asked how she had been.

Olivia admitted that she and Alex got lonely when Scott went out of town on business; he would not return home until the following Monday.

Emily suggested that they meet in Atlanta on Saturday for lunch and carry the children to Six Flags over Georgia that afternoon.

Olivia promised to meet her at the Hard Rock Café in Atlanta the next day at eleven o'clock.

That evening when Scott called. He asked her to fly to New York with Alex to spend the weekend. He wanted to take Alex to see the Statue of Liberty.

"Alex gets so restless when we travel," she said.

"Ask your mother to keep Alex," he said. "You never go any place and enjoy yourself."

"I don't want to leave Alex for the weekend with Mother. Besides, I have promised Alex a treat tomorrow. Emily wants us to meet her in Atlanta tomorrow. We plan to take the children to Six Flags Over Georgia."

"Don't let my son get on those dangerous rides with you."

"I am not crazy. You know I will not allow Alex to ride anything that is dangerous. I do want him to enjoy the rides for children."

"Are you going to ride with him?" he said.

"You know I would not let him ride without standing by his side or sitting with him," she said.

"I will call you tomorrow," he said.

"In case I miss your call, what is the name of the hotel where are you staying?"

"I'm at the Forbes Hotel, room number 151," he said and gave her the telephone number.

She made a smacking sound on the phone and said, "I love you. The next four days will be long and lonely without you. Alex wants to speak with you."

"Hello, Daddy. We miss you. Mother has promised me a big surprise tomorrow."

"Is your mother hiding a magic trick up her sleeve?" he said.

"I don't know," he said. "Uncle Jo can pull money from his ears. He says he will teach me his magic trick."

"Do you suppose she plans to surprise me and come to New York," he said.

"I hope so," Alex said. "New York is cool."

Scott laughed and said, "Kiss Mother for me. I love you, and I will see you on Friday."

Olivia put the chicken in the oven for dinner and sat down at the table to read the paper and go through her mail. When she picked the paper up, an envelope addressed to Olivia Bradford fell on the table. She thought Emily must have a lot to say to write her a letter. She tore into the envelope and got the shock of her life.

Olivia Bradford,

"I am writing this letter to give you a fair warning. I know you live with Scott Porter; and I know you have a son for him. If he promised to marry you, then he lied. Scott has a wife and has no intentions of divorcing her. He calls you a stupid whore behind your back. I advise you to move far away from here and take your bastard son with you. If you continue living with Scott Porter, you must take the consequences."

Speechless, Olivia threw the letter down and ran to the back porch to check on Alex. Her fear turned to laughter when she spotted Alex's dark head peeping above the boxwoods. She walked over to him and said, "What are you doing?"

"I am making a gopher house," he said. He pulled his buried foot out of the damp dirt to show her the house.

"That is a nice gopher house." Then she squatted down and kissed him on the cheek. "I love you, my son. Let's go into the house."

He touched her face and said, "Mama, why are you crying?"

"I will explain everything to you one day," she said as she took his hand. The feel of his small hand wrapped around her fingers overwhelmed her with love.

"Stop that crying, Mama. I can look after you; I am a big boy," he said, and he took extra big steps as if to tell her he would take care of her.

After she got Alex settled with toys to occupy his mind, she called Scott.

"Calm down. I'll get a flight out of New York as soon as possible. I will be home early in the morning."

"I don't think it would be safe for you to come here. I am afraid of what this crazy person will do next. The idiot threatened me and told me to move far away or take the consequences. Are you involved with another woman?"

"Hell no, I am not involved with another woman. The person who wrote that letter probably does not know either of us. Some folk get their kicks out of playing pranks and scaring others. This crazy person wants to scare you."

"The letter sounded very convincing. I am afraid this person will harm Alex."

"Stop worrying; I will find out who wrote that letter. I'll see you tomorrow morning."

After she hung up the phone, she called Emily and explained why she would be unable to meet her in Atlanta the next day.

Emily felt disappointed. She could not understand who would threaten Olivia. She asked Olivia to keep in touch and let her know what happened.

The next morning while Olivia cooked breakfast, the doorbell rang, and Olivia froze. She slowly made her way to the door and peeped out before she unlocked the door. She fell into Scott's arms and cried. He comforted her and explained that he would find out who had sent that threatening letter; he did not want her to worry another minute.

Scott went to Alex's room and got him up to eat breakfast. Alex kept him busy answering questions about New York. After they finished eating, Alex ran outside to play.

Olivia discussed moving to another city; she wanted to keep Alex safe. She could not have a peaceful moment until she felt safe.

Scott pulled her into his arms and tried to kiss her, but she pushed him away and went to the porch to check on Alex.

Scott followed her and tried to talk to her; he did not want her to move.

She ignored Scott and called Alex to come into the house.

Scott took a bath and dressed to go to work. He told her he did not have time to stay and eat lunch. He carried them to McDonalds, Alex's favorite fast food restaurant. They had an early lunch and Scott left to go to his office.

The next morning after breakfast, Olivia asked Scott to stay at his place until he found out who had written her that letter. She feared for his safety, also.

He refused to stay away from her. If Steve Brinson failed to discover who threatened Olivia, he planned to give the letter to the authorities and let them handle the criminal.

Olivia begged him not to go to the authorities. She feared they would print and spread details about her personal life in newspapers and on television. Gossip about her would ruin Alex.

He tried to make her see that their safety meant more than anything else. No one had a right to scare her and run her away from her home. Besides, their personal life should not concern anyone else.

How could she stop worrying? She would not feel safe until she moved away from Boulder Bluff.

After Scott left, Olivia thought about what he had said. Scott had money; he had millions, but she did not want him to spend his money for nothing. How could a private detective find out who had written that letter?

As Scott drove to work, he worried about Olivia's emotional state of mind. He also wanted to keep his good reputation as a successful businessman, but her safety meant more to him than a bad reputation.

When Scott got to work, he called a meeting with his supervisors, went over production for that week, and took inventory to determine what he needed to fill orders for the shipments going out the next week.

After the meeting, he went back to his office to call Detective Brinson. Before he finished dialing his number, his secretary buzzed him to pick up line one.

Scott refused to take the call; but his secretary convinced him that he should take emergency calls.

With Olivia's safety in mind, Scott quickly picked up the phone and said, "This is Scott Porter speaking."

"Scott, darling, your voice is like a dream come true," she said with a British accent.

"Who is this?" he said.

"Never mind who I am," she said. "Listen to what I have to say."

"Scott came forward in his chair." If you want money, you are out of luck, my dear," he said.

"I don't want money from you; I want to ruin your perfect little reputation."

"I don't have time for idiots and prank calls," Scott said.

"Don't hang up that phone," she said. "If you value your good name and your business, you will listen to what I have to say. I know about your affair with Olivia Bradford. If you continue living with her, I will tell all of your rich friends as well as the entire congregation at the Baptist church just how damn sorry you are and ---"

Before she finished her threats, Scott slammed the phone down and looked at it with a furrowed brow. Olivia had been right; the woman sounded like a nut case. Her laugh still pierced his ears; and her accent threw him for a loop. She had obviously changed her voice to conceal her identity. He leaned back in his chair with thought. Why had this crazy woman threatened Olivia and tried to blackmail him?

Steve Brinson answered his phone right away. He did not like to discuss cases on the phone and made an appointment to see Scott the next day. He had to leave his office after lunch to take his wife to the doctor.

When Scott got home that evening, Alex ran to him for a hug. Scott picked him up and said, "I bought you a surprise in New York, but I forgot to give it to you. Go look in the front seat of my truck."

Alex's eyes grew wide with excitement. He squirmed from Scott's hold and ran out the front door. He came back with a broad smile and held his bright red dump truck up for Olivia to see. "Look what Daddy brought me, Mother."

"That is a nice dump truck. Do you want to take me for a ride?"

"Mother, I cannot take you for a ride in a dump truck; I haul sand and rocks in my dump truck."

Olivia and Scott laughed as Alex ran out the back door to his sand pile.

Scott did not want to tell Olivia about the threatening phone call he got; but he felt that he must tell her. He put his arms around her and said, "The letter you got came from a woman."

"How do you know it was a woman?" she said.

"I got a threatening phone call from a woman," he said.

"This woman is crazy! We must think of Alex's safety. We must not see each other again until this lunatic is stopped." Olivia felt as if the woman watched and waited for Scott to leave home each day.

"I have an appointment with Steve Brinson tomorrow. He is the best private detective in Georgia. He will find out who this idiot is and why she threatened us."

"He cannot find this woman," she said. "I am going out of my mind."

"Stop worrying and let's enjoy this night together. You and Alex can go to my place and stay," he said.

"We will definitely not stay at your place."

"I'm not going to let a lunatic control our lives," he said. "Let's go to town and pick up something for dinner."

"I'm not going out in public with you. Do you want to get us killed? I don't feel safe with you near me; I don't feel safe when you are away."

Scott finally talked her into going with Alex and him to get dinner.

Alex got excited when they crossed the bridge near the house. "Look at the water, Daddy. Mama brings me here to watch the water falling on the rocks."

"The waterfall fascinates him," Olivia said. "During the summer, young folk stand on the huge rocks and dive into the lake. At times like this, I feel like diving from one of those huge rocks and disappearing forever."

"Mama? If you disappear, Daddy and I will find you."

Scott laughed and said, "Mama talks foolish sometimes. She knows we would go find her."

Olivia did not want to disappear; she wanted Scott to marry her; she wanted them to be a happy family who took vacations together and went out to public places without being ridiculed. Most of all, she wanted to feel safe and secure.

"I am afraid and unhappy; I do not know how much longer I can live like this."

"Daddy makes me happy," Alex said. "He takes us places and buys me toys."

Scott looked at Olivia with concern and said, "I will put a stop to this harassment. Stop worrying."

"Daddy, what does harassment mean? Is harassment a big hairy animal? Is it a monster?"

"Harassment is a monster that daddy will stop before it knocks our door down."

The next day, Scott went to Steve Brinson's Private Detective Agency. Many blue moons in June had passed since Scott hired Steve. After his father's death, Scott hired a truck driver from another country. Thankfully, Steve found that the employee had a clean record.

Steve's office, like other older buildings, in the middle of the city had no elevator. Scott climbed stairs to the third floor and entered a large office paneled with knotty pine. Lights hung on heavy chains from high ceilings and shed light on antique furniture, a large wooden desk, and wooden filing cabinets that shined like a mirror. On one side of the room, a book case with leather bound law books reached the ceiling. A smaller book case on the opposite wall held other bound books and magazines that looked undisturbed.

Steve looked up from his paper work, pushed his chair back, and stood to shake Scott's hand. "Good to see you, Scott. You should visit more often."

Scott explained that he lived with Olivia Bradford and they had a son. She got a threatening letter that ordered her to stay away from him or take the consequences. Then he got a phone call from a woman who threatened to tell all of his friends and the congregation at his church that he lived with a tramp and she had a bastard son for him.

Steve asked if he looked at his caller identification when she called.

Scott explained that the call came from an unknown number.

Steve believed the woman wanted money. He asked Scott if Olivia would suffer a great loss if this woman made their affair public.

Olivia's reputation concerned Scott. He feared that she and his son, as well, would suffer from the public display of their lives. He added that he would be willing to pay the woman to keep her mouth shut.

Steve advised him to never bend to the demands of a blackmail scheme. This woman would drain his bank account dry and start on his property. He suggested that a tap installed on their phones would enable him to record calls and pin-point her location and identity. Then he could have her arrested for her harassment. He added that she would not stand a chance in court; judges did not cater to anyone who tried to blackmail innocent citizens.

Scott needed to know his enemies. He wanted Steve to take the necessary steps to catch the crazy bitch.

Steve advised him not to take another call from the woman until he got the wire taps installed on his phones.

Scott thanked Steve and asked him to give him a call when he got ready to install the wire taps.

On the way back to his office, Scott called Joseph and asked him if he could meet him at the club for lunch. He could talk with Joseph about Olivia, because he knew about Scott's personal life.

Scott and Joseph got to the club at the same time. After they ordered dinner, Scott talked about his trouble and his visit with Steve Brinson.

Joseph agreed with Steve; the woman wanted money. He knew of no enemies Scott had in that town or the church. In fact, everybody liked Scott and had good things to say about him.

Scott explained that he did not want Olivia or Alex to suffer; and he did not want to lose his business nor his friends.

Joseph assured him that real friends would try to understand his situation; they would certainly not turn against him.

Scott disagreed with Joseph. He knew exactly how Christians reacted to situations like his. The church members usually expected sinners to confess their sins and make amends. Since Scott had done neither, he did not expect them to accept his situation; but he could not live without Olivia and Alex. He intended to continue living with them. He loved them; they were his reason for living, and he wanted to be with them the rest of his life. Besides, he felt responsible for their safety.

Back at his office, Scott' secretary, Jan, buzzed and informed him that a woman called from an unknown number and would not give her name.

Scott refused to take the call and asked his secretary to tell the woman that he had gone home for the day.

This woman's blackmail scheme did not make sense. She committed a crime when she threatened Olivia and him. If she did not want money, she must have other more important reasons for ruining him.

As the day wore on, Scott had sudden insight. Laura's Mother and her sister, Lisa, blamed him for Laura's accident. They accused him of encouraging Laura's hiking trips. He should have asked her to stay at home; he should have gone with her.

Scott did not argue with them; he ignored them; but he had never neglected Laura. He had paid a big price for Laura to have the best of care since her accident. He should remind them that they had never paid one dime on Laura's care; he had spent more money than they would see in their entire life. What could they possibly gain by ruining him?

That evening when he got home, Olivia seemed more content. He sat down at the table with her and his son. They enjoyed the delicious meal she had cooked and had a peaceful night. Scott did not tell her about the call he refused to take from that crazy woman.

CHAPTER TWENTY-ONE

Caught on Tape

THE NEXT MORNING, Steve Brinson came to Scott's office with his equipment to record his phone calls. Afterwards, he installed wire taps on Scott and Olivia's home phones. He explained how the machine recorded messages and the location of the caller. He stressed the importance of stalling the caller to allow time to get the location of the call.

Alex stayed right under his Daddy and watched everything Steve Brinson did as he worked on their phone.

After Steve and Scott left, Alex asked a thousand questions that Olivia could not answer. He must ask his daddy, since she knew nothing about wires and machines. Neither did she tell him why Mr. Brinson installed wire taps on their phones.

Olivia felt better about having equipment to record the anonymous caller's conversation. On the other hand, what could she do after she learned the caller's identity? She did not want to go to the authorities and tell them the details of her life.

That weekend, Scott and Olivia thought the prank calls had ended. Scott grilled hamburgers Friday night, because Alex liked to help him cook. On Saturday, they went out to dinner; on Sunday, they carried a picnic lunch to the park. Alex had fun swinging, climbing, and playing with the other children.

Back at the office on Monday, Scott met with the foreman over each department as usual. His secretary interrupted the meeting and asked him to pick up the phone in the conference room. When Scott asked who had called, his secretary told him Ned Levine, the head supervisor over the sewing room needed to talk to him right away.

Scott picked up the phone and Ned complained about a machine on line three that he could not repair; and Mr. Walton, the repair man, had taken the day off.

Scott assured him that he would contact Mr. Walton and get the machine repaired before the end of the day.

The week passed and neither Scott nor Olivia got a threatening message from the crazy woman. They spent a wonderful weekend with Alex at the beach.

After Scott left for work the next Monday, the phone rang and Olivia let it ring four times before picking up. The caller identification indicated an unknown number.

"Hello, bitch!" the voice said.

Too shocked to reply, Olivia remained silent.

"Bitch, are you still there?"

Surprised by her courage, Olivia blurted, "Who is this?"

"You don't know me; but I know you! You are a stupid whore!" the voice screamed. I warned you to part ways with your sweet Scott; but you spent the weekend with him."

"What do you want from me?" Olivia said.

"If you value your life and the life of that bastard child of yours, you will leave Scott Porter alone. He is married! You should know by now that he will never marry you. Are you stupid?"

"I am not stupid!" Olivia shouted; but you are a coward! Are you afraid to tell me your name?"

"I am sure you can find out my name," she said. "Your rich boyfriend has enough money to get anything he wants. "How much does he pay you every week? Do you work by the week or the hour?"

"You are insane!" Olivia said.

"Where is your son?" the woman said.

"My son has gone to visit his grandparents," Olivia lied.

"I did not call to talk about your little bastard," she said. I called to tell you that Scott Porter tells lies. I would suggest that you and your son move to another state for your own safety."

Olivia slammed the phone down and ran to check on Alex. She found him sleeping peacefully. She sat down on the edge of his bed and kissed him.

Back in the kitchen, Olivia got a cup of coffee, sat down at the table, and pulled her cell phone from her pocket. Scott had not had time to get to work, yet. She did not want to call her mother and listen to her warnings and accusations. She put her cell phone on the table and worried. Was Scott having an affair with that crazy woman? She had called her a bitch; she had called her son a bastard. She should have cursed the woman; but she had been too frightened to defend herself or her son.

When Alex came into the kitchen to eat breakfast, he noticed his mother crying. He ran over to her, patted her back and said, "What is wrong, Mother? Did the monster peep in the window and scare you?"

"I am not afraid," she said. "Are you ready for breakfast?"

"First, I will go outside and chase the monster away." He walked out the back door and she watched as he stood on the porch, waved his arms, and spoke to the monster. When he came back into the kitchen, he said, "The monster ran away. He is afraid of me."

At eight thirty, Olivia called Scott; but he had gone to a meeting. She hung up and called Joseph.

"Your voice is like a nice piece of music," Joseph said. "How are things going?"

"I am not singing," Olivia said. "I got a threatening call from the crazy woman this morning. Scott is in a meeting and I am afraid to let Alex go outside to play."

"Keep your doors locked. I will come over and check things out." Joseph said, and he left his office immediately.

Olivia felt safe after Joseph got there. Alex ran to him with laughter and said, "Mother, Uncle Joe is here."

Joseph picked Alex up, gave him a hug, and said, "You are getting big. Let me see those muscles."

Alex wiggled from his arms, jumped down, and pumped his arm to show his muscle. Then he held his hand up for a high five and dashed off to his room to play.

Joseph stayed and had lunch with Olivia and Alex. When he started to leave, he reminded her to keep her doors locked. He assured her that the crazy woman who called her likely made prank call every day to people she did not know.

After the meeting, Scott found a note on his desk to call Joseph Harrington.

Joseph explained that Olivia got a threatening phone call. He had gone over to check on her and Alex. She seemed calm when he left.

Scott thanked Joseph, hung up and called Olivia. He told her he would be home within an hour.

Before Scott got on his coat to leave, his secretary buzzed and told him he had a call on line one.

The woman called his name with that same British accent and asked if he had given any thought to getting his life straight.

Scott took his time with his reply; he wanted the machine to trace the location of her call.

"Are you still there?" the woman said.

Scott told her that he lived one day at a time and tended to his own business. He advised her to do the same and asked why his personal life interested her.

His remark made her angry; she screamed that she knew about his dirty secret, and she would make her and his bastard son disappear.

Scott declared that she must be a witch with magical powers. Then he asked how much money she wanted.

Once again, she told him that she did not want his money and repeated her threat.

Scott warned her that she had committed a criminal offense by her threats; and the Georgia Bureau of Investigation would knock on her door soon.

With disregard for his words, she bluntly asked if he loved that whore he lived with.

He insisted that his personal life should not concern her; and he hung up.

When Steve Brinson told him the name and address of the anonymous caller, Scott got angry. He had suspected Laura's sister, Lisa, from the beginning; but he did not understand why she had threatened him, Olivia, and his son.

After turning questions in his mind, he realized that Lisa had loved him since he dated her in high school. She had always been jealous of Laura. Now she wanted to kill Olivia and his son.

Scott left Adam Sinclair in charge of closing the plant and went with Steve Brinson to pay Lisa Cane a visit.

When Lisa opened her door and saw Scott with Steve Brinson, she tried to close the door; but Scott put his foot against the door, pushed it open, and walked into her house with Steve close behind him.

She moved fast feet behind them and told them to get out of her house. They ignored her and looked around the living room before taking choice seats.

"Who do you two think you are? I have not invited you to come into my home."

"I am Scott Porter and this is Detective Steve Brinson."

"I know who you are, stupid."

"I am not quite as stupid as you think, and Mr. Brinson is a damn genius."

Steve laughed as he pulled the small recorder from his pocket and turned on the speaker.

When Lisa Cane heard her voice and the threats she had made to Olivia Bradford and Scott Porter, her eyes widened with fear and she looked as if she might faint, but she tried to bluff them.

"What does your stupid machine prove?" she said.

Steve informed her that his stupid machine could put her in prison for life if Scott pressed charges against her for attempted murder and blackmail. He told her to listen carefully to the threats she made to Scott and Olivia Bradford. He added that the judge may be interested in a letter she had written to Olivia Bradford with additional threats.

"Get out of my house," she said.

Steve stood up and told her that Scott would press charges against her and she would be arrested before sundown. He had come with Scott as a witness and she could not deny the charges.

She broke down and tears streamed down her face as she looked at Scott and asked how he could treat her poor helpless sister with such disrespect.

Scott expressed his love for Laura and provisions he made for her to have the best of care; and he would continue to provide for her the rest of her life. However, Laura could no longer respond to him or communicate with him; she did not know him or anyone else; he did not believe his relationship with Olivia Bradford hurt Laura. In fact, he believed that Laura would want him to have a life.

Steve spoke up and asked Lisa what she planned to do.

She pulled a Kleenex from the box on the end table, blew her nose, and held her head down as she spoke, "I won't call Scott or Olivia Bradford again. I want Scott to apologize for his disrespect toward my family and me; he had chosen to live with another woman, and he is still married to my sister, who has no say in the matter."

Scott wanted to slap Lisa. He stood up and pointed his finger in her face as he spoke, "I will never apologize to you for anything I choose to do. You are an idiot!"

Steve warned her to tend to her own business. He added that she must not tell lies or spread gossip in any form, shape, or fashion about Scott, Olivia, or their son, Alex. Otherwise, he would file a complaint with the authorities.

At the door, Steve bid her a good day; but Scott had nothing more to say to the bitch. He wanted to call her a bitch outright; but he left well enough alone and tipped his hat to her as he walked out the door.

Steve bragged that this case had been easier to solve than he thought it would be. Then he asked Scott why his own sister-in-law wanted to blackmail him and ruin his reputation.

Scott believed that Lisa's jealousy made her threaten Olivia and him. He had been out with Lisa a few times during their high school years, but they never went steady and he had no special feelings for her. Then he met her sister, Laura and fell in love with her on the first date. Since that time, Lisa had hated him and kept her distance from him. When by chance they ran into each other, Lisa cut him down with smart remarks. After he asked Laura to marry him, Lisa refused to be in her own sister's wedding. She never visited Laura, unless she knew that he would not be there.

Steve believed that Lisa wanted his attention. He added that a jealous woman with revenge on her mind was worse than getting stung by a nest full of wild hornets.

Scott thought they had made Lisa lose her stinger.

Olivia felt relieved when Scott told her the news. She had been unable to get a good night's sleep since the crazy woman threatened her. Tonight, she snuggled close by Scott's side and slept better than she had slept in months.

When summer came, things seemed normal again. Lisa stopped her threats and let them live in peace. Scott stayed busy with his business and trips out of town; Olivia stayed busy caring for Alex, cooking, washing, and house work.

Olivia felt happy and safe. Her happiness showed in everything she did with Scott and Alex. She still wanted Scott to marry her. She wanted them to live like other families; she didn't want to feel ashamed when they went to public places. She wanted to bring her son up the way he should go and take him to church on Sunday with Scott sitting by her side.

Alex looked forward to the birthday party his mother promised him in September. He would soon be four years old; and he felt grown. He asked Olivia every day how many more days before his birthday.

CHAPTER TWENTY-TWO

House Fire

THE GRANDFATHER CLOCK struck twelve times at midnight and awoke Olivia. She felt the other side of the bed and realized that Scott had not come home, yet. When she heard Alex crying, her heart fell. She rushed across the hall to his bedroom and saw smoke boiling up the stairs. She grabbed Alex from his bed, ran down stairs and called the fire department. Flames whipped the ceiling as she edged her way to the door.

As Scott drove toward Olivia's, a loud siren and flashing lights startled him. He pulled to the side of the road for the fire truck to pass; it disappeared over the hill and Scott broke the speed limit to discover its destination.

When Scott topped the hill, he stretched his eyes with shock at the flames that licked Olivia's house. He felt as if his heart would literally beat out of his body. He skidded the wheels and jack-knifed his truck as he came to a halt. He went crazy with worry about Olivia and Alex. He jumped out of his truck and screamed her name as he groped his way through the thick smoke toward the house. Firemen surrounded the house and high streams of water fell on the flames. The smell of burning rubber made him sick. Before he got to the steps, flames had spread from the backside to the front porch. He started to run through the flames when two firemen pulled him back to safety. He fought them and shouted, "Olivia and my son are in that house. I have to save them."

When Olivia fell into his arms and he felt Alex's small hand on his face, he grabbed them in a tight hug.

"Mama, where is Jasper? We have to go find Jasper."

Scott tried to console him. "Jasper probably ran into the woods to feel safe. He will come back tomorrow."

"Jasper won't have a house when he comes back! He will run far away."

"We will come back and look for Jasper tomorrow," Scott said.

Olivia cried as they stood together and watched the flames swallow everything they had. "What will we do? Where will we live? We have no clothes; we have nothing. I need my robe."

Scott pulled off his coat, wrapped it around her shoulders. Clothes nor the house mattered to him. He thanked God that Olivia and Alex got out of the house alive.

"Lisa wants us dead," Olivia said. "That lunatic set my house on fire and tried to kill us. I will never feel safe again as long as I live near that crazy woman."

He tried to convince her to move into the house with him, but she refused. She feared that Lisa would burn his house, too.

One of the firemen walked over and said, "Miss, I straight switched your car and saved it. I parked it across the road."

"Thank you so much," Olivia said. "At least we have a way to travel."

The fire Chief believed the fire started under the floor near the middle. He explained that fires usually started from flaws in electrical wires or appliances. They would know more about the cause of the fire when they got the fire inspectors' report. The firemen would stay there several hours to keep the fire from spreading to the trees behind the house. Before he walked away, he ruffled Alex's hair and said, "I am happy that your son and wife got out alive. They are lucky."

Scott thanked him for the good job his firemen did to save his family and get the fire under control.

As the fire chief walked toward his truck, he turned back to Scott and said, "Be careful about walking under those burned rafters." Then he turned to the group of firemen and said, "Boys, I will see you in the morning. I'm going on to the house."

Scott finally convinced Olivia to follow him to Joseph's house. He had a furnished garage apartment that his son, wife, and two children stayed in when they visited. Joseph would be happy for them to stay there as long as they wanted to stay.

Joseph welcomed Olivia and Alex. They followed him across his lawn to the back side of his house, where the neat apartment set on a two car garage. They climbed the stairs and Alex got a head start. Then he jumped from one step to the next toward them. Scott scolded him and he walked back up the steps.

Inside the apartment, Alex ran from one room to another. He announced that the house looked cool and he liked it. Uncle Joe had put toys in the bedroom for him to play with and he had a television like the one in his room at home.

Joseph picked Alex up and swung him around. He told Alex that he could watch cartoons on television and the stuffed animals could sleep with him to keep him safe.

"Thanks, Uncle Joe," Alex said and dashed off to his bedroom. He had always called Joseph his uncle, and this made Joseph proud.

After they got Alex settled, Olivia and Scott followed Joseph back to the living room.

Joseph suspected that Lisa Cane set fire to Olivia's house and urged Scott to file charges against her.

Scott wanted to file a complaint, but they had no proof that Lisa set the fire.

Joseph told them to call him if they needed anything and he would see them later.

After Joseph left, they went to bed, but Olivia cried most of the night.

The next morning, Scott carried them to I-Hop for breakfast. Afterwards, they carried Alex to spend the day with his grandparents. Scott promised him they would find Jasper.

Mr. and Mrs. Hollister had heard the bad news, but they wanted to know the details about the fire.

Olivia knew nothing about how the fire started, but the fire destroyed everything they had.

Her mother insisted that she and Alex move in with them. Olivia turned down her offer and explained that she wanted to rent an apartment until she found a house to buy.

Olivia's mother offered to go with her to shop for clothes, but Scott had already taken the day off to go with her.

After they left Olivia's parents, they went to the mall and shopped for clothes and other things they needed. Then they went back to the burned house to find Jasper and look over the damage. The fire completely destroyed the rooms on the left side of the ground floor and damaged the adjoining rooms beyond repair. Smut buried the furniture and the entire contents of the house.

Scott pointed out that the burned rafters looked dangerous. They quickly darted around the burned rubble and went back outside. Olivia called to Jasper as they searched the woods behind the house. Minutes later, Jasper came from a clump of bushes and ran to her. She sensed his fear by the way he clung to her with his claws. She cuddled him to her breast and soothed him with words to calm his fright.

Scott opened the truck door and pulled her close as he spoke, "I am glad we found Jasper. Alex loves that cat."

"Alex wants a dog, too; I promised him a puppy when he gets old enough to take care of it."

As they drove back to her parents to get Alex, Olivia thought about moving to another town far away from Lisa Cane. She asked Scott if she could move into his house in Brunswick.

Scott complained about the distance from his business. He could not drive seventy five miles two ways each day; and he wanted to live with them. They could live with him for the time being, and move to Brunswick after he retired. They could not spend the rest of their lives running from Lisa Cane; he intended to show that bitch that he had rights, especially the right to a life with his son and the woman he loved.

Olivia tried to make him realize the danger of moving into the house with him. Lisa Cane would kill them all. She wanted revenge for her sister, because Scott cheated on Laura.

Scott argued that he had not cheated on Laura. She merely existed from one day to the next, and he only paid for her care. He assured Olivia that she and Alex would like living with him. After all, he wanted to marry her very soon.

Olivia did not want to hear any more of his promises. They could not get married until he divorced Laura. If Lisa Cane kept interfering, Scott would never be free. Right now she wanted to get settled again for Alex's sake and her sanity.

Alex ran to them when they pulled into the drive. When Olivia got out with Jasper in her arms, Alex ran to her and happily danced around with excitement. He took Jasper and held him as they walked back into the house to thank her parents for keeping Alex and tell them good bye.

The next day, Scott got up early. He wanted her to rest. He often stopped at McDonalds on the way to work and picked up breakfast.

Olivia got up at eight and fixed breakfast for Alex. She felt lost in Joseph's kitchen, but she had bought groceries and had everything she needed to cook several meals.

After breakfast, Alex called to Jasper and went to his bedroom to watch cartoons, while Olivia washed the dishes and made the beds. Her cell phone interrupted her house chores, and she quickly answered thinking Scott had called to check on her and Alex.

"Olivia, are you alright?" Tom's familiar voice shocked her to silence.

"Olivia, are you still there?"

"I am still here," she said.

"I heard that your house burned and I wanted to make sure that you and your son were alright."

"I lost everything in the fire; but I am thankful that Alex and I got out alive."

"Olivia, if you need anything at all, please call me. I still care about you and I wish you would at least consider being my friend and keep in touch. After you hang up, you will have my new phone number. Please call me."

"Thank you for your concern, Tom; but I live with Scott now. We have our son, Alex, to think about."

"Where are you staying since your house burned?" Tom said.

"Alex and I are staying with one of Scott's friends until I find another house."

"I wish you well, Olivia. I will be in touch."

Tom hung up and Olivia stood in a stupor and looked at her phone. She wondered who kept Tom informed about her. Did her mother call Tom? Why did her mother keep trouble stirred for her? If Scott knew about Tom's call, what could he say? He had a wife, and her needs came first. He had no right to say anything to her about talking to her ex-husband.

That evening when Scott got home, she had supper cooked. He laughed and joked with Alex; but Olivia had nothing to laugh about. Joseph would not take any money for rent, and she hated to impose on him any longer.

Scott promised to go with her to look at apartments the next weekend.

CHAPTER TWENTY-THREE
Snoopy Landlord

LENA STEWART SAT in her rocker, fanned gnats, and watched the busy traffic in front of her house.

When Scott Porter walked up the steps with Olivia and Alex, Mrs. Stewart pushed her glasses down on her nose, and cast a hard glance at them. She mentioned that she had not seen Scott in years and commented on the handsome little boy. She said nothing to Olivia.

Scott asked to see the apartment she had advertised for rent.

Mrs. Stewart wiped the sweat from her face with the wadded Kleenex in her hand, pushed her glasses back in place, and asked who wanted to rent the apartment.

Scott introduced Olivia as his friend who needed to rent a furnished apartment. He explained that her house recently burned and she lost everything.

Lena Stewart twisted her fingers nervously and asked Olivia who would be living with her.

Olivia quickly informed her that her son, Alex, would be living with her.

Mrs. Stewart explained that she and her sister, Mary, lived in the house all alone; and she had rules that her tenants must follow. Visitors must come and go at decent hours. She did not allow tenants to throw parties or have company after eleven o'clock at night. She added that a single woman with a child had no business entertaining men in the first place.

Scott flashed $60.00 for advance rent and Lena Stewart grabbed the money quicker than a frog grabs a fly. She got up from her rocker, opened the door, and asked them to follow her.

As they walked down the long hallway, the smell of Vicks Salve spread a clean, medicinal smell around them. They passed a large sitting room furnished with antique furniture; an oriental rug partially covered the pine hardwood floor that shined like a mirror. They moved on past a large room near the back of the house and saw an old lady with thick, gray hair stacked on her head. She sat in a padded, high back, cane rocker and rubbed her crooked fingers as if trying to pry them open.

Mrs. Stewart turned to them and complained that her sister, Mary, stayed in that dark room most of the time. She came to the table for her meals and went back to her chair.

She unlocked the door on the left at the end of the hall, and they walked into a large living room furnished with a leather sofa and two armchairs. Then they followed her to a small kitchen with an adjoining breakfast room. Next, they walked back across the living room and entered a large bedroom with double windows covered by shades. Mrs. Stewart raised the shades and light fell on a double iron bed that centered the wall to the right. A white rocking chair with a red velvet padded seat sat next to the bed. The opposite wall held a white chest and dresser with antique gold trim. Next to the bedroom, she showed them a large bathroom with a bathtub supported by four curved legs. Next to the tub, a sink leaned to one side as if propped with a stick; the mirror above the sink sat out from the wall and made it impossible to lean over the sink without bumping one's head. On the other wall, a rusty commode with a round knob handle made a leaky noise that came from the tank. Last of all, they entered a small bedroom furnished with a bunk bed and a small chest. The room had no windows, but it looked clean.

Olivia had lived in luxury compared to the apartment; but she wanted to get Alex settled. She hated to impose on Joseph. She took the apartment; but she did not plan to live there longer than necessary.

Mrs. Stewart went to her side of the house, and Scott helped Olivia move what little she had bought into the apartment. Since they had no groceries, Scott offered to take them out to eat that night. He promised to be back by seven o'clock.

Alex had already looked out the back windows and saw that the backyard had no slide, swing, monkey bars, or sand box with toys like he had at his other home. He did not like the apartment.

Olivia tried to get him in a better mood; she promised him that they would soon move into a nice house with a big back yard; and she would buy him toys to play with like the ones he had at the other house.

Before Olivia got settled in the apartment, Lena Stewart called Christine Wimberley, Scott's mother-in-law, to tell her the news. Scott Porter rented an apartment from her for his woman, Olivia Bradford. She had a son named Alex. Scott had paid the woman's rent in advance.

Christine Wimberley called Scott some dirty names. She asked Lena Stewart to keep her informed and thanked her for being a dear friend. Then she asked if she minded her paying Olivia Bradford a visit; she had a few things to say to that piece of trash.

Olivia expected Scott at seven that evening. She heard a commotion on the front porch and peeped out the window to see if Scott had gotten there early. To her surprise, Mrs. Stewart walked around in the yard.

Olivia did not like the nosy woman. She flung the curtain down with anger and worried. Minutes later, the door slammed and Olivia took a relaxed breath.

An hour later, Scott knocked on Olivia's door. Her heart took a shallow dip when his eyes met hers. She pressed a hush finger to her lips and looked down the hall as she tugged at his sleeve to come inside. He grabbed her, swung her around, and told her how much he loved her. Then Alex pulled at his arm and asked Scott if he loved him, too. He squatted before Alex and took him into his arms with a tight hug.

The pounding at the door startled them. Olivia opened the door to find Mrs. Stewart with wide eyes of curiosity. She explained that she had heard a man's voice and came to see if they were alright.

Alex ran to the door with excitement and told Mrs. Stewart that his daddy came to take them out to dinner.

Mrs. Stewart apologized; she claimed that she did not recognize Scott's voice.

Olivia slammed the door in her face and listened to her steps fade across the hall. Then she turned to Scott and complained. She could not live there with that nosey woman coming over to check on them each time he came to visit.

They went out to eat supper, rode around town, and returned to the apartment by nine. Scott walked Olivia to her door and waited for her to turn on the lights. He kissed her and Alex good night and told Olivia to keep her door locked. He had to go back to his office and catch up on his paperwork.

Before Scott reached the front door, Mrs. Stewart met him and questioned his being there. He told her she had no business keeping tabs on him, and Olivia would find another place to live the next day.

Mrs. Stewart eyed him like a dog grading his bone and changed her tune. She did not want Olivia to move out; she heard him walk down the hall and thought an intruder had broken into the house. She added that he should visit before nine o'clock at night.

He told her she should go back to her side of the house and stay there if she wanted Olivia to rent the apartment.

By this time, Olivia and Alex had heard the commotion and joined Scott.

Mrs. Stewart looked at them in their huddle and went back to her apartment.

Alex wanted to know why the mean old lady said bad things to his daddy.

Scott squatted in front of Alex, hugged him, and told him not to pay any attention to the old lady. He asked him to take good care of his mother.

Alex smiled and showed Scott his muscles.

Scott kissed Olivia and told her he would call her the next day.

After Scott left, Olivia tucked Alex into bed and waited for him to say his prayer. She smiled when he asked God to take care of his Mama and Daddy, the familiar prayer he always said. Then he asked God to make that old lady leave his daddy alone. Olivia held her laughter and kissed him goodnight. At the door, she looked back at him and turned out his light.

Olivia finally fell asleep; but a loud noise awoke her. Her brain always felt fuzzy when she first awoke. She sat upright in bed and realized the noise came from the windows. "Scott, is that you?" she yelled, and the noise stopped. She moved to the edge of the bed; someone moved around in the room. Fear for Alex made her jump to her feet. She ran to his room, flipped on his light, and took him into her arms. Then she made her way to the outside door and ran down the hall to Mrs. Stewart's door.

Olivia's scream brought Mrs. Stewart to the door right away. Olivia told her someone had broken into her apartment through the bedroom window.

Mrs. Stewart told her she expected no less. After all, she practically lived with a married man.

Olivia wanted to knock Mrs. Stewart against the wall and beat her to a pulp, but she stood silent and held tightly to Alex.

Then Mrs. Stewart told her to sit in her living room until the cops came to check out her apartment.

Minutes later, officer Dan Purvis knocked on the door. Mrs. Stewart introduced him and explained that Olivia had heard an intruder in her apartment.

Officer Purvis followed Olivia and Alex to her apartment; Mrs. Stewart went back to her apartment as if nothing had happened.

The officer checked out every room. He found that both windows in her bedroom had been pried open with a crow bar.

Back in the living room, he sat on the couch and asked a dozen questions, including the time and exactly what she had heard and seen.

After the officer finished writing his report, he assured Olivia that he would keep a watch over her apartment the rest of the night, but she should have new locks put on her bedroom windows and her door.

Before closing the front door behind him, Officer Purvis warned Olivia that the intruder had not come for a friendly visit, and she should be careful.

Olivia thanked him and went back inside her apartment. She blocked the door with chairs and put Alex in bed with her.

Alex questioned her about the mean monster that came through the window.

Olivia assured him that the cops would catch the monster and lock him away.

Alex finally fell asleep, but Olivia lay wide-awake and worried the rest of the night.

The next morning when Scott called, Olivia told him about the intruder.

He promised to be there as soon as he could make the drive.

Scott could do nothing to help. She asked him to come have dinner with them that evening and spend the night with them.

He promised to be at her apartment at six thirty.

After she hung up, she went across the hall and asked Mrs. Stewart if she could borrow the Morning Star.

Mrs. Stewart reluctantly handed the newspaper and asked that she bring her paper back.

Olivia promised to bring the newspaper back and thanked her.

Back in her apartment, she sat at the kitchen table and searched the ads for a house. She finally found a three bedroom house that seemed suitable; any house would be better than this apartment. She called West Real Estate Agency and made an appointment.

She and Alex went to MacDonald's for breakfast and carried hamburgers home for dinner. As they ate, she explained to Alex that she could not give him a nice birthday party like she had promised but she and his daddy would buy him a cake and something special on his birthday.

Alex said, "How many days before I turn four years old?"

"Your birthday is next Saturday," she said.

"Can we go to Disney World for my birthday?"

"We have to find a house and move before we can celebrate your birthday. Maybe we can go to Disney World when you turn five."

"That will be cool," he said. "We will have a new house, too."

At two o'clock that evening, Olivia drove two miles beyond the city to the red brick two story house similar to her house that burned. Alex got excited when he saw the house. They pulled into the drive and Mrs. West pulled in behind them.

They followed Mrs. West up the steps and across a large front porch. They entered a foyer that led to a large living room on the right and bedrooms on the left. The large brick fireplace in the living room impressed Olive. Beyond the living room, a dining room and modern kitchen with a breakfast nook took her attention. She liked the cabinets and bar as well as the countertops that blended well with the beige tile. Then they walked down a hallway to a large family room with a beautiful staircase that led to three large bedroom upstairs. Each of the bedrooms had a bath room and walk-in closet.

As Mrs. West discussed the house and asking price, Olivia heard Alex shout, "Mother, come look at the back yard."

They walked out the back door, stood on the porch, and watched Alex as he ran around in the back yard. Olivia liked the tall chain link fence surrounding the yard.

When Scott got to the apartment late that evening, Olivia had supper waiting. Alex ran to him with the story about the monster. Scott assured Alex that the cops would catch the monster and break his fingers and toes. He should not worry another minute.

Alex laughed and quickly changed the subject to the house he and his mother visited. His eyes widened with excitement as he described the back yard.

Scott promised to build him a big sand box and buy him a dump truck just like the one he had.

Alex reminded his daddy that he would be four years old on his birthday.

Scott had not forgot his birthday. He already had his birthday present.

Alex wanted to know what he bought.

Scott explained that he could not tell him and spoil his birthday surprise.

Then Alex wanted to know what spoil meant.

Scott explained that spoil meant to mess thing up.

Alex still did not understand; but he changed the subject to the nice cake with candles his mother promised him and talked about going out to eat on his birthday. Then he bragged that his mother promised to take him to Disney World on his next birthday, when he turned five years old.

Scott asked if he could go with them to Disney World.

Alex smiled up at his daddy and said, "You can go with us, Daddy. You know we won't leave you at home," and he grabbed Jasper and went to his room.

Olivia explained that Mrs. West asked one hundred and seventy-five thousand for the house, but she would get more than one hundred and fifty thousand from the insurance on the burned house. She would only have to borrow twenty-five thousand plus the closing fee. She wanted to talk with him before she made her final decision.

Excitement in Olivia's voice told Scott that she wanted to buy the house. He thought she should call Mrs. West and ask her to hold the house for her. He offered to give her enough money to finish paying for the house and the closing cost.

She smiled and thanked him. She bragged on the floor plan and the large bedrooms. She liked everything about the house; but the yards looked a mess. She would worry about the outside after they moved into the house.

Before they finished eating, they heard a knock at the door.

Scott went to the door and jerked it back as if expecting Mrs. Stewart. Instead he faced Christine Wimberley, Laura's mother. Her dark eyes pierced him with hatred; but she asked if she could come inside to talk.

Olivia stared at the tall woman with curiosity. Her bleached blond hair and bright red lipstick did not compliment her fair skin.

Scott said, "Olivia, this is Laura's mother, Mary Wimberley. Then he said, this is Olivia Bradford."

Mrs. Wimberley moved a hand over her bleached blond hair and blinked her eyes with her reply, "I know who you are, Miss Bradford; and I cannot say that I am pleased to meet you." Then she turned to Scott and said, "I would like to speak to you in private."

"Anything you have to say to me; you can say in front of Olivia. We do not keep secrets from each other," Scott said.

Her fair skin turned red with her angry voice, "Mrs. Stewart tells me that you paid this woman's rent and practically live with her." Then she turned to Olivia and said, "Scott is still married to my daughter, Laura. You have no morals what-so-ever to be living with a married man. Worse yet, I understand that you have a child for him. Your cheap affair is a shame and disgrace to my family."

"Olivia is single; and I am a married man without a wife," Scott said.

"Scott, I have always admired you and cared deeply for you; but I can no longer tolerate your disrespect for my daughter and my family. When you married Laura, you took vows for better or worse, and you should keep those vows. I understand you have lived with this woman for several years."

"Mrs. Wimberley, have you given any serious thought to my situation? Have you considered that I have feelings and needs that Laura can never satisfy again? You know as well as I do that Laura will never recover; she will never recognize or speak to either of us again. I have remained married to Laura only because I feel responsible for her, and I pay for her to have the best of care."

"You do not care about Laura!" she said. "You have shamed Laura's good name with your adulterous affair."

"I love Olivia; and I love my son, Alex. As soon as Olivia gets moved into her new home, we will live together again as a family. You cannot control my life. What I do is none of your nor Lisa's business. Lisa has also threatened us. Worst yet, I believe she burned Olivia's home. She will likely be charged with a felony and serve time for her threats and harassment. I hired a lawyer and a private detective to uncover the dirt you and Lisa have spread about us. If either of you stick your noses in my affairs again, I will have you arrested."

Mrs. Wimberley called Scott a liar and accused him of adultery and neglect.

"Since you do not appreciate my generosity and concern for Laura, I will file for a divorce from Laura and leave you with the responsibility of caring for her. I would suggest that you walk out that door and forget everything you said; otherwise, my lawyer will contact you."

Mrs. Wimberley gave him a vicious stare and walked toward the door. He rushed ahead of her and said, "Here, let me get the door for you."

Olivia had tears in her eyes. She ran to Scott and he held her as she poured out her heart. "What are we going to do?"

Scott believed that Mrs. Wimberley encouraged Lisa to write the threatening letter to Olivia as well as harass them with threatening phone calls. Mrs. Wimberley hated Olivia, because she had given him a son and she could never call Alex her grandson. She took pleasure in Scott's misery, because her daughter suffered. He also believed that Lisa hated her sister.

Regardless of their crazy motives, Olivia feared for their lives. She expected them to continue their harassment.

Scott wanted her to call Mrs. West right away and close the deal on the house.

Alex asked if they could move into his new house tomorrow. He complained that he did not like the mean lady that lived across the hall, and he did not like the monster that came into his bedroom to scare him every night.

Scott hugged him and explained that his mother would have to pay for the house before they moved; but they would move soon. In the meantime, they could move into the house with him.

In addition to the threats from Laura's sister and mother, Olivia worried about Scott's friends and his business. Would they turn against him?

He took her in his arms and tried to make her feel at ease. His friends as well as his business were the least of his worries. He made no sales in Porterville; his shipments went to large cities all over the United States and foreign countries; he paid his employees decent salaries and treated them special; they liked working for him. Besides, his employees needed a job and could find no better place to work, especially those without an education.

Scott gathered them in a huddle and kissed them good night. He wanted them to go out for supper the next evening.

The next morning, the fire chief's report did not surprise Scott. An arsonist set the fire beneath Olivia's house. The electrical wiring had nothing to do with the fire.

Scott went to see Joseph immediately.

Joseph shook his head with disbelief. Lisa Cane's sociopathic behavior had convinced him that she took pleasure in Scott's pain and suffering; she would not stop until the authorities stopped her. He advised Scott to go to file a complaint against Lisa Cane for burning Olivia's house. He also advised Scott to cancel his business trips and stay close by Olivia and Alex until he could stop the lunatic. He added that she apparently wanted them dead.

Scott explained that the authorities would ask him to present proof that Lisa Cane set the fire and he had no proof.

Joseph reminded Scott of the threatening letter and phone calls from Lisa Cane. He believed the authorities would consider his evidence and at least question Lisa.

Scott finally admitted that he had not reported Lisa to the authorities, because he wanted to protect Olivia's reputation. The authorities would slap Olivia's name across the front page of the newspapers in Boulder Bluff and towns nearby; and everybody would spread gossip about her.

He asked Joseph to go with him to visit Lisa Cane the next day.

The next day, Scott picked Joseph up at his office at five o'clock. Scott pulled into Lisa Cane's drive, and Joseph waited in the car.

When Joseph heard Scott yelling, he got out and rushed into the house. He found Lisa sitting in an armchair with her legs kicking and her arms flying toward Scott as he slapped at her and cursed her. Joseph ran up behind Scott, grabbed his arms, and pulled him away from Lisa.

Scott went after Lisa again; he called her a crazy, psychotic bitch, and accused her of trying to kill Olivia and his son by setting fire to her house. He threatened to kill her if she tried to harm Olivia or his son again.

Lisa denied his accusations and swore that she had nothing to do with that house fire. She claimed that she had done anything to harm his whore and had never laid a finger on her.

Scott called her a lying dog and reminded her of the tapes he had with her harassing calls.

Lisa Cane stood and pointed a finger in his face. He had no proof that she set that house on fire and she would call the cops to him if he touched her again.

Scott laughed in her face, shoved his cell phone toward her, and begged her to call the cops.

When she moved away from him, he grabbed her in a choker and threatened her. She squirmed from his hold, ran to the door, opened it, and ordered him to get out of her house and take his lawyer friend with him.

Scott tried to grab her again; but Joseph pulled him back. Before going out the door, Scott threatened to take her to court if she came near him, Olivia, or his son again.

Lisa gave him an angry stare as he and Joseph walked out the door. Then she shouted that she would kill him if he ever came to her home again.

Scott started after her again; but she slammed the door and locked it.

Joseph finally urged Scott to get into the car; and Joseph drove back to his office. When he started to get out, he told Scott to call him if he needed him.

The next week, Olivia closed the deal on the new house, and Scott went with her to buy furniture. Olivia had a lot of work ahead of her, but she and Alex moved into their new home without curtains over the windows. Scott covered the windows with sheets until she could make curtains. She had already bought a new sewing machine and material to complete the project.

On Saturday, Olivia and Scott carried Alex to MacDonald's to celebrate his birthday. On the way, they stopped by the bakery and picked up the cake she had ordered. After they ate hamburgers and fries, Alex blew out his candles and made a wish. Alex shouted with excitement when he opened his present. "Thank you, Daddy. Look Mother! Look at my pretty red dump truck."

Two months later, Olivia had everything organized. Scott moved in with her and Alex; they once again lived in peace.

CHAPTER TWENTY-FOUR
Murder or Mercy

THE SHRILL SCREAM of an ambulance echoed through the city and continued to whine as it came to a halt before Hillcrest Manor. The red bowl whirled with flashes of light and bounced across the entrance of the nursing home as two men rushed down the walk-way and pushed a gurney through the double doors.

The head nurse walked out the door behind them, stood on the lawn, and watched as they rolled Laura Porter to the waiting ambulance.

At the St. Joseph's Hospital in Savannah, Laura's parents and Lisa Cane sat on one side of the room and Scott sat on the other. Lisa buried her face in her hands and shook with tears. Her mother got up and went to the restroom; she came back with wet towels and shoved them toward Lisa. Lisa pressed the towels to her face and held them there for minutes before looking around the waiting room.

Lisa's tears disgusted Scott. He could see through her act; and he despised her for more than one reason. She had always been jealous of Laura; yet, she put on a big show of sympathy each time she visited Laura at Hillcrest Manor.

Scott got up and walked down the hall; the thoughts of Laura dying stirred a knot in his chest. He wondered what had happened to her. He had visited her that evening and she seemed the same as usual. Other than the brain damage that caused her paralysis, she seemed healthy.

Scott reached the emergency room entrance and stood to wait for the doctor. He wanted to hear what he had to say about his wife, before he talked to her parents and her hateful sister, Lisa.

A few minutes later, Doctor Hawkins came through the door. He extended a warm hand to Scott; but he had bad news written on his face. He put a hand on Scott' shoulder and informed him that Laura had an overdose of valium.

Scott looked at the doctor with shock and disbelief as he spoke, "An overdose? You must be mistaken. How could Laura take an overdose? The nurses gave her all of her medication."

Doctor Hawkins explained that he had prescribed the valium to help Laura sleep; but Laura had enough of the drug in her blood to kill a horse. He had pumped her stomach; and ordered IV fluids; but he could make no promises for her recovery. He added that he had done all he could do, and the man upstairs must do the rest.

As the doctor walked toward the waiting room, Scott followed to see the reaction of the family to his words.

Lisa broke down and directed her loud accusation toward Scott, "Someone tried to kill my sister!"

Laura's mother turned accusing eyes on Scott, also; but she remained silent.

To Scott's shock and surprise, Mr. Wimberley walked over to him, patted his shoulder, and said, "Scott, you have always been good to Laura, and I appreciate everything you have done for her. I certainly do not blame you for her condition. I loved Laura more than anything on this earth, but she did not have a life after the accident. I want you to know that I understand your situation."

Lisa jumped up and shouted, "Dad, Mother is ready to go home. We cannot do anything for Laura. That overdose Scott gave her will probably kill her."

Mr. Wimberley patted Scott on the arm and said, "Don't pay any attention to Lisa; she is upset and doesn't know what she is saying."

Scott thanked Mr. Wimberley and turned away without a reply to Lisa's accusation; but he wanted to slap her out the front door.

As Scott drove toward the Holiday Inn, he turned angry thoughts about Lisa and Mrs. Wimberley. After all of their harassment, Lisa had the brass on her face to accuse him of trying to kill Laura. He wanted to set them straight. He had provided well for Laura. She had everything she needed to make her as comfortable as possible. He had spent a fortune since he put her in the Hillcrest Manor Nursing Home. How could they accuse him? He had loved Laura since their first date, and they had been happy before she had the accident. He still loved Laura in his own way; but he no longer loved her like a husband loves his wife. Olivia had helped him forget Laura; now he loved Olivia with all his heart.

When Olivia's phone rang at two o'clock in the morning, the sound of Scott's voice alarmed her.

He explained that Laura had been carried to St. Joseph's Hospital in Savannah, and he would be staying overnight in Savannah at the Holiday Inn. He asked her to meet him there as soon as she could make the drive. He needed her.

Olivia dreaded telling her mother about Scott's wife. She did not feel like hearing her mother's lecture. She also hated leaving Alex with her parents; but Scott needed her more than Alex needed her tonight.

Olivia packed their bags, while she braced her courage to call her mother. After she explained what had happened, her mother nagged her about the right thing to do. She had warned her that nothing good would come of her situation, but she never listened to her advice.

Olivia interrupted with her question, "Do you want Alex to come for a visit?"

Her mother stopped her nagging and said, "I am always happy to see my grandson. I would like for him to come live with us."

Olivia explained that she only needed her to keep Alex overnight, or a day or two at most. She hung up and went to awake Alex.

Alex got excited when she told him he could spend the night with his grandparents. He sat up on the edge of the bed and asked when.

When she said he could go right now, he got up, put on his bedroom shoes, and lay back down.

After Olivia finished packing their overnight bags, she went to the kitchen and left food for her cat, Jasper.

On the way to her parent's house, Alex went back to sleep. When Olivia stepped inside her parent's door, her mother met her with twenty questions to answer before she could get Alex settled. Just as she reached the door to leave, her father came into the living room. He wanted to know what Scott had done this time. Olivia told him that she would explain what had happened later; she had a long drive.

As she drove toward Savannah, she thought about her parents' attitude toward Scott. She hated for them to bad mouth him. On the other hand, she felt grateful to have a mother and father who loved and cared for Alex; they treated him special.

After Scott got to his hotel, he felt drained of energy. He tried to rest, but the doctor's words kept haunting him. He could not believe someone wanted Laura dead. Who would benefit? He could think of very little that Lisa or her mother had ever done for Laura, except bring flowers to her that she never noticed or smelled. If Laura died, they would blame him; and the authorities would name him as the number one suspect for her death. Her parents nor her sister would be suspects. He looked toward the heavens and said, "God, please don't let Laura die."

When Olivia got to Savannah, she went directly to the Holiday Inn. The girl at the desk directed her to the fifth floor; room 550.

Scott answered with the first knock. He grabbed her, held her tightly, and told her how much he loved her. Then he broke down with tears and his voice shook as he explained what had happened to Laura. She had an overdose of Valium and the doctor gave him no hopes for her recovery. Lisa had accused him of trying to kill Laura; but Laura's father, Mr. Wimberley, had actually been supportive and told him that he did not blame him for Laura's condition.

Olivia begged him to get some rest and stop worrying. She believed that the truth would come out and clear him of any wrong doing.

After Scott lay down; Olivia unpacked her bags, and took a bath. Back in the bedroom; she found Scott sound asleep. She wanted to talk to him, but she did not disturb him;

he needed the rest. She worried that he had not eaten supper. She had not eaten supper, either, but she had waited to hear from him. She called room service and order dinner.

While she waited for her dinner to arrive, she walked out on the patio and looked out at the explosion of lights falling on the city. The breeze hit her face, and she could smell freshly cut flowers. She spotted the source of the sweet smell; clematis grew on the post at the end of the terrace. She walked to the sliding door and stepped back into the hotel room. She looked at Scott and felt sad for him; he had called her to be with him for comfort and had fallen asleep.

The waiter finally came into the room with the rolling table filled with covered trays. He pushed the table to the center of the room and lifted the lid from a delicious looking dinner: roast beef, creamed potatoes, green beans, and a garden salad. She thanked him and sat down to enjoy her meal.

As she ate, she kept looking at Scott; she wanted to awake him and talk; she wanted him to make love to her. She needed him, and she felt sure that he needed her. Then she thought of his terrible situation. He had worried about his deathly ill wife to the point of exhaustion.

Olivia finished eating, got dressed for bed, and snuggled close by Scott's side in hopes that he would wake up, but he never moved a muscle. She finally fell asleep.

CHAPTER TWENTY-FIVE

Till Death do we Part

ON DECEMBER 16, 1990, at six o'clock in the morning, a nurse from St. Joseph's Hospital called Scott and told him that Laura Porter had died that morning around five o'clock.

Scott cried and Olivia comforted him with the only words she knew to say; "You still have your son and me; we love you so much; we will stand by you until you get through this terrible time."

After Olivia's kind words, Scott felt better. He got up pulled her close, kissed her, and expressed his need for her and his son. He did not know what he would do without them; he loved them more than she knew.

Since he had to go to the hospital, she packed her overnight case to go back home. Scott called room service to take her luggage to the car.

As Scott walked with her to her car, he explained that he would not be there to have supper and spend the night with her and Alex; he had to make arrangements for Laura's funeral and take care of some business at his office. He kissed her and wished her a safe trip home.

When Olivia cranked her car, he rushed back to the window to tell her he would call that evening. She threw him a kiss as she drove away.

Back at her parents' home, Alex met her at the door. He wanted to show her his tree house that his grandfather built.

Olivia did not have her mind on a tree house, but she pretended that she liked it and wanted to spend the night with Alex in his house one night. She did appreciate her father's efforts to make Alex happy. He had painted the small room and decorated the walls with pictures of Bat Man and Disney characters.

Back in her mother's kitchen, she answered questions about Laura Porter, how she died, and the arrangements for the funeral. Olivia only told her part of the story. Why did she ask about Laura's funeral arrangements? She had no intentions of going to her funeral.

Then her mother insisted that she eat dinner before going back home. Olivia could not resist her mother's fried chicken. The green beans, potato salad, and country fried corn bread also hit the spot.

After dinner, Olivia quickly helped clean the kitchen and made excuses to get back home. Her mother and father followed them to the car and made a big fuss over Alex. He told his grandfather that he wanted to come back and live in his tree house for a whole year.

Olivia kept the conversation going with Alex as they drove home. She did not want him asking questions about her trip to Savannah.

That evening, Scott called to let her know that he would be unable to come spend the night with them. He had made arrangements for Laura's funeral; but he still had to catch up with work at his office and meet with his supervisors later that day.

Alex had a fit to talk to Scott, and this pleased him. "How is my big boy?"

"When are you coming home?" Alex said. "I miss you, Daddy."

"I will see you tomorrow. I want you to take care of Mother."

"I am four years old," Alex said. "I am a big boy; big boys can keep monsters away."

"I know you are a big boy. I love you, and I will see you tomorrow."

Alex gave the phone to Olivia and disappeared down the hall to his room to play.

That night, Olivia turned and tumbled for hours before she finally fell asleep. She slept later than usual the next morning. Alex awoke her when he jumped on the bed and said, "Wake up sleepy head; it's time for the little bear to be fed. I want pancakes and bacon, please."

Olivia grabbed him in a tight hug and said, "You are getting to be a big bear, and you can soon go out and find your own breakfast."

Alex followed her to the kitchen and she fixed his breakfast. She had no appetite; she worried about Scott. After two cups of coffee, she felt better.

Before they finished eating, Scott walked into the kitchen and Alex ran to meet him. Scott swung him around and gave him a tight hug. As he walked to the cabinet to get a plate, he paused behind Olivia's chair and kissed her.

Olivia got up, poured him a cup of coffee, and sat with him to talk while he ate.

After Alex went to his room, Scott told her about the funeral arrangements. He had not slept much the last two days and excused himself from the table to take a nap.

Scott had burial rites for Laura Porter on Sunday, December 18, 1990, at three o'clock in the evening at the First Baptist Church. People filled all seats in the church, stood at the back, and outside the church.

When the preacher began reading: "The Lord gives and the Lord takes away," Scott broke down with sobs and rushed out the side door of the church to grab his composure.

Olivia did not go into the church with Scott; she waited in her car parked in the church parking lot. She wanted to be there for him; she wanted to give him the love and support that he needed.

Scott felt like an outsider at his own wife's funeral. Lisa's mother nor her sister spoke to him. Lisa had accused him of murdering Laura; Mrs. Wimberley had told him that he had no business living with another woman while still married to her daughter; she had also called Olivia dirty names. Scott still respected Laura's father and got along well with him. He was thankful that he had Olivia and Alex to lean upon. Olivia believed in him, and Alex worshiped him. Olivia would stand up for him; she knew he had not harmed his wife. He also still had many friends; but a few of his friends had grown distant even before Laura's death. He blamed Lisa and Mrs. Wimberley's gossip for their sudden change.

After everyone left the grave-side service, Scott went to Laura's casket and pulled a white rose from the arrangement. He placed the rose on her heart and said, "Till Death do we part. I kept part of my vows; I stayed married to you through all of your suffering, and I kept you. You are in a better place. Good bye, my love. May we meet again in heaven?" With the prayer still on his heart, he walked toward the parking lot where Olivia waited for him. After he sat down and closed the door, Olivia took his hand to show him she cared; but she could think of nothing good to say.

"Let's go home," he said.

Back at home, they heard the phone ringing before they unlocked the door. Adam Sinclair, an employee and friend of Scott's, called to tell him that Laura's sister, Lisa Cain, had called everyone in town and spread slanderous lies about his affair with Olivia Bradford. He had left Laura for his whore who lived in Boulder Bluff. While her poor sister lay dying, Scott had spent the night in the Holiday Inn with Olivia Bradford. She also lied about Scott's not visiting Laura months before she died.

Scott hung up with thoughts of calling Lisa Cane and giving her a piece of his mind; but his call would make matters even worse. He could not believe the difference in two sisters. Laura had been a kind, gentle, and loving person; while Lisa had a conniving, hostile, and downright overbearing nature. Lisa had always been jealous of Laura. She pretended she loved her sister; but Scott had known all along that Lisa hated Laura.

Olivia fixed sandwiches and tea for dinner, and Scott ate with a hearty appetite; but he had little to say. Olivia did not press him for words. Neither did she complain when he went to the bedroom to take a nap. She understood that he needed to mourn the loss of Laura. Before leaving the table, he asked her not to answer the phone, unless her parents called. He kissed her and went by Alex's room to speak to him before he went to bed.

Alex had yellow and red Legos scattered all over the floor surrounding him. "I am building a tree house like the one Granddaddy built for me."

"Wow, I didn't know you had a tree house."

"I will show it to you when we go back to Granddaddy's. You can spend the summer with me in my tree house."

"I am too tall to enter your door," Scott said in a low voice.

"You can sit on a limb next to my window," Alex said in a squeaky voice.

Scott squatted next to him and hugged him tightly as he explained that he needed a nap.

After Scott went to bed, he stared at the ceiling and relived his life with Laura from the day they met and their short time together before and after the accident that changed their life forever. Now someone had given his helpless wife an overdose to kill her. In spite of Laura's condition, he did not want her to die. He had loved her with all of his heart. Somebody had to put those pills in her mouth; Laura could not feed herself or hold a cup in her hands. The authorities would point an accusing finger at him for killing his wife. They would advertise his affair with Olivia; they would tear down her reputation. Most of all, he worried about Alex. What would he tell his son? How could he explain to his son that he had a wife and she had been murdered? He did not mind the authorities questioning him; but he did not want them to touch his son and smear dirt in his face. He loved and needed Olivia and his son more than ever. He believed deep down in his heart that Laura would approve of Olivia and love his son. He finally fell asleep, but not a sound peaceful sleep.

CHAPTER TWENTY-SIX

Interrogations and Confrontations

THE PHONE CALL from the local precinct the next morning did not alarm Scott. He expected the call. In fact, he thought they would arrest him immediately after Laura's funeral; but he did not think he had anything to worry about.

When he told Olivia that he had to go in for questioning about Laura's death, she felt helpless. She wanted to go with him; but he thought her presence with him would make matters worse.

Scott went to Joseph's office before going in for questioning.

Joseph met him at the door and offered him a chair in front of his desk. He expected the authorities to call him in for questioning. They always tagged the spouse as the first suspect in a murder case. He explained the lawful procedure he would face. After they questioned him, they would question Laura's next of kin, especially her sister, mother, and father. Next, they would question all of the nurses at the nursing home who came in contact with Laura daily. Then they would likely question Olivia and may even question Olivia's parents.

Scott got up, walked across the room, and hit his fist in his palm, and cursed. Olivia had never laid eyes on his wife. She knew nothing about Laura. Besides, she would never kill anyone.

Joseph wanted to prepare him for the worst, while he hoped for the best. The district attorney did not know Olivia, but he had heard the gossip about their affair and about their son. He advised Scott to refuse to answer any of their questions until he had his lawyer present; he may also refuse to answer questions that may incriminate him with his lawyer present. He should listen carefully to each question the detective asked before he gave his answer.

Scott thanked him and Joseph walked him to the door. Then he slapped him on the back, and assured him that the authorities only had circumstantial evidence against him. He had visited Laura the night they rushed her to the hospital, but her mother, father, sister, and friends visited, also. He claimed that he could tear circumstantial evidence apart when he cross examined their witnesses. He promised to meet Scott at the district attorney's office as soon as he made a few phone calls.

Scott walked into a large interrogation room with double windows covered by white shades. A long, metal table sat in the center of the room surrounded by gray, steel, straight chairs. The bright, well lit room with its solid white walls had no decorative art or flowers.

A man came to the door and asked Scott to come with him. Scott followed him to another room, where a tall, skinny, man with a sullen face rolled his fingers in smut and made an imprint on a form. Then he gave Scott a towel to clean his fingers and sent him back to the interrogation room.

A few minutes later, a short, husky, man with black eyes, dark complexion, a fat nose, and fat lips that fit his fat face walked into the interrogation room. Three puffs of gray hair combed neatly back from his forehead reminded Scott of the pouches on the pet hamster he once owned.

The detective slapped a folder down on the table and took a chair across from Scott. He leaned back with straight shoulders and revealed his fat belly that stretched the buttons on his navy suit. He raised his thick brows and widened his dark eyes as he spoke, "I am Detective Gary Jones. I wish we had met under different circumstances, Mr. Porter." He quickly read Scott's Miranda rights and explained that his job required proper procedures in questioning the next of kin in Laura Porter's murder. He opened his folder, went through several papers, pulled out a form, and picked up his pen to write as he began his questions.

Scott informed Detective Jones that he would not answer any questions until his lawyer arrived.

Jones got up, grabbed his files, and left the interrogation room.

Twenty minutes later, Joseph arrived; and Detective Jones followed him to the interrogation room. After they got seated, Jones began his question. First, he got Scott's life history from his birth to present.

Scott started working with his father at Porter Manufacturing Company when he turned ten years of age. After his father died, he took over the plant.

Next, he wanted to know how long he had been married to Laura, and how they got along.

Scott met Laura in high school and they fell in love. Their love for each other had grown stronger with every passing day. They got married right after graduation and had been married five years when she had the accident. During this five years, they had been happy and never had any serious marital problems. Laura wanted children; she worried about being unable to get pregnant.

As expected, Mr. Jones asked about his relationship with Olivia Bradford and wanted to know if they had a son.

Scott saw no need to tell him anything about his personal life. Mr. Jones obviously knew about Olivia and his son. Scott explained that he had known Olivia more than five years. They fell in love and he wanted to marry her, especially after she got pregnant with their son; but he felt responsible for his wife and could not divorce her.

Then Mr. Jones asked when, where, what, how, and why details of Scott's activities from the time he got up until he went to bed on December 15, 1990.

Scott arrived at his office on December 15, 1990, at seven thirty A.M. He went to Buck's Grill for lunch and got back to his office around one o'clock. At five o'clock, he left his office and went to the Ocmulgee Country Club, where he played golf about an hour; then he ate dinner and had a few drinks with his friends at the club. He arrived at Hillcrest Manor at seven thirty on December 15, 1990. He stayed with Laura about an hour. He got home around eight-thirty, took a bath, and watched television until he fell asleep. The phone call from Karen Cato at Hillcrest Manor awoke him some time before ten o'clock. She called to inform him that she had called an ambulance to take his wife, Laura, to St. Joseph's hospital in Savannah. He arrived at St. Joseph's hospital after eleven that night. Doctor Hawkins, Laura's physician, told him that Laura had an overdose of valium, a drug he had prescribed for her with specific orders for the amount and times she should be given the drug. After Doctor Hawkins told him that Laura could have no visitors, he left the hospital around one o'clock and went to the Holiday Inn, where he spent the night. At six o'clock the next morning, on December 16, 1990, the nurse at St. Joseph's Hospital called and told him his wife did not make through the night. Then he made arrangements for her to be taken to the funeral home and he went there to arrange her funeral and pay the bills.

Next, Detective Jones asked about insurance policies.

Scott had a five hundred thousand dollars life insurance policy on Laura; but he also had a five hundred thousand life insurance policy on himself that he had made out to Laura in case of his death. They had bought the insurance right after they bought the house for financial protection.

He felt the need to tell Detective Jones about the threatening phone calls he and Olivia got from Lisa Cane. He also wanted to tell Detective Jones about Mrs. Wimberley's visit and her threats. He remained silent for Olivia's sake, since the information would make Detective Jones suspicious of Olivia's involvement in Laura's death to get even with Lisa and Mrs. Wimberley.

A knock at the door interrupted Detective Jones. The man with the sullen face came into the room and handed Detective Jones a sheet of paper with finger prints stamped across the page. Detective Jones placed the page of prints into his folder, and pushed his chair back. He had finished with his interrogation; but he advised Scott not to leave town. He added that he would likely call him in again to answer additional questions.

Joseph walked with Scott outside and talked. He did not think Scott had anything to worry about and assured him that he would be there for him whenever he needed him.

As Scott walked toward his car; Laura's sister, Lisa, pulled into the parking lot. Scott stepped up his pace and faced her. He wanted to slap hell out of her lying face; but he kept his cool.

Lisa turned her head and pretended not to see Scott.

Scott yelled at her, "Lisa, why are you running from me. Are you afraid to face me with the lies you have spread around town about Olivia and me?"

She stopped and stared at him with anger as she spoke. "You killed my sister, you bastard."

"I did not kill Laura! In spite of her condition, I loved her. For months, I sat by her side, held her hand, and talked to her; but she did not respond to me; she did not recognize me or anyone else. I still visited her every day, unless my job took me out of town."

"I do not want to hear your lies," Lisa said. "Since you got tangled up with Olivia Bradford, you have ignored my sister."

Scott softened his voice. "Lisa, I have tried to figure out why you hate me so much. After Olivia and I got your threatening phone calls, you took your dirty game further; you set fire to Olivia's house and tried to kill her and my son. Then I finally realized that your hatred toward me stems from the fact that I dumped you for Laura in high school. After you threatened Olivia and me, I realized that you really do not hate me; you still love me. Since I never gave you a second thought, you hated and tried to destroy everyone I love."

"Shut up, you lying bastard!"

"You are the liar," Scott said. "You cannot deny your reaction to Laura's first date with me. I remember how you acted. You tried to turn Laura against me with the lies you told; but you failed. I married your sister because I loved her; and I loved her during our entire married life. Your jealousy of Laura's beauty and intelligence made you hate her, because you are neither beautiful nor intelligent."

"I loved my sister; and I wanted the best for her. That sorry woman you have been living with makes me furious. I hope you both pay for what you have done to my sister. You don't care who you hurt. You would jump in bed with any whore who paid you a little attention."

"Why don't you pay me a little attention, Lisa; see how far your attention toward me gets you."

"Go to hell!" she said and started to walk away from him.

"Lisa, I have one other question. What happened to your husband? I liked Robert Cane. He was a decent man; you did not deserve a nice fellow like Robert. If I remember correctly, you ran him off six months after you married him. Robert learned the truth about you the first week after he married you. You showed your true colors and Robert got out of your trap before you carried him through the wringer. His intelligence beat you at your game. Then you stuck your nose into my business and tried to convince all of my friends in this town that I killed Laura. You have the best motive, Lisa. Did you kill your sister because you are still in love with me?"

"Hell no, you lying bastard! I have never loved you! I hate you. I have nothing else to say to you. As she walked away, she turned quickly and said, "I will see you in court; I hope they throw the book at you."

Scott yelled back at her, "I will go to my grave to stop you from ruining another life. I have enough money to hire the best detectives; they will hound you the rest of your life."

As Scott drove home he thought about how Lisa acted when he started dating Laura. Lisa pretended that his relationship with her sister did not bother her, but all of their friends knew that Lisa wanted him to marry her; she was jealous. After he married Laura, Lisa seldom came around and had little to do with Laura. After he put Laura in the nursing home, Lisa visited her every day for the first month. Then she seldom visited her sister. The night Laura got the overdose of valium, Lisa had visited her for the first time in months. He thought Detective Jones should check the visitors chart at Hillcrest Manor Nursing Home.

Lisa Cane carried her tall, slender figure across the interrogation room with straight shoulders and a pretense of confidence; but worry could be read in her eyes. She dressed in expensive clothes and had a good figure, but men seldom noticed her face. She had a long crooked nose similar to pictures he had seen of witches' noses.

Detective Jones came into the interrogation room, introduced himself, took a seat across from her, and explained his duty. He asked her to tell him when she last saw her sister, Laura Porter, alive.

She cried as she answered the question. She and her mother visited her sister around six o'clock on September 15, 1990. Her Mother dropped her off at her home around eight o'clock. Sometime after nine o'clock, Miss Cato at Hillcrest Manor called her mother and informed her that they had sent Laura to the St. Joseph's Hospital in Savannah. She went with her parents to see Laura; she looked like death warmed over beneath the oxygen mask they had strapped on her face. They soon moved her to ICU and allowed no visitors. She died the next morning and she never saw her poor sister again. Then she raised her voice in anger and accused Scott Porter of killing her sister. She added that Scott wanted his freedom to marry Olivia Bradford. She added that Scott's whore has no friends and she had heard that she had mental problems.

Detective Jones warned her that she must not make accusations and jump to conclusions; he wanted facts that could be proven. Then he asked her when she last spoke to Scott Porter.

She admitted that she had seen Scott in the parking lot a few minutes earlier. He started an argument with her. She called him a sociopath and told him that he should be put behind bars for killing her sister. Then she explained why she disliked Scott Porter. A few months before Laura's murder, Scott and a private detective named Brinson came to her home and accused her of making threatening phone calls to Scott and his whore, Olivia Bradford. She knew nothing about their accusations.

"Has your sister ever spoken to you or made an attempt to speak since she had the accident?" Mr. Jones said.

"She never talked to me, because she did not recognize me. She did not recognize any of my family or her husband, Scott. Since her accident, she could not help herself; now she cannot defend herself. I want revenge for her death. I want Scott Porter to die a slow, agonizing death for my sister's murder."

"Miss Cane, I am sorry for your loss, but you must forget any plan for revenge and let the law handle this case."

"If your brother-in-law killed your sister, would you not seek revenge?" Lisa said.

"In the first place, you cannot prove your brother-in-law killed your sister."

"I know Scott killed my sister; Olivia Bradford has a son for Scott and he wants to marry her to give his son a name; he could not marry Olivia with my sister still living."

"I have no further questions, Mrs. Cane. I may call you in later for further questioning."

Christine and Nathaniel Wimberley met Lisa as she walked toward the exit doors of the district attorney's office. They talked about her interrogation a few minutes and parted ways.

Christine walked into the interrogation room with sophistication. Nathaniel Wimberley moved his tall figure across the interrogation room close on Christine's heels. He pulled out a chair for Christine before taking a seat next to her. At sixty something years of age Mr. Wimberley still had a handsome face framed by light brown hair that had thinned and receded on top. He sat with relaxed shoulders and rested his elbows on the table, while Christine sat with perfect posture and moved her dark eyes around the room with curiosity.

When Detective Jones walked into the interrogation room, Mr. Wimberley stood and shook his hand. Mr. Wimberley mentioned that Mr. Jones looked familiar and asked if he ever attended the First Baptist Church. When Mr. Jones replied that he had never entered the doors of that church, Mr. Wimberley told him he must have seen him at a football game or on the golf course.

Mr. Jones Walked around the table, laid his files down, and took a seat across from them and explained the procedure.

When Detective Jones asked about their relationship, Nathaniel Wimberley's blue eyes pierced Detective Jones with resentment. He hated folk prying into his personal life. Mr. Wimberley moved a hand across his head as if frustration had taken his thoughts. Then he patted Christine Wimberley on the shoulder and bragged that he had been married to this woman thirty-five years. He talked about their life together and their two daughters. Then he talked about Laura's accident and how it had torn their family apart.

When detective Jones asked the Wimberley's about their activities just before they sent Laura to the hospital, Mr. Wimberley explained that his wife, and his daughter, Lisa, visited Laura late that evening. He admitted that he seldom visited Laura; he could not bear to see her stare in space and lie in that bed. She could not speak or move; the accident took her life; she merely existed.

Mrs. Wimberley quickly interrupted and explained that they never gave up hope; they expected Laura to get better with time.

Mr. Wimberley looked at his wife and shouted that miracles like that never happened. Their daughter died the day she fell and hit her head at Stone Mountain, and she should face reality.

Mrs. Wimberley broke down and shook with her tears.

Mr. Jones got up and walked around the table to comfort Mrs. Wimberley. He gently patted her shoulder with compassion. He understood her sadness under the circumstances. The loss of a child must be the worst thing in the world for a parent to live through.

Mr. Jones dismissed them and told them he may call them later if he had additional questions about Laura Porter.

In the meantime, Scott had stopped to tell Joseph about the argument at the precinct with Lisa Cane. He felt sure that Lisa had informed Detective Jones about his affair with Olivia and accused him of murdering her sister. On the other hand, she definitely did not tell Detective Jones about the threatening letter she wrote nor the phone calls. Neither did she tell Jones about her mother's visit to Olivia's home and her cruel accusations.

Joseph thought Lisa Cane should be at the top of the list of suspects in Laura's death. He believed that Lisa planned to kill her sister before she threatened Olivia and him. She had either given the pills to her sister or hired someone to do her dirty work. He had seen and heard enough to know that Lisa wanted money. If the court found Scott guilty, Lisa could file a civil suit against him for the wrongful death of her sister. If Lisa won a civil suit, the court would likely award her and her family the 500,000 thousand dollar life insurance policy he had on Laura as well as Porter Manufacturing and everything else he owned. Then Joseph asked how he got along with Laura's father.

Scott had always got along well with Laura's father. Laura's accident did not seem to change her father's attitude toward him. In fact, they had played golf together, gone out to dinner, and been good friends. He added that Mr. Wimberley still came by to see him now and then.

Scott believed that the nurses who cared for Laura should be questioned first about her death. They gave her medication prescribed by her doctor and they fed her every day.

Joseph suggested that they hire a private detective to question suspects before Laura's family brought him down with a murder rap and left him holding an empty bag. A detective could hopefully get valuable information for his defense. He knew that Laura's parents nor Lisa Cane would allow a private detective to come into their home; but the nurses and others may shed some light on Laura's death. He added that he hoped there would be no case against Scott, since the authorities had no real evidence to take the case to court.

Olivia met Scott with open arms and Alex begged for Scott's attention with questions about the mean cops. He wanted to know what they said to him.

Scott explained that the cops only wanted to question him about a crime.

Alex wanted to know what a crime meant.

Scott saw that he should not have mentioned the word. He did not know what to say.

Olivia saved him by asking Alex to please go and play with his new video game while she talked to daddy.

Alex hugged his daddy and said, "I will tell the cops that my daddy is the best daddy in the whole world." Then he ran down the hall to his room."

The love Scott felt for his son at this minute made tears come to his eyes.

Anxious to hear about his ordeal at the precinct, Olivia asked him to come to the kitchen. She perked coffee, but Scott needed something stronger than coffee. He grabbed a bottle of Jack Daniels from the cabinet and poured a stiff drink before sitting down at the table.

Scott's confrontation with Lisa about the lies she had spread and her accusations made Olivia see red.

Scott believed that Lisa's actions were displaced aggression; she took her hate for her sister out on him and Olivia; then she killed her sister. Joseph wanted to prove that Lisa framed him for murdering her sister in order to file a civil suit against him.

Olivia did not like the idea of Joseph presenting the letter, taped phone calls, and fire report in a court room; but Scott needed the evidence for his defense; she must grit her teeth and be strong for Scott's sake.

Likewise, Scott hated to drag Olivia's name through the dirt. He held her close and promised her that he would make it all up to her one day and they could live in peace like a happy family should live.

Olivia felt sure that Lisa Cane and Mrs. Wimberley framed Scott. They hated him for loving her and Alex. What could she do? She could do nothing to help him; she must protect her son.

The next morning after Scott left for work, Olivia got Alex settled at the table to eat breakfast and sat down to read the morning paper. The phone interrupted her reading. She had expected the call from Detective Jones; yet, she felt faint when she heard his voice.

Jones asked her to come to the police station for questioning in Laura Porter's murder at Eleven o'clock.

After Olivia hung up, she looked at Alex and convinced herself that she must be strong for his sake.

Olivia did not want to ask her mother to keep Alex. She did not want to answer her questions. Neither did she want to tell Scott that she had to go in for questioning. He had too much on his mind already, but she had no one else to keep Alex.

When Scott got to Olivia's, he suggested that he and Alex go with her to the police station; they could stay in the waiting room.

Olivia protested; she did not want her son to go to the police station, especially not under the circumstances.

Scott agreed to stay home with him.

Olivia walked out without giving an explanation to Alex. Before she opened the car door, she checked her surroundings. She had become paranoid about the cops; she felt as if they watched her house day and night. They probably thought she had killed Laura Porter.

As she drove she thought about all the bad things that had happened since she met Scott. Now Lisa Cane had framed Scott for his wife's murder. She felt shaky when she got to the police station; she took a good breath and walked into the foyer, where a woman behind a glass partition directed her to the third room on the right.

When she walked into the interrogation room, Detective Jones stood, extended his hand, and introduced himself. Then he asked her to have a seat, and began his questions.

Right away, Olivia sensed that Detective Jones had already convicted her of Laura Porter's murder. First, he asked how long she had known Laura Porter.

She had never met Laura Porter; she had only seen pictures of Laura and Scott.

Next, he asked her whereabouts the night they admitted Laura Porter to the hospital.

She stayed at home with her son, where she spent the majority of her time every day.

Then he asked if she had an alibi.

Olivia had only her son for an alibi. She had no visitors; Scott had to work late and stayed at his place that night.

After this, he wanted to know how she learned about Laura Porter's overdose and her death.

Scott called and told her that Laura had been admitted to the St. Joseph's Hospital in Savannah; he asked her to come to the Holiday Inn, where he stayed. She drove her car to Savannah and nobody went with her. She spent the night with Scott. The next morning, the nurse at St. Joseph's hospital called Scott and reported that his wife died. Scott went back to the hospital and she went home. That evening, Scott went to Porterville and made funeral arrangements for his wife.

Then Jones asked how long she had known Scott Porter, her relationship with him, when she gave birth to their son, and commitment Scott had made to her for their future.

Olivia left out the details of how she and Scott met and tried to make the story short. She had known Scott about five years; she admitted that Scott stayed with her sometimes; she gave birth to their son, Alex, on September 28, 1986. Scott loved Alex and provided well for them. Then she admitted that Scott had promised to marry her many times; but he felt responsible for his helpless wife, who needed constant care, and he could not live with his guilt if he divorced her.

After getting the details of her life with Scott, Detective Jones wanted to know about her previous relationships.

Olivia felt her face get hot; she resented Detective Jones asking personal questions about her past. Her previous relationships had nothing to do with Scott or Laura.

Her refusal to answer Detective Jones' question made him angry. He raised his voice and accused her of killing Laura Porter so she could marry Scott Porter and give her son a father.

Olivia sat and stared at Detective Jones with fire blazing from her eyes. Then she calmly said, "Mr. Jones, I do want Scott to marry me; I want us to be a family more than anything in this world; I want my son to have a father. In spite of my long held dream to be Scott's wife, I have a conscious. I did not kill Laura Porter. I would never take another human being's life, unless one threatened to take my life or my son's life."

Detective Jones sat and looked down at his notes and did not meet her angry eyes again. Then he said, "What do your parents think about your living with Scott Porter? Do they get along with him?"

"When I told my parents about my pregnancy, I also told them that Scott could not marry me, because he had a wife. They got very angry. After my son, Alex, came into their lives, they accepted our relationship. They never said anything negative about Scott again."

"I have no further questions today, but I may have other questions later. I do not think it wise for you to take a long vacation or a flight to another country until we solve this crime."

Olivia looked at him with disbelief before she got up. Then she shoved her chair with a bang against the table and made her way to the exit doors.

When she got home, Scott wanted to know what Detective Jones asked her.

She claimed that Detective Jones asked the usual questions. She did not mention Jones questioning her about her previous relationships. Neither did she tell him that her parents would likely be questioned. Scott knew that her parents disliked him. Olivia did not want him to worry about what her parents may say about him.

CHAPTER TWENTY-SEVEN

Search Warrant

THE NEXT MORNING when Scott walked into Steve Brinson's office, Steve moved his tall stout frame around his desk and met him with a firm hand as he offered his condolences in Laura's death. He had gone to the funeral but did not want to bother Scott in his time of grief.

Scott explained that he wanted to hire him to do some detective work.

Steve leaned back in his chair as if studying the situation. Then he asked if the authorities had accused him of killing Laura.

Steve seemed pleased that they had only called Scott in to question him; but Lisa Cane's accusations and the lies that she had spread all over town about his affair with Olivia made him look guilty. Steve believed Lisa Cane tried to make Scott look guilty to keep the cops off her tail. He thought Scott should have spilled the beans on Lisa Cane and her mother.

Scott thought the nurses at Hillcrest Manor should be held accountable for the dosage of medicine they gave her.

Steve assured Scott that he would begin his investigation right away and do everything he could do to help him.

After Scott left, Steve thought about Laura's murder. Of course, Scott would profit from his wife's life insurance. On the other hand, Laura's family may have a life insurance policy on Laura, also. He had been in the private detective business long enough to know that relatives or close friends are usually found guilty of murdering their loved ones; but the suspect in this case happened to be his good friend. Scott Porter did not kill his wife; and he would go down fighting to get evidence needed to clear him of a crime he did not commit.

First of all, Brinson wanted to question Judy Brooks, the nurse who had taken care of Laura Porter since her accident. He got her address from the receptionist at Hillcrest Manor. Brinson looked at his watch as he pulled into the drive before the small wood frame house. Most folk were up and around by ten, but he heard no sounds as he climbed the steps. He stood on the small porch, rang the doorbell, and waited. After the third ring of the bell, a tall slender lady who looked to be in her fifties met him. She had a figure like Dolly and the low cut housecoat she wore revealed the cleavage of her breast. She had fair skin and eyes that sparkled like sapphires behind her glasses.

"I am Detective Brinson. May I come in and ask you a few questions about Laura Porter?"

She stretched her eyes and pushed at the puff of blond hair piled on top of her head as she invited him to come inside. She apologized for the boxes stacked on the floor and explained that she had just moved into the house and had not finished unpacking.

As he followed her to the kitchen, he weaved around boxes stacked in his path and sat down at a small maple table. He readily accepted the cup of coffee she offered and helped himself to the cream and sugar on the table. As he sipped his coffee, he explained his visit and asked how long she had known Laura and Scott Porter.

She had known Laura and Scott since they were young children. They both came from fine families and had seemed happily married until Laura's accident. She had cared for Laura more than five years.

Next, he asked about the night Laura had been given an overdose of valium.

She had worked that night and fed Laura supper at five thirty. Laura ate with a hearty appetite, but she always ate most of her meal. At seven o'clock, she checked on Laura again and found her asleep. Laura's chart showed all of her vital signs to be normal all that day until nine thirty that night when she took her vital signs again. She found that Laura's blood pressure had bottomed out and she barely had a pulse. She immediately reported Laura's condition to the head nurse, Karen Cato, who called an ambulance around nine forty-five.

Then he asked if Laura had visitors that day other than her relatives.

Laura's mother and her sister visited her; they came into the room while she fed Laura that evening. Several of her friends from her church visited every day; but she would have to look at the visitors' chart to recall their names.

Before leaving, he asked if she saw or heard anything unusual that night.

She heard nothing unusual that night.

He thanked her for the coffee and gave her his card. "If you think of anything important that you forgot to tell me, call me after one o'clock in the evening. I'm out of my office every morning."

As she walked Steve to the door, she bragged on Scott Porter; she thought he treated Laura special, and he visited her almost every day. She wore a beautiful diamond ring the day they brought her into the nursing home. Scott told the nurses that he never wanted Laura's wedding rings removed from her finger.

Steve agreed that Scott Porter had a big heart; he provided well for Laura, gave thousands to charity every year, and gave money to the needy in their hometown.

She added that Mr. Porter had plenty of money to give, but he worked hard for his money.

Steve understood her thinking; Scott Porter had been his good friend for years and he knew him well.

After introducing himself to Karen Cato, head nurse at Hillcrest Manor, Steve Brinson explained his visit.

He followed the short, stout nurse to the waiting room near the foyer and sat in an armchair across from her. She looked to be in her late forties; she still had dark hair and an attractive face.

With hands tied in her lap, she stared at him with piercing dark eyes that seemed to read his thoughts. She quickly explained that she did not know anything about Laura Porter's death. She had already told the police everything she knew. They called her to come down to the station the day Laura Porter died. They questioned her for hours, and she did not sleep a wink that night.

Steve had no information from the police and asked if she would mind answering a few important questions that might be helpful for Scott Porter to have closure in his wife's death.

Nurse Cato admitted that she seldom went to check on patients, unless they required medical attention or emergency care. She mostly checked charts to make sure patients were fed, bathed, and given their medication on time and in the correct amount. The nurses had not recorded any unusual activity on Laura's chart that took her attention until Mrs. Brooks checked Laura at nine thirty and found Laura with a weak pulse and low blood pressure. She had called an ambulance immediately. She made it clear that she nor any of the nurses knew anything about Laura's overdose until they got the doctor's report from the hospital. She added that her nurses were the cream of the crop and they had never had a patient to die from their negligence. She saw nothing out of the ordinary the night they sent Laura to the hospital.

Next, he asked if she remembered who visited Laura the night she got the overdose.

She could not remember all of Laura's visitors that day; but she did remember that Laura's mother and sister visited her that evening. In fact, she had spoken with Laura's mother briefly when she and Lisa signed in. She paused and told him that Hillcrest Manor had strict rules; all visitors signed in at the front desk before they visited patients.

He asked if he could see the reports she had on Laura Porter the day she had the overdose of valium.

She hesitated before reviewing Laura Porter's chart with him. Then she allowed Steve Brinson to check the visitor's roster.

"Do you think they will arrest Mr. Porter?" Mrs. Cato said.

"If they have the evidence, they will arrest him."

"I don't like for killers to run around free."

"Are you afraid the killer might return to Hillcrest Manor?"

"I don't think the killer would be that brave, but I would not want to meet up with a psychotic killer in a dark alley."

"I understanding your thinking," he said and gave her his card. "Call me if you think of anything that would help Mr. Porter.

She looked at the card and said, "I will do that, Mr. Brinson."

Steve Brinson left Hillcrest Manor with nothing more than he already knew. He had to find someone who knew something that he did not know to help Scott.

Scott had not seen Olivia the entire week; but he talked with her every day on the phone. He explained that he had to visit Steve and Joseph every day; and he worked overtime at the office to keep up with his paper work.

Olivia understood. She would always be there waiting for him. In spite of her patience and love for Scott, the stress from not knowing what the next sunrise might bring made her want to take Alex and skip the country.

The next morning on the way to work, Scott called Olivia and asked if she and Alex had a good night.

Alex always slept like a little bear; but she had been miserable without him.

He asked her not to cook supper; he wanted to pick up something on the way. He expected to be there by six o'clock that evening.

Olivia wanted to cook supper for him; she wanted them to have dinner like a normal family.

Scott did not want her to go to a lot of trouble; but he liked her cooking and he looked forward to having dinner with her and his son. He needed them more than ever.

At twelve o'clock, Scott left his office, drove to the Burger King, picked up a hamburger and fries for lunch, and ate as he drove to Steve Brinson's office.

Scott left Steve's office disappointed; he had not made any progress in his investigation.

Back at the office, Scott got a stack of mail and started working. He wanted to catch up on his work early and spend the entire weekend with Olivia and Alex.

His office phone kept interrupting his thought; and he remembered that his secretary had not come back from lunch, yet.

When Scott answered his phone and heard Detective Jones' voice, he wanted to hang up in his face. Then Scott's eyes widened with shock at Detective Jones's request.

"Mr. Porter, I have a search warrant to search your home. My men will be at your place as soon as you can get there."

Scott asked him to give him about an hour and he would meet them at his house.

Scott hung up and called Adam Sinclair to his office. He asked him to lock up if he did not get back before Six o'clock.

On the way home, Scott called Olivia to let her know what had happened. He explained that he would be unable to have dinner with them, since Detective Jones had a search warrant to search his home; but he still looked forward to spending the weekend with her and Alex.

Olivia believed the cops were trying to slap him with a murder wrap, a murder that Lisa Cane committed.

Scott met the cops at his door one hour later. His anger showed as he unlocked the door and shoved it back. He invited them inside and told them that he had nothing to hide. He added that could search every crack and corner, but they would find nothing to incriminate him in Laura's death.

"We are doing our Job," Detective Wiggins said.

Scott followed the two cops to every room and watched them tumble his clothes and rummage through the pockets of his coats neatly hung in the closet. Then Detective Wiggins went to his bathroom. Scott watched him open his medicine cabinet and put something into his evidence bag; but he could not see what he got.

After the cops finished their search, Detective Wiggins informed Scott that the district attorney would contact him to discuss their findings.

Scott didn't worry about what Detective Wiggins had taken. His medicine cabinet only had his prescription for high blood pressure, over-the-counter pain medication, and first aid supplies.

Scott went to the kitchen, made a pot of coffee, and sat down at the table to call Olivia. The cops had tumbled every room in his house before they left. He felt as if he should stay home over-night to protect his property.

Olivia completely understood and asked him to come and have supper with them the next evening.

CHAPTER TWENTY EIGHT
Arrested for Murder

THE NEXT MORNING, Scott got to his office earlier than usual. He went to the club to have lunch with Joseph and went back to his office. Before he got seated behind his desk, his secretary asked him to pick up the phone on line one.

Detective Jones' voice made him furious. He wanted Scott to come to the precinct for questioning, and he should come as soon as possible.

As Scott drove to the police station, he smelled something fishy and Lisa Cane came to mind.

Two cops met Scott when he walked into the police station. They read him his right and arrested him as a prime suspect in his wife's murder. They led him to an office on the left and asked him to empty his pockets. They took all of his personal belongings. Then they got his fingerprints again.

Afterwards, they escorted him to the district attorney's office. The tall husky man looked up from his paperwork, stood up, and extended a hand to Scott as he spoke, "I am District Attorney Mark Kramer. Have a seat."

Before Mr. Kramer began his questions, Scott asked him why he had been arrested.

The DA started in on Scott like a mad bull flashing his horns for the kill. He asked Scott the same questions Detective Jones had already asked him. Scott reminded him that he had been questioned and Detective Jones had everything in his report.

Kramer slapped an empty prescription bottle before Scott and said, "This empty bottle is a prescription for thirty valium found in your medicine cabinet in your bathroom. The State Crime autopsy confirmed that an overdose of valium found in your wife system killed her. According to the date on the bottle, you filled this prescription for valium the morning before Laura Porter got that overdose of valium."

Scott sat and looked at Kramer with shock and disbelief. "I have never filled or refilled a prescription for Laura. She took valium before she had the accident, and she ordered her own medications. After the accident, the nurses ordered her medications; and they were supposed to follow the doctors' orders for the dosage they gave her."

"The date on this empty bottle states otherwise. If you did not refill her prescription, then who did? How did this empty bottle get into your medicine cabinet in your bathroom? Does anyone else have a key to your home? Does Olivia Bradford have a key to your house?"

Scott looked at Kramer with anger and remained silent.

Mr. Kramer hit his fist on his desk and shouted, "Mr. Porter, does the cat have your tongue? Why don't you tell me the truth? Go ahead and admit that you killed your wife. You killed your wife so you would be free to marry Olivia Bradford!"

"I did not kill my wife; and I will never confess to a murder that I did not commit!" Scott said.

Then Kramer reminded Scott that he lived with Miss Bradford and they had a son together who needed a father.

Scott insisted that his son had a father who loved him. He admitted that he wanted to marry Olivia, but he could not divorce his wife; he felt responsible for her.

Then Mr. Kramer revealed another shocking surprise. He shouted that a witness had seen him go into the nursing home after visiting hours and leave by the back door.

Scott stood up and called Kramer a liar. Then he asked the DA for the name of this mysterious witness.

Kramer would not disclose the name of the witness; but he informed Scott that the male witness volunteered the information.

Scott denied his accusation and assured him that his witness had lied to cover the real killer's tracks. He added that he knew when and where he went that night; he could account for his actions every minute of that day, but he could not prove that he stayed home that night, because he had no one there with him.

Two officials came into District Attorney Kramer's office and escorted Scott to his jail cell. Scott felt as if rusty hinges moved his legs as he walked down the long corridor.

After the door clanked behind him, he sat down on the hard bunk bed and thought about calling Joseph. Since they allowed him only one call, he called Olivia.

Olivia felt devastated when she learned what the detectives found.

Scott asked her to call Joseph and tell him he needed to talk to him as soon as possible.

Less than an hour later, Joseph came to the jail. Scott told him that he knew absolutely nothing about the empty pill bottle they found in his bathroom.

Joseph felt sure that someone planted that bottle in his medicine cabinet. If the druggist had a record of the prescriptions he filled that day, he should know who ordered the medication. He talked more than an hour about what steps he needed to take for a strong defense.

Before he left, he told Scott that he would appear before the judge within forty-eight hours for an information hearing. The district attorney would inform the judge about the charges against him and the evidence the law officers found. The empty prescription bottle for valium found in his medicine cabinet would likely give them enough evidence to deny his request for bail.

Joseph further explained that in some cases the judge held a preliminary hearing within ten day after a person's arrest to determine if the DA had enough evidence to carry the case to court. Then he explained the disadvantages of a preliminary hearing. The DA could use circumstantial evidence to suggest that he killed his wife. The DA could also present evidence that he obtained illegally as well as hearsay, such as the gossip and lies the Mrs. Wimberley and Lisa had spread about his affair with Olivia.

After Joseph left, Scott worried. How could he prove that he did not fill that prescription? Who took the pills and planted that empty bottle in his medicine cabinet? He was at home all alone when the killer gave Laura those pills. He moved two steps backwards with each step he made to move forward. He had always faced danger with courage, but he had been charged with murdering his wife. He had lost his ability to reason and felt as if he would go crazy. He had suddenly become helpless, a weakling wedged between two bricks with cement. He felt as if an anchor had pulled him under and he could not resurface; he could not breathe. He buried his face in his hands and cried for a long time.

Scott finally sat up, took a deep breath, and tried to clear his head. He was not about to confess to a crime that he did not commit. How could he prove his innocence? He could not prove his innocence unless Brinson came up with more evidence to clear him. What should he do next? What could he do? He could do nothing behind bars. If the judge approved his bail, he could help Detective Brinson and Joseph with his defense.

He finally turned the sheet back, fluffed the pillow and lay down. He was as sleepy as a bear in December, but he did not sleep; he lay for hours and stared through the darkness with thoughts of his predicament. He could not give up and lose self-control; he had to be strong and clear his name for the sake of Olivia and his son. They needed him; they depended on him. He would never kill anyone, unless he feared for his own life or the life of Alex and Olivia. Of course, he was not completely free from guilt; he had an affair with Olivia and she had a son for him. He had committed adultery, but the lies that had spread about his affair with Olivia seemed unfair. His father's familiar words came to mind, "Son, you cannot clean a chimney without smearing the smut." The public had smeared the smut about his and Olivia's affair; but she still loved him unconditionally. He had thought that he and Olivia would get married and have a good life; they could travel and do the things they dreamed about doing. He had been selfish to place Laura's physical needs before Olivia's needs. He should have divorced Laura the day he met Olivia. If he had cut all ties with the Wimberley family before Laura's death, they could not point fingers at him now. He loved Olivia more than life and she loved him; but they would never be together. He closed his eyes and thought about the last time he made love to Olivia. "No!" he said aloud, "I can't think of Olivia at a time like this."

The next day at nine o'clock, Scott stood before Judge Nathaniel Solomon for an Information Hearing to determine if the district attorney had enough evidence to hold him for trial.

District Attorney Mark Kramer stood and spoke directly to Judge Solomon. "Mr. Porter is accused of giving his wife, Laura Porter, an overdose of Valium on December 15, 1990, while she was confined to the Hillcrest Manor Nursing home in Porterville, Georgia."

Then Kramer presented the empty pill bottle found in Scott Porter's bathroom cabinet and pointed out that the prescription for valium had been filled the day before Laura Porter died from an overdose of the drug. Next, he informed the judge that Porter visited his wife at Hillcrest Manor that night at seven-thirty. Then he explained that Scott Porter had no alibi for the time between his visit and the time the head nurse found Laura Porter and called an ambulance to transport her to the St. Joseph's hospital in Savannah at nine forty-five. According to the autopsy report, an over dose of valium resulted in Laura Porter's death on December 16, 1990, at the St. Joseph's hospital in Savannah, Georgia. A guilty verdict in said charges may result in a prison term for a number of years to life, or may even result in a death sentence.

Judge Solomon looked at Scott and said, "Mr. Porter, how do you plea to the said charges?"

"I plead not guilty, your honor," Scott Said.

Joseph Harrington stood and said, "Your honor, I ask that you allow my client bail until his trial. Scott Porter is an outstanding citizen and owns his own business. He has never been arrested or charged with even a misdemeanor."

Before Judge Solomon had time to reply, DA Kramer said, "Your honor, the evidence against Scott Porter for the death of his wife has been presented. The State demands that Scott Porter be held without bail until his trial."

"Bail is denied," the judge said. "The Evidence presented by the DA suggest that Mr. Porter murdered his wife. This case warrants a trial by a jury."

Before the guards led Scott back to his cell, Joseph assured him that he would do everything he could to present evidence that would clear him of the murder charges. He asked him to try to get some sleep and he would talk to him the next day.

Later that evening, Olivia met Scott in the visitor's room. She cried and Scott knew nothing good to tell her. She told him Alex cried all morning, too. He wanted to come with her; but she didn't want him to see his daddy in that horrible jail.

Scott understood. He asked her to tell Alex that he loved him very much and he would be home soon.

They talked about his trial the entire hour. The prosecution obviously wanted to prove that Scott was guilty of premeditate murder in the first degree.

On the other hand, Joseph assured Scott that the prosecution had a weak case and a jury would never convict him with the circumstantial evidence presented by the state. Joseph wanted to prove that someone put that empty pill bottle in Scott's medicine cabinet to frame him.

Olivia asked the names of the witnesses for the defense. She wanted to testify for him. He definitely did not want her to testify. He explained that Joseph had more than enough character witnesses and he would also be allowed to cross-examine all of the witnesses for the State. He added that Detective Brinson continued his investigation and he hoped he found a witness who knew something about Laura's murder that would help his defense.

She tried to say comforting words; she did not want him to worry about her and Alex. They would be there to support him until the end of the trial and she felt sure that the jury would find him innocent of all charges after Mr. Brinson and Joseph presented their evidence. The jury would see that Lisa Cane framed him.

The guard came in and Olivia kissed Scott goodbye. She told him she would try to visit him at least once a week. She hated to ask her mother to keep Alex and Mrs. Sanders had not been around Alex but a few times over the years.

Scott understood. He looked forward to her next visit. He promised to call her every day and keep her informed about Brinson and Joseph's progress in his case.

The next week Scott learned that his trial would be held in the circuit court within two months from the said date of Laura's murder.

Joseph did not think Scott should testify, since the prosecution could cross examine him and try to tangle his mind with the information he had already given them. He explained that he looked forward to tangling the State's witnesses when they testified against him.

After Joseph left, Scott thought about how hard he had tried to be honest and do good deeds. He had abided by the laws of man; but he had failed God's test. His affair with Olivia ended the freedom he had left. Many of the citizens and a few of his good friends believed he murdered Laura for his freedom to marry Olivia. He felt betrayed; their gossip shattered his hopes of proving his innocence. How could his friends turn against him? Olivia had said these so called friends were not his friends in the first place; they had only pretended to be his friend.

The next day, Joseph came back to the jail to talk with Scott. He explained that he and the DA had exchanged copies of their witness list. He showed Scott both list and asked if he could think of others who may be good witnesses.

Scott could think of no other witnesses, unless Steve Brinson uncovered a witness with knowledge of the murder.

The next evening, Steve Brinson visited Scott. He had questioned the janitor at the nursing home and learned that he had seen a man leaving Laura Porter's room a little after nine o'clock on the night the ambulance carried her to the hospital. Scott concluded that the janitor must have told DA Kramer about this mysterious visitor. DA Kramer claimed that a witness saw Scott leaving his wife's room that night after nine o'clock.

Steve reassured Scott that the janitor did not tell Kramer this visitor looked like Scott Porter. In fact, the janitor made that clear to him. Joseph concluded that DA Kramer had lied to Scott in an effort to get his confession; he wanted him to admit that he murdered Laura. Then he described the man the janitor saw and asked Scott if he knew anyone who fit the man's description.

Several of Scott's employees matched the man's description; but not one of them had a criminal record or reason to harm his wife. He had never had any trouble with any of his employees.

Steve believed the janitor's testimony would help Scott's defense and perhaps get an acquittal of all charges.

CHAPTER TWENTY-NINE
Trial - State Witnesses

DURING THE LAST week of February 1991, Scott Porter sat with his lawyer, Joseph Harrington, and waited for his trial to begin. He had seen Olivia sitting on the front row behind him; the sight of her made him feel more confident, but he still felt as if the other spectators as well as the jury had already judged him guilty and sentenced him. He wanted to sleep until the night mare ended.

Judge Nathaniel Solomon entered the court room, and everyone stood with respect to his presence. He hit his gavel, asked that everyone be seated, stated his name and said, "The State of Georgia on behalf of Laura Porter, plaintiff, versus Scott Porter, defendant. DA Kramer for the State and Lawyer Joseph Harrington for the defense may present their opening statements to the jury.

District Attorney Kramer moved quickly from his table and walked before the jury. He explained that the State wanted justice for the death of Laura Porter, who could no longer defend herself. He declared that the State intended to prove that Scott Porter premeditated his wife's murder after he fell in love with Olivia Bradford, who had an illegitimate son for him. In addition, Scott Porter wanted money; he had taken out a five hundred thousand dollars life insurance policy on Laura Porter. He asked the jury to act as Laura Porter's eyes, ears, and voice as they weighed the evidence presented. Then he raised his voice and pounded his point. Regardless of Laura Porter's disability, she did not deserve to die in order for Scott Porter to live the good life with his mistress. He added that Scott Porter deserved no less than life in prison for murdering his wife and asked that the jury seek justice for Laura Porter with a guilty verdict for first degree, premeditated murder. He thanked the jury for their undivided attention and walked back to his station.

Joseph Harrington stood before the jury and paused to look at each of the jurors to get their attention. Then he explained that Scott Porter had been Laura Porter's eyes, ears, and voice since an accident paralyzed her; and he had stood by her since that accident. He declared that the evidence presented would prove that Scott Porter did not murder his wife; a jealous woman framed Scott Porter for her own selfish gain. She wanted money and she wanted revenge. He asked the jury why Scott Porter visited his wife every day and spent thousands for her to have the best medical care. Then he answered his own question: Scott Porter loved his wife. His need to be loved in return did not prove that he killed Laura Porter; his needs proved that he was a human being. He demanded that the jury listen carefully to the evidence presented and find Scott Porter innocent of the ridiculous murder charge.

The judge called for a recess and advised the court to reconvene at one o'clock.

Joseph Harrington explained to Scott that the State would call witnesses first; but he could cross examine any or all of the witnesses if he saw that they may help his case.

After lunch, the judge brought the court to order at one o'clock and instructed the DA to begin calling witnesses for the state.

First, District Attorney Kramer called Coroner Theodore Drake to verify the cause and time of Laura Porter's death.

Coroner Drake testified that Laura Porter died from an overdose of Valium on December 16, 1990 at approximately five AM.

Next, the DA called Karen Cato, the head nurse at Hillcrest Manor. He asked questions to verify the exact time she had called an ambulance for Laura Porter and to give evidence from Laura's chart that cleared her and the other nurses of any wrong doings.

Karen Cato testified that she called an ambulance for Laura Porter after Judy Brooks took Laura's vital signs at nine thirty PM. Laura's chart showed that her blood pressure had bottomed out and she had a weak pulse.

Under cross examination, Joseph Harrington turned the head nurse into a witness for the defense. Cato testified that Scott Porter practically stayed at the nursing home for a month after Laura's accident. Since that time, he visited Laura almost every day; he brought his wife flowers, candy, cards, and showed kindness and compassion toward her. Mr. Porter requested that his wife wear the beautiful wedding rings he had given her; he did not want anyone to take the rings from her finger.

Then the DA called Robert Wiggins, the police officer who searched Scott Porter's home.

Mr. Wiggins testified that he found an empty prescription bottle for valium in Scott Porter's medicine cabinet that had been filled on December 15, 1990, the day before Laura Porter died from an overdose of the drug.

Under cross examination, Joseph asked the officer if he had checked the empty prescription bottle for fingerprints.

Wiggins told the court that the bottle had been checked for fingerprints. They found three sets of finger prints: the pharmacist, the delivery boy, and one set of unidentified prints.

Joseph asked if the unidentified prints belonged to his client, Scott Porter.

Wiggins replied that the third set of prints had not been identified.

Then Joseph turned to the jury and said, "How can the prosecution explain the fact that Scott Porter's finger prints were not found on the empty prescription bottle that the detective found in Scott's own medicine cabinet? Was Scott Porter framed?"

DA Kramer shouted a loud objection and said, "Scott Porter wore gloves when he handled that prescription bottle."

"Scott Porter never touched that empty bottle!" Joseph said. "Scott Porter seems like an intelligent man to me. Do you think he would put this empty bottle back in his own medicine cabinet for the authorities to use as evidence against him?"

DA Kramer stood up and shouted "Objection! Scott Porter had to put that empty bottle in his medicine cabinet!"

Judge Solomon hit his gavel and asked the two lawyers to enter the bench. He looked from one to the other as he spoke, "Mr. Kramer, Mr. Harrington, you must stop arguing and shouting in my court room. Stick to the facts in the case." Then Judge Solomon hit his gavel and recessed court until the next morning at nine o'clock.

The next morning, Judge Solomon called for order and asked District Attorney Mark Kramer to resume questioning for the State.

First, DA Kramer, called Mr. John Bridges, the druggist from Bridges Pharmacy, to the stand.

Bridges testified that an unidentified person called in an order for Laura Porter's prescription at nine o'clock AM on December 15, 1990. The person who called asked that the prescription be delivered to Scott Porter, Route one, Box 110, Porterville, Georgia."

Under cross examination, defense lawyer, Joseph Harrington asked Mr. Bridges if he had talked with the person who called and requested that Laura Porter's prescription be refilled.

Mr. Bridges admitted that he had taken the call. The caller asked him to fill Laura Porter's prescription for valium.

Then Harrington asked if the phone identified the location or the name of the caller.

Bridges told the court that the phone identification showed an unknown caller and no number showed up on the phone.

Harrington asked Mr. Bridges if he had ever spoken with Scott Porter on the phone before.

Mr. Bridges testified that he had spoken with Scott many times on the phone.

Harrington asked Bridges if the caller had given his/her name.

Bridges said the caller gave no name; he assumed that he had Mr. Porter on the line, since he gave his address.

Harrington asked Mr. Bridges if Scott usually stated his name when he called in a prescription.

Mr. Bridges paused and told him that Mr. Porter always stated his name when he called in a prescription, but he had been busy and had not given the call much thought at the time.

Harrington asked Mr. Bridges if Scott Porter usually called in orders for prescriptions to be filled.

Mr. Bridges told the jury that Scott Porter never called for Laura's prescription to be refilled; but he had called and ordered prescriptions for himself. However, he had never asked for medications to be delivered; he always came to the drug store and picked up the medication he ordered. He added that Laura Porter called often and asked that her prescriptions be delivered to her door but not to her mail box.

Mr. Kramer objected. "Irrelevant, your honor. Laura Porter did not make that call to Mr. Bridges."

Judge Solomon reminded Harrington to refrain from asking witnesses questions that ended in irrelevant answers.

Harrington said, "Mr. Bridges, isn't it a fact that you do not know who called in that order for Valium?"

"Objection," DA Kramer said. "Mr. Harrington is leading the witness."

Harrington quickly changed his question, "Mr. Bridges do you know who called you and order Laura's prescription for valium?"

Mr. Bridges said, "No, I do not know for sure who called in the prescription for valium."

Harrington said, "Thank you, Mr. Bridges. I have no further question."

Next, DA Kramer called Kacey King, the delivery boy from Bridges Pharmacy, to the stand.

King testified that he delivered a prescription to Scott Porter's mail box on December 15, 1990, around eleven o'clock; and he went on to deliver other orders on his route.

Under cross examination, Harrington asked King if he had ever delivered drugs to Mr. Porter's mail box before.

Kacey King testified that this was the first prescription he had ever delivered to Scott Porter's mailbox and he had worked for Bridges Pharmacy more than ten years. He added that Mrs. Porter had ordered prescriptions before her accident that he had delivered; and she always met him at the door when he delivered her orders.

Next, the District Attorney called Gulliver Hayes to the stand.

The tall, slender man slowly walked to the witness stand and took a seat. He looked at Steve Brinson and turned back to the DA.

DA Kramer asked Mr. Hayes to tell the court where he worked.

"I work as a janitor at Hillcrest Manor Nursing Home."

Mr. Kramer asked if he knew Laura Porter.

Mr. Hayes told him that he had known Miss Laura all of her life; and he knew Mr. Scott Porter, too.

DA Kramer asked Hayes if he saw any visitors coming from Laura Porter's room on December 15, 1990.

Mr. Hayes testified that he saw a man leaving Miss Laura's room that night around nine o'clock. He said he was mopping the hall; the man passed right by him and left by the exit doors at the back that they always kept locked. He had no idea how he got inside. Visitors came in the front door and left by the front door. He added that the man messed up his clean floor and he had to mop again.

DA Kramer asked Mr. Hayes how the man got out if the doors were locked.

Mr. Hayes told him that the door would open from the inside to go out; but visitors could not get in from the outside.

DA Kramer scratched his head and asked how the man got into the building.

Mr. Hayes said he had to come into the building through the front door or an open window.

DA Kramer asked Mr. Hayes to describe this man he saw leaving Miss Laura's room.

Gulliver Hayes stretched his eyes and said, "I got a good look at the man and he looked like a hulk. I never saw him before then. He was a big, tall, white man with a big gut. He must have weighed more than two hundred and fifty pounds. He had smut black hair and dark skin; he looked like he had a beach tan."

DA Kramer asked Hayes if he saw a man in the court room that resembled the man he saw that night.

Gulliver Hayes looked around the room and focused his eyes on Scott Porter as he spoke, "I don't see a soul in this court room that looks like that man I saw leaving Miss Laura's room. The man I saw was not Scott Porter, if that's what you are asking. I know him and I talk to him often when he visits Miss Laura."

"I have no further questions," Mr. Kramer said.

Gulliver Hayes had said all that needed to be said, but Harrington wanted to plant the picture of the man deeply into the jurors mind. Under cross-examination, Harrington asked Mr. Hayes if he was sure that the man he saw leaving Laura Porter's room looked nothing like his client, Scott Porter.

"I can tell you for sure; that man was not Mr. Scott Porter."

"Thank you, Mr. Hayes. You may step down. I have no further questions." Harrington said.

District Attorney Kramer gave Harrington a dirty look before he called Christine Wimberley to the stand.

Mrs. Wimberley painted a bad picture of Scott Porter to the jury. She told about his adulterous affair with Olivia Bradford; she told that he had a son for this kept woman; and she called him a brutal murderer who killed her daughter.

Mrs. Wimberley accusations of Scott's adultery with Olivia Bradford made Harrington see red. He shouted an objection.

Judge Solomon sustained Harrington's objection with words of warning to Mrs. Wimberley about stating her personal opinions; but the jury had already heard her damaging words about Scott.

Under Cross examination, Harrington asked Mrs. Wimberley questions that required a yes or no answer and put her on the spot. "Mrs. Wimberley, did you go to Olivia Bradford's apartment uninvited, threaten her, and treat her with disrespect?"

"I went to speak to Olivia Bradford," she said.

"You did not answer my question, Mrs. Wimberley. Did you or did you not threaten Olivia Bradford and treat her with disrespect in her own apartment?"

"I guess you would call my visit to Olivia Bradford's apartment a threat and disrespectful, but …"

"I have no further questions."

Next Kramer called Laura's sister, Lisa Cane, to the stand. Lisa pointed an accusing finger at Scott Porter. She told the court that Scott killed her sister, because he wanted to marry his whore, Olivia Bradford.

Harrington shouted an objection, and the Judge quickly sustained his objection with a warning to Lisa Cane about her personal opinions. He added that he would hold her in contempt of court if she made another derogatory remark about the defendant's personal life.

Harrington cross examined Lisa Cane and tangled her hair. "Miss Cane, did you write Olivia Bradford a letter and threaten her life as well as her son's life if she did not stop seeing Scott Porter?"

"Objection," Mr. Kramer said. "Letters written by Miss Cane have nothing to do with this case."

Harrington said, "Your honor, this letter has everything to do with this case. My client has been framed for Laura Porter's death."

Judge Solomon said, "Mrs. Cane, answer the question."

"I do not remember," Lisa said.

Harrington said, "Let me refresh your memory, Mrs. Cane," and he placed the letter in front of her. "Would you read this letter to the court?"

"You cannot force me to read this letter!" she said.

Judge Solomon ordered Lisa Cane to read the letter.

The court room gasp with shock as they listened to her threatening words to Olivia Bradford. Then Lisa shouted, "Olivia Bradford had no business living with my poor sister's husband. Besides, she had a bastard son for him."

Judge Solomon warned Lisa Cane about her personal opinions again.

Harrington came back before her and said, "Mrs. Cane, did you call Scott Porter from an unknown number and threaten his life if he continued seeing Olivia Bradford?"

"Objection!" DA Kramer said. "I do not see how Miss Cane's conversation with Scott Porter has anything to do with Laura Porter's death."

Judge Solomon said, "Objection overruled. The court needs to hear what the witness has to say."

"I do not know what you are talking about," Lisa Cane said.

"Miss Cane, do you understand the penalty for lying under oath? You not only called Scott Porter and threatened his life; you also made several threatening calls to Olivia Bradford. Is this not correct?"

"I told you I do not know what you are talking about."

Harrington said, "Did you frame Scott Porter for killing your sister because you are still madly in love with him?"

The court room got so loud that Judge Solomon hit his gavel and called order.

"Objection," DA Kramer said. "Lisa Cane's relationship with Scott Porter previous to his marriage to Laura Porter is irrelevant."

Judge Solomon ordered Harrington to ask only question related to the case.

"Your honor, Lisa Cane's answer to my question is the key to Laura Porter's death."

Judge Solomon looked at Lisa Cain and ordered her to answer the question.

"I did not frame Scott Porter; I do not love him; I hate him."

"Isn't it true, Miss Cane, that you hated your deceased sister, because she took your boyfriend from you? "

"That is a lie!" Lisa shouted. "I never loved Scott Porter."

Judge Solomon hit his gavel and called order. Then he asked the witness to answer the questions and stop yelling in his court room.

Then Harrington looked at the jury and said, "I never mentioned the boy's name; but Lisa Cane knew the boy I spoke of was Scott Porter."

Lisa voice shook and tears streamed down her face as she spoke, "I loved my sister and I did not want Scott Porter to mistreat her as he had mistreated all other women he went with."

Harrington said, "Miss Cane, I have one other question. Did you set fire to Olivia Bradford's house in an attempt to kill her and her son?"

District Attorney Kramer shouted an objection; but Judge Solomon overruled his objection.

Lisa Cane screamed, "I did not set fire to her house; I never laid a hand on the bitch!"

Harrington looked at the jury and said, "As you can see, Lisa Cane does not want you or the public to know her true feelings; she hated her sister and loved Scott Porter. When Scott refused to have anything to do with Lisa, she wanted revenge; she killed her sister and framed Scott for her murder. I have no further question."

Lisa Cane stepped down from the witness chair and rushed to her seat next to her mother near the front bench.

DA Kramer called Nathaniel Wimberley, Laura's father, to the stand and asked him if he could tell the court anything about Scott Porter that was relative to her murder.

Mr. Wimberley broke down and cried as he talked about Laura. He told the court that his daughter seemed happily married to Scott Porter. Then Laura went on that darn hiking trip to Stone Mountain and fell. This accident had caused her to be paralyzed and changed her as well as Scott and her family's life forever. He told the court that he and his family had lived in hell for the past seven years. Laura's accident tore his family apart; they never had a decent family gathering at Thanksgiving or Christmas, they never had a decent conversation; his wife never spoke a kind word to him and they no longer had a marriage; he no longer had a family; he and his wife had grown miles apart. They still prayed to God for Laura's recovery; but she died the day of her accident. Then he stood up, looked at the jury and asked, "What would you do if your child turned to a vegetable without the ability to speak, stand, walk, or show any feelings?"

The spectators gasp with shock and got so loud that the judge called for order in his court. Mr. Wimberley's words made him look guilty of killing his daughter out of mercy; but he did not realize what he said until it was too late.

Under cross examination, Harrington turned Mr. Wimberley into a witness for the defense. He asked Mr. Wimberley to tell the court how he got along with his son-in-law, Scott Porter.

Mr. Wimberley told the court that he knew of no finer person anywhere than Scott Porter. He said that Scott treated him with respect and went out of his way to be nice to him. Scott had invited him to dinner more times than he could remember; and they played golf together. He added that Scott had also been good to Laura, both before and after her accident. Then he looked out at spectators and told them that Scott Porter did not kill his daughter.

The sure sound of Mr. Wimberley's voice pleased Harrington, and he was happy that the jury heard him testify. He had no further question and Mr. Wimberley stepped down from the witness stand.

Scott smiled at Mr. Wimberley as he made his way to his seat. Each time Joseph Harrington asked a question, Mr. Wimberley answered in Scott's favor.

Judge Solomon announced adjournment for the day and added that court would resume at nine o'clock the next morning.

CHAPTER THIRTY
Trial Defense Witnesses and acquittal

THE NEXT DAY at nine o'clock, the judge instructed Joseph Harrington to call witnesses for the defense.

First, Harrington called Scott's house keeper, Louise Sanders, to the stand.

Mrs. Sanders moved her tall, slender figure to the stand and sat with perfect posture.

Harrington asked Mrs. Sanders how long she had known Scott Porter.

Mrs. Sanders looked at Harrington as if he should know the answer to his question and said, "Why I have known Scott Porter since the day he came into the world. In fact, I fixed his bottle and changed his diapers. I kept house for Scott's parents before Scott's birth. After Scott married Miss Laura, he hired me to keep house for them."

Next, Harrington asked Mrs. Sanders how Scott and his wife, Laura, got along.

Mrs. Sanders told the court that Scott Porter treated Miss Laura like a queen. She added that he also bought a castle for her; and bought her everything she wished for. She said one only had to be around them a short while to know how much they loved each other.

DA Kramer objected. He claimed that Mrs. Sanders could not prove that Scott and Laura Porter loved each other by her observation.

The judge sustained the prosecution's objection.

Mrs. Sanders raised her voice and declared that she had good eyes and ears; and she knew a good thing when she saw and heard it. She added that she got a subpoena to testify as a character witness, and she wanted to tell everybody in that courtroom that Scott Porter was a fine man with a big heart. He had always been good to her, her family, and everybody else who came around.

Then Harrington asked Mrs. Sanders about the pills Laura took.

Mrs. Sanders said, "Why Miss Laura took valiums to help her sleep as far back as I can remember good."

Next Harrington asked if she knew anything about the valium delivered to Scott's home on December 15, 1990.

She told the court that she knew all about the valiums. She had worked at Scott's home that day. In fact, she had gone to the mail box to get the mail as she did every time she went to Mr. Porter's home. She found a white paper bag with Bridges Drugs stamped on the front. She took the bag as well as the newspaper and all the other mail addressed to Mr. Porter into the house.

Then Harrington asked her what she did with the pills.

She testified that she first pulled the stapled bill from the bag and put it in Mr. Porter's desk drawer, where she put all the bills that came in the mail. Then she took the pills out of the bag and threw the bag in the trash can. Before she put the bottle in Mr. Porter's medicine cabinet, she discovered that bottle was empty!

The uproar in the court room interrupted her testimony and the judge called order.

Mrs. Sanders continued. She told the court that she even opened the cap on the bottle and looked inside. That bottle didn't have a thing in it, not even cotton. She said she thought it mighty unusual for a smart pharmacist to send Mr. Scott an empty bottle. She added that she thought somebody had been tampering with Mr. Porter's mail; but she put the empty bottle in the medicine cabinet, anyhow, with Mr. Porter's other medication.

Harrington Said, "Mrs. Sanders, Did you tell Mr. Porter about the prescription you found in the mail box?"

"I did not see Mr. Porter that evening. I went on to the house before Scott got home from work. I drive my car to and from work and I seldom see Mr. Porter until he comes with my pay check. The next thing I know, Mr. Porter got accused and arrested for Miss Laura's murder."

Harrington asked if she called Scott and told him about the pills.

Mrs. Sanders said, "I saw no need to tell Mr. Porter about the empty bottle. I forgot all about it myself, and Mr. Porter never asked me anything about the prescription that came in the mail. The bottle was empty, anyhow. What would Scott want with an empty pill bottle? He didn't have no pills to give Miss Laura; and he did not kill her."

The judge had to call order in the court again.

Harrington told Mrs. Sanders he had no further questions.

Before Mrs. Sanders could step down, DA Kramer rushed up to the witness and raised his voice. "Mrs. Sanders, why did you not come forward with the information about the empty pill bottle when you heard that Mr. Porter had been arrested?"

She told the court that nobody asked her anything about the pills until this day and she didn't say anything, because an empty bottle wasn't worth a dime.

Everybody in the courtroom laughed, except Lisa Cane and Mary Wimberley.

Frustrated with her answer, DA Kramer shouted, "Mrs. Sanders, did you take the pills from that bottle, leave an empty bottle, and keep the pills for yourself?

She turned a question back to him. "What do you think I would do with a bottle of valium pills? I got my own medication; I don't take other folk medicine."

DA Kramer hung his head and told her he had no further questions. He walked back to his table with a look of disgust on his face. She had made the State's case worthless. The pills had been the only evidence he had for holding Scott Porter in the first place.

Next, Harrington called private detective Brinson to the stand. He asked Brinson to tell the court why Scott Porter hired him as a private investigator several months prior to his wife's murder.

Steve told the court that Scott Porter hired him to investigate an anonymous letter sent to Olivia Bradford as well as anonymous phone calls Scott and Olivia received.

DA Kramer objected to Brinson's testimony. He told the judge that Brinson's investigation before Laura Porter's murder had no relevance to the case.

Before the judge had time to sustain the testimony, Harrington explained to the judge that the information Brinson gathered would prove that Lisa Cane lied on the witness stand. Brinson would also show that Scott Porter had been framed for the murder of his wife by a jealous woman who wanted money and revenge.

Judge Solomon overruled Mr. Kramer's objection; he wanted to hear the evidence Steve Brinson gathered.

Harrington asked Brinson to tell the court what he learned from his investigation.

Steve testified that he installed wire taps on all of Mr. Porter's phones as well as Olivia Bradford's home phone. In less than one week, he had pinned down the guilty party.

Harrington asked Judge Solomon's permission to play the taped calls.

"Objection" District Attorney Kramer shouted.

Harrington explained to Judge Solomon that Lisa Cane accused his client of killing her sister; and the tapes would explain why she had accused Scott.

"Objection is overruled," Judge Solomon said. "Play the tapes."

Steve Brinson came forward and set up the tape recorder. The court room gasp with shock as they listened to Lisa Cane's threats and vulgar language on the taped calls.

Harrington said, "Mr. Brinson, what else did you uncover with your investigation?"

"The handwriting on the letter sent to Olivia Bradford matched Lisa Cane hand writing."

"Objection!" DA Kramer said. "Is Mr. Brinson a handwriting analysis expert?"

"I am not an expert on handwriting, but I hired an expert, John Tyson. He obtained Lisa Cane's handwritten reports from Atlanta Designs, where she used to work," Harrington said.

Judge Solomon overruled DA Kramer's objection.

Harrington said, "Lisa Cane cannot deny making the threatening phone calls nor writing the threatening letter. The court heard her voice and Mr. Brinson proved that she wrote the letter. She lied on the witness stand. I have no further question for Mr. Brinson.

DA Kramer cross examined Steve Brinson and tried to tangle his testimony; but Steve stuck to his story.

Next, Harrington called Officer Dan Purvis, a local police officer, to the stand. He asked him to tell the court why he had been called to Olivia Bradford's apartment previous to Laura Porter's murder.

Purvis testified that an intruder broke into Olivia Bradford's apartment and Mrs. Lena Stewart, who rented the apartment to Mrs. Bradford, called him to investigate. The intruder had broken a window and entered the apartment. He found the room ransacked with her clothes scattered on the floor as well as make-up and jewelry scattered on the dresser. He also found the drawers and cabinets in the kitchen and bathroom disarranged. He concluded that the intruder wanted something that they did not find. Then he told the court that he had all of the details in his report.

Dan Purvis stepped down and Judge Solomon announced adjournment for the day; court would resume the next morning at nine o'clock.

Lisa Cane rushed from the court room and left her parents behind.

Olivia waved to Scott before they took him back to his jail cell.

That night, he slept for the first time since his arrest. He felt as if the jury would find him innocent of murdering his wife.

The next day, court began a nine o'clock. Harrington called Scott's two main supervisors and his secretary as character witnesses. They all testified that Scott Porter treated his employees fairly and helped their families in times of need. They had never worked for a more honest or compassionate man.

Last, but not least, Scott Porter took the stand. Harrington tried to talk him out of testifying; he believed that Scott had a strong defense and he felt sure that the jury would find him innocent of all charges without his testimony; but Scott wanted the jury and citizens of Porterville to know that Lisa Cane had lied about everything she had said about him.

First Harrington asked Scott how he met Laura and about their marriage.

Scott testified that he fell in love with Laura when they were in high school. After they graduated from college, they got married. They had a good marriage until Laura's accident. She never recognized him or spoke to him again.

Next, Harrington asked Scott about his relationship with Lisa Cane.

Scott told the court that he dated Lisa Cane also in high school. He broke up with Lisa after he met Laura. He added that Lisa was jealous of her sister and refused to be in her sister's wedding, because she still loved him.

Whispers buzzed and excitement stirred the court room.

The judge called for order and Scott continued. The jury perked their ears as he described Lisa's fits of jealousy and violence as well as her threats to kill Laura if he did not break up with Laura. Lisa tempted him by her sexual gestures and told lies on Laura. Then she went back to Laura and told her lies about him. She told Laura that he had begged her to marry him and bragged about things he had bought her as well as lies about their sexual relationship.

Scott's words made Lisa see fire. She stood up, pointed a finger, and shouted, "Liar! Liar! You are a big liar!"

The judge called for order and warned Lisa Cane, "You must be seated; I will hold you in contempt of this court if you open your mouth again."

Scott Porter made Lisa grit her teeth. Who did he think he was? She moved her eyes around the court room and back to the jurors. She sensed that the jury believed Scott; they thought she was a crazy sociopath, a psychotic killer, who killed for pleasure. She could not actually deny that she wanted to kill Scott Porter. In fact, killing him would give her pleasure.

Scott continued his testimony. He told the court that Lisa Cane did not stop her threats with the phone calls and letter; she burned Olivia Bradford's house and tried to kill her and his son, Alex, just as she said she would do. He believed that all of her destruction stemmed from her jealousy, and she wanted revenge.

District Attorney Kramer objected and told the court that Scott Porter had no proof that Lisa Cane set fire to Mrs. Bradford's house.

The judge sustained his objection and told Harrington that his client must have proof of his accusations. Personal opinions and here say had no place in a murder trial by a jury.

Scott said, "Your honor, I reached my conclusion about Lisa Cane after I learned that she threatened to kill Olivia and my son. I have proof of her threat on tape."

Judge Solomon said, "None the less, you do not have proof that she set fire to Olivia Bradford's home."

The court room got loud and the judge called for order.

Then Scott shouted that Lisa murdered Laura, her own sister, and framed him for Laura's death in order to file a civil suit and take everything he owned.

In spite of the prosecutions' sustained objection, Scott had made Lisa look like a bag of trash; he had convinced the jury that she was a bitch and her dead sister an angel living with the saints in heaven. She felt more angry and embarrassed than she had ever felt in her life.

After the court room got quiet again, Harrington turned his attention back to Scott and asked if Mrs. Wimberley, Lisa's mother, had a motive for framing him for her daughter's death?

DA Kramer objected again and accused Harrington of leading the witness.

The judge hit his gavel as the court room buzzed. "There will not be another out-burst in this court room! Then he warned Harrington that he must not put words in his client's mouth.

Harrington shook his head in the affirmative and told the judge that he would change his line of questioning.

Harrington walked back before Scott Porter and asked if he could think of anyone else who would want to frame him for the murder of his wife.

Scott told the court that Mrs. Wimberley backed Lisa in all of her criminal acts; in fact Mrs. Wimberley helped Lisa frame him.

DA Kramer jumped up with an objection and accused Scott Porter of jumping to conclusions.

To Harrington's surprise, the judge over-ruled the prosecution's objection and told Harrington he would allow the testimony, but he should get to his point.

Harrington turned back to Scott and asked why he believed that Mrs. Wimberley and Lisa Cane framed him for the murder of his wife, Laura.

Scott told the court that Mrs. Wimberley wanted his money.

Mrs. Wimberley shot up and shouted, "You have lost your mind, Scott Porter. I wouldn't do anything to harm my own flesh and blood for all the money in the world. Besides, I have money of my own. I loved Laura, and I did everything I could for her since her accident. I am sorry to say that Laura's death made all of my efforts seem in vain."

The judge hit his gavel and said, "You must control your urge to speak Mrs. Wimberley; if you interrupt this court again, I will hold you in contempt."

Mr. Wimberley stood and told the judge he had something to say to the court that made sense.

The judge asked him to enter the bench.

The court room got as quiet as a chapel as Mr. Wimberley made his way to the front of the court room and faced the audience. He moved his eyes from the jury to the spectators as he spoke, "I want the jury and all the people in this court room to listen carefully to what I have to say. In spite of the trouble my daughter, Lisa, and my wife have caused Scott Porter, I have high regards for the man; and I appreciate everything he has done for my daughter, Laura. I do not want Scott to go to prison for a crime he did not commit. After the authorities arrested Scott, I thought they would let him go. I did not think the case against him would stand up in court without evidence against him. Someone framed him; that's plain to see. I loved my daughter with all of my heart, but I believe my Laura is in a better place; she can rest in peace now. I know that some of you cannot believe a Father could speak those words; but not one of you have walked in my shoes; not one of you have walked in Scott Porter's shoes. Laura has been dead for years; she could not communicate with us; she could not take care of her basic needs; and she did not recognize us. I faced the reality of her situation right after her accident; she would never get any better. I just want the family I have left to come back to me. Scott Porter loved my daughter; he paid for her to have the best of care as long as she lived; I know he did not murder her. I beg this jury to find Scott not guilty of murder. Let Scott and my family finally have some peace and live again.

The court room got so loud that the judge had to call order. Then he called the prosecuting attorney and the defense to the bench. After speaking to them briefly, he asked them to be seated. Then Judge Solomon announced to the jury and court that he had made the decision to dismiss all charges against Scott Porter for the murder of his wife. He thanked the jury for their time and patience in listening to the witnesses and dismissed the jury. Then he spoke directly to Scott," Mr. Porter you are free to go home." Judge Solomon hit his gavel three times, stood, and disappeared to his office located behind his platform.

Olivia ran to Scott and he embraced her with a tight hug before they made their way through the crowd to the parking lot. There he grabbed Olivia, swung her around with happiness, and put her on her feet. He held her tight as he told her he loved her and how much he had missed her and Alex. Then he said, "Let's go home and celebrate."

On the drive home, he apologized for the misery she and Alex had lived through during the trial.

Olivia talked about how happy it made her to have him back at home, where he belonged.

He suggested that they go to her house and spend some time alone before they went to her parent's to pick up Alex.

Her smile told him that she wanted to be alone with him, also.

When they got home, he held her hand as they walked to the door. Just inside, he pulled her to him and kissed her. She moved in a trance with him to the bedroom. His need for her and her need for him made them anxious to satisfy their desire. She quickly undressed and threw back the covers. He slid next to her and the warmth from her body made him crazy. She snuggled close to him; he moved his lips from her cheeks to her nose and found her lips. Her response from his passionate kiss demanded more. Her excitement mounted and she screamed his name as a flurry of pleasure flooded her body and took her to paradise, a place where everything was beautiful and sweet. Her love and need for him made him a happy man, happier than he had ever been.

His arms about her made her feel secure, relaxed, and content. She still felt the pleasure he gave her. He lay silently by her side and slid his fingers over her long, dark hair.

"I have a wonderful secret to tell you," she said.

"What is your secret? Tell me now; I cannot wait," He said.

"I am pregnant!"

Scott sat upright in bed and shouted, "I am so happy. This time you will have a little girl and she will have your beauty. How far along are you?"

"I am more than two months, but I did not want to tell you while you were in jail. I was afraid you would worry."

He grabbed her and kissed her and whispered words of love. She smiled up at him and said, "This pregnancy will be a happy time. We have nothing to worry about now."

She dozed off to sleep; when she awoke he was looking at her.

"I was watching you sleep. Are you as happy as you have made me?"

"I am always happy when you are here with me."

Their love for each other made all other things in the world seem small and worthless. All of his money and the things he owned meant nothing without Olivia and his son. He talked about their wedding and their future as she dozed.

Later that evening, they went to pick up Alex. They agreed not to tell her parents about the baby until Olive started showing.

Mr. and Mrs. Hollister acted excited and happy about Scott's acquittal. Mr. Hollister asked Scott to go with him to his shop to see his latest project, a Cedar toy box he had built for Alex.

The designs of Superman that Mr. Hollister had carved on the box impressed Scott most of all. He mentioned that he knew where his daughter got all of her creative talents.

At last, Mr. Hollister seemed to accept Scott as his son-in-law. Scott told him that he and Olivia wanted to get married in June by the Justice of Peace in Porterville, his hometown. He wanted him and Mrs. Hollister to attend the wedding and asked if they would keep Alex while they went on their honeymoon.

Scott's news made Mr. Hollister happy. He would be pleased if Alex stayed with them. In fact, he would like for Alex to spend the summer with them.

Mr. Hollister and Scott had the best visit they had ever had. He and Mrs. Hollister loved Alex more than anything or anybody; they tried to please Olivia and Scott, because they never wanted Alex taken away from them. Olivia concluded that their love for Alex had changed them into decent parents and accepting in-laws.

CHAPTER THIRTY-ONE

Shocking Letter and Burglary

SCOTT WENT BACK to work the next week. After he left, Olivia thought of the ordeal he had been through and she thanked God that he was free at last. She still wondered who killed Laura Porter. Did Lisa Cane kill her own sister? She should be punished for her lies and psychotic behavior, but Scott never made a case against her, because he did not want her nor Alex to get hurt. Now that Scott had been found not guilty and set free, she did not care about her reputation. Besides, DA Kramer had already exposed Olivia's life history. She wanted Scott to file a complaint for Lisa's harassment. She thought she should be punished.

Alex interrupted her thoughts with his laughter. She found him in the den on the floor with Jasper. He had tied his stuffed tiger to the string and pulled it in a circle as Jasper tried to catch the tiger. He loved Jasper and Olivia thanked God that they finally found him after the house fire.

That evening, Olivia called Emily. She had not kept her up to date on the trial; but Emily had called her several times and inquired. When she told Emily the good news about Scott's acquittal, Emily shouted with happiness. She asked Olivia to bring Alex for a visit soon. They would find something exciting for the children to enjoy. Olivia promised to visit soon and told her to take care.

That night Olivia asked Scott to press charges against Lisa Cane for her harassment. Since Lisa lied to DA Kramer about Scott, Olivia feared that Lisa's would continue to harass them.

Scott asked her to try to forget everything that had happened. After all, Mr. Wimberley had saved him from a guilty verdict the day he stood and told the court that Scott Porter did not murder his daughter.

Olivia disagreed with Scott. She believed the jury would have found him innocent of all charges against him, because of Mrs. Sanders' testimony as well as the janitor's testimony. He had been an eye witness to a stranger leaving Laura's room the night she had been given the overdose.

Scott kissed her and said, "Honey, let's not think about Laura's murder; let's be happy that we are together. I am the happiest man in the world now that I have you and Alex in my life. We can get married tomorrow if you wish."

His words were music to her ears, but she still wanted Lisa Cane punished. She said nothing more about the trial or Lisa, but she would never forget the hell Lisa put them through.

One morning after Scott left to go to work, Olivia fixed Alex's breakfast and went to get the paper. She discovered an envelope addressed to Olivia Bradford. She wanted to scream; she suspected that Lisa Cane had started her harassment again. She drew a breath of disgust and went back into the house.

Back in the kitchen, she laid the paper on the table and started to open the letter when she noticed that it had no stamp or return address. Someone had personally delivered the letter to Scott's mailbox.

Alex asked if she got a letter from Grandmother and Grandpa.

She could not tell him the truth; she explained that the letter came from an insurance company that sold car insurance; they wanted her to take an insurance policy with them.

Then Alex asked what policy meant.

She explained that an insurance policy paid for damages when a person wrecked their cars.

He continued eating his breakfast and Olivia turned back to the letter written with a black sharpie pen in bold print on yellow construction paper.

Dear Olivia,

I hope you are happy and all is well since Scott Porter's trial is over and he is a free man. Your problems are solved at last. Now Porter is free to marry you and your little boy will have a daddy.

Olivia, you are loved more than you will ever know.

BG

Olivia felt as if all of the blood in her body drained to her feet. She lay her head down on the table and breathed deeply to keep from falling out of the chair.

Then she felt Alex's small warm hand on her face. In his sweet little voice he begged her to sit up and talk to him.

"Sweetie, Mama has a terrible headache, but it will go away soon and I will be fine," she said and kissed his cheek; but she feared that that her headaches had just begun.

Alex ran down the hall and came back with a bottle of aspirin.

She asked where he found the bottle of aspirin.

He smiled and told her that he stood on the stool next to the sink and got the aspirin out of the medicine cabinet in the bathroom.

She warned him about climbing as well as touching bottles of medicine.

He bragged that big boys knew how to climb and jump without falling. He kissed her brow and told her that his medicine would cure her head ache in a jiffy.

After Alex went back to his room to play, Olivia sat at the table and searched every pocket of her brain in an effort to put a name to the initials B.G. She knew of no one called B.G. She went through the alphabet matching letters to B. She thought of Billy, Tom's best friend; but Billy's last name, Miller, did not begin with a G.

Suddenly a flash of lightening hit Olivia's brain; she had called Billy Miller a stinking Billy Goat since she first met him at Tom's dinner. The B.G. signed to the letter stood for Billy Goat. Did Tom have anything to do with Laura's death? She could not tell Scott; she could not tell her parents; she could not tell a living soul; she must carry the secret to her grave. Could she live with her guilt? Why should she feel guilty? She had done nothing to cause Laura Porter's death.

The first week of summer came and Olivia talked to Scott about taking Alex to the beach that weekend. He wanted to go to the beach, but he had to go to the office first and check on inventory and orders. He also needed to talk to Adam Sinclair and let him know what he needed to do and how long he would be gone.

On Friday after lunch, Scott called Olivia and asked her to go to his house and get his suitcase. He wanted her to have their bags packed to go to the beach when he got off work at five.

As they drove to Scott's house, Alex asked question about the beach and talked about building sand castles.

When they got to Scott's house, they discovered a white, 1989 Chevrolet Camaro parked in the drive. Olivia thought the car might belong to Mrs. Sanders; but she did not want to get surprised by a burglar. She called Scott.

Scott knew of no one who owned a 1990, white, Chevrolet Camaro; Mrs. Sanders had a beige Buick. He told Olivia to back out of the drive, pull down the road a safe distance, and call the cops.

When the cops pulled into Scott's drive, Olivia pulled in behind them. She told them that Scott wanted them to check the house. She explained that she nor Scott knew anyone with a 1990, white Chevrolet Camaro.

Before they reached the front door, a tall woman with blond hair ran past them to the end of the porch and jumped to the ground. Before she got to her car, the cops caught her. Mr. Wiggins handcuffed her, stated her rights, and told her she was under arrest for breaking and entering.

Lisa Cane twisted, kicked, and yelled, "Get your damn hands off me! I came here to get my sister's personal belongings."

Mr. Wiggins reminded Lisa that everything that once belonged to her sister now belonged to Scott Porter. He added that she had committed a crime when she broke into Mr. Porter's home.

"Scott Porter is a lying dog! This is my sister's home and everything in the house belongs to me and my mother now. My father says he doesn't want anything."

Mr. Wiggins forced Lisa to get into the police car.

Olivia could not believe what Lisa had said. The cops had a monster to deal with. She backed out of the drive way and let the cops pass. She only got a glimpse of Lisa Cane's angry face as they drove away.

"Mama, who was that mean woman? Mama, the cops tied her hands behind her back. She looked scared in that big police car. I'll bet they take her to Jail."

"Her name is Lisa Cane, and jail is where she belongs," Olivia said. "The cops lock up burglars in Jail and she broke into your daddy's house."

"Daddy says that house is my house now," Alex bragged.

"What am I going to do without a house?" Olivia said.

"When we move into my house, you can live with us," Alex said.

"Gee, thanks," Olivia said.

She thanked God that they finally caught Lisa. She hoped they gave her a stiff sentence for her criminal behavior. Had Lisa Cane been the guilty party who broke into her apartment? How many other houses had Lisa broken into before and since that time?

She felt sure that Lisa had set fire to her house. She prayed that they could live in peace with Lisa locked away. Maybe she had been wrong about Billy's involvement with Laura's death.

After she called Scott and explained what happened, he went directly to the police station and filed charges against Lisa Cane for breaking and entering his home. After he filled out the forms requested, Scott asked Mr. Wiggins if he had searched Lisa for stolen goods.

Mr. Wiggins found Lisa Cane's purse packed with jewelry. Among the stolen jewelry, they found a diamond ring and band worth at least four thousand dollars.

When Mr. Wiggins showed Scott the jewelry, he picked up Laura's wedding rings and said, "Lisa Cane has no conscious! Only a low down, sorry person would steal her dead sister's wedding rings. I wanted Laura buried with her rings on her finger; but the undertaker assumed that I wanted the rings. When I went to his office to pay for her burial, he gave me the rings. I put them in the jewelry box with the rest of her jewelry."

We will return everything Mrs. Cane took from you; but we need to keep the jewelry as evidence for a few days.

After Scott left Wiggins, he stopped by Detective Jones' office. Mr. Jones got up from his desk, shook Scott's hand, and invited him to have a seat.

Scott told him he did not have much time. He came by to ask if he had made any progress in solving Laura's murder.

"We stopped trying to solve Laura Porter's murder," Jones said. "We worked on the case several weeks after the trial, but we don't know any more now than we did the day Judge Solomon dismissed the charges against you. We could arrest Laura's family, but we can't prove that any one of them killed her. Neither have we identified or located the man seen coming from Laura's room the night she got the overdose."

"You may want to question Lisa Cane again. The cops just brought her in for breaking into my house. Her criminal act should give you clear insight as to her involvement in Laura's death. I never pressed charges for the harassment she put Olivia and me through, because she promised that she would never bother us again. She broke that promise today, and I am considering opening up that can of worms again."

"If you still have the tapes to prove her harassment, bring them in to my office, and I will see what I can do about adding additional charges made against her for burglary."

"I am happy that you finally decided that I had nothing to do with Laura's death. I told you the truth from the beginning."

"I finally realized that you were innocent of the charges against you, but I could not speak up in court. I was just doing my job. Mr. Porter, please accept my apology."

Scott shook his hand and said, "I can't say that it has been nice knowing you, Detective Jones. I will ask Steve Brinson to bring those tapes to your office tomorrow. I will see you at Lisa Cane's trial. Good day, Mr. Jones."

Olivia tried to talk Scott into delaying their trip to the beach. She thought he needed to stay home and protect his property.

Scott had already made plans to go to the beach. He surprised her; he had taken the entire week off. They stayed four days in Panama City at the Cavalier.

In July, the Justice of the Peace in Porterville married Olivia and Scott in his office at the court house. Her mother, father, and Alex were the only ones invited to their wedding. Afterwards, they went on a honeymoon to Hawaii, and Alex stayed with Mr. and Mrs. Hollister. Scott made Mrs. Olivia Porter the happiest woman in the world.

After they got back home from their honeymoon, Olivia finally agreed to move into the house with Scott. She should have felt proud to live with him in the beautiful two-story mansion with its expensive furniture and fine art; but she did not like the idea of living in a house that had Laura's touch in every room. She wanted them to have their house, a house with her furniture, curtains, and decorative art.

Alex did not put up a fuss about moving to his house. Besides, his house had a big back yard with swings, a slide, a sand box, and plenty of room to ride his bike.

Scott promised Olivia they would sell the house and move to his house in Brunswick as soon as he retired. He planned to let Adam Sinclair run his business, because he wanted Alex to take over Porter Manufacturing as soon as he graduated from college.

They lived happily under Scott's roof as a family and enjoyed every minute of the days they spent together. They carried Alex to the park to play with his friends and had picnics; they went out to eat; they went to movies; and they invited friends over for dinner. Olivia had met all of Scott employees; they treated her with respect and kindness; they loved Alex.

In August, Alex started to pre-kindergarten at the public school in Porterville. Then in September they made Alex's fifth birthday wish come true; they carried him to Disney World.

Before seven the next morning, Alex awoke them and announced that he turned five years old today. They sang happy birthday three times that day and made Alex the happiest little boy in the world. After breakfast they went to Magic Kingdom Park, Disney Animal Kingdom, and the water park. They ate lunch at the Seafood Palace and went to the Steak House for supper. Olivia and Scott had never been more exhausted, but the excitement and happiness Alex experienced made the trip worth the flight and every step they made.

At last, Olivia was Scott's legal wife and the happiest wife in Porterville. Scott was the best Father any child could ask for. Alex worshipped his daddy. He tried to walk, act, and talk like Scott; he mimicked everything Scott said. Olivia also had her mother and father back in her life and they grew to love Scott even more than they ever loved Tom.

She never heard from Tom again; but she often thought about him. He would always have a special place in her heart, because he had been her first love. She had to admit that he had not been the best husband. She finally got the cream of the crop when it came to husbands.